YOU MUST REMEMBER THIS

ALSO BY KAT ROSENFIELD

No One Will Miss Her

YOU MUST REMEMBER THIS

A NOVEL

KAT ROSENFIELD

WM

WILLIAM MORROW

An Imprint of HarperCollins*Publishers*

HarperCollins books may be purchased for educational, business, or sales promotional use. For information, please email the Special Markets Department at SPsales@harpercollins.com.

FIRST EDITION

Library of Congress Cataloging-in-Publication Data

Names: Rosenfield, Kat, author.
Title: You must remember this: a novel / Kat Rosenfield.
Description: First Edition. | New York, NY: William Morrow, [2023]
Identifiers: LCCN 2022016107 | ISBN 9780063207394 (hardcover) | ISBN 9780063207417 (ebook)
Subjects: LCGFT: Novels.
Classification: LCC PS3618.O8383 Y68 2023 | DDC 813/.6—dc23
LC record available at https://lccn.loc.gov/2022016107

ISBN 978-0-06-320739-4

23 24 25 26 27 LBC 5 4 3 2 1

In memory of Helen Janet Varkala Kelly
August 13, 1915–April 9, 2020

Fire and Ice

Some say the world will end in fire,
Some say in ice.
From what I've tasted of desire
I hold with those who favor fire.
But if it had to perish twice,
I think I know enough of hate
To know that for destruction ice
Is also great
And would suffice.

—ROBERT FROST, 1920

YOU MUST REMEMBER THIS

PROLOGUE

2014

CHRISTMAS EVE

She knows he's there even before he speaks. She feels the weight and warmth of him as he sits down beside her, the firm press of his hip against the small of her back. His fingers curl gently over her shoulder as he leans in, and she smells his breath, warm and sweet, tickling her ear and sending a delicious chill down her spine.

"Miriam," he says. "Are you awake, my love?"

"Yes," she whispers. For him, she is always awake. She always has been. Ready to rise at the touch of his hand, ready to offer her mouth to be kissed. She rolls toward him, reaching out, and feels him catch her by the wrist. He has strong hands. A workingman's hands. It has been a long time since he was up at dawn to labor at the docks, a long, long time, but the calluses, those relics of labor long since abandoned, never went away. Her own mother once shuddered over those hands—"Your beautiful skin, Miriam! How can you bear it?"—but Miriam would only smile and shrug, because the truth was, she loved the feel of his fingertips, the light scrape against her skin. When he touched her, it felt the way she imagined it would to be embraced by an animal, something big and powerful like a bear, holding her gently between its huge rough paws. He could have torn her to pieces.

But he didn't. He wouldn't.

"Will you come to bed? Isn't it very late?" she asks, squinting at the place where she thought her bedside clock should be, but isn't, which is strange. The room is dark, all shadows, with only the barest glimmers of moonlight shimmering outside a window that is beginning to feather with frost. Her husband is somewhere among the shadows, but she cannot see his face, only the back-and-forth movement of his head as he shakes it, *No*. He is wearing his hat, she can see the curve of it, and she hears the light crunch of canvas as he shifts beside her. *His coat,* she thinks. He's wearing his coat. But why? She shivers again, this time with confusion, her skin suddenly crawling. Why is he awake in the middle of the night? Why can't she see his face?

But then he laughs, and after a moment, she laughs, too, and the creeping sensation of dread disappears.

"Did you forget?" he asks gently. The hand holding her wrist unclasps, winding its fingers through hers.

"Forget?" she repeats, feeling stupid. "I don't—but I've only just woken up. What is it?"

"It's our night. Our special night. The reach has frozen over."

"It has?"

"Darling," he chides, "you did forget."

Her whisper is indignant. "I did not."

"No?"

"Of course I remember."

"Then let's go." The shadow shifts off the bed with a creak, and she hears him moving across the floor. She slips her legs out from beneath the covers, setting her feet carefully side by side, curling her toes into the braided rug. The air is cold against her bare legs, startlingly so, but her mind still feels clouded and half-asleep. She blinks, trying to clear the cobwebs, trying to make the hulking shadows resolve into familiar shapes. An armoire there, the bedpost here. Her things. Her room. Why does it feel so unfamiliar? A person shouldn't feel so lost, so confused, sitting on the edge of her own bed.

One of the shadows moves.

"Theo?" she says, and sees the bob of his head, the peaked brim of his cap as he passes in front of the window to kneel beside her.

"Here, let me help you," he whispers, and she lifts her feet obediently at his touch, one at a time, feeling them disappear into the warm depths of a pair of fur-lined boots. She feels his breath again as he tightens and ties the laces, this time against her bare legs below the hem of her nightgown, and the heat rises in her face. Not with embarrassment, but with anticipation. Their special night.

Of course she hadn't forgotten. Not now, not after so many midnight trysts that she knew the way by heart, stealing out in the black and bracing cold, down to the water's edge. She would hug the wall along the staircase, treading carefully to avoid the creaky spots, waiting at the bottom to be sure that the coast was clear—only no, she thinks, shaking her head, that was before. She'd been only a girl then, breaking her father's rules, giddy and defiant. But it's her house now. Her own, and her husband's. She could make as much noise as she likes. Except—

"The children," she exclaims suddenly, her voice loud in the dark, and he puts a hand to her cheek.

"Shh. They're asleep. They'll be fine."

She blinks again and loses time. One moment, she was rising to her feet, shuffling in the heavy boots toward the bedroom door. The next, she is outside, the wind whipping at the hem of her nightgown, the flagstone path through the garden at her feet.

A fog has crept in, blanketing everything, blotting out the dark sky and the glittering stars. Only the moon is still visible, casting its bleak light as if through a veil. There is a blanket over her shoulders, and she pulls it around her, gazing uncertainly into the night—but there, there he is. A lamplight bobs in the distance, a soft whistle summons her from where she stands. She begins to walk. She knows the way, whether he's beside her or not.

The house looms behind her, huge and dark, as she descends the first set of steps. Down the hill, through the formal gardens where she once played hide-and-seek as a girl. Past the massive topiaries, now bare and overgrown, that would be trimmed come springtime into perfect spheres. Past the long, high wall where you could pick up a path that led into the woods, or descend another, longer set of steps to reach the long pier that stretches into the bay.

This is where she used to walk out to meet him, in the shadow of the hedges, where a hulking juniper and the sheer stone wall kept her hidden from prying eyes. Not that anyone is awake in the house now, nor could anyone have seen them through the thick and drifting fog. When she looks back, the house is hardly there at all. It would be nothing but a looming shadow, if not for the single light shining from a window on the top floor.

She frowns. Something darts through her mind, a flicker of memory that is gone as quickly as it came, leaving behind a sense of unease. Something about the light. Something not quite right. She hesitates . . . but he appears again beside her, and the flicker chases itself away.

"Scared of the dark?" he says, and she giggles. A silly question. He knows better.

"I was just . . ." she says, and leaves the sentence unfinished, realizing she doesn't know how it ends.

He looks at her curiously and reaches out with the hand not holding the lantern. "Should we walk hand in hand?"

"Like we used to," she says, almost like a question, and he nods.

"That's right, my love."

The darkness closes in as they walk between the trees. The flickering lamp, where is it? Has the light gone out? When she looks down, she sees that his other hand, the one not holding hers, is empty. No matter. There's moonlight, just enough. She can see the broad white expanse of the reach up ahead, where the path ends and the cove begins, where they will step together onto the ice. There's another flicker, this one stronger: *I dared him,* she thinks suddenly, and the memory fills her with delight as she moves forward, more quickly now, tingling with the thrill of what has been and the anticipation of what comes next. That had been the first time, on a night even colder than this one. She had walked onto the ice herself and dared him to follow, turning away without even waiting to see if he would. She knew he would. She had been sure where he was afraid, sure enough for both of them. Not just of the way across the reach, but of what waited on the other side. The cabin, with its little stove and a cord of firewood at the ready. No bed, but a bearskin rug that would serve the necessary purpose. A hideaway for two. His hands slipping under her nightdress and around her waist, acquainting themselves with the curves of her body, the beautiful friction of his calloused fingertips against her skin. She had been so young, they both had, full of blazing passion, with a beautiful life ahead. A boy and a girl.

But Miriam is not a girl anymore.

And when she turns, her husband is no longer beside her. "Theo?"

The wind rises as the moon is swallowed by the fog, and she goes to pull the blanket tighter around her shoulders, but there is no blanket. It's gone, along with the moonlight, along with him. The flimsy fabric of her nightdress whips around her legs, and she shivers, looking down. There are her feet, warm in their boots, the laces knotted tightly. Below them, gritty snow over an endless expanse of white.

She is standing on the ice.

The wind blows harder. She peers into the murk, her heart beginning to race, her eyes searching in vain for the invisible shore. It could be ahead of her or behind, the fog so thick she can no longer see or remember which way she came. She reaches out, frantic, looking once more for his hand, but clutches only the air. There's nothing and no one. Nothing but the wind, raw and tinged with salt. She calls his name as the fog parts, and then she sees him. Just a silhouette, hardly there at all.

He is not there at all.

Instead of his voice calling back to her, there is only the soft sound, somewhere very close by, of rushing water.

If she had been given another moment more, she might have come back. She might have remembered that it had been more than fifty years since she had walked this way, fifty years since she had last crossed the reach on a cold winter's night. She might have remembered that her husband wasn't here, couldn't be, because he was dead, and had been for many years. She might have seen that her own hands, clutched across her sunken chest, were gnarled and marked with liver spots; she might have felt the arthritic flare in her hips.

She might have realized who and what she was: an old woman shivering in her nightdress, lost and alone in the dark.

And she might have remembered that just yesterday, a man on the news had warned that climate change was still bringing warmer winters—and that in the past ten years, the reach had never fully frozen until at least February, if it froze at all.

But there isn't time. Not enough for a memory. Not even enough for a scream. Her shuffling feet have taken her in the wrong direction, and the white ice beneath her isn't white anymore, but black and thin and groaning. The groan becomes a crack. A dark mouth opens up beneath her. Miriam gasps once at the cold as it rushes up to meet her. The dark mouth closes over her head.

In the great stone house standing high on the hill, the light behind the upstairs window goes out.

I.

DECEMBER

I woke to the sound of footsteps. Angry and rhythmic, a march back and forth right under my window.

I peeled my eyes open, reaching automatically toward the night-stand, grunting when the phone slipped out of my fingers and clattered to the floor. The house creaked and settled, buffeted lightly by the wind. I groaned along with it. I'd slept badly again, uncomfortable in a house and a bed that didn't belong to me. It had been easier in New York—if not easier to sleep, then easier to feel like it was okay that I didn't. Restless nights were just part of the constant noise and movement of the city; there, I was like a single cell that belonged to a huge, quivering organism as fidgety and restless as I was.

Maine was different at night. Too dark and too quiet, except for the eerie muttering that gave the house its name and that set my teeth on edge. I had been at the Whispers just over six months, but I wouldn't feel at home here if I stayed ten years.

Beyond the warped and wavy glass of my bedroom window was a copse of barren trees with a few dark evergreens nestled among them, the yellowing grass of the lawn. Beyond the trees, just a glimpse of cold gray water, where the bay crept inland and became a river. Mine was one of only a few rooms without a view. The house sat at the mouth of the harbor, perched on a high point with a steep descent toward the water on one side. Every room there was outfitted with porches and balconies so that its occupants could take in the sea, but my bedroom was on the other side, where a white gravel piazza spanned the length of the front facade, tapering at one end to a narrow driveway that snaked away through the trees.

This was the source of the noise: my mother was out there, marching back and forth on the gravel to a point about twenty feet from the front door—the place where a person would first be able to glimpse a car as it came around the curve approaching the house. I could see her through the window every time she reached her destination. Ten steps out, a pause, then a heel turn. Ten steps back, another turn, another ten steps, repeat.

Even from three stories up, the scuffing of feet was audible, and this was not an accident. Nervous noise was Dora Lockwood's preferred mode of communication when she was unhappy: taps, clicks, heavy footsteps, the conspicuous roar of the vacuum cleaner. Anything but actual words. One of my most vivid memories from childhood—one of the last ones my father was still around for—was of her sitting at the dinner table, methodically plucking ice cubes out of a glass and crushing them between her teeth. Not speaking, barely touching the food on her plate, just sipping at the melted ice water and then going to town on a new cube. Crunch, crunch, crunch.

It kept on until the glass was nearly empty and I thought I was going to scream. My father was pretending not to notice, but the tension in the room was unbearable, and I was sure that it was going to be a prelude to something—a conversation, an argument, a fistfight. My parents had been not talking about things for so long. But when the cubes were gone, Mom had just gotten up and cleared the dishes in a way that felt like the period at the end of a sentence, as though she'd said all she'd had to say.

Dad left for good pretty soon after that. I think he was already planning to, but if he wasn't, the thing with the ice would've pushed him over the edge. He lived in Santa Monica now and was married to a very blond, very tan woman who did crystal healing ceremonies for cats with emotional problems—or if not that, exactly, then something equally ridiculous, where the only thing more annoying than the existence of the job itself is how happy and #blessed the woman doing it seems to be. My father and the cat whisperer had two kids, twin girls. Vivacious and well-adjusted eighteen-year-olds. They looked just like their mother and ran a moderately successful YouTube channel where they posted hair-braiding tutorials. I tried one once, but all I ended up with was a rat's nest that took an hour to comb out and took about half my hair with it, which seemed like it should be a metaphor for something. The YouTube twins were my father's greatest creation. Me, I was the rough draft that got stuck in a drawer when it turned out that no amount of work would ever make it into something good.

I was only nine at the time of the ice-crunching incident, and it took me a while to realize what a significant moment it was, a first glimpse at some essential truth about the woman who'd given birth to me. My mother's unhappiness was like a cage, but not one she was trying to escape. She just liked to rattle the door to remind you that she was in there. Crunching ice cubes, clicking her fingernails, walking back and forth on the loud driveway in a pattern that just happens to pass underneath her sleeping daughter's window: all of these were ways of signaling her anxiety without ever having to talk about it. God forbid she *do* something about it.

I once told my therapist that Mom was a living lesson in the difference between communicating and making noises. I was pretty proud of that, I thought it was clever, but the therapist made this sniffing noise and said wasn't my phrasing *interesting,* since many languages sounded like nothing but noise to people who didn't understand them.

"Have you ever tried talking about this with your mother?" she asked.

"She'll just turn it around on me," I said. "I don't need to hear another lecture about what a disappointment I am, how I don't have any direction and need to be more of a go-getter."

"I see," the therapist said, and then glanced at her watch. "Ah, well, our hour is nearly up. We'll continue this next week."

I didn't keep that appointment. Among other things, I was pretty sure that it would involve another snotty comment about how my perspective was *interesting,* which we all know is therapist-speak for *Actually, you're the asshole.* But it was probably for the best. It wasn't long after that things in New York fell apart and I had fled up the coast to Bar Harbor, tail tucked firmly between my legs. That was June. Now it was December, and Mom and I were still living in the big ramshackle mansion that had seven bedrooms and four parlors and expansive grounds and a wide-open view of the sea, yet somehow it still felt not quite big enough for the both of us. If I was going to unpack my childhood issues, it could wait until we were back in different area codes.

I found the phone where it had fallen and picked it up, unlocking it with a swipe. It was almost dead. I'd fallen asleep without plugging it in, mid-scroll, eyes glued to the social media feeds of people who weren't my friends anymore—or, if I was really being honest, never had been. The screen said it was 10:28 A.M., but the sky outside the window was the same depthless gray that it had been yesterday afternoon. The color wouldn't change until the sun went down somewhere behind the cloud cover, and the gray became black. It was my first New England winter, and I hated it. New York had been cold, too, but at least it still felt alive, with the traffic rushing and the stoplights blinking from green to yellow to red, the storefronts full of twinkling lights, the streetlamps decked out with colorful banners that flapped in the wind as it howled down Fifth Avenue. The apartment I'd shared with roommates in Greenpoint was always warm—usually too warm, superheated by an ancient radiator that sometimes got overexcited and spewed hot water all over the carpet—and there was always somewhere to go, something to do. But here the arrival of winter felt like the whole world dying, the color bleeding out of everything until it was all just shades of stone, slate, granite. The seasonal businesses in town went dark when the last of the leaf peepers left, their windows all shuttered, and the trees without their leaves looked like skeletal hands, clawing at the sky. Even the house was made of yellowed stone that could look almost golden when the summer sunlight hit it just right, but by the time Thanksgiving rolled around, it had faded, too, to the dirty, desaturated color of an old corn husk.

The footsteps outside paused and I leaned closer to the window to peer down at the driveway, only to find myself locking eyes with my mother, who was staring up at the house with her arms folded across her chest. She waved impatiently, then pointed at her wrist, which was bare, but the message was clear enough: *It's time. Get down here.*

I extended my index finger, mouthing the words *one second,* and paused with my legs dangling over the side of the bed. I looked at the phone again, tapping the text message icon even though I already knew there would be nothing new.

There was nothing new.

My thumb hovered over our last exchange. His message read: GOODNIGHT BABE. Mine said: NIGHT. I'd been trying to seem nonchalant, but now it felt like a trap: if I followed it up with GOOD MORNING, I'd look too eager and lose the upper hand.

Five minutes later, I stepped out the front door, hugging my arms across my chest. My hair, untouched by a stylist since I left New York, was returning to its natural state like a garden that someone had stopped bothering to take care of—dark, lank, perpetually tangled. I'd pulled it unbrushed into a messy bun and thrown on yesterday's jeans with ankle boots and a thin sweater with a high neck that looked vaguely Victorian, something I bought on impulse with my thumb when it popped up in a targeted Instagram ad. I'd been doing a lot of that this year. I'd tried to pretend that moving up to the coast would be like my own personal Walden, an escape from the unrelenting grind of late capitalism to a world of wool sweaters, muddy boots, no makeup, long walks on the beach at dawn. But this was all bullshit; I didn't suddenly start living my best life in Maine. I was just bored and cold, and spent most of my abundant free time wrapped up in a blanket and sweats on the sofa, shopping for clothes that I had no place to wear— except when I drove an hour to visit Mimi at her living facility on the mainland.

For the past three months, I'd been making that drive nearly every day and staying as long as I possibly could.

Mom greeted me with a frown. "Oh, honey, get your coat, it's too cold," she said. Then, after a beat: "You look nice, though. Is that new?"

I ignored this, knowing that a yes would eventually come back to bite me in some future conversation about how I needed to learn financial responsibility, which always struck me as funny given the giant seaside mansion looming behind us like a giant flashing sign that read: THESE PEOPLE HAVE TOO MUCH MONEY. My mother had always worked, but not because she needed the income; she just wanted to feel normal among the other PTA parents in our New Jersey suburb, where everyone was *comfortable,* in a normal upper-middle-class sort of way, but nobody had the kind of wealth that made things weird. I was an adult before I learned the truth. My great-grandfather had been a rich man; his daughter, my grandmother, had been a savvy investor; and her three children, of whom my mother was the youngest, would inherit a life-changing amount of money when she died, a fact that was getting harder to ignore as my grandmother sank deeper into the grips of dementia. Some families had skeletons in the closet; mine had a twenty-million-dollar elephant in the room. One night not long after I'd moved in, my mother had gotten a little bit drunk and admitted that one of the bitterest bones of contention in her divorce was the existence of a prenup, which ensured my dad didn't get a dime when they split up. Apparently Mimi had insisted on this. She also hadn't missed the opportunity, when it was all over, to say *I told you so.*

I gestured back at the house. "Couldn't we just wait inside?"

"Mother will want us to be here to greet her."

"We *are* here to greet her. We could even come out as soon as we see the car. She doesn't need us lined up out here like the staff of Downton Abbey."

I hugged myself tighter and traced my mother's steps, looking out toward the road—still no car—and then moving left, out to the point where I could look past the house toward the bay. December had been raw and wet. We'd had two snows, and there were still drifts here and there on the lawn, long stripes of white where the shadow of a tree had shielded it from the sun. But mostly it was misty. In the past week the water had been invisible more often than not, and the property seemed to end abruptly just beyond the lower garden, obscured by a wall of fog pressing in from the bay. Quiet mornings were punctuated by the blaring horns of unseen barges as they passed through the harbor toward the river.

But today the view was clear, and I could see that the dark water was half-frozen. Big chunks of loose ice bobbed sluggishly with the current, and farther out, the islands that dotted the bay looked like they were edged with gray lace.

According to my grandmother, the stretch of water between the mainland and the islands used to freeze solid in the winter, so you could walk clear across. On my last visit, I'd heard all about how she used to cross the ice under cover of dark in her youth. She would sneak out to meet her lover, the man who would eventually become her husband, carrying a lantern to light her way across the frozen reach. My grandfather had been dead for fifty years, but Mimi seemed to remember their love affair like it was yesterday—while struggling to recall things that had actually happened yesterday or last week or even within the last decade. That was all right with me: I loved losing myself in her past, all the stories I had never heard because she'd always been too busy traveling or serving on this or that charity board to be an ordinary grandma. Her life was more vibrant and interesting than mine had ever been, or probably ever would be, and she would talk to me for hours about her childhood, her travels, her family, her husband. Especially him. Theo, the love of her life. The look on her face when she said his name was something magical, and the way they'd been robbed of a long life together was downright cruel while also being incredibly romantic. He'd been killed in a boating accident when Mimi was in her thirties, and she loved him so much that she'd never remarried. It was like something out of a movie, the most gorgeous, tragic love story. Compared to that, what happened to me in New York was nothing, the emotional equivalent of a stubbed toe.

Most important, not only was Mimi happy to share, but she was always happy to see me. Even on the days she didn't recognize me because she was lost somewhere in the past, she'd still greet me warmly, like a girlfriend who'd stopped by for tea and gossip. In all my months of visits there had been only one bad moment, when I walked through the door to her apartment and she sat bolt upright and screamed at the first glimpse of me. "You!" she'd shrieked. "You viper, you bitch! I know what you've done!"

I had made the mistake of taking a step toward her, and she sprang up like she wanted to fight me, lurching dangerously to one side, nearly colliding with a table. She didn't seem to even feel it. She hissed at me, "Get out," and then the hiss was a howl. "Get out, get out, get *out*!"

My sprint to the nurse's station down the hall was the fastest I'd run in years. But when I went back with an aide to my grandmother's room, Mimi was sitting down again. She just looked at us and said, "Oh, hello," like nothing had ever happened.

The staff called it "an episode." They said it was just one of those things, and we were lucky that it wasn't a regular occurrence, and that we would be luckier still if it didn't happen more frequently as her condition got worse. Mom got nervous then and started saying that maybe I should limit my visits if they were upsetting her—but less time at Willowcrest would have meant more time here, in a house that felt more like a museum than a home, while my mother made noise instead of conversation and said, "Oh, nothing," if I tried to ask serious questions about what was going on. Instead, I started going most days, getting in the car right after breakfast and staying until the staff said visiting hours were over. I said I wanted to spend as much time with Mimi as possible, to hear all the stories she had to tell while she was still here to tell them. I told her Mimi deserved to know she wasn't alone, that she had a family who loved her. It wasn't the whole truth, but it had the desired effect: my mother walked away and never brought it up again.

Now she came up beside me and looked out at the bay, the island, the ice. "Will you please get your coat? You're making me cold."

"All right, all right." I hesitated, hovering my thumb over the text-ing app again. Mom's eyebrows went up and she moved closer, angling for a view of the screen. I stuffed the phone in my pocket.

"Who are you texting with?"

"Nobody."

"Someone back in New York?"

"No," I said too quickly. I scooted past her, headed toward the front door.

"A man?"

"Where would I find one of those?"

"I just want you to find someone to take care of you," Mom called after me.

"Because that always works out great," I said, under my breath.

"What?"

"Nothing. I was just—"

Just thinking that you of all people should know you can't count on a guy to take care of anything, I thought but didn't say. Not just because it was mean, but because I could hear the thrum of a motor, the light crunch of tires on gravel. A moment later, a white van with the Willowcrest logo on the side appeared, winding its way through the trees and then around the final curve toward the house. I uncrossed my arms from my chest and waved. Behind the wheel, the driver raised a palm in greeting.

My mother took a deep breath and blew it out in a loud sigh. "Oh, good," she said. "They're here."

2.

I thought I could make a life in New York. Or at least I thought I could take up space there until I figured out what my life was supposed to look like. I had moved to the city after college and got a job as a marketing assistant at a company that made flavored water—not that I cared about that, I didn't even like the product we made, but I'd needed something to do and it was the first offer that came my way. Everyone I had known at school had scattered after graduation, moving to the West Coast in search of tech jobs or disappearing into grad school, law school, medical school. I envied them: they all knew exactly what they wanted to be when they grew up, while I was still wrestling with the idea of growing up, period. My mother had finally told me, in a rare direct conversation, that our family had enough money that I could do basically anything I wanted. I had "the privilege of pursuing my passions": that was how she put it.

The problem was, I had no passions. I think maybe Mom hoped that the money would change this, transform me overnight into a provocateur, an artist, an ambitious entrepreneur. As if the only thing keeping me from being a more interesting person was a lack of funding. She didn't understand that knowing I could do virtually anything just made me more afraid of everything, immobilized by too many choices and the certainty that no matter what I attempted, I was going to fail and crash and burn. Having a safety net didn't comfort me. Actually it made it worse. A safety net just felt like a scary promise: you're going to fall.

I snuck a last furtive look at the phone—3 percent battery, no new messages—and then joined my mother as she trotted toward the van. Two men wearing parkas over their Willowcrest polo shirts disembarked from the front seats while my mother peered into the back, where a lone silhouette was visible. Mimi. She tapped a finger to the glass. "Mother?"

The younger of the two men—dark-haired, broad-shouldered, the kind of guy my thirstier girlfriends back in New York would have referred to as "a snack"—flashed us a winning smile and reached out to shake Mom's hand. "Hi, Ms. Lockwood."

"Hi, Adam," she said.

"Sorry we're a little behind schedule. Miss Miriam had a little nap on the way here, but she woke up about a mile out. She's having a good day. She certainly recognized the place right away, soon as we came through the gates."

Marcus, whose face was narrow and fox-like below a receding hairline, grunted over his shoulder as he opened the back door of the van. "She said she heard whispers."

"Oh," Mom said, her expression brightening. "That's the name of the house, or it was, a long time back. The Whispers. All these big old houses had names."

"The Whispers," Adam repeated, looking up at the house.

"It's the wind," Mom said. "If it hits the gables just right, it sounds like someone muttering."

"Sounds spooky."

"It's terrifying," I said, stepping forward with a smile.

"This is my daughter," Mom said. "But you've met."

He grinned. "Of course. We all live for Miss Lockwood's visits over at Willowcrest." He looked back and forth between me and Mom. "Miss Lockwood and Miss Lockwood. This could get confusing."

"It would also make me feel like an old maid in a Jane Austen novel," Mom said dryly, "so let's stick with first names. Dora and Delphine. We used to call her Del until she threw a tantrum about it."

"In my defense, I was twelve at the time," I said.

"True," Mom said amiably. "At that age, you threw a tantrum about everything. Isn't puberty awful? Now, where's Mother's chair?"

"Here," Marcus said, rummaging at the back of the van. "Let me just get these bags, and then—"

His voice was cut off by an indignant squawk from inside as the silhouette in the back swiveled its head. "I don't want the chair!"

Adam turned away, reaching to open the van's side door. It swung back to reveal Mimi—full name Mrs. Miriam Caravasios—sitting ramrod-straight with her hands folded neatly in her lap like a proper lady. Her white hair was curled just above the shoulder of her dark wool coat, and her nails were neatly painted a bright poppy red. Willowcrest had a contract with a local salon, and my last visit had coincided with Mimi's turn with the manicurist. I had picked the red, a shade called Harlot, because I knew that it would make Mimi laugh and my mother disapprove.

She turned her head as the door opened, locking eyes with Mom, who instantly stood up straighter like she'd just been caught slumping at finishing school.

"I don't want the chair," Mimi said again, an edge creeping into her voice.

"Miss Miriam, you've got quite a welcoming committee here," Adam said with a smile, reaching across her lap to unbuckle her seat belt. She lifted one red-tipped hand, settling her fingers over his shoulder, keeping her gaze on Mom.

"Two people is not a committee," she said, her expression so pinched with disdain that I nearly burst out laughing. Mom just sighed.

"Diana and William are flying up this afternoon. They're probably in the air by now. Richard—that's my older brother, he lives in L.A.," she said, looking toward Adam, who had finished unlocking Mimi's seat belt and was helping her swing her legs toward the door. He nodded back, and Mom continued, "Richard stopped off to see friends in Portland on his way up. He says he'll be here this evening, but then again, he said that yesterday, so . . . we'll see."

Mimi frowned. "What about Jillian?"

Uh-oh, I thought.

Mom shook her head. "Richard isn't married to Jillian anymore, Mother."

"Not Jillian, then," Mimi said, waving a hand impatiently. "The one after Jillian."

"He's not married to her anymore, either." Mom chuckled a little. "Or the one after that. Richard is three for three on divorces, Mother. And his boys are spending the holidays with their wives' families. But look, your granddaughter is here."

Mimi made a *harrumph* noise, but the corners of her mouth lifted as she looked at me. "Well, hello, granddaughter," she said. "That's a lovely blouse."

"Thanks, Mimi," I said, and then shivered violently as a sudden gust of wind blew straight through the thin material of my sweater. Everyone laughed.

"Let's all go inside, we'll just need to unfold the ch—" Mom began, then stopped and looked aghast as Mimi scooted forward, one hand still resting on Adam's shoulder, and stepped down from the van as nimbly as a cat.

"Don't fuss, Theodora," the old woman said, the smile gone from her face. "I'm perfectly capable of walking on my own."

That's the problem, I thought, watching my mother's unhappy expression as she watched her mother walk toward the house, one hand nestled gently into the crook of Adam's arm. It was hard to believe that Mimi was dying. Her white hair was still thick and glossy, her cheeks pink, and though she had the deeply lined face and slightly shrunken look of a person who had lived for eighty-five years, she moved with the confidence of someone half her age. The running joke at Willowcrest was that she had a different kind of mobility issue from most residents: she was *too* agile, surprisingly quick on her feet. Some dementia patients lost their coordination at the same time as they lost their minds, which came with its own risks—bad falls, broken hips—but this was its own problem. Mimi had a habit of slipping away when somebody's back was turned, wandering into other residents' rooms or rattling for entry at locked doors. Once, just a few days after moving in, she'd managed to sneak into the cafeteria as it was closing after lunch and walked away with one of the tubs from the salad bar. She'd consumed fully half of it by the time someone noticed that Willowcrest's newest resident was sitting alone in one of the inner courtyards, eating egg salad out of a bucket with her bare hands.

But that was funny, not dangerous. Willowcrest was safe for someone like Mimi precisely because it seemed like you could leave. On the surface, it was a posh little village, with shops and restaurants and even a Victorian-style greenhouse where you could spend an afternoon reading under a palm tree. A place designed to make people feel free while also effectively and quietly imprisoning them. A resident like my grandmother could manage something like the egg salad incident, even enjoy her resulting reputation as a bit of a troublemaker, while we and the staff knew she'd never even gotten close to one of the few and firmly locked exits.

The only problem with Willowcrest was that it wasn't home.

And Mimi deserved to be home for Christmas, in the house where she'd been a child, a wife, a mother—and where she'd returned at the end of her long life, after decades away, as if she'd known it would be over soon. It was why we were here, and why everyone else would be, too. My mother and her siblings rarely spoke, and rarely agreed on anything when they did, but somehow they'd managed to plan this holiday reunion at the house that would eventually become just another asset to fight over. Maybe because everyone understood that it was now or never, that we wouldn't get another chance. Even if her body lived to see another December, Mimi would be gone by then. Lost in the fog like one of the shadowy boats drifting out there on the bay, sounding its mournful horn as it drifted past unseen. I thought of the way she'd looked at me, the way she'd said, *Hello, granddaughter,* with that cheeky smile. "Granddaughter," and not my name—because she'd forgotten it.

It all comes full circle, I thought, watching her approach the broad stone steps. It was a journey she must have made thousands of times, passing over the threshold of her family home. She glanced up at Adam, who smiled down at her, and tightened her grip on his arm.

"I've got you," he said.

Mom, who had been clicking her tongue almost unconsciously from the moment Mimi began walking, made a little squeak like she was being strangled.

"Mom," I said, my voice floating out low and cautious through gritted teeth. "Let it be."

But I didn't need to say anything: Mimi was up the steps in seconds, still holding tight to Adam's arm, waiting for him to reach out with his free hand to open the door. I felt Mom relax next to me—and then she chuckled. "They sure don't make nurses like they used to."

"He's not a nurse," I said automatically. "You need a degree for that. He's a personal caregiver."

Mom raised her eyebrows and gave me a sidelong glance. "Well, I wouldn't mind if he gave me some personal care."

"*Mom,*" I hissed, but started giggling. Adam looked back at us with a knowing grin. It was impossible to tell if he'd heard. If he did, I guessed he didn't mind.

As she stepped over the threshold, Mimi paused once more. The wind rose as she turned into it, whipping her hair back from her face. The open doorway framed her in darkness as she stood, gazing east toward the trees and the sea beyond. She looked beautiful and blissful, as if the years had receded to reveal the young woman she used to be. And inside my head, a single thought passed like a whisper.

She's home.

3.

1942

SUMMER

She is thirteen years old. Just a girl and young like a sunrise, with pink cheeks and blue eyes and hair the color of dark honey. Her face holds the promise of incredible beauty beneath its childish roundness. People look at her as though she's a flower, just waiting to bloom. She is small-boned but long-limbed, with her mother's slim ankles and shapely legs. Mother was a chorus girl before she became Papa's wife, and Miriam has her prettiness, her grace.

The fierceness, she gets from her father.

All summer long, she has felt herself standing on the precipice that separates a girl from a woman, not afraid to fall but also not quite ready to leap. Knowing that this part of her life will soon come to an end. She has a sense that she'll miss it when it's gone, even though being a lady looks like its own kind of fun. She has always loved the freedom of her wild girlhood, the small rebellions that her mother is always promising to punish her for. *Next time, Miriam,* she says. *I mean it.*

They both know she doesn't mean it. Her parents pretend to be dismayed by her untamable nature; their only daughter is forever trailing an untied ribbon from her hair, a loose thread from her hem. She turns up with her shoes missing and her stockings all stained with grass, until her mother sighs and says fine, she can run barefoot, as long as it's only here at the Whispers and there's no company to offend—but even then, they know this definition of "company" will be invoked rarely if at all. On the day they arrived at the house for the summer, Miriam left her shoes under her bed, and there they've stayed, collecting dust. She has never been asked to fetch them, not even when the local garden club came to take tea on the veranda and inspect her mother's roses, or when the two young ladies whom her brothers had been courting since last August arrived one evening with their families for dinner and dancing, wearing their prettiest silk gowns and pearls.

One day Miriam will put on her own silk dress and heeled shoes and take a seat at the great maple table in the dining room and make boring grown-up small talk with the boring grown-up guests. One day she'll have a suitor of her own to bring her flowers and whisper things in her ear that make her blush. The sensation of his breath on her neck will melt her.

One day he will kiss her with a mouth that tastes like salt water as the whole world burns.

But not now. Not yet. This summer, she is shoeless and sun-kissed and free to do as she pleases—and if any of those young ladies are scandalized by the sight of Roland Day's youngest daughter running in bare feet across the lawn at dusk to chase fireflies, they have the good sense not to say so. Their host, for all his generosity and good humor, is not a man it would be wise to offend.

• • •

But on this particular August evening, Miriam is not barefoot and not happy, either. The summer is coming to a close, and the country is at war; in only a week, her family will leave the Whispers and return to their home in Egg Harbor, New Jersey. This summer is the last they'll have here together as a family. Robert, the eldest, will be married before the year is out; Edward, younger and more idealistic, has announced his intention to enlist instead of continuing his education. Her father will be busy and absent, traveling often for business, and Miriam and her mother will be left to themselves, alone and quite lonely.

For all these reasons and more, she wishes she could kick off her shoes and run. Across the grass, through the gardens, along the shoreline where the pink granite rocks are still warm from the heat of the sun. She wants to fling open her arms and drink up the sky, the sea, the whole world.

Instead, she is stuck indoors playing hide-and-seek with an idiot.

Tonight's dinner was one she was not allowed to miss, the kind where children were expected to be seen but not heard, unless someone spoke to them, in which case they were expected to answer politely and using the proper honorifics. The guests, a family called Chandler whose house sits on the other side of the bay and which they insist on referring to as "the cottage" despite the fact that it's at least as big as the Whispers, were here to be impressed by Roland Day's many successes, including his lovely and well-mannered daughter. The Chandlers also have three children, including a son the same age as Miriam, whom she has been told she must be nice to. His name is Harold and he has pale blond hair, gangly legs, and a bright red face because he went outside today and forgot to wear his hat. Miriam thinks Harold looks like a freshly cooked crab. She also thinks he's a real dummy, and not just because a kid with his complexion should have learned to stay out of the sun by now.

When she asks him if he's read any good books lately, he says he doesn't like to read, and she has to fake a sneeze to conceal her look of horror. But she plays her part just like she's supposed to. She uses the proper fork; she says *please* and *thank you* and *no, sir,* and *yes, madam.* She dabs delicately at the corners of her mouth with her napkin, as if to keep from marring her lipstick, even though she's not old enough yet to be wearing any. She understands that the glorious freedom she enjoys here at the Whispers comes with an unspoken agreement that she'll play the role of the mannered and dutiful daughter on the rare occasions, like this one, when her parents require it.

But then dinner is over, and Papa tells her to go and play with the Chandler boy and his younger sisters while the grown-ups gather on the veranda to watch the sunset and talk about whatever grown-ups talk about. He waits for the rest of the children to turn away before he leans in with a wink and says, "Perhaps you should all stay indoors, darling. And try not to embarrass him. If that boy gets any redder, he'll burst into flames."

Miriam suggests hide-and-seek and volunteers to be it first, since it is her house. She leads the group out of the dining room and into the front foyer, where two long hallways stretch away into the house and a grand staircase rises toward the second floor. She points: upstairs is out of bounds, but anywhere in the north wing is fair game. The little Chandler girls clap their hands and scatter off into the shadows as Miriam sits on the staircase, closes her eyes, and begins to count. But when she reaches ten and opens them, she sighs. Stupid Harold is still standing exactly where he was, staring at her. Outside, the sky is deepening, and shadows are beginning to pool in the hallway. She hears the clink of glassware and the tinkle of laughter from the veranda. It sounds very far away.

"You're supposed to hide," Miriam says, and bites her tongue to keep from adding *dummy.* "I'm going to close my eyes and count to ten—"

"Mumma said that you and me are going to get married," Harold says, staring at her. His face doesn't look so red in the dark, but his strange pale eyes are unsettling, the pupils like big black holes. Miriam's mouth drops open. Now she doesn't have to bite her tongue at all; she couldn't speak if she wanted to. Harold takes a step toward her and makes a sort of clumsy half bow. "I want to give you a kiss."

"Oh," Miriam says faintly. "Oh, no. No, thank you." But Harold takes another step toward her, and the little pink lips at the center of his very red face start to pucker, and Miriam realizes with dismay that Harold intends to give her the kiss whether she wants it or not. And so she does the only thing she can think of: she stands up and taps him hard with her index finger, right in the center of his chest. Harold's puckered mouth transforms into a little O of surprise. He stares at her.

"I found you. So you're it," Miriam says gaily, and skips away into the house. She doesn't look back to see what Harold is doing, but some small part of her wonders if she's made a mistake, if the Chandler boy will turn out to be what her mother would call *persistent*. Persistent is not necessarily a bad thing. Miriam's own father was persistent, which is why Mother ended up married to him and not some other suitor, of which she had many. But Miriam does not want persistence from Harold. She doesn't want anything from Harold at all. She nearly sighs aloud with relief when his voice rings out from the foyer.

"One," he says glumly. There's a long pause, and a sigh. Then even more glumly: "Two."

Miriam darts through a dimly lit parlor and into her father's library, inhaling the familiar scent of pipe tobacco and old books. Harold is nearly done counting, but she lingers just inside the open door, waiting. Listening. Hide-and-seek is Miriam's favorite game, and she its undefeated champion, because she figured out long ago that the secret to winning isn't staying hidden. It's staying in motion, creeping from one hiding place to another, concealing yourself in spots that the seeker already investigated and found empty. Sliding unseen around corners like a ghost. Sometimes, when she's feeling especially mischievous, she'll make it into her own game and begin following the person looking for her, daring herself to get closer and closer. Nobody has ever caught her doing this, but it's thrilling to take the risk—and to see the way that people begin jumping at every creak and shadow the longer the chase goes on, as if they can sense they're being hunted.

The house itself is built perfectly for this game, although Miriam won't understand the reasons why until she's older. Her father bought the land for his house around the turn of the century, but he didn't finish building the Whispers until 1920. Just in time to make it a wedding gift for his beautiful young wife—but also to outfit the place with cubbies and passages to hold the illegal liquor that ran like a secret river through the dark harbor outside. Roland Day was an ambitious and deliberate man and rarely touched a drink himself. But he knew a good investment when he saw one: at the height of Prohibition, his great stone house above the bay was one of the biggest bootlegging hubs in the state.

He was already quite a rich man by the time Miriam came into the world, red-faced and screaming, on a dark and wild day in 1929. Papa liked to joke that she arrived furious, having gotten a bad stock tip from the stork who dropped her at their door. He could afford to joke, of course. The bulk of his fortune wasn't sitting in any bank when the market crashed. While his neighbors struggled, he thrived, even surpassing some of them in wealth, a fact he speaks of with dark and contemptuous pleasure. Mother tried to explain it once: These men used to sneer at Papa for being new money, a self-made man. But now he had assets, things those sneering neighbors desired.

• • •

Miriam is beginning to understand, barely, that she herself is one of those coveted things—and that Papa has plans for her. But what she knows without a doubt is that the house is full of wonderful places to hide, especially if you're a young girl whose hips are exactly half as wide as a case of whiskey.

Still, she doesn't want to spend an hour tiptoeing from place to place, dodging Harold Chandler and his puckered pink lips until it's time for the guests to go home. When she's sure he's far enough away not to hear it, she unbuckles her shoes, peels off her stockings, and leaves them stuffed behind a potted plant. Then she slips through a side door and runs.

Her bare feet touch the soft, warm grass as the sun dips just below the tree line, streaking the sky with pink. Behind her, the house looks like a great jewel, its windows shimmering gold with electric light, a beacon above the sea. She hears voices on the veranda, but they're only murmurs; nobody shouts her name, and she knows they haven't seen her. A moment later, she is behind the garden wall, down the steps that lead to the water, out to the long wooden pier that stretches into the bay. Once last summer she woke in the middle of the night and saw her father standing here, smoking, surrounded by the bobbing shadows of his men as they unloaded a small boat by moonlight. But this evening, with the sun still fading, she is alone. The wind dies and the water turns glassy, and then she sees him. Out in the bay a lobsterman's boat is passing, and a boy—or maybe a young man—is standing on the bow beside the stacks of rickety traps. His face is half hidden by shadow, but she can tell from the tilt of his head that he has seen her. That he is looking at her.

He looks at her for a long time.

Miriam looks back and continues looking, even when she can no longer tell which of the specks on the horizon is him. Even as someone calls her name from far above, in the sharp tone that tells her she will be scolded when she gets back. She stays just a moment more. She breathes in the scent of salt water, of sea mud, of the sun-warmed wood beneath her feet. The speck on the horizon is gone now. The path where the boat traveled ripples in the dying light, the faintest of disturbances, the only sign that it was ever there at all.

4.

By the time I first set foot in the Whispers, it was a shadow of its former self: cracked and creaky and full of locked doors, cluttered rooms, no company but stacks of old books and magazines and the muttering of the wind. What I knew of its history came mostly from an old brochure I'd found in one of the boxes that were stacked up in the library: built by my great-grandfather in 1920 as a wedding present for his new, young wife, back when Bar Harbor was a summer playground for the rich and famous. Partially destroyed in one of the famous fires that swallowed half the state in 1947. Restored the following year, when Mimi married my grandfather, turning it into a love nest twice over.

Mimi had left Bar Harbor for New Jersey after her husband died, but she was smart enough to keep the house, and to eventually realize its romantic history made for a great marketing pitch. Bootlegger's Historic Seaside Château. For decades, the Whispers had been in the care of a management company that rented it for wedding parties or corporate retreats. But a few years ago, without explanation, Mimi had canceled her contract with the management company and moved back to the coast—and here she'd stayed alone, quietly losing her mind where nobody was around to see it. I used to wonder if she was already sick then, or if rattling around in all that empty space with nothing to keep her company except her memories somehow unmoored her. It took five years for her dementia to progress to the point where someone finally noticed, in what my mother called *the first incident.* The old man who served as the Whispers' winter handyman was driving up at twilight to change out the furnace filter when he came around a curve and found Mimi standing dead center in the road. Her hair was wild, her feet were bare and bleeding, and when he called her name, she just stared—until he walked up and put a hand on her shoulder. Then she shrieked—like a banshee, he'd said—and sank her teeth into his forearm.

Mom had moved to Bar Harbor within the month. "Someone should be with her," she'd said, and when I tried to point out that someone didn't have to be her, she laughed ruefully. "If not me, who?"

She lasted six months up here, just her and Mimi. Long enough for the doctors to recommend that Mimi relinquish her car keys, take her pills, and get any outstanding affairs in order. It was also long enough for us to find out that just because Mimi needed care, that didn't mean she would want it or accept it—and long enough for there to be a second and third and tenth incident, all different from the first one, as she became more forgetful, more frightened, and finally, angrier and more defiant and sometimes cruel. My mother hadn't been back to the Whispers in decades, and it was a maze of hallways and doorways and places to hide, places she didn't know existed but that Mimi knew by heart. She would disappear every time my mother's back was turned. Sometimes Mom would find her. More often, she would wander the house for hours, calling out while the shadows lengthened outside.

Eventually she would sit down and give up, which was when Mimi would emerge from wherever she'd been and stalk past her like an imperious queen.

"Don't fuss, Theodora," she'd say.

It wasn't funny, except that it sort of was, an eighty-five-year-old woman who still got off on playing hide-and-seek—but a creepy, nonconsensual version where the other person was always it whether they wanted to be or not. Even Mom would laugh about it when she called me afterward, usually three glasses deep into a bottle of wine, and I'd laugh, too. But under the laughter was the ominous sense that things were going badly and getting worse. That there would come a time, very soon, when Mimi wasn't safe at home anymore.

Actually, that time had come and gone. My mother's hesitation wasn't about Mimi, but about herself: she'd sold her house and packed her things and moved back north for one thing, and one thing only. If Mimi went into a care facility, she hadn't just failed. She had no backup plan. Nothing to do, nowhere to go. No purpose.

Really, I did her a favor by blowing up my life and getting kicked out of my apartment. My mother needed someone to take care of, and I'd had nowhere else to go.

Marcus set the folded wheelchair down inside the door. My grandmother, still holding Adam's arm, scowled at it and turned away, her gaze drifting around the room as if she were taking inventory. Nothing missing, everything in its place. Two tall mirrors stood on either side of a pair of pocket doors, which opened to the formal dining room; a long wood table and threadbare oriental rug were visible through the doorway. She glanced at her reflection in one of the mirrors, then turned to gaze up along the gleaming wooden staircase that took two turns on its way to the second floor.

Marcus was looking around, too. "This is some place," he said to me. "You and your ma have been living here just the two of you?"

"We only really live in a few rooms." My mother came up abruptly behind me. "The cost of heating the whole place alone would bankrupt us."

Marcus chuckled dutifully but continued to stare at the dark hallways, the peeling walls, the cracked ceiling. "It must have been something once upon a time."

"It's seen better days," Mom said. "That wing there was practically destroyed in 1947. The fire, you know."

"My uncle was there," Marcus said. "They had every man on the island out there trying to fight the fire. He said he never saw anything like it. You're lucky the whole place didn't go."

"Sometimes I wish it had." She smiled weakly, gesturing toward the dark hallway that opened up to our left. "We keep it all closed up, but—"

A sharp voice broke in. "You changed it," Mimi said, glaring at my mother.

Mom sighed. "Mother, I've done no such thing. Everything is just like you left it."

Mimi's voice was getting louder. "No. You changed it. You changed . . ." She trailed off, her eyes flitting from place to place, lingering on an empty space just over my shoulder. "Where's the plant?"

Mom looked in the same direction and shook her head, frustration creeping into her voice. "There's never been a plant there, Mother."

"But my shoes," Mimi said, her voice faltering. "How will I find . . ."

"I think she's just tired. Let's get these things to her room," Mom said, turning to Adam as Mimi's voice dropped to a low mutter. She pointed. "There's a back bedroom here on the first floor, just past the kitchen that way."

"The one with all the hats?" I said. In the years that Mimi had lived here alone, she'd managed to fill up the house with clutter that was worthless but bizarrely, carefully curated. One room had housed a collection of at least three dozen dining chairs, none of which seemed to match; another had been crammed floor to ceiling with boxes that turned out to contain old, moldy copies of the *Ladies' Home Journal*. But the most interesting was the little room off the kitchen that had contained a bed, a nightstand, and about a hundred hats of all shapes and sizes that looked like they'd dropped through a wormhole from the 1950s. I had even briefly thought about starting an Instagram account for the hats, which seemed like a great idea right up until I opened one of the hatboxes and found, nestled alongside a black wool pillbox covered with white feathers and a twee little veil, the desiccated corpse of either a very large mouse or a small rat.

I'd clapped the top back on the hatbox and kicked it under the bed, and that was the end of that project. It was also the last time I'd gone poking through any of Mimi's collections.

My mother snorted a little. "I moved the hats yesterday. If you hadn't been so glued to your phone, maybe you would have noticed. Anyway, it's a bit cold and small, but it's got its own bathroom. And I don't want her attempting stairs." She moved to my grandmother's side, gently taking her arm. "Okay, Mother? We're going to get you settled in, right here on the first floor."

Mimi blinked and pulled her arm free. "But that's Shelly's room." She looked back at us, her gaze jumping from face to face, the imperious tone back in her voice. "Where is Shelly?"

A funny thing about Mimi was that her confidence was contagious: even though she wasn't making sense, the rest of us began shuffling and looking around as if the mysterious missing Shelly might suddenly materialize from behind a door. Marcus turned to Adam. "Do we know a Shelly?"

"Oh," Mom said abruptly. "Shelly worked here. A long time back, when I was just a little girl. She was my nanny, too, wasn't she? Mother?" Mimi didn't answer and Mom shrugged, turning back to the group. "I was so young, I hardly remember her. But that back bedroom was hers. I think it was actually the servant's quarters when the house was first built."

"Servants! Fancy folks," Marcus said, and everyone laughed.

"Like you said, once upon a time," Mom said. "I don't think anyone lives like that anymore. At least not around here."

"What happened to Shelly?" Adam asked, and my mother shrugged.

"I'd guess she's still in town, unless she retired somewhere. She had a son about my age . . ." She trailed off, furrowing her brow. "Anyway, I think Mother might feel better if she could lie down for a bit. Would you bring her bags?"

"Sure thing," Marcus said. "The chair, too?"

"No," Mimi said, fully alert again. Adam and Marcus exchanged bemused looks.

Mom shifted her weight uncomfortably and sighed. "I guess it's not necessary. We'll keep it here just in case. Delphine, maybe you and Adam can find room for it in one of the coat closets?"

"I'll look," I said while my mother took Mimi's arm again and began to lead her away down the hallway on the right.

Mimi took a few steps, then cast a fearful look back over her shoulder. "Is Theo coming?" she said.

"He'll be here for dinner," Mom said without missing a beat, and looked relieved when Mimi hesitated only a second before nodding— knowing this impossible promise was one she'd never have to keep. Mimi's short-term memory was almost completely gone. Sometimes I would visit her in the morning, only to have her call the house in tears just a few hours later, asking why no one had come to see her. It was like a dark, ironic twist on all those live-laugh-love memes, the ones like "Be present" or "Stay in the moment": Mimi was so present that yesterday no longer existed for her. As soon you left her alone, it was like you'd never been there at all.

Marcus followed my mother, all three of them disappearing through the doorway at the end of the hall. Adam smiled at me as an awkward silence descended. I hadn't expected to be left alone with him, and my mind was blank—except for the memory of my mother, saying *I wouldn't mind if he gave me some personal care*, which wasn't helping the situation. I bit my lip and tried to think of something to say.

Instead, he broke the silence. "So, uh, this is a really huge house," he said finally.

"Yeah, but like she said, we don't use all the rooms," I said, relieved to have something concrete and boring to discuss. "Most of them are full of random stuff anyway. We only go into that wing a few times a week to run the taps and flush the toilets, so the pipes don't freeze."

He made a show of looking impressed. "Toilets! Toilets, plural? How many bathrooms are in this place?"

"Seventeen," I deadpanned, then laughed as his mouth dropped open. "Just kidding. There are four. Oh, five if you count the crazy powder room. Check this out," I said, crossing the foyer to the staircase. The wall underneath the stairs was made of the same dark wood as the banister, inlaid with decorative paneling. A carved rosette sat at the center of each panel; I grasped the one nearest my hip and twisted. There was a click as a hidden catch disengaged and a seam opened up in the wall. I stepped aside, pulling the door wide to reveal a narrow space with a commode at one end, a pedestal sink at the other.

"Oh, wow," Adam said, peering in. "That's really cool. It's like a secret passage. Except with a toilet in it. Is this the only one?"

"Yep," I said. "I mean, as far as I know. I mostly go back and forth from my room to the kitchen to the sofa. I haven't actually checked every room for a secret bathroom."

"So you're saying, there *could* be seventeen bathrooms."

I laughed. "There could. Toilets stashed in the walls, the ceilings—"

"And if you find them all, you unlock the key to a secret VIP bathroom where the toilet is made of solid gold," he finished.

"That's pretty specific," I said. "Is this a dream of yours?"

"Yes. And since you made fun of it, when I do get a solid gold toilet, I'm not letting you use it, no matter how nicely you ask," Adam said, grinning. "So what's in the spooky wing where nobody goes?"

"Just rooms. Boxes. Lots of furniture covered in drapes."

"You've never explored?"

"If you've seen one mummified mouse, you've seen them all," I said, and he laughed.

"But it's such a cool place. Would you ever open it back up?"

"It's not up to me," I said, before realizing that there was an unspoken second half to the question—that there would come a time when it was up to me, or at least, up to whoever inherited the Whispers after Mimi was gone. I grimaced.

"I'm sorry," Adam said.

"No, it's fine. It's just strange. And sad. This place was home for my grandmother, but when she's gone, it's just going to be another asset to fight over." I was suddenly, painfully aware of how ridiculous I sounded, complaining about the terrible burden of owning a huge seaside mansion to a guy who lived in one room above someone's garage. "Sorry, you don't need to hear about this."

"No, it's interesting," he said. "But your mom wouldn't stay here? You wouldn't? It is a pretty awesome house. If I had a place like this, with all those memories, I don't know that I would want to let go of it."

"Not my memories. I'd never set foot in this place until this year. Once Mimi is gone, none of us have a reason to stay."

"Well, maybe you'll find a reason," he said, and the awkward silence descended again. Adam had a way of making very direct, intense eye contact—probably a skill he'd picked up at Willowcrest, so the residents always felt like he had their full attention—but even though I'd known him for months, I couldn't get used to that penetrating stare. It made me feel *too* seen, exposed, like there was nowhere to hide. I fought the urge to reach for my phone.

"So what are y—" I started to say, and then nearly sighed with relief at the sound of footsteps from the hallway. My mother reemerged with Marcus close behind her.

"How's Mimi?" I asked.

"Fine," Mom said, but she had a funny look on her face; clearly the homecoming wasn't going as she'd hoped. Then she blinked and looked at Adam with a start, as if she'd forgotten he was there. "Oh. Did you give Adam the tour yet?"

I shook my head.

"Well, he should know his way around." She turned to Adam. "Is now a good time? We'll be quick."

Adam nodded. "Absolutely. Unless you need to get back, bro," he added, turning to Marcus.

Marcus shook his head. "Take your time. But I do need, uh, the lavatory, if you don't mind."

Adam laughed and snapped his fingers. "Oh, man, you're gonna love this. Miss Lockwood, can he use the secret toilet?"

The three of us climbed the stairs as Marcus disappeared underneath them. I'd always been wary of that bathroom for fear that the noise would be broadcast through the house by the same weird acoustics that made it whisper when the wind came up, but the last thing I heard was a cheerful "Hey, neat," as he stepped into the room, the last syllable clipped as the door closed behind him. After that the only noise was our footsteps and the familiar creaking of the staircase.

Mom sighed as a loose step squealed under her feet. "One more thing to fix." She turned at the top of the stairs and began moving down the hall, gesturing at doorways and keeping up a running commentary—"Bedroom, master bedroom, bath, parlor, there's a balcony there, that's a linen closet"—but a sidelong glance at Adam showed that he wasn't really paying attention. He kept looking backward like he was afraid he'd be lost or lingering in front of the oil paintings and faded photographs that lined the walls. The paintings were seascapes, views of the bay and outlying islands that someone had probably painted while staying at the house. The pictures were mostly of the house itself. Adam paused in front of one, a black-and-white photograph in which three men wearing old-fashioned tennis whites were posed in front of the entrance, in the same spot where we'd met the Willowcrest van. One of them was shorter and older than the others, with brooding dark eyes and a luxuriant mustache—but the way he stood between them, with a hand resting on each of their shoulders, you could tell it was a father and his sons.

"Who's this?" Adam said.

My mother walked over and leaned in close, eye to eye with the tallest of the two sons. "Ah, that would be my grandfather and my uncles. That's Edward on the left and Robert on the right. Uncle Bob. Edward, I never met. He was killed in an accident before I was born."

Adam raised his eyebrows. "That's Miss Miriam's pop, there in the middle? Damn, he looks intense."

Mom laughed. "Considering he made his fortune selling illegal liquor to the mafia, I'm sure he was. Edward and Bob were his sons from his first marriage. They were quite a bit older than my mom."

I drifted away while they talked—Adam wanted to know if there were more photographs; Mom said they had been mostly destroyed in the fire, but Mimi's family albums were probably stored in the attic—and wound up at the end of the hall, where a window offered a view of the sea. The mist was coming in again, in wisps this time, so that the islands out in the bay winked in and out of view as it drifted past. The last time I'd looked out this particular window was on the day I moved in, when I'd wandered all over the house feeling desperately sorry for myself, reliving the highlights reel of my humiliating departure from New York as if I could change how it ended. Last conversations, last meetings. My last view of Colin as he'd closed his bedroom door in my face, and his voice, floating out through the crack just before it clicked shut, saying, "You're just kind of basic, Delphine."

Unlike Mimi, I had nothing wrong with my memory. I could recall every excruciating detail—right down to the exact shape and shade of the mark I left on the door when I kicked it.

My mother was still talking. "Anyway, we'll stick you in the apartment suite on the third floor. It has its own bathroom and kitchenette, so you can prepare meals if you want to, or of course you're welcome to dine with us. I'd like you to feel at home while you're here, but don't feel compelled. We just appreciate it so much, all you've done for my mother. And I have to ask just once more, you're positive you don't need some time off for Christmas? Even on Christmas Day? Your family—"

Adam held up a hand to stop her, but not before I noticed the way he flinched when she said *your family*.

"It's just another day for me," he said. "My mom passed a long time ago and I never knew my dad. And I guess I have some extended family in Brazil, but that's a long flight to see people I've never met. I've pretty much always spent Christmas at work. A lot of people in care homes get lonely this time of year so they'll really go all out with the decorations and activities. But this—I mean, this house, and a family? I'm really honored you'd let me be a part of it."

"Well, Willowcrest is lucky to have you," Mom said. "But Mother will be so happy to have you here. You're her favorite, you know."

"Well," Adam said, smiling, "we're not supposed to have favorites, but just between us, the feeling is mutual."

Some time later, Mom and I stood on the piazza and waved as the Willowcrest van trundled back down the driveway and out of sight. Adam had promised to be back around dinnertime, as soon as he'd finished his last shift and circled home to pack a bag. My mother waited until the van was gone, then raised her eyebrows. "So, that was interesting."

"What?" I said, distracted: in my pocket, my phone had just vibrated with an alert.

"He's, what, thirty? There's no wife, no girlfriend?"

"It's not easy to meet people. I don't know if you've looked at Tinder up here, but it's pretty slim pickings."

"I don't Tinder," Mom said. "Wait, or is it 'I don't have Tinder'? Is Tinder a verb or a noun?"

"It's a hellscape, is what it is," I said.

"You could always meet someone the old-fashioned way."

"Oh, are we talking about me now? I thought it was Adam's love life you were worried about."

"I guess you're the expert," Mom said. She was quiet as we walked together back toward the house. I hung back for a moment as she climbed the steps, tugging out my phone, smiling as I saw a single alert on-screen. One new message.

Good morning 😊

I nearly skipped up the steps, pulling the heavy door closed behind me. As I did, my mother spun around, her eyes wide. "Oh!" she said and snapped her fingers. "Do you think he might be gay?"

"What?" I said, bewildered.

"Adam!"

"Mom, for the love—"

The sound of a motor from outside silenced both of us, although my mother at least had the decency to look embarrassed. There was the slow crunch of tires on gravel, a car door slamming, and the sound of rapid footsteps approaching. Mom and I looked at each other.

"I guess they forgot something," she said, walking past me to open the door. But as she did, she leaped back in surprise. A tall, slender man with luxuriant gray hair and an eggplant-colored puffer coat stood in the doorway, the handle of a rolling suitcase gripped in one hand. His other hand had been raised to knock, but now he waved at us with a grin. His teeth were very white.

"Richard!" Mom squawked and stood aside as my uncle strode through the door, set his bag down, and wrapped her in a brief hug.

"Little sister," he said, and turned to nod at me. "And progeny. All grown up."

"Hi, Uncle Richard," I said. He took a few steps and leaned in to give me a perfunctory kiss that landed mostly in the air next to my cheek. I kissed the air next to his.

"Well," he said, looking around, raising his voice so that it echoed against the high ceiling and marble floor, "what do you say, kids? Shall we set the place on fire now, or get good and drunk first?"

5.

Richard stuck around long enough to register his disappointment in the weather ("disgusting"), the condition of the house ("dilapidated"), and my mother's appearance ("Have they not heard of moisturizer in Maine?") before whisking himself and his bags upstairs in search of a shower. He reappeared just as my grandmother finished her nap, the two of them arriving in the kitchen from opposite entrances and stopping abruptly at the sight of each other. My mother came up behind Mimi and squeezed her shoulder.

"There's Richard, Mother. He's come to visit with you."

"Richard?" Mimi said. She frowned, shooting a narrow glance back over her shoulder at my mother. "He looks old."

Richard let out a bark of laughter. "So do you, Mom. We're none of us spring chickens here, are we. Even young Del is looking a little pinched around the eyes."

My mother cleared her throat. "She doesn't like that nickname, Richard," she said, and I felt myself gripped by equal parts gratitude and frustration. All Richard had done since he'd arrived was snipe about everyone and everything, like he was trying to make himself feel better by making the rest of us miserable; something about being here, whether it was the family reunion or the house itself, was obviously making him uncomfortable. My mother always said that Richard moved to the West Coast for the weather, but I was beginning to wonder if there wasn't another reason why he'd moved so far away—and why, in all these years, nobody had ever suggested he come back.

"Oh, beg pardon, Del-*pheeen*," Richard said, running his hands through his damp hair. "Christ, what a name. Honestly, Dora, whose idea was that? No, don't tell me, I guess we all know the answer to that one. You'd never be that pretentious. That guy you married, though . . . well. Delphine Lockwood. It's like a poor person's idea of what a rich person would name their kid."

My mother looked like she'd swallowed a bee. Speaking up on my behalf had been hard enough; defending herself, or her choice to marry a man who'd turned out to be a disappointment at much more than choosing baby names, was beyond her.

I flashed Richard an unfriendly smile. "How about this," I said. "You can call me Del, and I'll call you Dick. So everyone gets a name that suits them."

Richard stared. Then he guffawed, and the tension in the room relaxed by a degree.

"Oh, I *like* you," he said, and sighed. "Touché, Delphine. And beg pardon, ladies. I'm cranky. I blame low blood sugar."

We ate an early supper at the farmhouse table in the kitchen, as the mist outside grew thicker and bolder, rolling up from the bay to press against the windows. Mom had made a batch of potato leek soup that she served with hunks of crusty bread; only I knew that the hunks were shaped the way they were not for rustic effect, but because we'd quietly, strategically sliced away the moldy spots before serving it. It was one of the quirks of the Whispers: food seemed to spoil here twice as fast as it did anywhere else, something about the dampness of the weather. I tapped out a text message under the table—PLANS

TONIGHT?—while the rest of the family small talked over my head. Richard asked Mimi how she liked Willowcrest and said that the soup could use more salt; Mimi said on the contrary, the soup was too salty, as were most soups, in her opinion. They argued halfheartedly while my mother scribbled on a notepad, making a grocery list.

"Do we need a vegetable?" she said. "For Christmas dinner."

"Yes, but only one," Richard said. "One vegetable, and we'll all battle gladiator-style to see who gets to eat it." Everyone laughed except Mimi, who had gone very quiet, staring toward the window that was practically opaque with fog.

"I think we should keep it simple. Roast turkey, mashed potatoes. We can have a cheese plate or something for an appetizer. I'll go to the market tomorrow morning, so if anyone wants to add anything to the list—"

"Booze," said Richard.

"Anything in particular?"

"Extra boozy booze." He paused. Then he snorted. "Oh my god, she's actually writing it down."

Listening to my mother and Richard spatting was unsettling, even though the two of them seemed more at ease than ever, relaxing into the same old patterns. Playing their roles. Her ability to suffer in silence was perfectly matched to his compulsive jabbing—or maybe she was like this simply because *he* was like that first. My mother once told me, in the most casual way, that he'd tried to get rid of her one summer, back when he was ten and she was just an infant. He'd put her in a basket and carried her down to the water, intending to float her out to sea. When I had asked if he'd gotten in trouble, she thought for a second and then said, "I don't know, but my parents apparently had a big fight about whose idea it had been to let him watch *The Ten Commandments*."

Their bickering stopped abruptly when Mimi dropped her spoon with a clatter. "I want to walk the pine path," she said.

I stood up, relieved at the chance to escape. "I'll take you."

• • •

My mother brought Mimi's winter boots from a closet and bent to lace them, pulling them tight and tying them twice over her protestations.

"I can put my own shoes on," my grandmother said, indignant, but Mom ignored her, looking over her shoulder at me instead.

"She can't get her laces tight enough. It's her arthritis, the doctor said it might flare up with the damp. You shouldn't take her too far. I want you to turn around after ten minutes—"

"My hands are perfectly fine," Mimi said, louder.

"—and I got some lavender balm to rub on her joints in the evenings."

"Okay," I said, and Mimi stamped one of her feet against the floor with a loud *thwap*.

"I said, my hands are fine," she nearly shouted. "Stop fussing, damn you!"

My mom stood up, hands on hips. "Don't be silly, Mother. I'm just trying to take care of you," she said, but there was an edge in her voice that made me think of those mafia movies where the mob boss wants a problem *taken care of* and everyone knows that somebody is going to end up dead.

"We'll be back soon," I said, and practically pulled Mimi out of the room.

I held her arm as we walked through the gardens and past the rear wall, but she shook my hand away when we reached the path. There was more snow here, nestled in hollows between the trees and crunching under our feet. I was glad my mother had tied Mimi's boots tight, and sorry I hadn't taken the time to fetch my own from upstairs.

"I don't need help," Mimi said.

"That makes one of us," I said. I wasn't kidding: my feet were threatening to slide out from under me every time I moved too quickly. "I haven't walked on this path before. You'll have to show me where to step."

"It's not far," she said. "I know the way."

"Did you walk here with Theo?" I asked, even though I knew the answer. This was familiar territory, not just under our feet but in her memory.

She smiled. "Oh yes, we love to walk. He would hold my hand. So gentle. Like I was a little bird and he was afraid he'd crush me." She sighed, her breath misting in the air. "I do love the pine path. Of course Theo prefers the water."

"What did he name his boat?" I said, even though I knew the answer.

"*Red Sky*. He named it after that summer when the island burned."

This was one of her favorite stories to tell, and mine to hear. The moment they finally came together, in the midst of fear and flame, and found each other.

"Tell me about the fire," I said, but she didn't seem to hear me. Her memories were like a series of interconnected rooms, each with several ways in or out. The strongest ones, like the story of how she met my grandfather, had dozens of entry points; she often ended up there no matter where she'd started. But today, instead of following the boat's name into the memory of that autumn when the sky was on fire, she followed the boat itself into a story I hadn't heard before.

"He used to come in just before sunset," she said. "I could tell which boat was his from a mile off, just from the way she sat in the water. He liked it when I stood out on the pier to watch." Her expression turned sly. She giggled like a girl. "He liked when I wore my cotton dress and stood facing into the wind."

I got her meaning instantly and laughed. "I bet he did. Men haven't changed much since then."

"That's right. They don't change. You're a smart girl. You know," she said, and faltered. "You know . . ."

"Tell me about your cotton dress," I said quickly, glancing at the sky. It was the same depthless gray as before, too early for her to be sundowning, but the path itself was twilit, the light filtered and muted by the pines. I wondered if it was confusing her. We needed to turn around. "What color was it?"

"What color was what?"

"Your cotton dress. The one Theo liked."

"It had blue flowers on it," she said. She began to walk faster. Purposefully, as if she'd remembered she was late for something. "Blue flowers and green leaves. Now, don't dally."

"Mimi, let's turn around."

"Oh no, dear. We're not there yet."

"We're not where?"

"Where the sea lavender grows. Didn't you want some? We'll bundle it up and hang it in the kitchen. Only, it's so cold. I wonder . . ." She paused, slowed, stopped. I breathed a sigh of relief: a tree had fallen across the path ahead, its tangled black branches an impenetrable barrier.

"Looks like this is the end of the road," I said. Mimi slipped her arm through mine again.

"No," she said. "The road goes on, on the other side. We just can't get there."

We meandered back the way we came, passing over our own footprints in the patches of snow. Mimi paused again as we came through the garden and pointed back at the stone wall, where the entrance was framed by two finials mottled with greenish lichen.

"There was a fox there," she said. She sounded unhappy.

"When?"

"Before." She glanced at me, then up at the house, which looked from this angle as though it might tumble over and crush us. "I think . . . I think it might have been a very long time ago."

The gray sky began to get darker by degrees shortly after three o'clock, while Richard got drunker by degrees as soon as it was past five. He was three whiskeys deep when my aunt Diana and her husband William arrived in their rental car and Diana came whirling through the room like a tornado, bustling around, shedding coats and scarves, kissing everyone, exclaiming over changes in hair and height—and hadn't it been so long? And wasn't it nice that we could all be together at Christmas, even if it was under sad circumstances, even if it was only this once? My mother went wide-eyed at that and shushed her, glancing nervously at Mimi, who was planted in front of the television, watching an episode of *The Great British Bake Off.*

"Doesn't she know she's"—Diana dropped her voice to a theatrical whisper—"dying?"

"Diana, please, we'll talk about this later," Mom said, and Richard tossed back the last of his whiskey and said, "I'm telling you both now, I will not be sober for this conversation." Then he poured himself another. By the time Diana and William took themselves up to bed, pleading exhaustion from all the traveling, he was what my grandmother would have called "pickled"—and probably to his face, too, if she hadn't begun nodding off in her chair.

My mother looked at the time and frowned. "I thought Adam would be here by now," she said. "I hope nothing went wrong. Delphine, do you have his phone number?"

I stared. "Why would I have his phone number?"

"Shit," she said. "Well, that's all right. But I guess I'll help Mother to bed myself, before she completely falls asleep."

Richard shot me a sidelong look, a lock of his white hair drooping limply over his eye. "I hope you're not expecting me to volunteer."

"You can both stay here," Mom said, rolling her eyes.

Richard waited until she'd walked Mimi off to bed before he spoke again. "So, Delphine," he said. "How's life?"

I got up to pour myself a fresh glass of wine. "Lately?" I said, cracking the seal on a ten-dollar screw-top bottle of Cabernet. Richard winced at the sound like I'd scratched my nails across a chalkboard; for all his complaints about my name, he was a huge snob about corks. "Lately, pretty uneventful."

"I surmised." He sipped his whiskey. "Want to guess how I knew?"

"I'd rather not."

Another sip. "You stopped posting."

"What?"

"On Instagram. Man, you were prolific. And then six months ago, *poof.* One picture out on the pier and then nothing. Zip. Like you died."

I blinked, so horrified by the first two words in Richard's monologue that I couldn't even begin to process the rest. "You follow me on Instagram," I said slowly. "I . . . did not know that."

He laughed. "Didn't think an old fart could figure out social media, huh."

"No, but I don't understand. I mean, why?"

"You popped up as a suggestion. Honestly, it took me a minute to realize who you were. The last photograph Dora sent of you was from your high school graduation, and that ridiculous name . . . Delphine Lockwood. I'm sorry, it is ridiculous. I thought you were some heiress, like that blond one, you know."

"Tinsley Mortimer?" I said automatically.

"The other one."

"Paris Hilton?"

"No, the one with the, you know, um . . ." He frowned, then snapped his fingers. "Kim Kardashian."

"She's not blond." I paused. Thought for a moment. "Okay, she's not blond right now."

"Uh-huh. So like I said, it took me a minute. Just a minute—then it clicked. So I followed you. I mean, not just you. I only got on it in the first place because that's where my daughter-in-law puts all the pics of the grandkids, and then I followed a bunch of dogs, too, just for the hell of it. But I'll tell you, your pictures were kind of a blast. You'd look at them and think, that kid's got a fun life. Always going places and doing things. And then, you know, poof."

"You said *poof* already," I said, and he chuckled. It was a cheerful sound, but it made me uneasy. I thought again of how he'd made that dig about my mother's appearance within minutes of stepping into the house: he'd laughed the same way then. Because it was all in good fun, and if you got upset, you were the weird one. Oversensitive. He was good at knowing just what to say so that you felt like you wanted to cry but knew you had to laugh.

"Do you want to know what I think?" he said.

I made myself hold eye contact. "I'm sure you'll tell me whether I want to know or not."

Another chuckle. He flashed me a sly, fox-like grin and said, "I think it was that guy. The one with the curly hair. A good old-fashioned New York heartbreak. That's why you left, isn't it? Am I right?"

I guffawed. I hadn't planned to, but I wasn't sorry when I saw Richard's eyes narrow, the look of a man who had overplayed his hand and ended up the butt of the joke. *Well, good,* I thought. Let him think he was wrong, so wrong that all I could do was laugh.

"Well, Dick," I said, "you tried."

He didn't need to know he'd succeeded, sort of. There had indeed been *a guy.* But to say that what happened to me in New York was about *a guy* was like saying that the *Hindenburg* disaster was about *a blimp.* Of course there was a blimp. But the important part was, the blimp exploded.

At first Colin was just my roommate, a stranger from Craigslist whose ad I responded to when I decided after a couple of lonely years that I didn't like living by myself (and when my therapist, the isn't-that-*interesting* one, said that maybe I should see this as a chance to expand my social circle). The apartment was a four-bedroom floor-through in a north Brooklyn townhouse, and the other residents were all a few years younger than me, fresh out of college and embarking on big lives in the city. I was offered the biggest room—which cost twice as much as the other, smaller ones, but half as much as the studio I'd been living in before—and this put me next door to Colin, who had cemented my acceptance at the place when he said I seemed like "a chill girl." He was charming and boyish, not too tall, with a wild mop of sandy hair and a beautiful jawline and a shelf full of poetry books that he seemed to have actually read. His room was a tiny space, possibly a former closet, that had once been connected to mine by a narrow doorway, but someone had made it into a fourth bedroom by covering the opening with plaster, a substance through which you could see nothing but hear everything. That was how I learned without asking that he was single, having recently broken up with a college girlfriend he called "unadventurous." She'd apparently moved back to Texas after graduation and wanted him to come, too, but Colin was young, hungry, angry, and anxious to taste all that life had to offer—and he knew that if he went to Austin, the girlfriend would see it as a step toward marriage, which was just so *ugh, conventional*. (This last thought was expressed in a full-on sneer, followed by a pause, after which he said, "No, of course not, obviously I'll still fuck her if she's in town.")

In other words, Colin was the worst.

Even I could see that now. But if you were me in that moment, socially adrift, no professional ambitions, aimless in every possible way and looking for something to latch onto, he sounded like something else: an opportunity, and maybe a challenge. The kind of girl Colin would have admired was the kind of girl I'd always wanted to be, fearless and cool and too interested in the world to ever be clingy. A "not like the other girls" kind of girl. If I could catch the interest of someone like Colin, it would mean I'd made myself interesting in a way I'd never been before—and I'd get a cute boyfriend in the bargain.

Of course, all of this was perspective I'd gained later, after everything fell apart. At the time, I was mostly thinking about the jawline.

In some ways, Colin seemed like my perfect match, or at least like I could be his, if I just rearranged myself into a slightly more compatible shape. We bonded over our complicated feelings about coming from money—feelings I had admittedly never had, but magically discovered shortly after he shared his—which he claimed to find revolting. His parents lived in a beautiful brownstone on the Upper West Side, but they were estranged, he told me, and he wouldn't accept a dime of their support even if they wanted him to (apart from the bajillion dimes in his trust fund, which didn't seem to count). He said the recession had awakened him to the vulgarity of his own existence, that people like him could have so much when others had so little. He said that Obama was overrated and Stalin was misunderstood. He told me he valued my perspective as "an older woman" (an ancient twenty-six to his twenty-three), and that he dreamed of dismantling both capitalism and the patriarchy in equal measure. He told me we should backpack in Peru and do ayahuasca together—or maybe he just said he wanted to do this, and I assumed I would be there, too.

It was hard to know afterward whether he had lied to me, or if he'd simply created a series of blanks that I could fill in by lying to myself. We never discussed the relationship, except to discuss how great it was that we never had to discuss it, but I thought that was because we both knew it was something special. After a couple of near misses, he came up with the idea to push our beds up against the shared wall between our rooms and use a knocking code so that the other roommates wouldn't know we were hooking up. The secrecy made it feel sexy and urgent, like we were having an affair; sometimes he'd text me at work, EVERYONE'S GONE, and I'd drop everything to run home and jump into his bed. He'd plant himself between my legs, lick his lips with a wink, and tell me to scream his name—until we heard someone on the stairs. Then he'd theatrically clamp his hand over my mouth lest we be discovered.

The fling lasted only three months. But in New York City, in that magical, romantic time when the days are lengthening and the trees are blossoming and spring is warming into summer, three months can feel like a blissful eternity. This was what I'd tell myself, anyway, when it was all over and I needed some kind of explanation for how I could have been so stupid, so blind. It was early on a Sunday morning when I heard his knock on the wall, the one that meant I should come over. But when I opened the door, he wasn't waiting for me: he was lying on his back, naked and thrusting, with his eyes squeezed shut and his crotch obscured by something bright pink and furry that he was holding in both hands—and in my confusion I thought, *Stuffed animal, he's fucking a stuffed animal,* a fetish that I immediately decided I was going to be totally cool about, cool and understanding like the chill girl that I was. Stuffed animal fucking? Sure, I could roll with that, and then the pink furry stuffed animal lifted up its head and looked at me and said, "Um, hi?" Because the stuffed animal wasn't an animal at all, but a girl with a bright pink punky pixie cut that looked absolutely great on her, a fact that was all the more enraging considering she was currently giving my boyfriend a blow job.

Colin opened his eyes. "Oh," he said. "I guess I hit the wall with my elbow, sorry. Uh, this is Claire?"

I closed the door.

I was back in my room, still trying to decide if I intended to be cool about this, too—or if I even had a right to be mad, although I *was* mad, and getting madder by the minute—when I heard Colin's door open and the soft thump of feet as Claire-with-the-pink-hair headed to the bathroom. A moment later, there was another knock on the wall. I waited, and then heard his muffled voice: "Delphine?"

This time I knocked on his door and waited for him to open it. When he did, I was relieved to see that he'd put some pants on, and that he looked at least a little chagrined. *Okay,* I thought. *Here comes the apology.*

"So, I've been thinking we should just be friends," he said.

I felt my mouth open and close, goldfish-like, no sound coming out. Finally I managed to squeak, "What?"

"It's just, I'm me," he said. "And you're . . . you."

"I don't understand," I said, and that's when he said it. Sadly but dutifully, like he was a doctor telling a patient the cancer had spread to her brain.

"You're just kind of basic, Delphine."

Of course I didn't tell Richard any of this. I also didn't tell him that Claire had become Colin's girlfriend and moved into his room after what seemed like five minutes, and that the sound of their moaning and thumping kept me awake all night long, and that he not only revealed to everyone that we'd been involved but told them I'd practically forced myself on him, so that for the next few weeks he avoided me while everyone else looked at me with a mix of disgust and pity every time I left my room. I didn't tell him that I got fired from my job, because I'd left work early to run home and sleep with Colin on the one day that my boss had some sort of flavored water marketing emergency and didn't believe me when I said I'd gone home sick. And I didn't tell him how I'd come home one day to find my roommates all waiting for me in the living room to tell me I had to pack my things and leave, or about how I'd started to cry when I asked where I was supposed to go and my worst roommate, a girl with a septum piercing named Clarissa, said, "We really don't care, as long as it's not here."

There's a saying about New York: you're always looking for a job, an apartment, or a boyfriend. If you're lucky, you're looking for only one of these things at any given time. If you're missing two, it's an emergency. If it's three, as it turns out, it's easier to just pack up and leave. So I did.

I peed in Colin's shampoo before I left.

I didn't mention that, either.

Richard was still staring at me, his face quizzical and annoyed. I was grateful when my phone buzzed.

"Excuse me," I said. Richard raised his whiskey in salute as I walked out of the room and toward the front of the house, pulling up the messages app as I did. Someone had dimmed the lights in the foyer down to their lowest setting, and everything was drenched in shadow—but I could see the mirrors on either side of the open dining room doors, the umbrella stand just inside the door, the outline of the staircase with its spindly woodwork. As my eyes adjusted to the dark, one patch of shadow stayed deeper than the others. My breath caught in my throat. The door beneath the staircase, the one to the weird little powder room, was standing open. I crossed quickly to close it, but as I reached for the rosette knob, a hand snaked out of the darkness and grabbed me by the wrist—and then another pressed hard over my mouth before I could scream. I made a muffled squeak as my heart beat wildly in my chest . . . and then I relaxed, giggling, as he stepped out of the dark.

"Not funny," I said, and Adam smiled.

"Surprise," he said. "Where's your family?"

I gestured back over my shoulder. "Here and there. But not right here."

"So we're alone."

"We are," I said. "For now."

"Good," he said, and wrapped his arms around me, pulling me back through the door beneath the stairs. I felt his breath hot against my ear as he buried his face in my neck.

"We'll have to be careful," I whispered, my hand finding the doorknob.

"But just until we tell them, right?"

"Yes. Until we tell them." I tilted my chin and his lips found mine. The door closed silently behind me as we kissed in the safety of the dark.

6.

1946

SUMMER

She is seventeen years old, and in full bloom.

The prettiness that she had as a child has grown past its promise of ordinary beauty into something less conventional, more striking. She's tall for a girl, her angular face framed and softened by a cascade of dark blond curls. Her blue eyes are set deep beneath prominent brows and slightly downturned, so that she always looks just a little bit skeptical, a little bit unimpressed. It's a useful look to have, since people—boys, especially—are always trying to show off for her. The expression on her face gives nothing away, on the rare occasion when there's anything to give. Miriam is rarely impressed by anyone, but particularly not by try-hards.

That doesn't mean she's cruel, of course. She likes people well enough, even if she'd like them better if they'd stop boasting and putting on airs, and anyway, she's been carefully taught that attention should be graciously accepted no matter the source. Better to have more than you want than to need it and have none at all: that's what Mother says, and Miriam knows she's right. One of her friends at school, a girl named Janet Reardon, is always going on about what a bore it is to be beautiful—which is awfully audacious coming from Janet, who is the prettiest girl in their class, a real stunner. She'll moan about how exhausting it is to have so many suitors, and so on and so forth, and while Miriam would never say so out loud, she thinks that Janet Reardon has her very pretty head stuck all the way up her own ass. She knows that most girls would give anything to be half as beautiful, and she also knows that Janet wouldn't trade places with one of those girls for anything, no matter how much she might like to pretend otherwise.

The weather in Bar Harbor is unseasonably cool this summer, with a fierce wind blowing off the water that sounds more like a howl than a whisper as it races past the house. It's a mournful sound, but then the Whispers has been a mournful place lately, full of empty rooms where nobody is coming to stay and empty chairs where people used to sit. Her brother Edward had come back from the war and promptly married the pretty girl he was courting during that hazy summer five years past. He is so busy in his new life that he can spare only a week to visit the coast this year, and then only because Miriam begged. Her other brother, Robert, is gone, too: rejected by the army for his poor eyesight, he married his own sweetheart and decamped to Kentucky with his father's blessing (both of them having agreed that there was good money to be made in the whiskey business, especially for a family with such a rich and storied history in liquor). And maybe it's seeing his sons scattered and starting families of their own, or maybe it's just Miriam noticing what she was too much of a child to see before, but Papa seems to have aged fifteen years just within the past two summers. His rich chestnut-colored hair is half-gone now and almost entirely gray, and the unhappy furrow that used to appear between his eyebrows when he scowled is now a permanent fixture, even when he's in good spirits.

To Miriam, it seems like the house and her father are suffering from the same sickness. The same loneliness. It's hard to believe that the Whispers used to be a bustling place in the summer, with parties and picnics and an endless series of guests coming and going, or that her father is the same man who used to keep his visitors entertained with wild stories and bawdy jokes, the gaiety lasting into the wee hours of the morning. Lately he's been talking of retiring, selling the house in the city and spending his remaining years here by the sea— unless, he says, a certain daughter thinks she might like to settle in the city house herself, someday soon, when she's married.

Miriam doesn't have a single solitary thought of getting married. None of the young men she knows are appealing enough to spend an evening with, let alone a lifetime. But she likes to see the smile on her father's face when he talks about this, and so she plays along. "I don't know, Papa," she says with a wink. "My future husband and I might prefer a seaside cottage ourselves, or maybe a château in the South of France. Or both."

"For my girl, a house on every continent," Papa says, winking back, and they both laugh. It's lovely to see him laugh.

Little red-faced Harold Chandler is a young man now, still prone to sunburns, and still dull as a doorstop. But Miriam has been thrown together with him often enough over the course of so many summers that he doesn't annoy her as much as he used to, and Harold has wisely avoided making any further attempts to pucker up and lunge at her. Instead, he and his sisters and Miriam enjoy a casual seasonal acquain- tanceship, one that rekindles each May and disbands without fanfare three months later—and because Harold is such a pale, indoorsy crea- ture, Miriam's relationship with him has largely consisted of eating luncheon at his parents' so-called cottage when it's too rainy to do any- thing else. But this year, things are different. Harold arrived in town in his brand-new birthday present, a Cadillac convertible—a blue one, with chrome hubcaps and soft leather seats and a push-button radio, and a sleek body that reminds Miriam of a sleeping cat. It's a beautiful car, Harold's pride and joy, and he's never prouder than when he can drive around town with a pretty girl sitting next to him. At least twice a week, he'll come trundling up the driveway to the Whispers and beep the horn, sitting there with a grin on his face and one hand resting casually on the steering wheel until Miriam comes outside.

"Want to go for a spin?" he asks, and Miriam, looking back at the house and thinking of the dreadful silence inside, of all the people who used to be here and are now, painfully, not, nods and hops in. It doesn't matter that she's only there to make Harold look good, as decorative as the silver hood ornament that's shaped like a woman with her hair swept back from her face. It's still nice to sit back in those soft leather seats and allow herself to be taken away.

Today she's up and out the front door at the first beep of the Cadillac's horn. The cloth bag that holds her towel and swimsuit bangs against her hip she runs across the piazza, her espadrilles kicking up gravel. It's the Fourth of July, the sun has finally chased away the unseasonable chill in the air, and the delicious heat has everyone feeling giddy. There's a rumor that one of their neighbors has procured fireworks, big ones, which Miriam will watch with her family from the broad veranda at the Whispers—but that's hours away, and the day is hers. She intends to enjoy it. Harold is waiting in the usual spot, his arm draped out the window, but the back seat of the Cadillac is full: Harold's sisters, Dodie and Peggy, are crammed in like sardines with a girlfriend each beside them. They're giggling and whispering to each other, and Harold's face is a shade of pink that Miriam has never seen before: not sunburn, but embarrassment.

"Miriam!" Peggy chirps. "It's so nice that you're coming with us. Harry was *sooo* worried that you might change your mind. Weren't you, Harry?"

"Shush, Peg," Harold says, blushing harder as Miriam arranges herself in the front seat. But Peggy doesn't shush. She leans over to listen as her friend whispers something to her, and giggles.

"That's a darling dress, Miriam," she says. "Did you bring your bathing suit? Pete, that's our man at the cottage, he says the water might be warm enough to swim."

"I brought it." Miriam pats the bag at her hip and fights the urge to laugh herself when Harold glances at it and turns a shade redder, as though just knowing he's in the presence of a bathing suit is more excitement than he can bear. His sisters aren't so restrained: Peggy exclaims, "Jeepers, Harry, even your *neck* is blushing," and the girls collapse against each other, giggling and shrieking.

"It's the sun," Harold says lamely. He doesn't look at Miriam at all as he puts the car in gear and pulls away from the house.

They take the long way toward the bridge that connects the island to the mainland, gliding along the winding coastal road with its endless views of the bay. There are white gulls in the sky and white sails in the water, so bright in the sunshine that Miriam can still see the shape of them when she closes her eyes. Eventually the road turns north, with tall trees looming on either side, and Miriam doesn't realize she's been dozing until Peggy suddenly shouts, "Harry, you've just missed it!" and her eyes fly open as Harold stomps the brakes. There between the trees is a narrow dirt road, climbing gently uphill. A few minutes later, the narrow road opens into a grassy clearing, where tire tracks mark the presence of previous visitors. They park beside the only other automobile, an old truck with rust coming up over the hood and some lobsterman's traps stacked in the cargo. A mosquito whines past Miriam's ear while the girls pile out of the back seat, all talking at once about whether they should have packed more sandwiches, and if they ought to change their clothes right here behind the car or somewhere in the woods, and where was the swimming pond anyway, and her gaze drifts along the edge of the clearing, to a spot where the flattened grass becomes a dirt footpath that disappears between the trees.

She's the first one into the woods, breathing a sigh of relief as the dazzling sunshine gives way to the cool and quiet of the forest. The path twists this way and that, the air is fragrant with the scent of growing things, and she has just enough time to wonder if it's much farther to the pond when the next twist of the path brings her around a huge mossy boulder and she sees it: the sparkle of sunshine on dark water. She walks the last few yards to emerge from between the trees onto a broad, flat rock that slopes gently downhill at one end to a little patch of bobbing lily pads—and then looks up with surprise at the streak of something plummeting through the air just off to her right. There's an enormous splash, and a moment later, a boy's head pops up in the water. A chorus of whooping and shouting goes up: twenty yards from her own rock, a sheer cliff rises from the water's edge to a rocky precipice high above the pond. A half a dozen of them are standing there, bare-chested and laughing and shoving, young men with the deep tans and hard muscles that come from hauling lines or digging ditches day in and day out.

There's another shout, another boy runs, leaps, splashes down, and Miriam suddenly feels like she's witnessing something secret and precious, like opening a love letter meant for someone else. She feels like an intruder. She's sure that the Chandlers' man wasn't supposed to tell them about this pond, or if he did, that it was only in passing, never expecting any of them to actually come here. This is not a place for seasonal visitors. It's for these boys, who spend their summers trawling the seas and combing the tide beds, sweaty and salty and standing knee-deep in muck, so that people like Miriam Day can eat freshly cooked lobster off fine china in their seaside estates. Boys who were too young to enlist, yet bore the burden of supporting their families when the older men were drafted. For some, it was a temporary hardship; for others, the ones whose fathers and brothers never came back, it would last forever.

They haven't seen her yet, and she wonders if she ought to just go, step back and disappear into the woods the same way she came.

And then she sees him.

She'd know him anywhere. She knows the shape of him: the tilt of his head, the lean lines of his silhouette as he stands against the sky. She knows him even though they've never met except at a distance, ever since that night when she ran away from Harold Chandler and stood on the pier as the sun went down. The boy on the bow of the boat. Since then, she has seen him countless times. His boat passes nearly every evening as it did that day, carving a shimmering path through the water as the last light slips from the sky, and nearly every evening, Miriam is there to watch it pass.

It has been four years since that moment, and she couldn't say when going down to the pier began to feel like a ritual—or when she realized that it wasn't really the sunset she was anxious to see, but him. Sometimes it would rain and she would be forced to stay indoors, wondering if he was passing by, and if, seeing the pier empty, he might wonder where she was. Did he feel the same magnetic pull as she did? Did he find himself thinking at odd times of the pier and the girl who stood there watching the boats, and the way the sun danced like liquid gold on the water as it stretched out between them? Sometimes she thought about waving or calling out to him, but then the moment would pass, and she'd be glad she didn't. There was something delicious about it, the tension, the two of them watching each other to see who would make a move and break the spell. Lately it had occurred to Miriam that if they were both the same sort of stubborn, things might continue on like this for another four years, maybe even forever. Maybe they'd stare at each other from a distance until they were old and stooped and gray, go to their graves without ever even having said hello.

But now here he is, standing far above her but still closer than he's ever been. He doesn't see her. He's focused, his body tense—and then he runs, leaps, and the sight of him with his arms outstretched is so beautiful that her breath catches in her throat. She watches him fold his body in the air and then plummet, headfirst, entering the water so cleanly that there's barely a splash.

"Gosh," says a voice behind her, and Miriam turns to see the rest of the group, four wide-eyed girls with Harold bringing up the rear. Dodie, the youngest, steps up next to Miriam and shakes her head. "Gosh, I wouldn't dare. Do you think— Oh, but look, there he is!"

Miriam turns back to see the jumper: resurfaced and swimming easily back to shore. His head swivels toward the sound of Dodie's voice, but he doesn't look at Dodie. He looks at Miriam and keeps looking, even as the rest of the group begins to chatter among themselves, setting out towels and kicking off shoes and settling down to their picnic. She isn't sure, but she thinks she sees him smiling.

The two groups make a point of ignoring each other, but Miriam no longer feels like an intruder; the boy from the boat keeps glancing at her and she at him, and it feels like a dance. Miriam looks at him, then looks away—and then looks over her shoulder to see Harold, who is sitting in the shade underneath a tree with a conspicuously empty space on the blanket beside him. She knows he wants her to join him; any moment, he'll stop shooting her hopeful looks and actually work up the courage to ask, and she realizes that if he does, she'll feel compelled to say yes.

"I think I'll go for a swim," she says, standing up.

Her bathing suit is the same bright yellow as the water lilies that dot the pond, a halter-style two-piece that reveals a strip of creamy skin just above her navel. When she comes out of the woods after changing her clothes, she can sense heads turning in her direction. Not just one, but everyone's. The men on the ledge and Harold's sisters and Harold himself, but he looks down at his own lap rather than meeting her eyes when she turns toward him.

"Are you sure you want to do that? There might be snapping turtles," he says, and she feels a flare of annoyance.

"Don't fuss, Harold," she says, more sharply than she means to. She tosses her dress over a branch and enters the water in one motion, gasping a little as it closes over her shoulders, and swims away from the bank without so much as a look back, not even when Peggy calls after her to ask if it's very cold. She doesn't stop swimming until she's halfway across, and then she rolls onto her back and floats, eyes closed, feeling the sun on her face and relishing the sense of being alone at last. Peggy and Dodie and their friends are still chattering away on the bank, but their voices are blissfully distant, just noise, like the birdsong in the trees or the occasional shout and splash of the local boys as they jump from the ledge. She drifts, weightless. Waiting. The trickle of water in her ears sounds like music—and then, very nearby, there's a splash, and a light spray of water against her face.

"Hello," a voice says, and Miriam's eyes fly open. Her head bobs briefly underwater before she resurfaces with a splutter. She knows even before she swipes the water from her eyes that it's him, and the skin on her arms ripples out in gooseflesh, not with the cold but with anticipation. Even with pond water in her eyes, and even with his hair slicked down to his head and the tip of his chin submerged, her first up-close glimpse of him is thrilling.

"Oh, hello," she says, and he grins, showing an even row of teeth with the slightest gap between the front two.

"Ah, she speaks," he says.

"Only when spoken to," she says.

"Is that why you've never said hello to me?"

"Why, what do you mean?" she says, her tone teasing. "Have we met before?"

"Only about a hundred times, by my count. 'Course we've never been formally introduced. I'm Theodore Caravasios." He smiles again. "Should we shake hands?"

Miriam laughs and extends her hand above the water, kicking her legs to stay afloat, and he clasps it briefly, sending another chill down her spine.

"I'm—"

"Oh, I know who you are, Miss Miriam Day. Your family is famous around here."

She blinks, unsettled. "You know my father?"

"Not personally. But most every man with a fishing boat knows Roland Day. He used to do a good business with a lot of them, back before the Depression."

"Fishing business?" Miriam says innocently, but the way Theo laughs, she can tell he knows that her father was pulling something a lot more lucrative than seafood out of the harbor in the dead of night—and that he knows she knows, too.

"That's right," he says. "Pretty funny-looking fish. Fetched quite a price, too, from what I hear. But that was before my time."

"Are you a fisherman, Theodore Caravasios?"

"A lobsterman," he says, and she can hear the pride in his voice. "Well, I will be, anyway. That's my uncle's boat I'm working on, but I'll have my own someday."

"Then maybe when you're the captain, you'll take me for a spin," Miriam says. "Instead of just floating on by."

"Just so long as you understand I intend to run a tight ship. You'll have to earn your keep."

"Fine by me."

"You say that now. But when the wind comes up and a big cold wave comes over the bow and drenches you from head to toe, you might say different."

She swims a few lazy strokes and looks back impishly over her shoulder. "Do I look like a girl who's afraid of getting wet?"

He laughs, a great, booming sound that echoes across the pond, and Miriam sees heads swiveling on the bank: Harold and his sisters and their friends have stopped whatever they were doing and are all looking across the water toward her. Harold has even ventured into the sun to stand right at the water's edge, his arms folded across his chest. Staring. Good and mad, probably, but Miriam doesn't care. She's had more fun in the span of this short conversation than in all the afternoons she's spent in Harold Chandler's company combined, and if that doesn't meet with his approval, he can go jump in a lake.

He can jump right in this one, she thinks. *This lake, in particular*—and then bites her tongue to keep from giggling at the image of Harold flopping angrily into the pond like a big pale frog.

Theodore swims up beside her. "I'm not sure your friends approve of me," he says, tilting his head toward the group on the rock.

"I wouldn't worry. I don't think they approve of me, either," she says, and feels a little flare of annoyance. The scowl on Harold's face is clear, even at a distance, and she can just imagine how Peggy and Dodie must be teasing him, always doing their best to make every awkward situation worse. Those obnoxious little girls are so keen to stir up trouble, to fan every spark into a five-alarm fire, and suddenly, all Miriam wants is to give them a taste of their own medicine. It's a mean impulse, the kind she'd never ordinarily indulge, but it's at this exact moment that Peggy says something to Harold that makes him whip his head around and shout at her, and the girls all erupt in a chorus of wicked, gleeful cackling, and the words are out of Miriam's mouth before she can think better of it.

"Why don't you swim on over with me right now, and I'll introduce you."

It takes only ten minutes for them to swim back to shore, and only half that time for Miriam to realize that this was a mistake. The girls' gleeful cackling had stopped the moment Theodore and Miriam began to paddle back; they were whispering to each other now, glancing periodically at the swimmers as the distance closed to twenty yards, then ten. Harold, meanwhile, is standing and staring, with his arms folded across his chest. But the idea of turning back is impossible to contemplate, and then just impossible, period, as her hand touches the submerged edge of the rock and she climbs carefully out of the water, slipping a little on the slimy surface. Harold rushes forward to help her at the same time as Theodore steps up beside her to do the same, and for a moment she is suspended between the two of them, one boy holding each hand, her toes frantically gripping for purchase in the greenish muck. Then Harold pulls, too hard, and she falls forward as he stumbles back, yanking her other hand free from Theodore's just in time to fling it out and catch her fall. One of her knees bangs hard against the rock and she gasps.

"Are you all right?" Theodore says, hurrying to help her up at the same time as Harold springs to his feet and snaps, "What the hell do you think you're doing?" in an angry tone Miriam has never heard before, and it takes her a moment to realize that Harold isn't talking to her but to Theodore, who gazes back at Harold with an unreadable expression on his face. The girls are standing in a huddle a few feet back, their eyes wide, and Miriam has time to think that if Dodie and Peggy and the rest were always trying to start fires, she might as well have shown up with a canister of gasoline. Theodore's friends are watching, too, looking down on the scene from their vantage point high on the ledge—and though the sun is still bright and warm, an ominous chill runs down her spine. She looks up at Harold and tries to smile. "Nothing to worry about," she says lightly. "I only bumped my knee, that's all. Harold, this is—"

"I asked you a question," Harold says louder, not even looking at Miriam, and Theodore stands up a little straighter.

"Miss Day asked if I'd like to be introduced to her friends," he says, mildly enough, but Miriam can see him shift his weight forward just a little, so that he's standing on the balls of his feet. Like a boxer, not swinging but ready to move if it comes to that—only it can't come to that, Miriam thinks, because Theodore would put Harold's lights out with one punch. He extends a hand toward Harold, like he did for her back in the water, but no smile this time. "And I said sure, I'd love to meet Miriam's friends. I'm Theodore Caravasios."

Harold stares but doesn't move. His face beneath his hat has turned pink at the mention of Miriam's name, as if someone just uttered a forbidden oath. He looks at Miriam.

"You," he sputters, then looks back at Theodore, his face twisting up like an angry little boy's. But he lifts his own hand, and at first it seems like it might be okay, like he might reach out for the hand-shake after all. Only he doesn't, and what happens next happens in slow motion—a moment that lasts long enough for Miriam to look at Harold's pinched face and think to herself, *Oh no,* and then, seeing his elbow drawing back, to think even more urgently, *Oh, NO,* and then there's the light *thwap* of flesh on flesh as he swings his arm forward and swats Theodore's proffered hand out of the air, like it's an insect.

Nobody moves. Nobody speaks. Even Peggy, who can usually be counted on to start giggling the moment her brother does something to embarrass himself, just stares with her mouth open and her hands clasped to either side of her face. It's not the violence, but the ridicu-lousness of it: that a slap could be so weak, so limp-wristed, and yet so rude all at the same time, and Miriam realizes two things at once: first, that Harold Chandler is a loathsome, pathetic little weasel who she will never speak to again if she can help it.

The second thing is that if she doesn't do something, he's about to have his teeth caved in.

Theodore tenses as if he's about to pounce, and Miriam leaps up, stretching her long arms and long legs, unfolding like a flower. In addition to those lessons about accepting attention graciously, Mother has explained that attention can also be cultivated and useful, that you could learn to move and speak so that every eye in the room is drawn to you. This was a woman's power, a different sort of weapon but no less effective when used correctly, and while Mother's lessons never explicitly addressed this situation in particular, Miriam sees the logic: if you are standing between two men, and they are both looking at you, then they cannot also be punching each other.

She allows her back to arch as she tosses her damp hair over her shoulder. Then she stands up straight, shoulders back, and walks right in between Harold and Theodore, both of whom automatically step back. The simmering tension that was in the air just a moment ago isn't gone but displaced: She holds the power now, and this could be the end of it. She could let it go as easily as she seized it, let it dissipate into the air. Catastrophe averted. She could even still make things right with Harold if she wanted to, taking his arm and asking him sweetly if they couldn't go home now, as she'd caught a little chill in the water.

But this isn't only about keeping Harold from taking a swing at Theodore or keeping Theodore from breaking Harold's nose. Suddenly it's hardly about the men at all. This is Miriam's moment, and everyone is looking. Waiting, watching, to see what she'll do—and Miriam herself suddenly has the strange sensation that she's waiting, too, floating somewhere above the scene, watching it like a movie and wondering how it might end. Her gaze rises up the sheer face of the cliff and fixes on the ledge high above, where the boys are still standing, watching, a group of gangly silhouettes against the brilliant sky. For the second time today, a wild thought flashes through her mind . . . and before she knows it, she's said the words. She points up at the ledge. "I think I'd like to try that."

For a moment, nobody speaks. Then Peggy lets out a high, nervous giggle, like a horse's whinny, and the other girls join in—as if Miriam has said something desperately funny, or maybe just something they desperately want to be funny. Harold snorts, a half laugh.

Theodore is the only one who doesn't smile at all. He cocks his head and looks at her curiously. "The cliff? You want to jump?"

Harold rolls his eyes and turns away, bending over to gather some scattered items from the rock. "Of course she doesn't. She's just putting you on. Miriam, where's your towel?"

"I didn't ask you," Theodore says, his eyes not moving from Miriam's face. "I asked her."

Harold scoffs, "Come on, Miriam. This is stupid. It'll be more fun back at the cottage anyway. Hey, *Miriam.* I said come on. What do you say?"

A smile tweaks at the corners of Theodore's mouth. "Well, you heard him. What *do* you say, Miriam? Because if you want to jump—"

"I said come *on,* we're *going,*" Harold whines, and Miriam turns to face him.

"I'll only be a minute." She turns back, takes a deep breath. "I want to jump."

Peggy squawks, "Oh, *Miriam*, but it's dangerous," and Theodore shakes his head.

"It's not. I've done it a million times. Never once hit the bottom."

Peggy falls silent, and Harold's eyes narrow. He hesitates, and for a moment, Miriam thinks he might give it one more try. A last stand, a last chance to lay claim to the girl he's been reliably informed is supposed to be his. Hadn't he told her that this was the plan, that even his *mumma* had said so? But he doesn't. Instead, he shoves a bag at his sister and stalks off into the woods. His parting shot at Miriam is tossed over his shoulder. "If you're not at the car in ten minutes, I'm leaving without you."

"I'll fall just as fast as I can, Harold," she calls after him, her voice sugary. Is this cruel? She doesn't think so. It's time Harold Chandler understood that she's a person with a mind of her own, not an ornament to be paraded around as if her only purpose is to make him look good.

Neither of them speaks as Theodore leads her along the rocks, past the bobbing lily field to a narrow dirt path that rises steeply between the trees. It's a short but hard climb, with bare roots and jutting rocks that she has to grab ahold of to keep her footing, and she keeps her eyes on the dirt beneath her bare feet. He doesn't offer help, and she doesn't ask for it; only once, the loose dirt slides out from beneath her and she feels the warm, broad weight of his palm against her hip, to keep her from falling. When she regains her balance, he takes his hand away, his fingers trailing momentarily over her bare back. The touch, rough and soft at once, is the most thrilling thing she's ever felt.

Eventually they emerge atop the cliff. Theodore's friends glance at her, some skeptical, some curious, but when Theodore says, "Clear a path, fellas," they all step aside. He comes up beside her as she approaches the edge.

"Well, here we are," he says. "It's wide open down there. All you have to do is jump. I can go first, to show you." He pauses. "Or we can jump together."

Miriam takes a deep breath, gazing out over the pond, the opposite bank with its own jagged cliffs, the dark copse of trees beyond. The water laps gently far below; the sun beats its fierce warmth against her bare shoulders. For several long moments she stands still, poised on the precipice—of the cliff, of the rest of her life. The air seems to shimmer, full of possibilities, and she thinks that whatever happens next, she will always remember this day, this moment, as the one where everything changed.

Very soon, everything will. At this very moment, in a hospital in New York City, a man with sweat on his brow and a drying bloodstain on his shirt is asking an operator to please ring the Day house in Bar Harbor. Moments later, the telephone in the drawing room at the Whispers will begin to trill. In another forty-five minutes, Miriam will arrive back home to find her father's car idling on the piazza with its doors flung wide open, her mother sitting in the front seat palefaced and clutching a handkerchief, as Papa frantically throws things into the trunk and shouts at Miriam to *get in, get in*. She will be told that her brother Edward, sweet and handsome Edward who promised he'd come to visit before the summer was out, has been struck by a city bus and may not live through the night—and her horror at the idea that she might have delayed their departure will consume her all the way home, only to be replaced by anguish when they learn that he died barely an hour later, before they had even made it over the state line into New Hampshire.

The Day family will not come back to Bar Harbor this summer.

It will be a long time before she sees Theodore Caravasios again.

Later, much later, Miriam will think of this moment and wonder if she ever had a choice at all. She will wonder if she jumped because she wanted to, or simply because the path that fate had chosen for her led in one direction: forward, over the edge into nothingness.

But in this moment, it doesn't feel like fate. It feels like a choice, her choice, and hers alone, and she doesn't need anyone—not even Theodore Caravasios—to show her how to make it.

"What do you say, Miriam?" he says. It's the same question Harold asked her—only this time, it actually feels like a question. His voice is curious and warm, and she turns to him with a smile.

"Geronimo!" she says, and leaps alone into the open sky.

7.

2014

DECEMBER

I was alone and cold when I woke the next morning, shivering under a blanket. I reached automatically for my phone, swiping it to check for messages and then chuckling at my own foolishness. For the next week, at least, Adam and I would be saying our good mornings and good nights in person.

Last night had been a very good night.

I shivered again, remembering. We hadn't dared stay long in the little powder room, but later, after everyone else was asleep, I woke to the creak of my door opening and the soft tread of his feet as he crossed the room, the weight of his body as he slipped into bed beside me.

"We have to be quiet," I whispered as he put his lips against my collarbone, my shoulder, my bare breasts.

"Quiet, I can do," he'd whispered back. "Just don't tell me to be quick."

. . .

The clock on my phone said 7:03 A.M., but the sky was the same flat gray as always, and the fog was thicker than ever. I listened for the sounds of people waking up, a creaking floorboard or the clink of coffee mugs, but there was nothing, not even the wind. Was I the only one awake? Maybe, I thought. Diana and William had gone up to bed just after they had arrived, but I didn't think they'd gone to sleep; when I passed their door two hours later, I'd heard the murmur of voices having what sounded like a whispered argument. Richard was still on West Coast time and would probably sleep until noon, just in time to wake up and have a three-martini lunch—if he'd even made it back to his room before passing out. Adam had told me he was setting an alarm for eight o'clock, which was when my mom usually started moving around. And Mimi—her room was just below mine, which thanks to the acoustics of the house meant that everything she did down there sounded like it was happening right next to me. I'd woken in the night to the sound of her climbing out of bed and pacing the floor, maybe to use the bathroom, but when I listened now, there was nothing.

If I got up now, I would have the place to myself—but what I really wanted, suddenly, was to get up and get out. Not forever, but just for a little while. Just to delay whatever was coming when Adam and I met again in the cold light of day.

I scurried downstairs in my socks, clutching my heavy winter boots in my hand. The last of yesterday's coffee was still in the pot; I poured it into a travel mug and set it in the microwave, taking it out before the one-minute countdown was done so that it wouldn't beep. Five minutes later, I was outside with my boots and coat on, the coffee warm in my hand, my breath visible in the air. A frost had settled in overnight, feathering everything in white. I trudged through the gardens toward the pine path where I'd walked with

Mimi yesterday, pausing in the spot where she said she'd seen the fox—remembering the strange mix of certainty and sadness in her voice, as if she'd known her mind was playing tricks on her. I looked around just in case, but there were no telltale paw prints in the icy grass, no signs of life at all. The house loomed, great and gray and still against the sky, its dark windows like sightless eyes. The world seemed to be holding its breath, waiting. The only thing moving was me, into the forest, into the fog. My feet carried me forward as my mind traveled back and found him waiting there.

Last night had been so exciting, all those long months of tension and anticipation burning away in an instant as we came together in the dark, and I'd been so caught up in the moment that it never occurred to me to think about what came next. That I would still have to run into him on the stairs or sit across from him at breakfast and pretend that he was just a friendly acquaintance, just a member of the staff.

It had been so much easier to pretend nothing was happening when nothing had really *happened*, when we weren't even a real couple because it was against the rules. When we talked about the relationship, it was all about what might eventually happen: Someday we'd go out on a real date without worrying that someone would see us. Someday we'd take a weekend trip way up north, snuggling up in a little cabin by a lake somewhere as summer gave over to autumn and the leaves began to turn. Someday we'd drive across the country in search of weird landmarks and greasy roadside food, stopping whenever and wherever we wanted to, with no particular timeline or destination in mind. Adam was all about someday: he had a lifetime's worth of plans for us before we'd ever even kissed for the first time. But when I teased him that he might be getting ahead of himself, he had gotten serious and quiet and said, "I'm not getting ahead of anything. I'm exactly where I'm supposed to be, and I know exactly what I want."

Adam put a lot of stock in what was meant to be. He told me he believed in fate, soulmates, all of it. In his world, there were no accidents.

Of course I thought it had to be bullshit. The idea of a guy who didn't play games, who wanted to make plans, who liked me just the way I was and wanted to organize *his* life to spend more time with *me*? This was clearly suspicious, a too-good-to-be-true scenario that I warned myself not to trust. I'd had a million flings that started out like this, guys who couldn't get enough of me one minute only to suddenly discover that I was just a little too *this* or not enough *that,* a few disappointing degrees shy of the girl they'd thought they were getting—a girl whom, no matter how hard I tried, I could never quite turn myself into. But then Adam was so demonstrably not like Colin or anyone else who came before him.

From the start, the relationship had felt different; it had to, when most of our time together was chaperoned by a rotating cast of senior citizens, including my grandmother. We had spent so many hours just talking, sharing stories while we walked or sat or did puzzles with Mimi, so that I felt I knew him better after only a few weeks than I'd ever gotten to know Colin even after we'd been hooking up for months. I knew he didn't like ice cream; I knew he played the guitar left-handed but swung a baseball bat from the right; I knew he rented a tiny apartment above an old lady's garage, shopped secondhand, and ate cheap, because he wanted to go back to school for his nursing certification. I knew the most expensive thing he owned was his winter coat. He told me about his childhood in Miami, raised by a beloved grandmother who had broken his heart when she passed away; he told me that it was his memories of her that spurred him to become a caregiver and work with the elderly.

And before I knew it, I was sharing things, too: I told him why I'd left New York, including the gory details. I told him that part of the reason I visited Mimi so often was because getting lost in someone else's past was preferable to dealing with my right-now. I even told him about my dad and the cat whisperer and the YouTube twins, and though I played it up like it was funny, he put his hand on mine and said he wished that hadn't happened to me, that it must have been hard.

But I didn't let myself fall for him. And when Adam talked about all the things we would do together someday, I kept my mouth shut. I told myself I'd learned my lesson when it came to making plans—and I told him that I didn't believe in fate, or anything like it.

And yet I couldn't help noticing how things seemed to be falling into place, as if God or the universe or some mischievous Christmas spirit had conspired to make this happen because it was supposed to, whether I wanted it or not. We were spending the holidays together, like a real couple, and all those *somedays* were suddenly more like *any day now*. I had resisted the fantasy, and it became real anyway.

Until we tell them.

This was where the scared and skeptical part of my mind, the one that always wanted to scoff and tell me I was making a fool of myself, usually would have stepped in to slap me across the face—but it was strangely silent today. Flummoxed. I could almost picture her, my inner cool girl, shrugging and throwing her hands up and saying, *I don't know, man, I don't know what's going on anymore. Do whatever you want.*

Instead, I heard another voice: Mimi's. She'd told me this story countless times, of how she'd found herself at the edge of something, side by side with a man she hardly knew. A young woman standing on a ledge high above the water, with the sun on her face and nothing but open sky ahead of her. She hadn't known then what would happen. There had been no promises, no assurances. There had only been a choice, to leap or not. He'd asked her what she wanted. And unlike me, she'd been unafraid to name it—and jump.

I stopped walking, draining the last lukewarm swallow from the mug in my hand. Ahead was the deadfall that would keep me from going farther, but that was fine: where I wanted to go was behind me. Back the way I came. Back to the house where there was a man waiting patiently for me to get brave. To make plans. To stop dithering over what-ifs and start thinking about what could be.

I smiled and whispered my answer aloud. Just like Mimi, I would leap—and allow myself to fall.

"Geronimo."

I hurried back the way I'd come, feeling bolder and surer of myself with every step. I had resisted thinking about a future with Adam for so long that now my imagination leaped wildly ahead, as if making up for lost time. I imagined us holding hands as we told my mother we'd fallen for each other. I imagined us signing the lease on a cool loft in some young, unspoiled city and using my trust from Mimi to start some kind of business, a coworking space or a cat café, the kind of thing that gets you interviewed for a "30 Under 30" list about young entrepreneurs who are giving back to their communities— and I imagined my father seeing the resulting article and calling me up, unscheduled, just to say he was proud of me. As I left the pine path and climbed up through the garden, I looked around at the gray hedges and crumbling stones with fresh eyes and thought it would be the perfect spot for a wedding, and then laughed out loud at how completely my imagination had run off the rails even as I pictured soft lights, sweet music, the two of us swaying gently together beneath the evening sky.

The skeptical voice inside me had fallen entirely silent, no longer interested in telling me *no* or *wait*, and I closed my eyes to linger there, to luxuriate in the fantasy. It would be summer, the height of summer, after the awful blackflies had died off but before the nights turned too cool for dancing. The hedges would be green, the light golden, and the dress—the dress would be ivory, of course, with lace sleeves and a full skirt and a modest neckline, appropriate for church, because her family had insisted they be married in one. Not my family, but Mimi's, and maybe this was why my vision seemed so real: not just because it could happen, but because it already had. My grandmother had danced in her white dress on this very spot with the man she'd vowed to love, honor, comfort, and keep for as long as they both would live. Was it so crazy to think that I might do the same?

I opened my eyes. Above me, the house still loomed, the windows still dark and empty—save one. My breath caught in my throat. A man's pale face was framed in one of the first-floor windows. He was holding very still, and he was staring at me. I stared back, raising one hand in a tentative wave, thinking that maybe it was Diana's husband, realizing almost at the same moment that it couldn't be. The shape of his face wasn't like William's at all, and his hair was black, not gray—and yet his face was oddly familiar, even as I became certain that I'd never seen him before. I dropped my hand. For a moment, the stranger in the window only stared at me. Then his mouth twisted. Sneering. I took an involuntary step back. The man disappeared.

Somewhere inside the house, my grandmother began to scream.

8.

Mimi's screaming tapered off to a wail as I sprinted back through the gardens and toward the house, the cold burning in my lungs. The piazza was crowded with cars now, including a beat-up truck with rusted fenders that hadn't been there when I left an hour ago. The front door was standing open and I ran through it, arriving just in time to see Richard stumbling up the stairs. He was still wearing last night's clothes and his hair was sticking out in all directions. The room was full of noise, Mimi's crying mixed with the urgent chatter of other voices. Richard shouted something at me that sounded like "Janet!"— which made no sense—and then pointed across the room. I turned my head to see Diana and William, who were huddled together and snapping rapid-fire questions at Adam, who was not answering them because he was whispering something to Mimi, who was standing with her back to him and her forehead pressed against the wall. She was still in her nightgown and still sobbing, shaking her head back and forth. I looked from Richard to Adam to Mimi and back to Richard twice more before I realized that the sneering man from the window was here, too, standing quietly beside the stairs with a canvas bag in his hand—only what I'd mistaken for a sneer was just how his face looked. Long and pinched, with heavy brows and a snarly upper lip that lifted at the center to expose his teeth but drew down sharply at the corners.

"Bloody hell!" Richard shouted, his voice booming above the cacophony. Everyone looked except Mimi, who kept crying, and the stranger, who looked at his feet. "Doesn't anyone have a sedative? Some Xanax?!"

Xanax, I thought, as the whole room stared. *Xanax, not Janet.*

"Oh, shut up, Richard," Diana snapped finally, at the same time as my mother appeared from the dining room door and said, "For god's sake, Richard, if anyone has *that*, it's you." Richard threw his hands in the air and stomped the rest of the way up the stairs, disappearing in the direction of his bedroom.

"What's going on?" I asked, but Mom only hissed, "Where were you?" and brushed past me without waiting for an answer. She said something hurriedly to the scowling stranger, then ushered him back through the open front door. He stared at me as he passed in a way that made me take an involuntary step back, his gaze pointed and angry. My mother followed him, pulling the door closed behind her. I glanced through one of the panes of glass in the casing and saw that they were paused halfway across the piazza, having an intense conversation that I couldn't hear over the sound of Mimi's weeping. Her sobs were starting to take shape, becoming words.

"I won't," she was saying over and over. "I won't, I won't!" She lifted her head to look at me, and I shuddered. There was no sign of the composed, confident woman who'd arrived here yesterday morning, or even of the slightly confused but amiable one I'd walked with in the afternoon. Mimi's skin was splotchy, her jaw quivering uncontrollably, her eyes bloodshot, her lips flecked with spittle. I gazed into her eyes, which gazed back at me without a shred of recognition or understanding—and that voice, the skeptical one that was always chiming in to tell me cruel and unbearable truths, chose this moment to break its silence.

She's going to die soon, it said, *but not soon enough. There will be months of this, horrible moments just like this one, while the lights inside her go out one by one, until all that's left is a walking, shitting, drooling husk that used to be a person. You'll wish she was dead a hundred times over before she ever takes her last breath.*

It was a horrible thought, one I never wanted and tried to banish as soon as it had come—but as I looked at Mimi's face, her empty eyes, I felt the truth of it and shuddered. Adam, who was holding my grandmother carefully by both shoulders, shot me a look over the top of her head that could have been confusion or maybe disappointment, and I looked back with a miserable shrug. The excitement and intimacy of last night seemed like a distant memory.

"I was just out for a walk," I said, even though the only person who'd asked where I'd been wasn't in the room anymore. Diana left her husband's side and took me by the arm, pulling me away from the others and down one of the shadowed hallways. Mimi's moans echoed eerily behind me.

"This is just awful," she said. She was wearing long, tasseled earrings that swung below the blunt line of her blond bob as she shook her head and kept swinging for several beats after she stopped. "Dora told me she had some bad days, but I never imagined—"

"This isn't normal," I interrupted. "Something must have happened. That guy, the one with the bag—"

"Oh, he's just a repairman or something," Diana said.

"He was watching me from the window."

She stiffened. "Watching you? You mean, like . . . a predator?" she said, her eyes narrowing, and I suddenly remembered that Diana was one of those people who was always sharing fake news stories on Facebook about women getting kidnapped in Walmart parking lots and getting sold into sex slavery.

"No," I said hurriedly. I would have said it no matter what, just to stop her from getting worked up, but it was true: there had been nothing predatory in the man's gaze.

I heard the front door open and close and my mother's voice saying, "Adam, can you take my mother back to her room and help her find some clothes, please."

"Of course," Adam said; I came back into the foyer just in time to see him disappear into the hallway opposite me, holding Mimi's arm with one hand and gently pressing her forward with the other. I wondered if he regretted coming here, and then thought dismally that if he didn't already, he would. Every person in the house seemed determined to show him, in their own ridiculous way, that he'd made a terrible mistake in getting so close to my grandmother. To my family. To me.

Diana had followed me back and started clucking, shaking her head again, her earrings swinging lightly. "A male nurse, Dora?" she said. "Is that really appropriate?"

"He's not a nurse, he's a personal caregiver," my mother and I said automatically, in unison. Mom looked startled and let out a little *ha!* sound that wasn't quite a laugh. She sat down heavily on the staircase and pressed two fingers into her temples, hard.

"I don't see what's so funny." Diana sniffed, and Mom rolled her eyes.

"Adam is a professional, and frankly, I'm grateful to have a strong young man around to help out with things," she said, and then tilted her head apologetically toward William. "No offense to any not-so-young men present."

William just blinked and shrugged, but Richard's voice floated down from above. "Too late," he said, appearing on the stairs. He'd changed his clothes and combed his hair, and was holding a small white pill between his thumb and forefinger. "I did find some Xanax, if Mother wants—"

"She doesn't," Mom said, and Richard shrugged and popped the pill in his mouth, swallowing it with a grimace. "If you say so," he said. My mother guffawed.

"You know, you could apologize," she said.

"For what?"

"Richard."

"What?!"

"You know we talked about this," Mom said darkly. "When she asks about Daddy, we should say he's at work, but he'll be home later. We *agreed*."

Richard snorted. "You agreed. I think it's obscene. I won't do it."

Diana looked back and forth between them, clasping her hands nervously. "Dora, do you really think that's wise—"

"I don't care about what's wise, I care about what's cruel," Mom said, her voice rising in pitch. "You haven't been here. You don't understand. When she doesn't remember and you tell her that he's dead, it breaks her heart just like she was losing him for the first time. I can't bear it."

The cough and rumble of a motor sounded and the old pickup truck I'd seen outside rolled past the window and down the driveway, the sneering man behind the wheel.

Diana cleared her throat. "Honestly, Dora, I have to wonder at your judgment. Are you just letting anyone walk into the house these days? That man was leering at your daughter, did you know that?" she said, pursing her lips.

My mouth dropped open. "That's not what I—" I started to stammer, but my mother just guffawed.

"Leering? Don't be ridiculous," she said. "Do you even know who that was? It's Jack Dyer. Shelly's son. You remember her, don't you? From when we were kids?"

Diana frowned, looking distinctly disappointed. An old acquaintance from childhood was much less exciting than a strange pervert on the premises, apparently. "Shelly? Barely. She was your nanny, wasn't she?"

"And yours," Mom said, but Diana shook her head.

"No. I remember when Daddy hired her. Mother was pregnant with you, so I would have been eight or nine. She was exhausted all the time, she couldn't keep up with the house. That's when Shelly came. But she hardly paid any attention to me and Richard. We were too old,

I guess. Although I seem to remember that she was very young and pretty. Richard even had a little crush on her—"

"I did not," Richard interrupted.

Diana shrugged. "Well, anyway. So that's her son? I don't remember him at all."

Richard snorted violently, and everyone stared. "Are you serious?" he said. Diana looked indignant, and he rolled his eyes melodramatically. "Good lord, sister. It was only the scandal of the century. Shelly got knocked up out of wedlock by a merchant seaman and decided to keep the baby. You can imagine how that played, at a time like that in a place like this."

I did the math: Jack Dyer looked to be about my mother's age, which would put his birth date sometime in the late 1950s. Not a great time to be pregnant and unmarried in a tiny New England town, that was for sure. Another few years and Shelly could've been an early crusader in the sexual revolution; instead, she'd gotten caught in the tail end of a Golden Age Puritan shame spiral.

"That's messed up," I said.

"It was a different time, young Delphine." Richard chuckled. "A merchant seaman could spray his merchant semen with wild abandon and then ride off into the sunset, footloose and fancy-free."

"Gross," I said.

"Anyway, it was quite the outrage. Our parents fought like hell about it. Dad wanted to get rid of her, and if Mother hadn't been so attached to Shelly, she would've been out on her ear."

"Daddy said that?" My mother looked shocked. Richard looked annoyed.

"What would you know about what Dad was like?" he said. "I doubt you even remember—"

"Shhhh," Diana said frantically, and gestured across the foyer. Adam was back and waiting at a polite distance, pretending not to listen, even though he must have heard. He smiled at me and I felt a flutter of gratitude.

"I made Miss Miriam a cup of tea and got her settled with Netflix," he said. "She's in the room with the green sofa, watching that baking show."

"Thank you, Adam," my mother said. "How is she?"

"She's okay. You know how it is: one second it's a crisis, and the next, it's like nothing ever happened. If you asked her now, I don't think she'd even remember why she was so upset."

Diana gave him an accusing look. "Why *was* she so upset?"

"There's never really one reason," Adam said cautiously, and Richard snorted again.

"This one's very diplomatic, isn't he," he said, as he descended the rest of the way downstairs and took a seat on the step beside my mother. "Very polite. Doesn't want to tell everyone that drunk Uncle Richard spent the night passed out on the sofa and woke up just in time to cause a great big scene." He chuckled again. "Well, I'll tell on myself. One minute I was having a late-night tryst with a bottle of scotch, the next I was waking up with a ripping headache, and there was a man who looked like an angry ferret standing over me and asking if the lady of the house was at home. It's all a bit fuzzy, but I believe I told him there were certainly no ladies here, and no gentlemen, either—"

"Asshole," Diana interjected.

"—and he wandered off, and I followed him, and then Mother stumbled in from God knows where in that ludicrous nightie, and she told us we were both trespassing and that her husband would have us arrested. And yes, in my cranky and hungover state, I may have rudely reminded her that she doesn't have a husband anymore." He gave me a wry look. "I am, as you kids say, the asshole. Mystery solved."

Diana looked at William and said, "God, I wish we'd stayed in a hotel," and stalked away down the hall. Her husband cast a wordless glance at all of us and walked away after her, and I had a sudden flashback to another holiday ten years previous, the last time Diana had come to visit us for Christmas. Like Mom, my aunt had been married and divorced once by the time she was forty; unlike Mom,

KAT ROSENFIELD / 90

she didn't have a kid hanging like a millstone around her neck, and she was desperate not to be alone, but also terrified of choosing the wrong man . . . again. Her first husband had been some kind of musician—I had a very old, very hazy memory of sitting at his feet while he sang and played a complicated, Spanish-inflected arrangement of "Puff, the Magic Dragon" on an acoustic guitar—and while they didn't talk about it much in front of me, I still gathered that he'd been a disappointment in the way that handsome men with guitars usually are. Diana had been between boyfriends on that Christmas ten years ago, and a little bit drunk, when she told my mom that she had given up entirely on sexy and exciting. She wanted nice, reliable, even boring: the Toyota Corolla of men. ("So, midsize and Japanese," Mom said, at which point Diana laughed so hard that she choked on her Chardonnay.)

I couldn't help thinking now that it seemed she'd gotten what she wanted: William was so bland that he barely registered as human, like someone had put half a personality in a man-shaped box and filled the rest of the empty space with foam packing peanuts. Certainly Diana never had to worry about him cheating on her, not just because it was hard to believe anyone else could like him enough to sleep with him, but because it seemed like he might wink out of existence entirely anytime they weren't together. It made me wonder again what they'd been arguing about when I passed their room last night.

Mom sighed. "I'm sorry about all this, Adam," she said. "It's . . . well. I'm just very sorry."

There was a moment where nobody spoke, where all the things my mother didn't say in the ellipsis between "It's" and "well" seemed to hover in the air. *It's a shit show. It's embarrassing. It's insane that a house full of grown adults can't stop squabbling and sniping at each other even when someone is dying.* Even Richard looked embarrassed. But Adam didn't: he crossed the distance between us in a few steps and dropped to a squat, eye level with my mother, as if he were talking to a child.

"Listen, Dora," he said, looking steadily at my mother, "there's nothing to apologize for. If this were easy, you wouldn't need me. I'm here because it's hard. Not just for your mom. What you and Richard and Delphine"—he nodded at each of us in turn—"what you're all going through, that's hard. And having Miriam here with you . . . don't get me wrong, it's good. But it was always going to be really challenging, and that's nobody's fault." He paused. "Except ours, maybe. Willowcrest is really focused on the residents, and that's mostly a good thing, but sometimes I think we don't talk enough about how rough this is on the families."

My mother took a shaky breath. "Thank you," she said.

Richard stood up. "Yes, thank you. I for one am delighted to know that Mother is under the competent care of a living saint. And since you all have things so well in hand, I think I'll go have a mimosa."

We all watched him stride out of the room, and Mom shifted uncomfortably. "You said not to apologize, but—"

Adam laughed. "I've been called worse. Don't worry about it."

"My brother has always dealt with things in his own way. Or not dealt with them." She sighed again. "Anyway, I guess I'd better go talk to him. To both of them. There's a lot to discuss, including some things I was hoping might wait until after Christmas, but . . ." She trailed off, looking at me. "Maybe you could keep Mimi company? Find something to occupy her? The things we're talking about, I don't want her overhearing."

I started to answer, but Adam stood up. "She's been talking about a bakery she used to go to back in the day. Over in Northeast Harbor."

Mom shook her head. "If there was, I'm sure it's long gone—"

"For sure," Adam interrupted, "but I checked online, and there *is* a bakery over there. Probably not the same one, but it might be a nice little trip anyway. I could get her out of the house and give you all some privacy."

KAT ROSENFIELD / 92

"Oh, that's a lovely idea," Mom said, sounding relieved. "You two can take her together. Adam, do you know where her boots are? You'll need to put them on for her, her arthritis—"

"I got it," he said, smiling. "I'll go get her ready."

I waited for Adam to disappear down the hall, trying to ignore how giddy I felt that we were about to be alone together—or at least alone together with Mimi, who would probably fall asleep and leave us free to talk. There was something about the way my mother had pivoted away from Diana's questions. A sense, very familiar, that there was something she wasn't talking about.

"What was he doing here?" I asked.

Mom blinked. "Hmm?"

"That man. Jack Dyer."

"Oh." She paused. "The furnace. He owns a local oil supply company. I was thinking of switching the account, because the guy we use now is, well . . . I don't need to bore you with the details."

"It's eight o'clock in the morning."

"Yes?"

"He just walked in here at eight o'clock in the morning, while everyone was sleeping, four days before Christmas . . . to talk about heating oil?"

She gave me a long look. "Delphine, someday, and I hope it's not for a while, but someday? You'll be the child of an aging parent, too. And you'll find out then that there's no such thing as a convenient time to take care of all the many, many things you have to take care of when your mother is losing her mind."

By ten o'clock, I was in the back seat of Adam's car as it traveled the long curves of the oceanside road. The fog had lifted and the sea stretched away to the south, the water dark and churning. Overhead, the clouds had cracked apart to reveal a thin, pale slice of blue sky. Mimi hadn't fallen asleep after all; she was alert, riding shotgun next to Adam, leaning forward to look through the windshield and keeping up a stream of chatter about the drives she used to take. She'd once known a boy with a Cadillac, she said, who would take her all around the island.

"But I was only a girl then," she said, and twisted in her seat to look at me. "A girl like this girl. How are you, dear?"

I smiled, not bothering to point out that I was a long way from being a teenager, as she'd been during those long-ago summer drives. "Just fine."

"In those days, we could have sat the three of us up front," Mimi said. "But this . . . this . . ."

"Subaru," Adam said, and Mimi made a face.

"This *Subaru*," she said, "they put this thing in it." She tapped her fingers against the center console.

Adam smiled. "But now there's a place for your elbow. And your coffee."

Mimi gave him a sly look. "That's not what it's for."

"It's not?"

"No," she said. "It's not for elbows. It's a blockade. To stop young people from canoodling."

"You know," Adam said, "I think you're right. But you know what else?"

"What?"

"I bet they find a way to canoodle anyway."

I watched and grinned as Mimi giggled and Adam winked at me over his shoulder. He was so good at this, at knowing just the right tone to take, gentle and playful but never condescending. Too many people didn't understand that dementia made a person sick, not stupid. I still remembered the time when the woman doing Mimi's pedicure had chirped, "And now we'll paint your little piggy-wiggies," like she was talking to a toddler, and then looked like she'd been slapped when Mimi plucked the polish right out of her hand, turned to me, and said, "Dear, would you paint them? This bitch appears to have gone soft in the head."

I chuckled to myself, and then felt a chill run down my spine as Adam's eyes briefly met mine in the rearview mirror. Something dark and delicious seemed to flicker there, and I thought, *Tonight.* Just the one word. Like a promise.

Mimi stayed in high spirits all the way to Northeast Harbor, but when we pulled into the small lot beside the bakery, she suddenly grew moody.

"We're here!" I said, unbuckling my seat belt.

"Here? Where?" She frowned. "I don't know this place."

"The bakery in Northeast Harbor."

"This isn't—" She faltered and seemed to shrink in her seat. "No, this isn't right. You must have gone the wrong way."

Adam and I exchanged looks. The tremble in Mimi's voice was a warning; there was no sense in trying to correct her.

"Well, damn, I probably did," he said, nodding agreeably and keeping his tone light. "It's so easy to get lost around here, isn't it? I'm sorry. But hey, since we're here, maybe we should just take a look inside this place? See what looks good? What do you say, Miss Miriam?"

Mimi gripped her seat belt with both hands. "I won't," she said, her voice rising in pitch. "I won't!"

He rested a hand on her shoulder. "Sure, okay. But I don't mind telling you, I'm pretty hungry. Maybe you and I can just sit here a minute, and Delphine can go inside and buy some, well, something."

"I think that's a great idea," I said quickly. "I'll be back before you know it."

Mimi still clung to the seat belt as if she thought I might try to haul her out of the car, but she nodded. "All right."

I hurried into the bakery, where a small bell rang above the door and the air was warm, thick with the smell of yeast and cinnamon sugar. There was a glass case lined with pastries to my right, and a chalkboard on the wall where someone had scrawled "Cranberry

Holiday Cake, $10" in red-and-white-striped letters made to look like candy canes. I saw tall jars filled with cookies, a dozen rustic bread loaves piled up in a pyramid.

I didn't see Jack Dyer until he was right next to me, standing too close, staring at me with the same scowl that I'd seen in the window earlier. He was close enough that I could smell him—body odor mixed with old smoke—and I stumbled back, hearing my aunt Diana's voice in my head as I did: *Watching you? Like a predator?*

No, I thought as I found my footing again. Not like a predator. It wasn't like that at all, because it was something much stranger. The way Jack Dyer looked at me, it wasn't like he wanted to do something bad to me. It was more like I had done something bad to *him.*

He spoke before I could, clearing his throat. "Didn't mean to startle you," he said.

"You mean just now or at my house this morning?" I said. It was meant to be a joke, but came out sounding peevish, and I winced.

"Your house," he repeated, the corners of his mouth drawing upward—and if I didn't like Jack Dyer's scowl, I liked his smile even less. "Your house," he said again. "Well, I guess it is. Since you live there. You know, I used to live there, too."

"You?"

"Ayuh. Long time ago. Never thought of it as my house, though."

I blinked, feeling stupid. Of course: Shelly had been the live-in housekeeper. With no husband and nowhere else to go, of course she would've stayed on—first pregnant, then with her baby.

"Sorry," I said. "I didn't realize."

"Your granny, she never mentioned it? Never talks about my mother?"

"Not really. There's a lot she doesn't remember anymore."

"Ah," he said. "Well, my ma sure remembers her."

"Does she?"

"Sure does. She's got some stories. Not that she's telling them now. Ma had a stroke a while back. She can't talk no more. I've been taking care of her."

"I'm sorry," I said again. "That sounds rough."

"It is what it is. We didn't have the kind of money to put her in a nice place like your granny." He paused. "Or take her out of it, nurse and all."

I couldn't say *I'm sorry* again, even if I wanted to—and I didn't. I thought that Jack Dyer had some nerve, to be so ungracious about Mimi when she was the one who'd given his pregnant unwed mother a roof over her head, a job, another chance despite the scandal. I gestured toward the door. "They're waiting in the car for me. I'd better get what I came for and go."

"And what did you come for, missy?"

Accompanied by Jack Dyer's fierce stare, the words felt like an accusation. I glanced around until my gaze settled on the chalkboard with the candy-cane lettering. "Cranberry holiday cake. You know, uh, for the holiday. Merry Christmas," I added lamely, and turned away. He didn't say *Merry Christmas* back—didn't say anything at all, just stood there—and I avoided looking at him as I paid for the cake and left. I hadn't noticed his truck as I walked in, but I saw it now, parked on the opposite side of the lot almost directly behind us. There was an old woman with long gray hair sitting in the front seat; even through the grimy windshield, I could see that one side of Shelly Dyer's face was slack, her mouth pulling down at one corner. As I watched, her hands came up in front of her face, holding something—like a child playing peekaboo, I thought, but she wasn't playing. The object in front of her face was a tablet, and she was pointing its camera at me. She was taking my picture. I thought of waving, then heard Jack Dyer's bitter voice in my head—*my ma sure remembers her*—and thought better of it. I also thought instinctively that I would not mention any of this while Mimi was in earshot.

"Success," I said cheerfully, brandishing the cake as I climbed into the back seat. The scent of sugar and cinnamon wafted under my nose.

Adam looked back, smacking his lips exaggeratedly. "Oh wow, that's something. Looks delicious. Doesn't it, Miriam?"

My grandmother turned her head, but not to look. Her eyes were closed and her expression was dreamy. She inhaled deeply and smiled. "Oh, darling," she said. "It's so wonderful."

In three days, she would be dead.

9.

1947

AUTUMN

She is eighteen, and the state is about to burn.

It's the first year that she's stayed long enough to see the little seaside village empty out at the end of the summer season—and to see her breath in the air in the morning, weeks later, as the trees began to blaze with autumn color. A change of seasons, and a change of scenery. For the first time, the Day family has come from Egg Harbor to the Whispers with no plan to leave.

At Edward's funeral, the minister had read from Ecclesiastes: "To every thing there is a season, and a time to every purpose under the heaven. A time to be born, and a time to die; a time to plant, and a time to pluck up that which is planted." Miriam could hardly concentrate on the words then as she clutched the hand of her brother's wife—the sweet young woman who had looked so beautiful all those summers past, dancing and laughing in a dress of cream-colored silk, now draped in black, a pale and hollow-eyed widow at twenty-three.

But she feels the weight of them now. They echo in her head as she stares out the window at the changing landscape, while Edward's little white dog, Patches, sleeps curled in a ball at her feet. She feels a kinship with the dog: both of them were planted in one place, now plucked up and set back down in lives that bear no resemblance to the ones they'd had. She also envies Patches, who doesn't seem to mind at all that his family situation has changed, just so long as he has one. Dwelling on the past is strictly a human concern.

For Miriam, the past feels like another life—and the future, a question with no answer. Before Edward's death, there had been talk of going abroad with her mother after school was finished, but nobody would think of leaving Papa at home now. Her school friends, who hugged her so tightly at their graduation parties and promised to write often, promptly disappeared into a whirlwind of college studies and travel and engagements that she finds out about from reading the newspaper rather than from their letters. Moving on with their lives while Miriam treads water, unsure and stuck in place.

A time to weep, and a time to laugh; a time to mourn, and a time to dance.

This summer had been full of mourning and not much else. Papa always said he'd retire and live out his remaining days at the seaside, and Miriam used to imagine that he'd spend years that way, a king in his castle, holding court in his favorite chair with a book and a glass of his very best scotch. Now she sometimes looks at her father and thinks, with quiet despair, that he's disappearing before her eyes. The formidable Roland Day is diminished, shrunken by grief, and the high back of his favorite chair looms over his hunched shoulders. The legendary parties where he entertained dozens of guests are a distant memory. The house has had only one visitor all summer, and he's no guest; he's more like part of the furniture, a coarse man of thirty or so whom Papa calls "my young friend from the old days." Mother calls him "that man." And the man in question calls himself Charles Smith, but Miriam noticed the first day how he and Father paused and exchanged looks before he introduced himself, which almost certainly means that his real name is something else—that he used to be someone else.

She's also noticed that when Smith is in the room, her mother always manages to be elsewhere.

It could be that she doesn't like the reminder of whatever he and Papa used to do, the winking way he says *the old days* that makes it clear they were up to no good. Maybe she worries that they still are. Or maybe it's simpler than that: pure jealousy, that Papa seems to have a rapport with Smith, who is coarse and badly dressed with fetid breath and brown teeth, that he doesn't share with anyone else.

But if Mother is lonely, she doesn't say so. Instead, she fills her time, and Miriam's, too, with luncheons and teas and card parties, dinners and dances. It's unsaid yet understood that there's no saying no to these engagements. Evelyn Day has worked hard to keep her society connections, not for herself but for her daughter; it's just as unsaid, and just as understood, that Miriam is being paraded through all these parties just so that all the biddies in attendance can tell their eligible sons how lovely she looks, which of course they do. A few of the sons have even come calling. They doff their hats as they come inside, and smile like sharks that have caught the scent of blood.

Miriam has enjoyed exactly one of these visits, and then only because Patches had come into the room, sniffed once at the interloper, and then lifted his leg and urinated extravagantly all over the suitor's shoes.

Harold Chandler, on the other hand, has not come calling. He and his Cadillac are elsewhere this year, and Mother keeps asking after him—but always in a sidelong way that suggests she's already heard something, maybe from Harold's mother. The summer is gone, and the Chandlers with it, before she finally asks outright.

"Did something happen?" she says, but Miriam doesn't know how to answer that, except to shrug and say, "No." It wasn't that something had happened. It was that something could have but didn't. If not for Edward's accident, if she hadn't left that very day—but there was no changing what was already past, the chance she had already missed. When she went back to the pond this summer, she found it empty, the lily pads growing thick and undisturbed. There was a forest of bobbing flowers now beneath the ledge she'd jumped from, which looked so impossibly high that the memory made her stomach do a somersault. She wonders if the boys stopped coming here, and if it's because of her. She wonders if she spoiled this place. She has looked for Theodore Caravasios, waiting on the pier at sunset, but none of the boats that pass by seem to be his. Maybe he no longer cares for her . . . or maybe he doesn't live here anymore. She had thought of writing him, and just as quickly thought better of it: what would she say? And now whatever they might have sparked is gone, and it's too late.

It's too late, and she burns with it.

Come the third week of October, the island begins burning with her.

A summer without rain has turned acres of wilderness into kindling. Some people swear they've seen the sky glowing red in its southern reaches at night, that they can smell the smoke as it wafts up the coast from Portland. Most of the town's seasonal visitors have already left, but those who stayed to see the autumn can talk of nothing else. At the next luncheon, Miriam picks at her crabmeat salad and listens as the women trade snippets of news overheard at the post office or market: towns reduced to ashes overnight, people stumbling out of the haze with soot on their faces, all of them clutching suitcases stuffed with every precious thing that was small enough to carry. Their hostess, a petite blonde named Mrs. Procter, shoots a glance at Miriam and mistakes her fascination for fear.

"Oh, but there's no need to worry, dear. My William spoke to a ranger just yesterday, and he assured me we needn't concern ourselves," she says, patting Miriam's hand. She's still patting, still smiling, when the fire whistle blows. It's loud enough to rattle the windows, loud enough to bounce off the top of the mountains and echo back from every cove. The first peal silences the chatter. By the third, every woman at the table is on her feet. They stare at one another, wide-eyed, in the silence that follows, waiting for the next whistle that never comes.

Only Miriam stays seated, biting her lip, staring straight ahead. Three blasts on the fire whistle isn't just a warning. It's a call to arms, a summons to every able-bodied man. In homes all over the island, they'll be standing up and making for the door, ready to beat back the flames.

And Theodore Caravasios, if he's still here, will be among them.

"*Miriam,*" Mother says, and she snaps to attention. She's alone at the table, her fork still in her hand, surrounded by abandoned plates and half-drunk glasses of punch; from the hallway beyond Mrs. Procter's dining room comes the frantic rustling and murmured apologies of five women struggling into their coats.

As Miriam looks toward the open door, their hostess suddenly reappears, gazing back and forth across the room with her hands fluttering and twisting at her heart. "Oh dear," she says to no one in particular. "The house may go, I suppose there's nothing to be done about that . . . but I simply must save my best pink hat."

Mother is too nervous to drive, and Miriam takes the wheel, carefully following the curves of the road that runs out of town and across the ridge back to the cove and the Whispers. Despite the shattering blast of the fire whistle, everyone outside and on the streets is oddly calm, continuing about their business even as blazing destruction creeps closer and closer. When Miriam sees men and trucks gathered in the road ahead, she slows the car to a stop and rolls the window down. The air is already hazy and tinged with the scent of smoke, but it's light, almost pleasant, as if a few men working to clear someone's yard had set a pile of leaves to burn. Even the men guarding the road seem cheerful and unafraid.

"Hello there," one calls, jogging up to the car.

Mother leans across Miriam's lap. "Where is the fire? Can we cross over?"

"Half a mile along Eagle Lake Road. That'll be closed off now, but you can make your way over the mountain road."

"Is there any hope of stopping it?"

The man chuckles darkly. "This fire? No, ma'am. We may be able to push it to Eagle Lake and contain it there, where there's water. Otherwise it'll continue on, all t'way to the sea."

Mother seems on the verge of saying something else, another foolish question, but coughs instead. The smoke has grown thicker in the minute since they first stopped, and another man points and shouts: in the distance, a spike of flame has appeared over the top of a hill. It hovers there like a cresting wave—and then the wave breaks, a cascade of fire rippling down, devouring the hillside.

"Best go now, young lady," the man says, and Miriam does, peering into the side mirror for one last glance at the men in the road as she drives away from them. Theo is not among them, but the hope of seeing him must show on her face, because Mother twists in her seat to look back, too. The fear in her eyes is briefly replaced with something more familiar: suspicion. "Do you know those men?"

"No," Miriam says, although it's not entirely true. There was one man, small and lean with ears that stuck out beneath his hat. She doesn't know his name, but he was there that day, one of the curious bystanders on the ledge who stepped aside so that she could leap. A witness. But that moment has been her secret for more than a year, and she isn't about to tell it now.

Evelyn Day narrows her eyes but doesn't say anything else. Instead, she gazes out the window, her lips moving, muttering to herself— praying, Miriam thinks, until she catches the tail end of a whisper and hears not an Our Father or a Hail Mary, but the words *green glass bowl*. Her mother isn't asking God to save them. She's making a list of the things she herself wants to save. Miriam is about to make a joke about Mrs. Procter and her hats, but then the car reaches the top of its uphill climb and the trees fall away, and she can't joke at all, only gasp. Over their heads whirls a mass of smoke that writhes and shudders like a living thing. Furious eddies of bright pink and dusky purple ripple through its blackened body. Dark furrows open and close in its billowing surface like hungry mouths. It spirals funnel-shaped into the heavens, so huge and endless that it is impossible to imagine there's a place in the world that isn't burning, where the sky isn't choked with black.

Mother's face is very pale. "Have you ever seen anything so terrible," she whispers, as the ash begins to fall.

By two o'clock, an evacuation order has come over the radio and the smoke is so soup-thick around the house that the view from every window is nothing but a blank wall, broken by the dark trunks of trees rising up here and there like girders. Miriam and her mother run back and forth through the hazy air, filling the larger of their two cars with boxes and suitcases that hold clothes, books, a handful of framed photographs.

Papa watches their packing with amusement until it tips over into scorn. "My dear," he finally says as his wife rifles furiously through drawers and cabinets, "is there truly any object in this house that I couldn't just buy you a second time?"

That's when Smith starts chuckling from the corner, and both women jump; they hadn't even seen him sitting there. Mother's face is as angry and wounded as if she'd been slapped. She looks out the window, out at the copse of trees that used to make the house feel beautifully secluded but which now makes it feel like a tinderbox surrounded by kindling wood.

"Perhaps it may miss us yet. Perhaps the wind will change," she says, but her voice is so strange and flat that Miriam will always remember it: this is the moment she understands that there is no hope, that the Whispers will burn.

Smith knows it, too. He shakes his head. "You know better than that." He turns to Papa. "And if there's anything in this house you feel keenly attached to, old man, I suggest you put it in that car . . . if the ladies left any room."

Despite the smoke, the radio says the fire won't reach them until early in the evening. The mood in the house is strange, like what Miriam imagines the decks of the *Titanic* must have been like in those long hours after the iceberg pierced the hull, when the boat had not yet begun to sink. There was still time, not to alter how things would end, but to prepare oneself for what was inevitable—or to pretend it wasn't. Even once they resume preparing to evacuate, crossing from the house to the cars and back while Patches sits curious and watchful beside the front door, nobody seems willing to say the worst aloud: that the next time they come back, it will almost certainly be to blackened ruins. Where will they go? Where will they live? Back to Egg Harbor, maybe, to scrape up whatever pieces remain of the life they used to have and try to make them into something new.

A time to get, and a time to lose.

It's time, it seems, to lose everything.

The Whispers looms magnificent as ever against the sky, like a man who's been told he will hang tomorrow at dawn and is determined to stand tall until his last breath. They drive out the front gate sometime just after four o'clock, Miriam's parents in their wine-colored Buick Special and then Smith in his battered black Ford, with Miriam in the passenger seat and a trio of nested boxes in between them, stacked so high that she can't even see Smith's face when she looks crosswise, only the creased top of his brown hat. Something rattles inside the boxes and she tries to remember what it could be—the clinking and clanking of china, or maybe tin—as she rests her forehead against the car window. A teakettle? A typewriter? The green glass bowl that Mother murmured over like a prayer while the sky turned black above them?

The little village is busy, the roads full of army jeeps and army men called in to help fight the fire, the trucks and men alike dressed in the same shade of olive drab. Smith pulls to the curb in front of the post office and lights a cigarette. Miriam's parents have parked just ahead and are standing on the sidewalk, arguing about whether to make space in the car by sending some boxes ahead by post. Miriam rolls the window down to listen, but the wind has begun to blow and carries their voices away; instead, she hears a group of men trading snippets of information about where the fire has already been and which roads are still open for evacuation.

"Shan't be long now," one of them says, his voice weary but calm. He gestures farther down the road, where a group of soldiers has piled into a jeep and is driving slowly toward them, followed by a truck filled with local men, all packed like sardines into the back with their faces turned to the wind. Soon this village will be a ghost town, abandoned to the flames while its residents head north, across the bridge to the mainland. Miriam and her family will be among them, and she wonders what will come after, and then decides just as quickly that it hardly matters. Her uprooted family will be planted again, if not here then somewhere else, and she resolves here and now to be peaceful about it. To accept the change with the same cheerfulness as Edward's little dog, who never seems to mind where he is as long as he can curl up beside someone familiar. It's a comforting thought: that wherever she sleeps tonight and tomorrow, it will at least be with the familiar weight and warmth of Patches at her feet.

But Patches is not here.

Miriam's stomach lurches horribly as she twists in her seat, peering back into the cluttered car. Hoping against hope for any sign of the dog, for a glimpse of white fur or a little *yip* to contradict what she already knows. She can see it in her memory: Patches at his post just inside the door, the curious cock of his head as he watched them pack up the car. He'd lain there quietly for an hour—right up until Smith stumbled over him so that he and his armful of packages nearly went sprawling. Smith had hollered, and Patches had fled back into the house, out of sight.

And out of mind. They'd left him behind.

"Oh no, oh no," Miriam gasps, and above the rim of the stacked boxes, Smith's hat twists in her direction. "We have to go back. The dog, we left him. We have to go back!"

There's a pause before Smith answers. When he does, the sound of his dark chuckling is the most hideous thing Miriam has ever heard. "Kid, have you lost your mind?" he says, and the chuckle turns into a hacking laugh. "There's no going back now. But don't fret, I'm sure your pops will get you another dog. Maybe even one of them fancy breeds, like a Pe—"

But Miriam never hears what Smith has to say. Not just because his voice is drowned out by the sudden shriek of the fire whistle, three quick blasts, and not just because of the sudden commotion as every one of the men standing watchfully on the street springs into action. Miriam isn't in the car anymore. She's running down the street, her shoes slapping hard against the pavement, her skirt whipping around her legs. She's waving and shouting at the truck full of men that has just passed, shouting at them to stop, *stop, damn you,* and then letting go a ragged sob of relief when it does.

"Are you going to Hull's Cove?" she gasps, and though the men exchange looks, a voice from the middle of the group speaks up.

"Ayuh, we're headed up that way. But the wind will shift soon, miss, and the fire's holding its own. I don't think—"

"I don't care what you think," Miriam says, and reaches her hand out. The man who spoke hesitates for only a moment, then reaches out and hauls her up into the truck. As he does, she looks full into his face and lets out a little laugh of recognition: it's the same man she saw in the street yesterday, the one with the prominent ears, the one who was there the day she jumped from the ledge. She almost asks him if Theodore is somewhere fighting the fire, but then the driver hollers back, "All set back there?" and one of the men thumps the cab roof in response, and it's all she can do to cling to the sideboards as the truck begins to roll forward.

"Always jumping into things, aren't you," says the man with the ears, chuckling, but then he turns away before she can answer and nobody else says a word. The last thing Miriam sees as the truck rolls around the corner is her parents, their faces stricken, their argument forgotten, gazing in her direction but not seeing her. Their eyes are lifted toward the sky, where a coal-black haze has risen up to blot out the sun. And just beneath it, flickering over the far-off top of the great hill that shadows the town, the light of the coming fire.

By the time they reach the turnoff to the shore drive and the Whispers, she can hear the distant roar of the flames. The wind coming down the road is fiercely hot, blowing dry leaves and dust that make her eyes burn and water. The truck slows just enough that she can drop off the back, and the man in the passenger seat leans out, shouting at her as they pull away.

"You've got a bit of time yet," he yells above the gusting wind. "But whatever you came for, get it and get back fast. Some men and equipment will be coming this way in no more than fifteen minutes."

Miriam nods.

Then she runs.

She reaches the house more quickly than she expected, her feet flying over the crushed stone drive as a haze settles between the trees, the light growing soft as a sunrise. The quickness of her journey is her first stroke of luck. The second comes when she runs up to the door and finds it unlocked—another thing forgotten in their hurry to leave—and the house as dark and quiet as a tomb inside. She calls the dog's name as she runs through the house, first toward the library where he sometimes slept at Papa's feet, then through the dining room, the kitchen, up the stairs and back down, her shouts of "Patches!" growing shriller as she searches his favorite spots and finds them empty. She goes again to the library, again to the kitchen, up to her room where she kneels to look under the bed and finds nothing but the dusty outline where her suitcase used to be. *I saved that but not him,* she thinks, and her next exhalation is half sob, half scream.

"Patches! Here, boy!"

But there's no answer, the dog doesn't appear, and now there's no time. Miriam's wristwatch tells her that she must leave now, leave or be found standing alone in the road as the fire comes over the hill. She's weeping in earnest now. Sobbing for the dog she can't find and for the brother she lost as she struggles to her feet and back down the stairs. Her eyes burn with the smoke and her own tears, and she sees with alarm how the shadows have deepened as she hurries back through the hall and down the stairs. She's still weeping when her foot catches on the last step and she stumbles, flailing gracelessly into the foyer, failing to regain her balance and instead sprawling flat on her belly. There's a terrible *whoosh* as the breath flies out of her lungs and then panic: she tries to take her next breath and finds her diaphragm frozen. She rolls to her side, fingertips scrabbling at the marble floor, clawing for air—and in the last moment before her diaphragm releases and her lungs draw another breath, she hears it.

Coming from the water closet under the stairs, the sound of tiny claws scratching against the door.

She flies to her feet, still gasping, and flings the door wide. A ball of white fur streaks past her, then doubles back to run between her legs. She reaches down to scoop the dog up, burying her face in his fur for just a moment before she tucks him inside her coat, clutching him tightly. She allows herself one moment more to wonder how he got trapped in the powder room and grinds her teeth in anger as she realizes the likeliest answer. Then she runs, out the way she came, out toward the drive and the road beyond, where she will climb aboard one of the equipment trucks and ride back to town. Already, she can see how it will happen: How she'll find her family where she left them, or maybe even somewhere along the way. How she won't apologize, just hold up the dog by way of explanation, knowing Papa will understand. How she'll tell her father, when the time is right, that his old friend Smith closed Patches up in the water closet, knowing full well that he would be trapped and left behind.

But she won't do any of these things. And when the truck that would have taken her back to the village passes by just minutes from now, there will be no girl standing in the road waiting to hitch a ride.

The trees that line either side of the drive are on fire. Flames encircle their bases like burning bracelets, then race upward to engulf the trunk, the branches, the dust-dry leaves. The air is filled with the crackle and burst of trees exploding, the heavy thud of branches as they plummet to the ground and keep burning. Miriam tries to take another breath and chokes, gagging on the smoke, whirling this way and that in search of a way out. She feels Patches wriggling against her, feels herself losing her grip. She dives after him as he slips from her arms, scrabbling across the ground to grab at a fistful of fur and skin, shouting at him to stay—and this is her third stroke of luck. As she scrambles after the dog, a thunderous crack sounds from overhead. A moment later, the highest trunk on the huge maple tree that hung out over the roof of the north wing splits cleanly in two, and crashes down in the place where she had been standing, raining down a cascade of sparks as it shakes free its burning leaves.

Miriam is dimly aware that she once again has Patches in her arms.

She is also dimly aware, as she struggles back to her feet and runs toward the sea, that her hair is on fire.

The gardens are already ablaze as she flees along the stone wall and down the steps, the fire leaping higher and higher as the hedges crackle and burn and burst, showering her again with sparks. She beats at her head with one hand to smother the flames as she flees across the smoldering grass and onto the pier. Thinking only of getting away from the fire and toward the water—and realizing only when she turns to look back, too late, that she wasn't thinking clearly.

There is nowhere to go. The fire is at the pier, and then on it. The first board begins to burn, then the second, the flames whipped by the wind. And Miriam, trapped on the rickety pier with a seven-foot plunge between herself and the churning, frigid sea, will either burn or drown.

She falls to her knees, holding Patches tight, and buries her face in his neck. The smoke billows toward her, the fire close behind it, and then it envelops her. The world turns black and choking. She sees nothing, not the sky above or the water below, even as her ears fill with noise. The creak and pop of the burning pier. The splash of the water below. The roar of fire and wind. The harsh and angry sound of her breath as it drags ragged into her throat and comes out as a retching, hacking cough. Her thoughts are disjointed and wild, images flashing through her mind. Mother and Papa, as they were when she saw them last, gazing at the horizon with fear in their eyes—and then as they used to be, dancing, laughing, twirling arm in arm. She sees her brothers, young and tanned and chasing her along the shore path after she dropped a piece of seaweed down Robert's collar. She sees Robert's eyes full of unspilled tears above his stubbled cheeks, and Edward's casket laden with white gardenias. She sees herself: running shoeless through the garden. Tiptoeing like a ghost through the house during hide-and-seek. Riding beside Harold Chandler with the sun on her face. Running to the edge of that rocky ledge and taking flight—and that split second, before she began plummeting toward the water, when she thought she might never fall at all.

She sees Theodore Caravasios, smiling and offering her a choice.

She chose to leap.

She's not sorry. She would do it again.

The cold takes her breath away as she plunges feetfirst into the sea and then surfaces, gagging, her feet reaching in vain for purchase against the ocean floor too far below. She had let go of Patches as she jumped, but he's here now, paddling around beside her, his fur matted down against his head, his small body being knocked here and there by the waves. But he stays afloat, he keeps swimming, and she thinks that the dog might make it to shore—and feels heartened by it, even as she understands that she will not.

She's just chosen a better way to die.

The needle-sharp cold of the October water is already beginning to dull, and Miriam knows this is how it begins. Already her fingers are numbing, refusing to clench; already her extremities and sodden clothes are getting heavy, dead weight that will drag her down. She gazes back toward the shore, where the upper peaks of the Whispers can be seen just above the swirling smoke. There are flames licking from the windows. The house is going. And so is she.

Miriam closes her eyes.

The freezing water begins to touch her ears as her legs slow their frantic treading. She sees death approaching, reaching for her. Soon its icy fingers will grasp her ankles and draw her down. But not yet. Not quite.

To everything there is a season. A time to be born, a time to die. A time to plant, a time to pluck up that which is planted. *A time,* she whispers, and her thoughts grow sluggish. *A time.*

Her ears are under the water. She cannot hear the fire anymore, or the creak of the boards, or the puff of Patches's breath as he swims anxiously in the tossing bay.

She cannot hear the splash of water against the hull of the fast-approaching boat.

She cannot hear Theo shouting her name.

But when a strong arm wraps her from behind and she feels herself pulled through the water, through and up and out—and when his mouth presses hot and fiercely over hers to blow life back into her lungs—she knows that there is time yet.

Time to keep, and to cast away. To embrace, and to refrain. To gain, to lose, and to love, to love, to love.

She opens her eyes. Beside her, Patches is pacing and whining, pushing his wet nose against her hand—and above her is Theodore Caravasios, his face inches from hers. She watches his expression change: from fear to relief, and then relief to anger, and then anger to something else. Something fierce and dark and all hers, if she wants it, and she does. She does.

"God damn it, Miriam," he says, and kisses her under the flame-tipped sky.

IO.

2014

DECEMBER

Christmas was coming, and Mimi was disappearing. The dreamy look she'd had at the bakery was on her face all the time now, as if her last mooring to reality had finally snapped and she was drifting away. Every day she was a little bit more diminished, a little bit less there. Instead of dying, she seemed to be slowly turning transparent, fading away until she was nothing but a shadow, a disturbance in the air—and then nothing at all, just gone.

She'd started having visitors that nobody could see but her. Old friends, former schoolmates, her mother, her brother Edward. They came to her out of the past or sometimes out of her imagination: one evening she fell asleep beside me and Diana while we were watching *Apollo 13,* then informed us the next morning that some nice young men had taken her on a trip to visit the moon. I woke that night to the sound of her getting out of bed, followed by the creak of her footsteps as she paced the room, back and forth. She was muttering, something unintelligible at first, but then her voice floated up from below, bright and clear.

"Is that you?" she said, so imperiously that I felt the absurd urge to reply. I listened as she paced for another few minutes, then heard the creak of her bed frame, the click as she turned the light off. And then a sigh, so soft that she could only have been talking to herself. "Forgive me," she whimpered. "I never meant for him to hurt you."

The next morning, I asked her politely if she'd had any visitors last night and what they talked about.

She smiled slyly. "He says it'll freeze soon," she said.

"Who?"

She giggled. "Why, the weatherman, of course."

I didn't bother to point out that the local weatherman was a woman, or that her forecast for the coming days, which we watched together every morning, was highs in the mid-thirties and more fog, endless fog. Mimi's weather reports were like the old songs she sometimes sang under her breath at odd moments, the conversations she had with herself in the dark. Just flotsam from the wreckage of her memory that had improbably bubbled to the surface.

"My goodness, the time," she said suddenly, twisting in her chair and looking toward the door. "Hasn't Shelly brought the tea?"

"I'm sure she's getting it now."

"I know what you must think of me," she said. "The scandal of it. But I couldn't turn her out."

I hoped she'd say more about Shelly. I wanted to know what had happened all those years ago—and why Shelly's son was still holding a grudge about it decades later. But Mimi had nothing else to say; she tipped her head back against the chair and fell deeply asleep.

I watched the slow rise and fall of her chest, envying the way she could slip out of consciousness and be immediately at peace.

The rest of us were not at peace. The incident with Jack Dyer had set the stage for a bigger conflict, one that erupted late that night after Mimi had gone to bed and all of us, Adam included, were sitting in the big living room where a Christmas tree should've been but wasn't. Adam, Diana, and William were playing hearts, Mom was focused on her phone, Richard was announcing for the third time that he couldn't find the DVD of *Holiday Inn,* and I was silently hoping he'd give up and decide to watch literally any other seasonal movie that didn't have blackface in it. (I was also hoping he wouldn't figure out that I'd hidden the *Holiday Inn* DVD, for this reason, between the cushions of the couch I was sitting on.)

"What about one of these?" I asked, indicating the Netflix "Holiday" menu, but nobody responded until Adam looked up from his hand and said, "Hey, is that *White Christmas?* My grandma used to love that movie. She was wild for Bing Crosby."

Diana laid down a card and snorted. "I'd rather watch *Love Actually.*"

"And I'd rather put both my eyes out with a hot poker," Richard said.

"So, how about *White Christmas,*" I said, smiling at Adam, who smiled back.

"And then stick the poker up my anus," Richard said.

Diana twisted in her chair. "Don't be disgusting. Do you remember that time that Daddy dressed as Santa Claus?"

"That wasn't Dad, it was Pop-Pop," Richard said.

"Oh no, I'm sure it was Daddy."

"It wasn't."

"It was!"

"Are you insane? Dad would never."

"Dora," Diana said, exasperated, "you remember. It was the year I wore that green tartan, and Richard—"

"I don't remember," Mom said, not lifting her eyes from her phone. Her thumbs kept racing over the screen.

"How can you not remember?"

"Because she wasn't born yet," Richard said. "Because it was Pop-Pop."

"I believe my wife," William said, but nobody, not even Diana, looked at him.

Diana looked at my mother. "We could resolve this so easily if we checked the photo album," she said pointedly.

Mom's eyes stayed on her phone. "I told you, I don't know where—"

"Didn't you say it was in the attic?" Adam said suddenly, and though Mom didn't look up, her thumbs stopped moving.

"Did I?"

"Yes," I said. "I remember, too. You said that the older photos were destroyed in the fire, but a family album might be in the attic."

Mom yawned. "Oh, I guess that's right. But let's not tonight. It's awfully late and dark—"

"And I'm sure that *Holiday Inn* DVD is around here somewhere," Richard chimed in, but Diana was on her feet and heading toward the door.

"I know I'm right," she was saying. "I'll just—"

Richard and Mom leaped up at the same time.

"Diana, those pull-down stairs are dangerous," Mom said, at the same time as Richard said, "For god's sake, sister, nobody cares," but Diana kept moving—and then Adam was on his feet, saying, "I got you," to everybody and nobody all at once, as if it were his job to keep the peace. By the time we reached the stairs he was ahead of everyone, leading the procession as we climbed to the third floor.

"It's at the end of the hall to the left," Mom said from somewhere behind me, but Adam was already there, flicking the light switch as if he'd lived here for years. The ladder stairs to the attic came down with a groan, and a scattering of dust fell into Adam's hair.

There was more dust under Adam's feet, and Richard pointed to it. "Gee, I hope that's not asbestos," he said, in a tone that suggested he'd like nothing more than for it to be asbestos, that asbestos was just the thing to liven up this boring party.

"There's a trunk," Mom was saying as Adam began climbing. "Actually, there's more than one. Big old-fashioned ones. I'm not sure which is the right one. Do you need a flashlight?"

Adam's voice floated down from above. "I've got my phone. Yeah, I see the trunks. Okay, just a sec—" He broke off, and for a while there was only the sound of objects scraping across the floor, old hinges creaking, the occasional cough. Then: "Huh." He reappeared in the opening above us. "The albums aren't here," he said.

Diana made a squawking noise. "What? But you've barely looked, they have to be—"

Adam's voice was apologetic. "Sorry, I mean, they definitely were here. I found one trunk with a big empty space where they could have been, and there's one photograph loose, wedged in the liner. But things are kind of a mess up here. There's a bunch of trunks open and everything's tossed around. Maybe someone came up looking for Christmas ornaments and ended up moving the albums at the same time?"

"Moving them?" Diana put her hands on her hips and glared up at him and then around at the rest of us. "Stole them, you mean."

"I can look some more," he said, but Diana ignored him.

"Somebody stole them," she said again. Her accusatory gaze skated past me, past her husband, lingered briefly on my mother, and settled on Richard. "You."

Richard put a hand over his heart and went wide-eyed. "Moi? If that's not the most ridiculous—"

"Of course you! You knew I wanted them! I told you I was planning to look at them with Mother on Christmas morning. Our holiday photos, her wedding photos—you know how she loves to reminisce about Daddy. I was going to . . ." She trailed off. Her voice was shrill. "It was going to be so lovely, and you had to ruin it. You *always* have to ruin it. You wanted to hurt me."

He scoffed. "I don't want to hurt you."

Diana's tone turned bitter. "Then you did it to upset Mother. And don't you dare try to tell me you don't have any bad blood with her."

Richard had gone very still. The hallway was dim, lit by a single low-watt bulb in a brass sconce on the wall—but it was clear from the way his features pinched together that Diana had struck a nerve.

"No," he said finally, "I won't deny that. Why should I? Maybe

I do want to hurt her. Maybe she hurt me plenty, and I'd like a little payback after all these years. But more importantly, maybe I think that the way you're all coddling her, pretending like she was some great mother, is a repulsive fucking farce, and you should all be ashamed of yourselves. Including you, you simpering little shit," he said, pointing a finger at Adam, who was frozen halfway down the attic stairs with his mouth hanging slightly open. "How's that? Enough honesty for you?"

Nobody spoke. My mother looked stricken. Richard said, "I thought so," pushed past me, and started down the stairs.

"You're going to tell me where you put those photographs!" Diana shrieked, and Richard's voice floated up, singsong, from somewhere on the stairs.

"Sisters," he crooned. "Sisters, there were never such deluded sisters!" Diana disappeared after him.

William, who had been so silent throughout this exchange that I hadn't even realized he was there, followed his wife—but as he left, he paused in front of Adam. "Welcome to the family," he said.

Adam didn't come back downstairs with us. "I don't want to be in the way," he said, and nobody had to ask of what. Richard and Diana were still arguing loudly in the kitchen, nominally about the photographs, but with so much bitterness and contempt that it was clear the missing mementos were just a front for a lifetime's worth of grievances. I came back in just as Diana stopped shouting and started wheedling: "You don't even have to tell me exactly where they are, just give me a hint."

It was entirely the wrong tactic to use on my uncle, who looked at her with open disgust. "If I knew where they were, and I'm not saying I do, but if I did? I certainly wouldn't tell you," he said, then grabbed his wineglass and a fresh bottle of red and added, "For your own good," before he stalked out of the room.

My mother came in and laid a hand on Diana's shoulder. Her other hand held the one photograph Adam had found wedged in the liner of the trunk. It was a picture of my grandfather, dressed for fishing, taken at a distance so that you could see both him and the name of the boat whose bow he was standing on: *Red Sky.* The photo was badly creased. On the back, in faded pencil, someone had written a caption: *Theo, August 1950.*

"Here," she said, "we'll find the rest, don't worry."

Diana sniffled. "He probably burned them. Or tore them into little pieces."

"I'm sure he didn't."

Another sniffle. "You don't understand. You were so much younger, you never knew how vicious he could be. You don't know him like I do."

I thought about Richard putting Mom in a basket and trying to float her out to sea. Mom didn't say so, but I thought she was thinking of it, too.

"I guess we all know Richard in our own way," she said hesitantly. "But I don't believe he took those photos."

"Oh, I suppose they just grew little legs and walked away," Diana snapped.

That was when I decided that Richard had the right idea. I was on my way up the stairs with my own glass of wine when I heard a creak above me and saw Adam come around the corner onto the landing. He was looking down at his feet, not yet seeing me, and I realized for the first time how tired he looked. Shoulders caved forward, the skin under his eyes as dark as a bruise. When I said his name, he jumped.

"I didn't see you there," he said as I climbed to the landing to meet him. "Isn't it a little early to be going to bed?"

"Just taking this party to my room." I brandished my glass and glanced down the second-floor hallway. It was empty, and the door to Richard's room was closed, but I lowered my voice anyway and leaned in. "I could take it to your room."

He smiled, and for a moment the air was full of sizzling tension.

But instead of reaching for me, he stepped away. "I think we'd better not," he said. "Just, you know, after everything tonight."

I shrugged with fake nonchalance and took my own step back. Just a chill girl, being chilly. "Sure."

He looked pained. "It's not you. I mean, it's not us. Nothing has changed. It's just complicated, being here with your whole family."

I tried to tell you, I thought. "Sure," I said, again, but he didn't answer, only looked at me like I should have more to say. There was a thick smudge of dust on one of his sleeves from his foray into the attic, and something wispy floating in the air just above his ear.

"There's a cobweb in your hair," I said, reaching out to pluck it away.

"Oh," he said. "Thank you."

For just a moment, I thought maybe he'd change his mind, take my hand, lead me upstairs. But when my fingertips brushed against his ear, he flinched.

An uneasy peace settled over the house after that. There were no more disruptions from Jack Dyer, no more eruptions from Richard, but there was also no happy whirlwind of activity, no laughter, no twinkling lights or warm embraces. There were no gifts piling up under the tree in expectation of a happy Christmas morning, because there was no tree at all. If my mom had been hoping that her warring siblings could put aside their differences just this once to enjoy the holiday and give Mimi the pleasure of seeing the family all together again, drinking eggnog by the fire while carols played softly in the background, she had to be disappointed. Instead, it seemed like everyone had made an unspoken agreement to avoid conflict by avoiding one another, so that I sometimes felt like I was living in a house with my secret boyfriend and a handful of ghosts.

For three days I sensed the presence of my relatives but rarely saw them except when we converged on the kitchen at mealtimes, where we ate hurriedly and then disbanded before the bickering could start afresh. Adam and I settled into a new routine, meeting for cramped but delicious late-morning sex in the little bathroom under the stairs, and then meeting an hour later for lunch as if nothing had ever happened. At night, I woke up to the sound of Mimi pacing the floor downstairs, walking circles around her bedroom and having one-sided conversations with herself, sometimes bursting into laughter that was somehow creepier than the muttering. Just once, she left her room: the pacing suddenly stopped and she hissed, "I see you," in a voice that made every hair on the back of my neck stand on end. Her footsteps pounded across the floor then, and I ran down the stairs to find her in the kitchen, trying unsuccessfully to open the door that led outside, thudding it repeatedly against the dead bolt that she didn't seem to notice above her head.

"Mimi?" I said, and she whirled, her eyes huge, her face furious.

"I won't go back there. *He's* in there. It's *his* room," she said, pointing back in the direction of her bedroom, her voice so clear and urgent that I had to force myself not to match her panic with my own. When I checked her room, it was chilly but empty. The only thing unusual was the way it smelled—a dusky, vaguely sweet aroma that I thought was familiar but couldn't place.

"You've seen him, haven't you? He's always watching me," Mimi muttered as I tucked her back into bed.

"Who?"

She leaned in, her voice a conspiratorial whisper: "The man with the brown teeth."

I practically ran back upstairs, taking the creaky stairs as quickly and quietly as I could. Trying not to think too hard about men with brown teeth, trying to ignore the creepy sound of the wind as it rose and fell outside. I'd left a light on in my bedroom and its glow greeted me as I came down the hallway and around the corner, spilling through the cracked door and onto the carpet. Beyond it, the familiar space of the hallway, the small window at the end that looked out onto the bay.

My breath caught in my throat.

A man was standing at the end of the hall. I could see the shape of him against the window, the hulk of his broad shoulders, the peak of the old-fashioned cap on his head. No brown teeth, but only because he had no face at all, no features, nothing but shadow, and I flailed back toward the wall just behind me, reaching blindly for the light switch. My fingers grazed over it, slipped away, then found it once more, and the hallway flooded with light and I turned back to see . . .

Nobody.

The air left my lungs in a whoosh as my knees went weak. I slumped against the wall. Ahead of me was the hallway, empty. Far behind me, at the opposite end of the hall, a door cracked open and someone—William, maybe—hissed, "Would you keep it down? People are trying to sleep."

"Sorry," I muttered, and turned the light off, plunging the hallway once again into shadow. I braced myself for that figure to appear again, like a horror-movie monster that could be seen only in the dark, but it wasn't there. *It never had been*, I thought, even as a wild, hysterical part of my mind suggested that oh yes, it was, this was just one of Mimi's many visitors, and if he wasn't here anymore, it was just because I wasn't the woman he came here to see.

I wondered what the difference was, really, between a ghost and a memory.

And for the rest of the night I didn't sleep badly, but only because I didn't sleep at all.

We still walked the pine path in the afternoons, but now with Adam on my grandmother's right-hand side. If she stumbled on the uneven ground, she inevitably reached for him, not me. Each stroll ended at the fallen tree, where she'd gaze into the dark impassable tangle of branches and then sigh. "We'll have to come back for the sea lavender some other time," she'd say. I started to imagine it growing wild on the other side, uncollected all these years, a purple forest trapped under the ice of the frozen tidal pools. If I came back in the summer, I thought, I could pick a bouquet for Mimi—and lay it on her grave.

Normally we would linger by the fallen tree, letting her reminisce about the times she'd walked here with my grandfather. But on our last walk, the day before Christmas Eve, Mimi was agitated; she turned away from the tree and pushed past us, moving quickly back down the path.

"Whoa there," Adam said. "Where's the fire, Miss Miriam?"

"I have to get back," Mimi said. "I shouldn't have left them alone."

"Who?" I said, but she ignored me and kept walking.

Adam sighed quietly beside me. The circles under his eyes were darker than ever, and I fought the urge to squeeze his hand.

"You look tired," I said to him.

"I am," he said, and gave me a wry smile. "I haven't been sleeping well."

I smiled back. "Maybe you need some company."

"Don't tempt me," he said, leaning in so that I could feel the warm tickle of his breath against my ear. He paused, and then, with one last glance at Mimi's retreating back, he took my face in both hands and kissed me hard, hungrily, on the lips.

Mimi had gotten far enough ahead of us that we had to hurry to catch up, coming up on her heels as she passed through the lower entrance to the garden. She was moving fast, faster than I'd known she was capable of, and seemed to have forgotten all about us. When I fell into step beside her, she glanced at me with surprise, then turned sharply away, taking the flagstone path toward the house's side entrance.

"She's supposed to have a bath before dinner," Adam called from behind me. Mimi had finished climbing the steps and didn't look back as she slipped through the door. I caught it just in time to keep it from slamming in my face, then caught her by the arm just inside the kitchen, where she'd paused as though she wasn't sure anymore where she was going.

"Am I—" she began to say, and faltered.

"Late for your spa treatment? Nope, you're right on time," I said, nodding at Adam as he came through the door behind me. He gave me a thumbs-up. "Everything's ready for you," I said, gently steering her forward. There wasn't actually a spa at the Whispers, but one of the first-floor bathrooms—the one adjacent to the suite that used to be a getting-ready room for bridal parties—was luxurious enough to pass as one. Her face brightened as soon as we walked in, and she sat obligingly on an upholstered bench, smiling and humming to herself while I unlaced her boots and eased them off her feet. But as I twisted the knob to set the warm water running, unfamiliar footsteps suddenly thudded across the floor above me, fast and heavy. The hairs on the back of my neck stood on end.

"Hello?" I called. The answer was a series of thuds as the steps picked up speed, then the slam of the front door.

"Mimi, I'll be right back," I said. I left the room at a run, taking a left down the hall and a sharp right through the back entrance to the dining room, coming through the pocket doors into the foyer just as Adam appeared in the opposite doorway.

"Are you all r—" he started to say, and then abruptly stopped as we both stared at what sat on the floor in between us. It was a wheelchair, the one I'd folded and stowed in a closet the day Mimi arrived at the house. Now it was sitting in the foyer, turned on its side, with one wheel lazily spinning in space. We both watched as the rotation slowed, then stopped.

"That," Adam said, "is spooky."

The sound of footsteps came again, these ones lighter and familiar, and I looked up to see my mother at the top of the stairs. She peered over the banister. "What's that doing out?" she asked.

"Are you okay?" I said. "Who was here?"

"Here? Nobody." She stared at me. "Last I knew, you three were out walking. Richard and Diana and William took Diana's rental to go look for a tree. And I was just up in the attic—"

"A tree?"

"A Christmas tree?" Mom said slowly, looking at me in the same way she had back in high school when she'd asked, very seriously, if any of my friends were into "smoking drugs."

I shook my head. "Sure. Okay. A Christmas tree. You didn't hear someone running around on the second floor?"

Mom's facial expression shifted; now she thought *I* was smoking drugs.

I approached the wheelchair carefully, half expecting that wheel to start spinning again. I sniffed the air. "Do you guys smell that?"

"Smell what?" Mom said.

"It's like cloves, or . . . I don't know."

"Is that . . ." She paused, and as she did, I listened—and felt my skin ripple out in gooseflesh. I heard it, too: the sound of water. Not just running, but splashing, splattering. For one horrible moment, we locked eyes.

"Where's your grandmother?" Mom said, her voice rising shrilly toward panic, but I was already running. Back through the dining room, back down the hall, back to the bridal-suite bathroom with its copper tub, the one Mimi liked best. The sound of water got louder as I neared the door, and I realized with horror that the carpet under my feet was soaked. I felt my lips moving, forming one word, half mantra and half prayer: *Please.*

Please let her be here.

Please let her be okay.

Please don't let me come around the corner to see her dead and pale and facedown on the floor, a pool of blood spreading from the place where she hit her head on the side of the bathtub.

Then I came through the doorway, my feet slipping beneath me on the wet tile, and the word died in my throat.

There was no body.

There was no blood.

There was only the tub, brimming over. An unused towel lying soaked on the floor. Beyond the windows, the vast gray expanse of the bay, now beginning to edge with ice. Nothing else.

And no one else.

For days, Mimi had been disappearing.

Now she was simply gone.

II.

We found her socks ten feet down the hall, so soaked and heavy that they'd probably fallen off on their own. After that, we found nothing.

Diana and William and Richard showed up lugging a Christmas tree, which sat abandoned in the foyer while we fanned out to search the house. For the next two hours, the six of us trudged back and forth and up and down like a live-action role-playing version of Clue. The library. The study. The kitchen. The hall. The countless bedrooms with their countless closets, all the weird nooks and crannies that were unique to the Whispers and that Mimi knew better than anyone. She could be anywhere and had to be somewhere, yet the quickness and completeness with which she'd vanished was unsettling, like the house had simply swallowed her up. The longer we looked without finding her, the more guilty and responsible I felt. I was helped along in this by my mother, who was making her disappointment known by stomping, sighing, and slamming doors, and Diana, who made her disappointment known by stepping in front of me and hissing, "This was extremely irresponsible of you, Delphine," before stalking away.

The only person who didn't give me grief, shockingly, was Richard—

maybe just because he was so delighted that here at last was a mishap nobody could blame him for. As the sun began to disappear below the horizon, I came back through the foyer to find him sitting in the discarded wheelchair, using one hand to spin himself in circles like a little kid who'd found a new toy.

"Is this really the best use of your time right now?" I said through gritted teeth.

Richard stopped spinning and set both feet on the floor. "Oh, piss off, Delphine," he said cheerfully. "I'm just having the tiniest moment of fun. I wouldn't begrudge *you* a little break from the search for coffee . . . or something, *heh-heh*, stronger," he added, waggling his eyebrows suggestively as Adam walked in from the direction of the kitchen. "And where have *you* been, young man?"

Adam flashed me an obvious "What's this guy's problem?" look before turning to Richard. "I just checked her room again. Is there a way to lock the doors after we've looked somewhere?"

"Now, that's smart," Richard said. "Strategic thinking. See, you don't even need me." His tone softened. "You could take a break, you know. She'll turn up. Why don't we all have a drink and—"

"Why don't *you* have a drink," I snapped. "Or seventy."

Richard shrugged. "You are your own master."

I shook my head with disgust and walked away, toward the shuttered wing.

"I already looked down there," Richard called after me, but his voice faded as I turned the corner. I walked to the end of the hall, opened a door at random, and peered in. I didn't think Mimi would have come this way. After all, this part of the house had been shut up and unused for more than a year, the vents closed and drapes drawn, and it was so cold that I could see my breath. Like most of the rooms in the north wing, this one was wall-to-wall clutter, with heavy curtains pulled over the windows and everything draped with dust sheets. But every hulking object, every shadow, looked suspicious. Even if Richard had already looked, she could easily be hiding here.

And so could somebody else.

I shuddered, thinking again of those heavy unfamiliar footsteps rushing across the floor above the bathroom, the wheelchair tipped on its side—things I'd pushed to the back of my mind after my grandmother's disappearance threw us all into emergency mode. And maybe it was nothing; maybe what had sounded like footsteps was just the creaking and settling of the house, and maybe Richard or Diana had pulled the chair out of the closet to get at something else and simply not put it back . . . or maybe I was desperately trying to convince myself that there was a reasonable explanation for all of this. That the house wasn't being haunted by disembodied footsteps or hosting a series of visitors nobody but Mimi could see.

I stepped through the door and paused again, letting my eyes adjust to the dim light, listening for the furtive movements or the quiet breathing of someone trying not to be found. I took a deep breath— and then erupted in a coughing fit so loud and so long that any hope I'd had of being stealthy was lost. The room was thick with dust. I could see it sitting like a film on every surface and smell it in the air.

"Mimi?" I called. There was a light switch on the wall and I flipped it, and a chandelier overhead brightened and then flared out just as quickly with a loud *ffftz!* that let me know I'd blown a fuse. The light from the hallway behind me went out, too, plunging the whole room into gloomy near darkness. In the next moment, I heard two things: a faraway thud followed by a male voice—Richard, probably—shouting, "Fuck!"

And second, from inside the room, the slow rustle of a plastic furniture drape sliding to the floor.

I whirled toward the sound, yanking my phone from my pocket and turning the flashlight on, aiming it wildly into every corner and seeing nothing out of place. Every hair on the back of my neck was standing on end, and I willed myself to cross the room, sweeping the flashlight beam back and forth, finally reaching the opposite wall, where heavy damask curtains covered the windows. I yanked one back, setting off another explosion of dust that in turn set off another coughing fit, then turned toward the window and screamed: a hideous ghostly face stared back at me, and my scream had tapered to a whimper by the time I realized I was seeing myself, lit from below like a ghoul by the glow of my own phone. I turned the flashlight off and looked out. There was the veranda, empty, with the twilit garden and bay beyond. The outdoor lights were still on, throwing a weak glow across the veranda that made everything beyond it seem darker still. Nothing moved—and then suddenly one of the shadows shifted.

Not quite empty, I thought as a fox materialized at the edge of the circle of lamplight and slunk cautiously into view. It stopped to sit, its thick tail curled neatly around its feet, and in my head, I heard Mimi's voice.

There was a fox there, she had said, and I wondered if this was the one she'd seen, its presence just striking enough to find a foothold in her failing memory. The fox sat unmoving, its eyes huge and unblinking in the dark. It seemed to be looking at me.

I turned back to the room. The light coming through the window was enough to see by, to ascertain that all the ominous lurking and crouching shapes were nothing more than furniture—and yet I still had the unshakable feeling that I wasn't alone, that I was being watched, that not only was I playing hide-and-seek but that somehow my role in the game had been flipped so that it was me, not Mimi, who was being hunted.

From behind me came the soft scrape of a footstep and the murmur of low voices, and I jumped. But it was no ghost, only my aunt Diana: she was standing on the terrace just outside the window, turned three-quarters away from me and talking urgently to someone I couldn't see. The fox, wherever it had come from, was gone.

". . . And tell him you need another month," she was saying as I got close to the window. I was about to tap on the glass, to let her know I was there, but I instinctively ducked out of sight as she began to turn in my direction and I saw the expression on her face: pure naked rage.

"That's going to be difficult," said another voice—William's—and Diana whirled away and began to gesture wildly.

"You shut the fuck up," she snapped, her voice high and hysterical. She was angrier than I'd ever seen her. I crept closer to the window, staying low, straining to make out the words. "I'm doing my part to clean up your mess, but I need time."

"Can't you just, I don't know, get her alone somehow?" William whined.

"What do you think I've been trying to do? Between Dora and Delphine and that goddamn male nurse of hers—and after this it'll be even harder, you know they won't let her out of their sight. I can't just—"

She stopped speaking so abruptly that I was sure she must have seen me, but when I looked, she had moved away from the window and was staring into the dark.

"What?" William said.

"I thought I saw . . ." Diana trailed off. "Come on." She strode purposefully away, with William following after, dragging his feet like a teenager who didn't want to be seen walking with his mom. I stood frozen, trying to make sense of what I'd heard. Diana needed something from my grandmother, that part was clear enough, but—

My thoughts were interrupted by a soft click behind me, and I turned to see the door open, a shadow moving into the room. I bit back a shriek.

"It's just me," Adam said softly. "I wanted to make sure you were okay. The lights—"

"That was me," I said. "I think I blew a fuse."

"Yeah. Your mom and Richard went down to the basement to fix it."

"I just saw Diana and William outside." I paused, debating whether to say more.

Adam crossed the room and pulled me against him. "So we're alone," he said, his lips brushing close to my ear. One of his hands slid around the curve of my hip, and I shivered, letting my head drop back so that he could kiss my neck.

"We should keep looking for Mimi," I said, but with no force behind it. It was just a line, the thing I was supposed to say; Adam squeezed me tighter and slid a hand up the front of my sweater.

"In a minute," he whispered, and then laughed against my neck. "Okay, five minutes."

"Five minutes," I murmured. I felt myself steered backward across the room, until my legs bumped against the edge of something. I looked over my shoulder to see a velvet sofa, uncovered, its dust sheet puddled on the floor beneath my feet. This was what I'd heard rustling in the room, but I wasn't thinking about that, wasn't thinking about what it could mean. I was thinking about Adam's hands on my skin, the cold kiss of the air on my bare belly as my sweater came over my head. He pushed me down onto the sofa and then sank to his knees, his hands briefly going to unbuckle his belt and then returning, heavy, to my hips. He buried his face against my abdomen. One hand slid up between my legs, and I gasped.

"God, I want you," he whispered. "I want you all the time, I can't stand it."

"You have me," I said, reaching for him. Letting my eyes close. Going by feel. My jeans were down around my knees and I kicked them loose, arching my back, lifting my hips to meet him. He moaned, and so did I. Taking his weight as he took me. He put his lips against my neck and I turned my head, feeling soft velvet on one cheek, the roughness of stubble on the other. I opened my eyes. The room was all shadow, gray on black, nothing moving.

But we weren't alone.

I froze.

Mimi was standing in the center of the room, watching us. I could just make out the bony slope of her shoulders, the pale planes of her face. Her eyes were pits, a single point of reflected light visible in each one.

"Adam." My voice was a weak whisper. I dug my fingers into his shoulders and pushed him away, took a deep breath. "Adam!"

"What," he started to say, and then turned his head. Mimi hadn't moved, didn't move, and I saw him see her—squinting into the dark, then scrambling backward as horror dawned over his face. I sat up, fumbling for my pants, but they were hopelessly twisted around my leg.

For one awful moment, nobody spoke, and nothing moved.

Then Adam stood, took a step toward her.

"Miriam," he said, his voice strangled, and Mimi stiffened. She raised her hand and pointed with a trembling finger—not at him, but at me.

"I always knew you were trouble," she hissed, and before I could say anything, before Adam could take another step, she turned and ran. Her bare feet made no sound as she skipped across the floor and into the shadows in a cluttered corner of the room. I fumbled for my phone and raised it up just in time to see her in the beam of the flashlight, disappearing through a narrow doorway that hadn't been there when I entered the room, and that disappeared as I watched, a hidden panel in the wall swinging closed behind her with a light click.

"Adam," I started to say, but he was gone, too—out the main door and down the hall, his feet thudding against the carpet. I jumped to my feet, tripping over my pants before yanking them back up to my waist and looking frantically for the shoe I wasn't wearing. A moment later I found it under the sofa, and a moment after that, I was out the same door Adam had left by, calling his name. The lights flared on above me as I reached the end of the hall, rounded the corner to the foyer, and felt my knees go weak—this time with relief. They were both there, Adam and Mimi. He was holding both her hands and peering into her face, saying something low and urgent; I came nearer and heard the words *really scared me*. She was staring down at her hands in his, frowning.

"Mimi," I said softly, and she turned to look at me. The angry expression was gone.

"Hello," she said. "Pardon me, I seem to have gotten lost."

I swallowed hard, my ears burning. For one ridiculous moment, I wondered if it was possible that she'd forgotten what she saw, but while the anger was gone from her face, the knowing look was not.

"Mimi, what happened in there—"

She cut me off with an embarrassed little laugh. "Oh, don't mention it, dear. A dreadful misunderstanding. I was looking for my husband, you see, and in the dark, I didn't recognize—well, no matter. He's explained everything," she said, gesturing at Adam.

I stared. "Oh. Um. Okay."

Mimi smiled. "Have you met my husband?"

I paused, trying to remember what the line was that we were supposed to use when Mimi asked about my grandfather, but was cut off by the sound of hurried footsteps coming through the house.

My mother entered at the other end of the foyer, her phone to her ear, clutching it so hard that her knuckles had turned white. "Yes, please do, thanks," she was saying, in a voice that sounded like a paper-thin veneer of calm laid over a deep well of panic. When she saw Mimi, she stopped dead, the phone dropping from her hand with a clatter. Richard, who had been walking just behind her, stumbled into her back with an *oof.*

"Mother?!" Mom shrieked, taking in Mimi's wild hair, her bare and dirty feet. "My god, oh my god. Her feet. Was she outside? Mother, did you go outside?"

The front door slammed as Diana and William appeared, both of them flushed and out of breath. "Dora, I found—" Diana started to say, and then broke off mid-sentence when she saw Mimi.

My mother didn't even look at her. "Mother," she said again, her voice rising. She shouldered Adam aside, grabbing Mimi's wrist hard, her fingernails digging in. "Where were you? Do you have any idea how worried—"

Mimi yanked her hand away and snarled, "You're *hurting* me!" Her eyes narrowed, and she stood up straighter, glaring at my mother. "Oh, but this is what you do, isn't it? You always did. Always crying.

Always *clinging*. I never had a moment's peace with you, not one single moment. It was always mother-mother-mother and daddy-daddy-daddy, a demand every damned minute, draining me like a little . . ." She trailed off, fumbling for the word while the rest of us stared in shock. Then her gaze sharpened, and she snapped her fingers. "Like a parasite. That's it, a little parasite. You sucked the life out of me, Theodora. You sucked the life out of everything."

Nobody spoke. Nobody moved. Even Richard had the decency to look horrified, staring at Mimi with his mouth half-open.

Adam cleared his throat and stepped up, catching my grandmother by the arm. "I'll take her to her room."

"Oh no you won't," my mother practically shrieked. She looked around wildly at each of us and then pointed at Adam. "Not you. If you'd been monitoring her properly, if you'd been doing your job, none of this would have happened!"

For the second time, there was nothing but silence. I burned with embarrassment for Adam, trying to flash him a sympathetic look, but he just flinched and looked at his feet.

After another moment, Mom shook her head and put her face in her hands. "I'm sorry," she said, her voice muffled. "I'm sorry. I didn't mean that. I'm just so tired—" Her voice broke, and her hands dropped away. She wasn't crying, not yet, but her eyes were filled with tears. "Excuse me. I need a moment."

She pushed past me, past Adam and Mimi, taking the stairs at a run. Her bedroom door slammed. The silence that followed was broken by the sound of murmuring—not a human voice, but the house itself as the wind began to rise outside.

I took my grandmother's arm and nodded at Adam. "I'll take her," I said under my breath. "She's clearly not herself right now."

Richard clapped his hands together sharply, and everyone jumped. "She's exactly like herself," he said cheerfully. "More than ever, really. Aren't you, Ma? But don't worry, it'll pass."

Diana laughed nervously. "She just needs a nap. Don't you, Mother? You sure scared us."

Mimi looked at her feet, with their red-painted toenails, and then at me. She looked bewildered. "Look at that," she said, all the acid gone from her voice. "I've had a pedicure."

I steered Mimi back toward her room, trying to ignore the sound of hushed conversation that rose behind us as we walked away. I worried that she might snap at me the way she'd snapped at my mother, but she seemed lost in thought, walking obediently beside me with her hands pressed together like a nun. When we reached the little back bedroom, I helped her sit down on the side of the en suite tub and ran warm water over her bare feet, watching the dirt swirling between her toes and down the drain. She was humming to herself, her hands resting in her lap.

I picked up her hairbrush from the side of the sink. "Let's get some of these tangles out," I said, beginning to gather her hair from the nape of her neck—and then stopping short. There was a mark there, just behind the soft curve of her jaw, a purplish oval that could only be a thumbprint. I could picture exactly how it had happened. Someone's hand coming up to grip her just under the chin. Grabbing her hard enough to bruise. Grabbing her like my mother had, just moments before.

"Mimi?" I said, but she didn't respond, just kept humming to herself. I set the brush down and reached for her hand, keeping my voice gentle, saying, "Mimi, did someone—" before she turned to look at me and something clattered from her hand onto the bathroom floor. I saw the glint of silver against the tile and leaned down to scoop it up. It was a pendant, a pale glass rectangle with a small glittering stone at the center that might have been a diamond, framed by a tarnished but delicate silver setting. It wasn't Mimi's taste at all, and I didn't think it belonged to her. Everything about it screamed 1920s, which would make it older than she was, and I'd never seen it among her things at Willowcrest, where she liked to bring out her jewelry box and ask me to help her select a necklace or a brooch before dinner.

"Give it back," she said, and I looked up to see her eyes fixed on me, dark and suspicious. "It's mine."

I put it back in her hand with a shrug. "Okay, it's yours. It's very pretty. Where did you get it?"

"Papa gave it to Mother," she said in a singsong little girl's voice. "And then my sweetheart gave it to me."

"I see," I said, biting my lip, playing along. This was one of the reasons it had taken so long for anyone to know that Mimi was sick: when she didn't remember something, she would simply invent a story to fill in the blanks, so persuasive and richly detailed that you'd never have guessed she was making it up. "When did he give it to you?"

"It's for Christmas," she said, and sighed again. "He said he can forgive if I can forget. He says he'll come for me soon. Maybe even tonight."

"Tonight?"

Mimi tilted her head. "Oh yes," she said. Her gaze was dark and intense, and her lips curled in a smile—the one I'd seen on her face so often when she talked about her unseen visitors and her overnight trips to the moon, the one that made her look like a little girl with a secret. She leaned in close, lowering her voice to a whisper. "He always comes at night."

12.

1947

WINTER

She is eighteen and shivering in the dark.

A few low-lying clouds have crept in to smudge the face of the moon, and the air is biting cold where it slides through the opening of her coat. She has a lantern in her hand but doesn't dare light it. Not yet. Not until she passes beyond the garden wall, where the flick and flare of the match will be hidden from the restless occupants of the grand house, now half-burned, that stands high above the bay.

It's been eight weeks since the terrible fires that swallowed nine towns and a quarter of a million acres of forest, leaving ash and ruin in their wake. Great swaths of the island are black and bald, the beautiful wilderness burned all the way to the ground, nothing left behind but the charcoal spikes of broken trees and the odd chimney where a house once stood. The seventy majestic cottages that lined Frenchman Bay, once known as Millionaires Row, are gone, including the stately shingled manor where Miriam was sitting at luncheon on the day when the fire whistle sounded its alarm. The Chandlers' seaside estate is nothing but rubble, rotting away under a light dusting of new snow. When Miriam's mother had wondered aloud whether some of the society families might rebuild their seasonal homes and come back next year, her father snorted.

"Rebuild *what*, do you imagine? Will they scoop the ashes into a little mound and plant a flag in it?" He shook his head. "The ones who live here all year round, of course they'll rebuild. What choice do they have? It's their home. But just look at it, Evie. The ruin of it. It'll be years before this place is even a ghost of what it was. And your Chandlers and your Vanderbilts and your Pulitzers, they'll be off to some new playground."

"And the Days?" Mother asked. "What shall they do?"

"Well," he mused, "the way I see it, the Days should stay right where they are. After all is said and done, it seems we're the proud owners of the finest damn house on this island."

"Half a house, you mean," Mother said, gesturing in the direction of the door, the foyer beyond, and the ashen wreckage beyond that. Through some divine intervention, or perhaps just the caprice of a changing wind, the fire had cleaved through the Whispers as cleanly as a blade, ravaging the north wing while leaving the rest largely untouched. But far from despairing at the destruction, Papa had seemed invigorated by it, suddenly infused once more with the fierce and hungry spirit that used to animate him as a younger man. Perhaps it was no surprise. Roland Day had always known how to make a fortune on the back of a tragedy, to see opportunity where others saw only obstacles. This was no different.

As angry as he'd been at Smith for letting Miriam vanish on the day of the fire, he wasted no time dispatching his old friend to spearhead the rebuilding, hiring contractors and carpenters and sourcing new lumber from the forests up north—and Smith, eager to prove he could still be trusted, had managed it all with lightning speed. The project would begin just as soon as the last snow melted. But for now, the house was like Mother said: half a house, and half the charred stone skeleton of what used to be the north wing's outer walls.

"'Every man's work shall be made manifest: for the day shall declare it, because it shall be revealed by fire; and the fire shall try every man's work of what sort it is,'" Papa replied, quoting Corinthians.

Mother raised an eyebrow. "And I suppose the fire revealed your manifest destiny to own the finest damn home in Bar Harbor?"

"Obviously." He paused to take a sip of whiskey. "And who am I to argue with the will of the Almighty?"

"Mmmm," Mother said, pursing her lips. "Well then, what does the Almighty say about installing a modern heating system in this very fine damn house?"

Papa had laughed and laughed then, with his head thrown back and both hands on his belly, as if he were afraid it would burst. But when he was done laughing, he'd patted his wife's hand. "You'll have the best that money can buy. And of course I know what worries you, my dear. For everything to go up in smoke like this, and after all your efforts, too. But"—and here he glanced in Miriam's direction—"I think that New York society will do well enough for our Mimi's prospects, when the time comes."

Miriam thought, and still thinks, that there was something in that glance. A knowing little gleam—or perhaps that's just her own guilty conscience, winking back at her from behind her father's eyes. Society or not, Mother's efforts have indeed been all for nothing, and they'll surely go to waste, because Miriam will not marry any of those eligible young men with their neat haircuts and tailored jackets. Not if they begged her a hundred times. There's only one man she wants, just one, and he is already hers.

Theodore Caravasios. Theo. Her Theo.

If what happened that summer at the pond had been a spark, what she feels now is a wildfire, one that could smolder for a thousand years, sustained by nothing more than the memory of his lips meeting hers that day, the taste of him lingering there amid the flavors of salt water and smoke. Her hero. Her savior. His boat had carried her—and Patches, too, plucked from the water and seemingly none the worse for wear—around the cove and up the river to Ellsworth, where she was reunited with her parents amid a throng of a thousand refugees from Mount Desert Island. Their elation and relief at finding Miriam safe was so great that they barely remembered to scold her for disappearing in the first place, and they had nothing but tears and thanks for the young man who had saved her life. Even Smith doffed his cap, smiled his awful brown smile, and shook Theo's hand. It wasn't until many days later that Mother suddenly seemed to grow suspicious and asked just how it was that she'd been so lucky, that Theo had happened to be there at exactly the right place and time to rescue her.

"Why, I've no idea," Miriam had said, blinking with wide-eyed innocence. "I imagine he was on his way to the town pier to help with the rescue effort and saw me go into the water."

Miriam had comforted herself with the knowledge that this was not a lie, even if it wasn't the entire truth, either. The roads off the island had been overtaken by fire, and several hundred people had been rescued by boat from the town pier by local fishermen—a group that surely would have included Theo if he hadn't been there to pull her out of the water. She had his friend to thank for that, the one with the prominent ears; he'd run into Theo on the ridge where a hundred men were working to contain the fire and told him where she went and why. He'd left at a dead run to get to his boat and arrived just in time. Meanwhile, her parents had lingered in town, berating Smith for losing sight of her and hoping she'd turn up, until they had no choice but to join the slow caravan of cars winding precariously through the wreckage and rubble of the burned island up to Ellsworth. The drive had begun well after dark and taken the better part of the night, with arcing flames and raining sparks threatening to engulf them all the while. Miriam, traveling by sea, had beaten them to safety by many hours.

What she didn't mention was how she'd spent those hours—those long dark chaotic hours wrapped up in Theodore Caravasios's arms, so cocooned by the tragedy unfolding around them that prudence seemed wholly unnecessary. Who would ever notice or remember one young couple embracing as the world burned down? He'd kissed her again and again and again even as the sky began to lighten and murmurs ran through the crowd, heralding the arrival of the first cars from the caravan. And while she felt deliciously invisible then, her mother's questioning look made her wonder. Maybe she was too certain. Maybe they had been seen, after all.

And so she is careful.

She has been meeting him in secret for many weeks, ever since the Day family returned to find the Whispers half-burned but still habitable. Waiting for sundown, watching from her window for the light of his boat out beside the wreckage of the pier, waiting for his signal: two short flashes, three long. Then she steals away, down the staircase and through the darkened kitchen, where she collects the lamp that she takes care not to light until she's down beyond the garden wall. A right turn takes her into the small copse of unburned pines that still stands by the water's edge and then to a quarter-mile walk down the path to the narrow inlet where the sea lavender grows in the summer. This is where they meet as often as they dare, for as long as they dare, shivering in each other's arms against the deepening cold.

But tonight is different. Even in the dark, she can see the unhappiness written across his face, the furrow of his brow as she reaches for him.

"The reach has frozen over," he whispers against her cheek. "I barely made it into the cove tonight, and then only because of the moonlight. I can't risk it again, Miriam. We won't be able to meet this way again until spring."

"Spring," she murmurs back. "It's too long. There must be another way."

"Only if you're ready to meet me where people can see us."

"And what if I am?"

"You say that now, but you don't mean it," he says gently, and she pulls back, wounded.

"Maybe *you're* the one who isn't ready," she says, and he laughs.

"I've been ready since the day I first laid eyes on you. And every day since, too. That day at the pond, I swam out to you knowing full well I might get nothing out of it except a punch in the jaw. But I was ready to fight for you. I still am."

"Is that so," she whispers, and he leans in to kiss her again, but she turns her face away. Not to rebuff him, but to gaze out into the dark, toward the reach with its black and quiet water, now covered over with ice. In her mind, an idea is beginning to form. Something wild and dangerous and exciting. She sifts through her memories—of the island out there in the bay that she so often sailed past on excursions in the summer, of the cabin she once glimpsed there, set back from the rocky shore, barely visible between the trees. And of something her father once said, about how an enterprising merchant could carry his wares around the coves by boat in the summer . . . and in the winter, when the ice lies twelve inches thick in those stagnant pools, by sled.

She pulls back and gazes up at his face, the curve of his forehead, the heavy brows with deep eyes underneath. "There's a place we could go," she says, "if you're not too afraid."

But he is afraid. She'll remember this later, the way he hesitated, and wonder if it was only fear of the ice that held him back or something more. If despite his pretty promises, he was never really so certain—of himself, of her, of what lay ahead of them beyond that frigid night. But in this moment, she simply feels thrilled by the idea that she might be the braver of them, leading the way and daring him to follow.

She steps onto the ice.

"Miriam," he calls softly, but she raises up her lantern and beckons him with her other hand to come. She can already see the island, dark and solid against the moonlit sky, and the ice beneath her feet is as firm as granite. When she shivers, it's with excitement rather than fear.

She takes another step, and another.

And after a moment, that endless pause, he follows.

They trudge together, not speaking, the snow crunching lightly beneath their feet. He stays a few steps behind her until her feet touch rock, and then steps up beside her. They are on the shore of the island, where a tumble of rocks gives way to a short stretch of beach, then a thick stand of evergreens.

"Where—" Theo begins to say, and Miriam holds her lantern up again. The light jumps against the rocks, the trunks of the trees, and between two of these, a glimpse of weathered wood.

"There."

Years ago, during the long and idle summers of her childhood, Papa would take the family out and around this island in a little sailboat. He never mentioned the cabin, and Miriam never asked about it, even though she often noticed it as they passed. It was just part of the landscape, as unremarkable as a rock or a buoy or the neighbor's house across the cove. But now its existence feels to her like destiny. Whatever purpose the cabin once served to the person who built it, now it seems like it stayed standing all these years just for tonight, just for her. For them. Four walls and a roof to shelter the lovers from the cold, from the world, from judgmental and prying eyes. The door creaks on ancient hinges when it opens, and the lantern light spills over bare floor, a tiny woodstove in one corner, a wooden platform that might be a bench or a cot, depending. There's a tin cup with the ancient remains of someone's coffee perched on top of the stove, and a bearskin tacked up on the wall just inside the door, dusty but intact.

"Well, it's hardly luxurious, but I think it will do," Miriam says, or begins to. Her last words are lost under Theodore Caravasios's lips. After this, there are only two pauses: one as Theo pulls down the dusty bearskin and spreads it over the floor, and then one more, sometime later, as he places a rough hand on each of her smooth, bare hips and asks her if she's certain.

Her yes comes with no hesitation, no fear.

Later she'll think about that, too.

Afterward, they lie together in a tangle, slick with sweat despite the cold. Theo is resting on his stomach with his face turned toward her and his eyes closed, and she looks for a long time at the broad landscape of his body. The rough hands, the ropy muscles, skin so sunkissed that even in the dead of winter his arms and shoulders are still a deep tan. She's contemplating the stubbled curve of his jaw when he opens his eyes and asks her to marry him.

"You know I'm out of my mind to even ask you," he says before she can take a breath to answer. "And you'd be a madwoman to say yes. I have nothing to give you, Miriam. Nothing to offer."

"Are you talking about money?" she says, and he frowns. She pushes her thumb into his furrowed brow, smoothing out the angry lines, laughing softly. "What would I want with money? I have money. Or my father does, more than he knows what to do with, more than I could ever need."

He frowns harder. "All the more reason he'll never give his consent. A man who knows the value of money knows better than anyone not to give his daughter away to a man who doesn't have any."

"Give me away!" She snorts. "I'm not a case of whiskey, Theo. Papa will listen to me. He'll see how good you are. And he'll see that I love you. How could he say no when I love you?"

For a long time, neither of them speaks.

Finally Theo stops frowning. "When will you tell them?"

Miriam bites her lip. "At Christmas, I think. He'll be in good spirits then."

"What will you say?"

She laughs, burying her face against his shoulder. "I've no idea. I suppose I'll have to start practicing my speech. At least I have a few days."

But she doesn't.

• • •

It's still dark, the moon now barefaced in the night sky, when she once again crosses the reach and races back down the pine path. It's cold, bitterly cold, but she hardly feels it. Her skin is warm with the memory of his body, her neck rubbed raw by the stubble on his cheeks, her lips bruised where he kissed her once more, fiercely, before they parted ways. She trips through the snowy garden like a drunken dancer, so careless in her joy that she realizes too late that she has forgotten to dim the lantern. She hurries to shutter it, thinking that it's all right, that they're all still asleep, that surely no one has seen her. She does not see the man standing in the shadows beside the door. She does not notice him fall into step behind her as she steals back inside—but when she turns to pull the door closed behind her, he's there. Looming, leering, his face inches from hers.

"Well, well," Smith says, and she lets out a small shriek as he catches her by the arm, plucks the lantern from her hand, and pushes her roughly inside. There's a grin on his face all the while, one that makes Miriam's stomach turn. She's terrified, and he's enjoying it.

"Let me go," she hisses, and Smith chuckles.

"Go where, young lady? Back out there? Back to him?"

"I don't know what you're talking about," she says weakly, and struggles as Smith laughs and grips her arm harder still—hard enough to hurt, hard enough to bruise.

"You know," he says, "your pa was awfully sore at me for letting you run away that day. Said I was supposed to keep an eye on you. Said I was supposed to keep you safe. He said you was a good girl, a *sweet* girl."

He grins wider, leaning in, hissing his rank brown breath into Miriam's face. "What do you say we wake him up, and see what he thinks of you now?"

Miriam stops struggling. In place of fear and panic, something else is rising: a cold rage, cold as the frozen sea, and she sees in Smith's face that he sees it. His terrible smile falters, his grip on her arm loosens by a single degree, and she's suddenly seized by an idea. Wonderful and terrible and fierce, the same impulsiveness that once sent her off a cliff with her arms outstretched, that she followed into the frigid night to lie in Theodore Caravasios's arms.

"You want to wake my father up? Here, this ought to do it," she says, and sinks her teeth into Smith's hand as hard as she can. Something crunches, there's blood in her mouth, and Smith screams and reels backward, and screams some more. From upstairs, there's a shout and the sound of doors opening, feet pounding.

Miriam wipes the blood from her lips and sits down at the table to wait.

13.

2014

DECEMBER

I woke up groggy on the morning of Christmas Eve, my tongue fat and my thoughts tangled. My brain had taken yesterday's events and remixed them overnight into a series of strange bad dreams in which I stumbled frantically through the house, searching without knowing what I was looking for, while from behind the closed doors came the sounds of moaning, sobbing, urgent whispering that abruptly cut off the moment I reached for the doorknob. In one dream, I was struggling to decorate an enormous Christmas tree while Richard and Colin, who looked just as he had when I'd last seen him except that he was now wearing Adam's Willowcrest uniform, kept pulling the ornaments down and smashing them on the floor. In another, the fox from the terrace had gotten inside the house, and I was chasing it from room to room, tracking its paw prints across the dusty floors until I realized with horror that the paw prints weren't paw prints anymore, but the tracks of a stranger's bare feet.

But it was the last dream, the one I had just before waking, that stayed with me. In it, I opened the door to the bathroom and found Mimi sitting naked in the tub, her knees drawn up against her chest. Water was running out of the faucet and the tub was overflowing, with water spilling onto the floor, and outside the window the sun was sitting so low on the horizon that it seemed to be sinking into the ocean. The sky was streaked crimson and gold, and Mimi lifted her hand and pointed.

"Sailor's delight," she said in a lilting little girl's voice, and she laughed in a way that sent chills down my spine. She turned to smile at me over her shoulder, her expression sly. "He'll be here soon."

"Who?" I asked, moving in slow motion to turn off the taps. Mimi only shook her head and laughed again.

"*You* know," she said, and as I leaned over, she suddenly caught me by the throat, pulling me in close while I fought to keep my grip on the slippery sides of the tub. She lifted her other hand out of the water, silver glinting between her fingers. She was holding the pendant, its chain threaded through the eye of a long, sharp needle, and in my dream, I watched helplessly as Mimi leaned forward while I squirmed and fought but couldn't get free. There was no pain as she popped the pendant into my mouth and pushed the needle through the soft flesh of my lips, through and around and through again, sewing them shut.

"Now it's your secret, too," she said, her eyes glittering. When she smiled again, blood rimmed the edges of her teeth. "I know you'll never tell."

My mother had never come back downstairs again the night before, after Mimi called her a parasite. In fact, everyone seemed shaken by it—not just the viciousness of their confrontation, but how quickly it was over, so fast that it seemed like something we'd hallucinated. When I got back from washing my grandmother's feet and helping her to bed, Adam wordlessly handed me a glass of wine and then poured one for himself, which under any other circumstances would have earned some sort of snarky comment from Richard, but he only stared into his whiskey glass, swirling the amber liquid in it around and around without drinking.

"Someone should talk to her," I said.

"Good luck with that," Richard said. "You should know, she'll never apologize. She never would. Even before her brain started melting."

"Richard," Diana said, and he rolled his eyes.

"I may be impolite," he said, "but I'm not wrong."

"I meant someone should talk to Mom. To my mom," I said. What I didn't say was that by *someone,* I meant *anyone but me.* I couldn't stop thinking about the way she'd grabbed Mimi, and about whether it might not have been the first time. If I measured the bruise on Mimi's neck, would it be a perfect match, the exact diameter of my mother's thumb? Was she taking out her anger at being thrust into the care-giver role on my grandmother, one rough touch at a time?

Adam touched my arm. "I'll talk to her."

"You shouldn't have to—" I started to say, but he gave my forearm a squeeze and cut me off.

"It might be better coming from a non-family member." He kept his eyes on me, but it was clear he was speaking to all of us. "I didn't know Miriam before, so I don't know what she used to be like. But I have known a lot of people with dementia, and I can tell you, this is something that's going to happen. After this, it's probably going to happen more. She's scared and angry, and she's going to lash out. You'll need to be prepared for that."

"Dear god," Diana said faintly. "For how long? How much longer can she go on like this?"

Adam was still looking at me, and in the moment before he turned to answer my aunt, I saw something flicker over his face. It was a dark, unhappy expression that was there and gone in an instant, and while I wouldn't grasp its full meaning until much later, I understood instantly that there was something, some awful truth, that he wasn't telling us. Something like the horrible thought I'd had on my own, not that long ago. *She's going to die soon, but not soon enough. You'll wish she was dead a hundred times over before she ever takes her last breath.*

"What's important is that you make the most of her good days," he said.

"That's not an answer," Diana said, and Richard snorted.

"Good lord, sister," he said. "What do you want, a timetable? Is Mother not dying fast enough for you to put a down payment on that condo in Key West?"

All the color drained from her face. "I already own a condo in Key West," she said, and Richard tilted his head with a quirky little smile. He didn't say it, but he didn't need to; we were all thinking it.

That's not an answer.

Diana's gaze traveled from Adam's face to his hand, still resting on my arm, and her eyes narrowed. Adam saw her looking and quickly turned away. "I'll go talk to Dora now."

Diana watched him go, waiting for the sound of his footsteps to recede before she spoke again. I thought she might lay into Richard, or maybe say something about Adam—*that goddamn male nurse of hers*—but the next thing out of her mouth was unexpected.

"Delphine," she said, her voice low, "does Adam eat pistachios?"

"What?"

She waved her hand impatiently. "Pistachio nuts. The kind with the shells on. Have you seen him eating them?"

"No," I said. "Why?"

William cleared his throat. "Are you sure?"

"Jesus, yes. What the hell? Did someone steal your nuts or something?"

Richard guffawed and Diana said, "Don't you *start*," as William reached into his coat pocket and retrieved an object that he laid on the kitchen counter. It was an empty bag of, yes, pistachios—the kind with the shell on.

"We found this outside," he said.

"Not just outside." Diana barged in, her voice impatient. "It was on the ground in that grove of trees. The one across the parking area." She paused. "If you stand there, you can see the front door."

I looked back and forth between them. "I don't get it. You think Adam has been sneaking out of the house to . . . to eat nuts? In the woods? Like in secret?" I started to laugh, too, unable to help myself.

"Well, not necessarily, but—"

"Oooh, no," Richard interrupted, "that's just one possibility. But— and this is the really exciting one—maybe it belongs to someone else. Some secret snacker who's been hiding in the forest, watching us come and go. Is that what you're thinking, sister mine?"

Diana frowned. "You don't need to make it sound so ridiculous."

"*Au contraire,*" Richard said, "I think it's intriguing. Pistachios, that's a very specific nut. Aren't police officers partial to pistachios? Maybe some old-school beat cop has staked out the place, surveilling all of us, snacking to pass the time." He paused. "Or maybe we're being stalked by squirrels."

I laughed again. "You're all being ridiculous. It's just litter. It probably blew in from the road."

William cleared his throat. "It's not litter."

Richard cocked his head. "No?"

William reached into his pocket again, then held out his hand. In it were a half-dozen shells.

"We found a whole bunch of these," he said.

"In the woods?" Richard asked.

Diana moved to stand beside me, picked up the glass of wine that Adam had left behind, and took a long swallow. "Some of them were in the woods," she said ominously, "and some of them were somewhere else."

"Where?" I said, but I wasn't laughing anymore. In my head, I heard Mimi's voice.

He always comes at night.

He's always watching me.

The man with the brown teeth.

Diana had let out a shaky breath. "Underneath your grandmother's bedroom window."

I thought about those shells as I lingered in bed the next morning, exhausted and uneasy. The spot outside Mimi's first-floor bedroom where Diana had found them was sheltered by a pair of overgrown evergreens, which meant that someone could easily have been lurking there without being spotted, but also meant that the shells themselves could have been left there months or even years ago by some handyman, a houseguest, even Mimi herself. There was a part of my mind, logical and insistent, that liked this explanation a lot. Surely it made more sense than the alternative: that someone was lurking nearby, hiding in the dark, spying on us through the lighted windows. *I don't really believe that,* I told myself.

And then I'd think of that shadow I saw in the hallway, the one shaped like a man. I'd imagine a pale face at the window, eyes like pits, lips peeled back to reveal a smile the color of bark.

I went downstairs and found my mother on her knees on the red oriental rug in the library, surrounded on all sides by papers, ledgers, and several photo albums that she was shuffling through with one hand while scrolling her phone with the other. She flipped the album closed and sat back on her heels as I came through the door. "Oh, there you are," she said. "Close the door."

I did, unsettled by the directness in her voice. The last time I'd seen her she was barely holding it together, but there was no trace of that now; she looked focused and intent on the task at hand . . . whatever it was.

"You found the photo albums?" I asked.

"Mm-hmm," she said, without looking up.

"Where were they?"

"Oh, you know," she said, and gestured around the room and then at the mess on the floor. There was a tube of paper near my foot that unrolled halfway when I prodded it with my toe, revealing a familiar outline. "Is that the blueprint for the house?"

"One of them. I thought I might be able to figure out where your grandmother disappeared to yesterday. Adam said it looked like she went through a servant's entrance at one end of the north parlor. Did you see that?"

"Not really," I said, not sure what Adam had told her, not wanting to say too much. It wasn't a lie, anyway: I hadn't seen the servant's entrance. I was too busy panicking and trying to get my pants back on. "But wherever she was, it's got a hell of a jewelry department." I had pocketed the glass pendant last night after Mimi fell asleep; now I pulled it out and handed it to my mother. "When I brought her to bed last night, she had this."

"You're kidding," she said. "I'm almost certain this was my grandmother's. I'll have to check it against the list."

"List?"

She smiled grimly. "Of missing heirlooms. She was hiding things before I moved up here. I guess it's pretty common with dementia. She was obsessed with the idea that someone might be trying to steal from her—so she stashed her valuables somewhere, and now—"

"She can't remember where she put them," I finished.

"Yep. I've been checking everything against a list from the insurance company, but there's so much missing I doubt they'll cover it all. She didn't happen to have anything else?"

"Just this."

"Twenty years from now, some lucky person is going to bump up against a trick panel in one of the walls and a pile of jewelry is going to come falling out like candy from a piñata," she said, sighing exasperatedly. "My grandfather really outdid himself when he built this place."

"Maybe his wife liked to play hide-and-seek, too," I said, and she rolled her eyes.

"Right, the wedding present story. Nice idea, but I'm pretty sure this house was built for money before it was built for love. Pop-Pop needed a place to stash all the liquor he was bringing in . . . among other things."

"Dead bodies," I said, joking, but Mom just raised her eyebrows. I guffawed. "Come on."

She shrugged. "He was a very old man by the time I came along. When he was younger, who knows? He did run a highly illegal business, and he had a reputation. Not a guy whose bad side you wanted to be on." She rolled the blueprints back up. "But that's not what I wanted to talk to you about. I want you to keep an eye on your grandmother today."

I felt myself turn red. "Mom, yesterday—"

She waved a hand in the air. "This isn't about yesterday. This isn't about *anything* that happened yesterday," she added, looking pointedly at me. "We don't need to talk about that. It was ugly, enough said."

All I could do was stare, but she wasn't even looking at me anymore; she had begun rifling through the papers again as she spoke, her brows knit together in concentration. "Did Aunt Diana tell you what she found?"

"The shells?"

"Yeah. Do you think we need to be—" *worried,* I was going to say, but she cut me off.

"No. I'm pretty sure— Aha!" She broke off, reaching for one of the photo albums. She flipped through it rapidly and then set it down, turning it toward me.

"Look at that," she said. I leaned in. It was a black-and-white photograph of two women smoking cigarettes, sitting at a wrought iron table on a broad veranda that I recognized instantly as the one behind the Whispers. One of the women was unmistakably Mimi, with her coifed dark blond hair and broad smile. She was tipped back in her chair and laughing at something the other had said, one of her bare feet kicked up in the air. The other woman was nobody I knew: she was small and wiry, with wide-set eyes, dark hair, and short, thick bangs. She was leaning forward and looking straight at the camera, smiling with her lips closed, her cigarette held forward as if she were offering it to the photographer.

"That's a cool picture."

My mom tapped her finger above the head of the dark-haired woman and said, "That's Shelly Dyer."

"Really?" I squinted, trying to connect the smirking beauty in the picture to the slack-faced, gray-haired woman I'd seen sitting in the truck outside the bakery. "Wow."

"And this," she said, flipping the page, "is Jack and me."

I leaned in to look at the photograph: two little kids, one a chubby-cheeked, short-haired toddler and the other an even chubbier-cheeked bald baby, sat together on a blanket with a plastic bucket in between them. The toddler had a little shovel and was digging in the sand with it. The baby had an identical shovel and appeared to be chewing on the handle. I laughed. "Which one is you?"

Mom gave me a funny little smile and pointed to the toddler. "That's me. I was about a year older than Jack."

"Are there more photos?"

"Oh yes. He and his mother lived here for several years."

"Does Diana know you found these?"

Mom flipped the album shut. "No, and I'd appreciate it if you didn't tell her just yet."

"Because once she gets her hands on them, she's not giving them back."

"She's welcome to them once I'm finished here," she said. "But I have a lot to deal with today, errands to run before the stores close, and I won't be here to monitor your grandmother. Can I trust you to do that?"

For a moment, I thought about asking her about the bruise under Mimi's jaw. But she was already on her feet, walking away, the photo album tucked under her arm.

"Of course."

Mom looked relieved. "Good. She'll like that. You're so patient with her." She hesitated at the door. "I think you should know, when we take her back to Willowcrest, she'll be moving into memory care. Having her here, seeing it up close, it's become clear that she's deteriorating. You should prepare yourself."

Adam had said nearly the same thing last night, but this was different. My mother's tone was cold, matter-of-fact—and did I hear relief in her voice? But then she smiled and said, "Let's enjoy today. Keep her company, listen to her stories. Savor the moment. You know."

I nodded.

I knew.

When I think of it now, I think of that—cling to it, the idea that before my grandmother was dead, she was already gone. Lost in another world where she was still young, still full of promise, still looking forward to a whole life with the man she loved. She was unusually quiet that day, perched on her favorite green sofa in the parlor, her eyes flicking this way and that. She watched as Adam and Richard and William wrangled the Christmas tree into an upright position. The tree was huge, fully filling up the space by the window, so wide that its outer branches scraped the spines of the books in the built-in shelves. The smell of balsam was everywhere.

"I think it's too—" William started to say, but too late, and there was a moment of petrified silence as the tree's top scraped across the ceiling, leaving a long dirty mark. The men looked in terror at one another, at me, at Mimi, and back at one another—and burst out laughing all at once.

"Oopsy-daisy," Richard said, setting off a fresh round of hysterics.

Mimi smiled serenely. "Our man Smith will take care of that," she said, and the smile became a smirk. "I'll see to it, don't you worry. He'll scrub it until it gleams."

"Who's Smith?" William said while Adam stared and Richard flailed wildly in a show of violently shushing him.

"He's the ghost of Christmas past," he said. "Or he's just some guy.

Either way, if Mother says he's going to clean the ceiling, I for one believe her."

"Papa says he has to do everything I say," Mimi said, and then the smile faded from her face. "He does, but he hates me for it."

The rest of us exchanged looks, but Diana walked into the room then, letting out an appreciative *oooh* when she saw the tree. She was wearing an apron and carrying a bowl of oranges, and the scent of nutmeg and cinnamon wafted in behind her. She'd found Mimi's recipe box stashed away in a kitchen cabinet and had spent all day industriously baking cookies, a pumpkin pie, and some sort of holiday cake flavored with oranges that was a recipe passed down from my grandfather's mother, the Greek side of the family. My mother had disappeared hours earlier to go to the market, but I thought that even if she came back empty-handed, we had enough sugar and alcohol to last the night—and that if things kept going as they had been, we might even enjoy ourselves.

"Someone should check out the attic. Dora said there are lights and ornaments," Diana said. She set the oranges on the coffee table and slid in beside Mimi on the sofa, pulling a box of whole cloves out of her apron. "Mother, how are your hands? Would you like to make pomanders? I've already pierced the rinds."

"How lovely," Mimi said, and began pressing the cloves into one of the oranges, her fingers moving deftly over the surface, transforming it into a spiked sphere. The smell of citrus and spice filled the room. If someone had walked in at that moment, they could have mistaken us for a happy, normal family having a Hallmark holiday, baking cookies and making crafts and being kind, not cruel, to one another.

I left Mimi with Diana sitting beside her and climbed the stairs to the third floor, then made my way into the attic. It was a mess up there, full of boxes and trunks that someone, maybe my mother looking for the missing-now-found photo albums, had rifled through and then left open and in disarray. The Christmas stuff was guarded by a box half-full of ledgers like the ones spread out on the floor in the library, and a trunk stuffed with men's work clothes, coveralls and flannel shirts and a waxed jacket that someone—my grandfather, maybe— might have worn on damp mornings when he left at dawn for the docks. I smelled dust and mold and a hint of ancient cologne as I shoved it aside, aiming my phone's flashlight into the dark behind it, looking for the string lights. I found them a moment later, just as my phone buzzed with a message. It was from Adam: a selfie with a caption that said, WAITING FOR U. He was in the little powder room under the stairs—I could see the wallpaper in the background—and he was holding an ornament above his head. It was the kind of thing you'd find in a bin at a dollar store: a brightly colored plastic frog in a Santa hat, straddling what looked like a rocket. I squinted and then guffawed.

Not a frog, I thought. *A toad. A toad riding a missile.* "Missile toad," I said aloud. "He's standing under the missile toad."

I grabbed a box of lights and started downstairs, still laughing, shaking my head. There was a time, not that long ago, when I would have had to pretend I was too cool for this sort of earnestness. I would have told the story to my friends and laughed along with them at Adam's expense, and when they asked if I had texted him back, I would have rolled my eyes and said, "Ugh, of course not," and then enjoyed their approving nods. But here in the privacy of this old, whispering house, surrounded by a bickering family whom I didn't need to impress, I could admit that I liked it. This was what I wanted. I was going to go downstairs and kiss my boyfriend under the missile toad, and I could imagine that stupid ornament hanging in a series of doorways, a reminder of the first holiday we'd ever shared. I could see the two of us laughing at it, embracing under it, one, two, five years from now.

Once, Adam had said that he believed things happened for a reason, that fate had brought us together. I'd laughed at him then, told him I didn't believe in fate.

But when I went down to the room under the stairs and let him pull me close, I didn't want to laugh anymore. I felt it, too: the rightness of it, the sense that every moment in my life had led me to this place. I was finally exactly where I was supposed to be.

Some kind of magic seemed to settle over the house in the hours that followed. I wrapped the tree in lights that miraculously came on and stayed lit, not a single dead string among them even though they must have been at least a decade old. I found boxes and boxes of ornaments, delicate glass balls and bead garlands in every color, and hung them on the branches until there wasn't a single space left that didn't sparkle. My mother came back with a giant charcuterie and cheese platter at the same time as Diana announced that she'd made pasta and salad, so that suddenly there was food everywhere, and all of us eating, drinking, talking about nothing except how good everything tasted and how beautiful everything looked.

Richard built a roaring fire as the sun went down, and one by one we gravitated toward it, settling into chairs and onto sofas, listening to the crackle and snap of the kindling and the voice of the rising wind under the eaves. My grandmother had been quiet and alert all afternoon, talking very little and looking up every time someone walked into the room, as if she was expecting visitors. But now she sat back in a chair close to the fire, letting her head rest to one side, lifting a hand to touch the crepey skin at the base of her throat. My mother came to kneel in front of her, taking her hands one at a time and massaging them with lavender cream, and Mimi sighed and said, "Thank you, dear," and that awful moment from the night before seemed like something that had never happened at all, nothing more than a bad dream. When Adam brought Mimi her evening pills, she swallowed them obediently. Her eyes stayed open, fixed on the door. In her pupils, wide and dark, the reflected firelight danced.

The house sighed. The wind rose. Adam stepped out to get more firewood and came back in with his cheeks flushed and his hair wild, blowing furiously on his hands to warm them. "It's gotten damn cold out there," he said, and the wind howled and rattled the windows as if in agreement. The lights flickered once, but stayed on, and the room filled with a series of relieved sighs and ripples of nervous laughter.

"Imagine," someone said, and the rest of us nodded, so in tune with the moment and with one another that one word was enough to understand: Imagine if the lights had gone out. Imagine no power on Christmas Eve, Christmas Day. Imagine that darkness, how complete. How terrible, how exciting. Imagine the flicker of candlelight on freshly fallen snow.

We drank and dozed as the night deepened, steeped in the comfortable silence and cozy intimacy that comes from being in a room where everyone is either a little bit drunk, a little bit asleep, or both. Diana turned on *Love Actually* while Richard pretended to vomit in protest. My mother, Adam, and I played half a game of Scrabble, then abandoned it when Mom played EXOTICS on a triple word score and gained an insurmountable lead. William fell asleep reading and then woke himself up with a sudden fart that everyone pretended not to hear until he'd excused himself off to bed, at which point the entire room collapsed into hysterics. Adam settled in beside me on the couch where I was stretched out with a blanket in my lap, taking care not to look at me but arranging himself on the cushions so that one of my feet was pressed against his thigh, the sweet sneakiness of it sending chills down my spine as much as the warmth of him against me. Richard stopped pretending to vomit at *Love Actually* and then sniffled loudly as the end credits rolled, so that Diana turned and gave him an incredulous look.

"Aww, Dicky," she said.

"Oh, shut up," he said, blowing his nose and then throwing the balled-up tissue at her.

And all the while, the house whispered while the wind rushed, rattled, roared.

Sometime later, Mimi suddenly stood up, wild-eyed and looking around the room. "Is he here?" She looked at me, at my mother. She stared at the tree.

"Who?" my mother said, and Richard yawned and said, "Santa Claus," and then stood up, too, and took my grandmother by the arm with surprising tenderness. "Come on, Mother," he said. "It's bedtime."

Mimi blinked at him indignantly. "I can't go to bed with *you*," she said, and Richard raised his eyebrows in mock offense. "What's so wrong with me?"

"You're my . . ." Mimi trailed off, gazing into his face, searching his features. "I'm not sure," she said in a small voice. "You look like someone. You look like my papa. But you're not."

"No, I'm not."

"Do you know him? My papa?"

From the corner of my eye, I saw my mother and Diana tense up. Anticipating something bad, something cutting, one of Richard's trademark barbs. The night would be ruined, all the magic gone. But he only slid his arm across Mimi's shoulders and smiled.

"Well, I knew him a bit," he said. "I haven't seen him in many years."

"It's been so long. But I need . . . I need to speak to him." Her voice grew tremulous. "I need to tell him before it's too late. I promised, but—" She broke off, looking around the room, and her face fell. "Oh no, but I've been confused. It's already happened. Hasn't it? I can't take it back."

"What's happened, Mother?" Richard said carefully.

Mimi shook her head. "They said it was an accident," she said, and her voice broke. "They said he must have slipped and fallen overboard."

A hush fell, and we all stared. The details of my grandfather's death were the one thing Mimi never talked about, and hearing her say the words aloud was unsettling, as if a taboo had been broken.

Diana piped up. "That's right, Mother. It was an accident, a terrible accident," she said, and my grandmother shook her head. Her voice was flat now, the tremble gone.

"They never found him," she said, and a funny little smile played

over her lips. "I remember now. An empty box, that's what I buried."
She paused. "They never found him, so they never knew. But I knew.
It was my blood, after all. My blood, on my hands."

"What is she talking about?" Diana said nervously. "Does anyone
know what she's talking about? Mother—"

But Mimi wasn't listening. She was staring into space now, lost in
a reverie, talking only to herself.

"But it doesn't matter," she said. "He came back for me. He always
comes back. I feel him beside me at night, I hear him whispering in
my ear." She lowered her voice and looked around furtively. "He's here
now, you know. In this very room. Only he thinks I can't see him,
because he's wearing someone else's skin."

Nobody spoke. The temperature in the room seemed to have
dropped ten degrees. Mimi turned her head, looking toward the dark
and empty doorway, and so did everyone else. All of us holding our
breath, as if the ghost of my dead, drowned grandfather might walk
through at any moment, pale and cold, reaching out with a hand that
the sea had long since stripped to the bone. The silence stretched out,
no sound but the crackling of the fire—until a log popped loudly
enough to make everyone jump, and my mother stepped up and took
Mimi's other arm. "Bed. Right now," she said firmly.

Richard sighed and stepped aside. "Shame. It was just getting interesting," he said, and then threw his hands up when my mother gave
him a dirty look. "Hey, this isn't my fault. She brought it up."

"Say good night, Mother," my mom said.

"Of course," Mimi said cheerfully, as if the preceding conversation
hadn't happened at all. "Good night."

She smiled then. I think a lot about that smile. Blissful, distant
and dreamy and already half asleep. Was she happy, there at the end?
Was she ready? I'd like to believe she was.

But it's because I want to believe it so badly that I know it might
not be true.

What I do know is that she looked at us. One after another, like she was trying to memorize our faces. Like she was fighting for this one last memory, even as everything else slipped away. "Thank you all," she said. "It's been so lovely."

If she had any other last words, I wasn't there to hear them.

People began to drift away after that, saying good night and wandering off to various rooms while the house muttered and groaned around us. Richard stood, yawning, and took a last look at Adam and me where we sat at opposite ends of the couch.

"You kids have yourselves a merry little Christmas," he said, and then, with an exaggerated wink: "Not that you weren't already."

I tried to keep my expression neutral. "What?"

"Oh, no judgment," he said. "Hell, I respect it."

"I have literally no idea what you're talking about," I said, and my mother turned in her chair.

"Richard, what *are* you talking about?"

I held my breath then, mentally running back through all the times Adam and I had snuck off together. We'd always been alone, I was certain of that, except for that one kiss on the pine path while Mimi's back was turned, a kiss there was no way he could've seen. *He's bluffing,* I thought. He doesn't know. He might suspect, because he's some sort of freakish savant with a goddamn sixth sense for when people are horny for each other, but—

Richard yawned and shrugged. "Apparently I don't know what I'm talking about. As usual, some might say."

"No kidding," I said, standing up, realizing as I did that I was very drunk. "Good night."

I was swaying my way upstairs when Adam caught up to me.

"You left your phone downstairs," he said, pressing it into my hand—but when my fist closed around it, I felt something else. There was a ribbon wrapped around the phone, and sitting on top of it, a small box wrapped in brown paper.

"What's this?"

"Something you can't open until Christmas," he said.

"If this is that freaking missile toad—" I started to say, but even as I looked at the box, I knew it wasn't. It was too small. So small that it could hold only one of a very few things, and when I looked at Adam's face, I was suddenly certain that I knew what was in it. Certain and thrilled and terrified.

"Good night, Delphine," he said, and before I could say anything else, before I could even decide whether or not to ask the obvious question, he was gone. Up the stairs, out of sight, and I didn't call after him. I stood, staring at the box in my hand. I stared at it some more after I went to bed, wanting to look inside, but also not wanting to, knowing that once I opened it, I might be opening a door I couldn't close. Outside, a thick fog was rising, rolling across the bay, blotting out the moon. I was still staring at the box where it sat on my nightstand when I fell asleep. Deeply and completely, a plunge into the dark. And for once, I didn't dream.

14.

Someone was pounding on my door. The sound matched the pounding in my head.

"Delphine?" My mother's voice. I struggled to peel my eyes open. Reached for my phone, but the screen stayed dark—dead. No charge. I turned my head to look out the window and saw fog, nothing but fog, as if the house had been picked up overnight and dropped into some other dimension, a deep gray void with no end.

I rubbed my eyes and shivered. The room was very, very cold. "What?" I croaked.

The door cracked open. "Are you sick? I've been knocking and knocking," Mom said, and heaved a sigh. "Your grandmother is playing hide-and-seek again. You haven't seen her, have you? She isn't in her room."

But nobody was worried. Not then, not really. After all, we thought we knew this game by now—and not just that, we thought we'd figured out that the winning move was not to play. Mimi would turn up when she got tired of hiding. All we had to do was wait.

"She does this because it gets a rise out of us," Diana was saying as

I came into the kitchen. "She always did love to make a stir. Well, I'm not worried. I *refuse* to worry. It's what she wants, for us to all lose our minds and run around like chickens with our heads cut off. I say, let's just wait. She'll come out when she gets hungry."

"You make her sound like a lost cat," my mom said, and Richard guffawed.

"Now, why didn't I think of that before," he said. "When she comes back, can we put a bell on her?"

Everyone laughed. Why not? It was funny.

It took an hour for it to stop being funny. We did start looking then, just like we'd done before. But we were annoyed, not scared, and the search had none of the urgency of the day before last. We dutifully fanned out, up the stairs, down the halls, in and out of the empty rooms—all the while expecting that we'd probably come back to the kitchen and find her waiting for us, eating the last of the cookies and smirking. The sky darkened and snow began to fall, huge fat flakes that accumulated quickly on the windowsills, the pathways, the bare branches of the trees. Diana abandoned the search in order to start making the turkey—still certain that Mimi would turn up by the time we sat down to eat it. But she stayed missing, and the snow kept falling, and finally my mother glanced out the window—at the foggy bay, at the swirling sky—and said, "I'm just going to check outside. Just in case."

"I'll come with you," I said, but by the time I had found my boots and coat, she was already gone, so I followed her footprints. Through the fresh fallen snow, from the front door to the side to the back, where they crossed the veranda and went down the stairs to the garden. The footprints turned right at the long stone wall, then veered away through the trees to the pine path.

I heard Adam's voice behind me then. He called my name, and I looked back to see him standing on the veranda, waving. I waved back, but I didn't wait. I kept going.

I think maybe, even then, I knew something was wrong.

And I think I knew because she did. My mother: her footprints danced away ahead of me, and I could see from the length and shape of her stride that she had started to hurry. The tracks disappeared down the pine path, into the darkness of the trees. I chased them. Faster, my breath coming in puffs, my heart starting to race. Matching my strides to hers, slowing down only when I came to the fallen tree in the middle of the path—but I was alone and climbed over it easily, the trunk cold and slimy beneath my hands, and in the back of my head I heard Mimi's voice saying, *The path goes on, we just can't get there,* and realized she was wrong. We could get there. We could have gotten here anytime, *she* could have gotten here anytime, because the tree wasn't really that big after all. Certainly not big enough to stop a spry and determined old woman from crossing over, from going out to the place where the sea lavender grows, where she used to walk so often as a girl, a young woman, a wife.

And that was when I heard it. A howl, wild and keening. It was a terrible sound, the sound of an animal trapped and dying, and every hair on the back of my neck stood on end as I listened between the trees, barely breathing, waiting. The howl ended. There was silence.

Then it began again.

I ran toward the noise, down the shadowed path to the place where the woods ended and the rocky coastline began, letting go of my coat so that it flapped open, but I no longer felt the chill. I ran even though that voice inside me, that cold and logical voice, was suddenly awake again and telling me, *No, don't, turn around,* because whatever was making that sound was something I didn't want to see. I ran, the trees passing in a blur beside me, until suddenly they fell away and I was standing in the cove, and the howl had started again, and the howling animal wasn't an animal at all, but my mother.

She was on her knees at the edge of the frozen reach, her hands bare, pounding her fists at the ice and snow that was already turning red with her blood. Her mouth was open, and she was screaming, and the scream was living anguish wrapped around a single word: *No.*

No, she screamed, *no, no, no,* as her fists hit the ice and her knuckles split open and the ice didn't crack at all. Not a crack. Not a flaw. It was clear, so beautifully clear, that frozen water smeared with blood.

He caught up to me then. Adam. He must have been coming after me, tracking my steps as I had tracked my mother's, running at the sound of her terrible cry. He saw me, and he saw what was in front of me, and he gathered me up in his arms and said, "Don't look, don't look."

But I had already looked. I had already seen.

I would never stop seeing it.

My mother on her knees, howling.

Her knuckles bruised and bleeding.

The snow, falling fast now.

The ice, and what lay beneath it.

Mimi's eyes were open. Open wide in her pale frozen face, open wide below the frozen surface of the sea that drowned her and then pushed her back to shore. Gazing into the flat gray sky forever and seeing nothing at all.

15.

1948

SUMMER

She is nineteen and luminous in her ivory dress. She walks over rose petals to meet him at the altar, a blushing, beautiful June bride. Later, one of her mother's friends will cluck and frown and say *what a shame* that there weren't more people there to see how lovely she looked. St. Saviour's is a small church already, and even then, as Miriam makes her way down the aisle, the pews are only half-full. But then, this is no grand society wedding. The invitees who might have made an event of it all declined to attend, sending regrets from their new summer homes in Newport, Cape May, Nantucket. The announcement that runs a week later in the New York papers will be small and mostly overlooked, except by Harold Chandler, who will angrily crumple up the page, put a match to it, and use it to light a cigarette. Just as Roland Day predicted, Bar Harbor's moment as a seaside enclave for the rich and famous is over—and the few families who returned after the fire have been as left behind as the island itself.

• • •

But Miriam doesn't care about any of that. She never wanted it: not the parties, not her picture in the paper, not the two-faced friends who would invite her to lunch and compliment her hat and then gossip furiously about her the moment her back was turned. She only wanted Theodore Caravasios.

And she has him.

There had been one terrible week in which she wasn't certain she would prevail. The chaotic confrontation that began when Smith screamed the household awake went on all the way until dawn. Mother had slapped her hard across the face, then burst into tears. Papa had raged and ranted for hours, scathing Miriam for her deception, her carelessness, the scandal she might have caused to the detriment not only of her own reputation but of her family's, too. There had been shouting, then pleas, then angry promises. Miriam would be sent away, he said—to a distant relative, to a convent, to a city overseas where she would never see that boy again, and she should count herself lucky that this was all that would happen, because what Papa really wanted to do was throttle that disgusting greaser with his bare hands. He cajoled and threatened; he begged her to tell him that she hadn't gone out into the night by choice, grabbing her hard by the shoulders and saying, "You tell me the truth, child. If he harmed you, if he forced you." That was when Miriam lifted her chin and looked him dead in the eye and said, "The only person hurting me is you, Papa," so that he reddened and released his grip, looking ashamed. Oh, they had fought.

But in the end, she was right. Her father would not, could not, stand in the way of her marrying the man she loved.

It was the first day of the New Year, a subdued affair at which the conflict hung like a dark cloud over everything, when Papa knocked at the door of her room.

"All right then, child," he said. "I've made up my mind. Your mother says I'd be a fool to allow it, and she might be right. But fool or no, it's done. I telephoned your Mr. Caravasios this morning . . . and I told him he has my blessing."

Miriam had flung herself off the bed with a shriek, embracing him so fiercely that she nearly sent both of them toppling. "Thank you, Papa," she said. After a long moment, she stepped back. "Does Mother know?"

"Of course. Whether she approves is another matter, but that's between you and her. As for me, I'm still not sure I approve. But," he added with a sigh, "I also know better than to enter a contest with my own daughter to see which of us can be more stubborn."

"I'd win, you know. I'd reject every suitor who came my way and become an old maid just to spite you."

He laughed at that. "You know, I believe you would."

"He's a good man, Papa. You'll see."

"Well," he said, "he seems to be. And I'll do whatever I can, whatever is in my power, to make sure that you and your young man have a happy, prosperous life." He paused, and smiled. "You, and anyone else who might come along. That's a promise, my dear. I know you love him, and I believe he loves you, too, and that's no small thing. But that's not why I'm giving you my blessing."

She stepped back to look into his face. "Why, then?"

Her father laid a hand on each of her shoulders and gazed unflinchingly into her eyes. The look on his face was one she'd never seen before: full of love, but also something darker, something savage. He looked like a man about to declare war.

"Because you're *my* daughter. *My* blood. If he doesn't do right by you, girl, I trust you to give him the hell he deserves. And I want you to promise me, Miriam. A promise for a promise. If the worst comes to pass, if it goes bad, you come to me. Do you hear? You come to me."

Gooseflesh rippled over her skin, but she met his gaze without flinching.

"I promise."

• • •

But it was a silly promise, one forgotten nearly as soon as she made it, swept away by jubilation at her engagement, the thrill of Theo's hand in hers as she introduced him as her fiancé, the excitement of planning the wedding that would take place in just a few short months. By the time she and Theo say their vows, it's the very last thing she's thinking of—and by the time she falls into his arms on their wedding night, this time pillowed by soft white linens instead of a rough and dusty bearskin laid over a dirty floor, she's not thinking of it at all.

And Papa keeps his promise. The newlywed couple has everything they could ask for, everything they could ever want—except a house of their own, but it hardly matters when the Day family already owns the finest damn house in Bar Harbor, now fully rebuilt and grander than ever. Maybe that's why, although it's supposed to be only temporary, Miriam and Theo stay on at the Whispers. First in Miriam's own bedroom, where they settle in immediately after returning from a honeymoon in Niagara Falls. (Miriam tries and fails not to smirk at the sight of Smith, struggling to drag her heavy luggage up the stairs.) A year later, Mother and Papa move into the rebuilt north wing, Smith exits for parts unknown, and she and Theo take the master bedroom, with its connected dressing rooms, private veranda, and sweeping views of the bay. Mother says it's to give them their privacy; Miriam suspects that it has more to do with the very expensive, very luxurious radiant heating system Papa had installed in the floors of the north wing. At any rate, she's glad—for the extra space, but also to have her mother still so nearby. She already suspects what the doctor will confirm in another few weeks: she's pregnant.

She's twenty-one when Richard comes into the world, squalling and red-faced, his little fists waving in the air even before his eyes open, like he's fighting an unseen enemy.

Twenty-two, and pregnant again, watching from the newly rebuilt pier at sunset as her husband's boat comes in, one hand resting on her burgeoning belly and the other holding Richard on her hip. Patches, seven years old and still spry, runs circles around her legs.

Twenty-three, and a mother twice over, to the rambunctious toddler who has begun to look more like Miriam's father than anyone else, and to a baby girl who was born two weeks ahead of schedule with a full head of thick, dark hair. Theo's uncle, visiting for the first time since the wedding, chucks the sleeping infant Diana under the chin and says, "This one's Greek for sure"—and then looks nervously over his shoulder when Roland Day scowls and harrumphs behind his newspaper.

Time moves like a river. Fast, faster.

She is twenty-five. Twenty-seven—no, twenty-eight, and this is when she realizes she's stopped counting her own birthdays, instead marking time by the number of candles on her children's birthday cakes. Seven for Richard, five for Diana. She marvels at how fast it passes, how she seems to turn around and find another year gone. So much has changed. So much has stayed the same. Patches is an old dog, white-muzzled and contentedly sleeping his days away, waking up only to follow the rays of the sun as they shift from window to window. He doesn't come down to the pier with Miriam anymore, and Miriam herself doesn't go as often as she used to. Theo has two boats now, the *Red Sky* and one other, called *Sprite*, that he charters from the marina on summer weekends for wealthy visitors to go deep-sea fishing. This side business was Papa's idea. For the first year, Theo's clientele consisted almost solely of Roland Day and his friends, but it's quickly become lucrative, more so than his own work. He wears a jaunty white captain's hat when he takes folks out on the water, also at Papa's suggestion; he says it completes the image, so that clients know they're in good hands, and Miriam thinks he looks terribly handsome, even though Theo privately grumbles to her that he thinks the hat is ridiculous.

Later, she'll remember this year as a good one. One of the best. Happy and busy and full of laughter, the family gathered for dinner in the evenings, the table set for six or eight or even ten. Papa hires a cook and a housekeeper and the Whispers is bustling once again, this time with amateur fishermen and their wives, who cluck delightedly over the children and often join Miriam for tea while their husbands are out on the water.

She is twenty-eight when Papa's health begins to decline, and he and Mother tell her they've decided to return to Egg Harbor. The winters are too hard, the doctors too far away. The Whispers succumbs once again to emptiness. The summer guests, who were always her parents' friends more than her own, send their regrets and stay elsewhere.

She has never been so lonely.

She shouldn't be. She knows it's absurd, when she's been so fortunate—and when she has this lovely home, two beautiful children, a loving husband to keep her company. Some people had tried to tell her that time would eventually cool their passions, that there would come a day when she didn't want to melt every time he looked her way, but they were wrong. She loves him as fiercely as ever, burns for him the way she always has. They even still slip out to the island as they did years ago on that one frigid night, waiting for the reach to freeze solid and then sneaking out like teenagers from their own house, laughing and clinging to each other as they cross the ice.

But then the winter of 1958 is unseasonably mild, and the ice never comes—and the next winter, it's as if he's forgotten. Not just the island, the cabin, those stolen moments in the dark, but Miriam herself. He leaves for the docks earlier, comes home later, lingers downstairs smoking or reading long after she's gone to bed. Sometimes he falls asleep down there and never comes to bed at all, so that when Miriam wakes up and stretches her hand out in the dark, she finds herself alone, his side of the bed empty and cold. He reaches for her less and less.

She tells herself things will change—they must—as the temperature falls, the frost creeps in, the world covers over in snow. She waits a week, and then another. On the last day of January 1959, with the temperature hovering near ten degrees and the wind blowing wildly over the snowdrifts, she walks the pine path alone to the cove. A hard walk, her cheeks burning against the wind, her arms crossed protectively over her tender breasts, a bone-deep exhaustion setting into her body before she's even halfway there. But she makes it, leaning out to poke a stick into the water. It goes two inches into the snow, and no farther. The ice is as hard as granite.

She smiles as she makes her way back along the path, imagining how she'll wink at him across the dinner table. "Wouldn't you know," she'll say, "the reach is frozen solid. It's pure ice all the way across."

She imagines how he'll smile at her. How he'll remember what he's somehow forgotten. How they'll wait until after dark, until the children are asleep. She imagines the delicious weight of him as he lays her against the floor, taking her by the hips and moving slowly inside of her.

As she reaches the garden wall, she falls to her knees and vomits.

At dinner that night, there is no wink, no smile. Instead, she passes the potatoes across the table and says, "We're going to have another baby."

Richard thinks about this for three or four seconds, then asks if they can name the baby Captain Kangaroo. Diana, confused, says that if they're having a baby kangaroo, she'd very much like if it could sleep in her room. Patches, resting against Miriam's foot under the table, makes a little *whuff* noise and twitches in his sleep. But Theo doesn't say anything, not for a long time, gazing at her with an unreadable expression on his face.

"Are you sure?" he asks finally.

"Pretty sure," Miriam says.

"You look so pale."

"I was sick earlier. I'll be all right."

There's another silence. Then he smiles, he smiles at last, and Miriam lets go of a breath she didn't know she was holding, her body flooded with relief she hadn't known she was craving.

"Well," he says, "that's some great news. Just wonderful. Although, too bad."

"What? What's too bad?"

He smiles. "Well, I took a little walk down the pine path this afternoon. Would you believe the reach has frozen over?"

She laughs with delight then, and reaches for his hand across the table, laying her other palm against her not-yet-swollen belly. She thinks that perhaps this baby is a sign of change to come, a way for them to find their way back to each other when they might have started drifting apart. She thinks, *We'll name it after him.* Theodore for a boy—and if it's a girl, why not, Theodora.

She is as certain of their love in this moment as she has ever been.

After all, they still have so much time.

16.

It was an accident.

Legally, I mean. Somewhere, someone typed that word—*Accident*—next to the words *Manner of death* in a file that had Mimi's name on it, and that was that. Case closed.

It was supposed to be satisfying, even a relief. An accident meant you could stop asking why and how and what if. It meant it was over, and there was nothing left to do but bury her and get on with your grief. No bang, no whimper, just a shrug. A life had ended.

An accident meant it was nobody's fault.

Richard gave us the news on the day he came back from the police station, where he'd signed the papers for the release of my grandmother's corpse.

"Did they say anything?" Diana asked, and his lips peeled back in a humorless grin.

"Oh yes. They told me that after a careful examination of the evidence, they decided that none of us murdered her. Isn't that comforting?" he said, and then walked off in search of a whiskey without waiting for an answer.

Of course it was easy for him to joke. He wasn't the one who was supposed to look after her.

He wasn't the one who didn't wake up when she crept off into the night.

The funeral was a blur, the pews of St. Saviour's church crowded with unfamiliar faces, everyone in black. The priest, a man in his fifties with kind eyes and prematurely gray hair, was unfamiliar, too—but he seemed to know Mimi, which surprised everyone, my mother most of all. When we traveled back to the house for the reception, he was among the first guests through the door.

"I'm so sorry," my mother said, even as the Reverend Frank was trying to say that *he* was sorry, for our family's loss. "She never told me she was going back to church. I would have—"

"She hadn't been to the church itself in some time, as I understand it," he said. "But I keep hours at a few retirement homes on the mainland, and I visited with her at Willowcrest many times. She was a remarkable woman."

I blinked. In all the hours I'd spent visiting Mimi, she had never said anything about visiting with a priest, and I'd never seen the reverend before.

"I never saw you. And she never mentioned you," I said, and then cringed as I realized how rude I sounded, but he just smiled.

"No, I don't suppose she would. Whenever we met, she often seemed to think it was the first time. But I believe our conversations were valuable all the same."

My mother began talking again and I looked around the room, wondering how many of the people here I would remember meeting, if I ever saw them again. Willowcrest had chartered a shuttle for the residents who wanted to attend, but the handful of elderly ladies who'd turned up were nobody I recognized, which confused me until Adam took me aside to explain that they attended every funeral they were allowed to, whether they'd known the dead person or not.

"Why?" I'd asked, bewildered. I had to stifle the world's most inappropriate burst of laughter when he shrugged and said, "They like the food."

There was one party present I did recognize, apart from Adam. Jack Dyer was here, dressed in a suit that was shiny at the elbows and looked like it had belonged to at least three men before him. Beside him in a wheelchair was Shelly, clutching the iPad that was apparently a permanent accessory, staring hard out of the one eye she could still focus with, and working her mouth like she was trying to chew her own tongue off. I'd heard from Adam that she was moving into Willowcrest. I wondered how she could afford it.

Shelly Dyer's good eye darted back and forth, watching everyone who was paying no attention to her, all the people walking around and past her like she was a piece of furniture. This must have been her first time back in the house since she'd lived here all those years ago, but it was impossible to read any emotion on her half-frozen face—until her gaze suddenly shifted and she was looking directly at me. I forced myself to stare back, to smile politely. Shelly's face may have been unreadable, but there was plenty of emotion in her single glaring eye, and whatever she felt about being back at the Whispers, it definitely wasn't friendly.

I felt a tap on my shoulder and turned to find Adam standing behind me. I hadn't been close to him since the day Mimi died, when he pulled me into his arms to try to keep me from seeing her body trapped under the ice, and now he was keeping his distance. Anyone looking at us would see nothing out of place, just a professional caregiver chatting politely with the grieving granddaughter of the woman he used to care for—only when I looked back, Shelly was still looking, her head shaking slowly side to side as if she'd seen something she disapproved of. Me? *Us?* Had she somehow seen with only one good eye what nobody else but Richard had noticed?

"I have to start getting the shuttle ready," Adam said.

"Okay," I said. I looked around and lowered my voice. "When will I see you?"

He grimaced. "I was going to ask you that. We need to talk."

My stomach twisted, and my face must have done the same, because he did reach for me then. It wasn't much, just a split second as his hand fell warm and heavy on my shoulder, but I felt myself relax.

"Nothing bad," he said. "Could you get away tomorrow night? Maybe even," and his voice dropped to a near whisper, "overnight? I know your family—"

"Yes," I said, not having the slightest idea how I would explain being gone for the night, only knowing that I'd do anything to make it happen. A beat passed, the space between us suddenly pregnant with tension. I couldn't stop looking at his hands, thinking about how it would feel to have them wrapped around my waist, my neck. The warmth and strength of him.

He walked away, motioning to the Willowcrest funeral tourists. They followed him out the door in a gaggle, bobbing and gossiping with their heads close together in a way that reminded me of chickens in a yard. My mother, stepping back through the door, smiled and thanked them for coming. When I looked back at Shelly Dyer, she had turned away; her gaze was aimed at the door, and so was her iPad camera. I watched her grip it with her good hand, scowling at the screen; her other hand rose, trembling, to tap it. The shutter sound was loud enough that one of the Willowcrest ladies turned her head as her picture was taken, looking for the camera. She gave Shelly a twinkly little wave. Shelly, apparently not interested in making friends, put the iPad back in her lap and resumed chewing on her tongue.

• • •

Twenty-four hours later, I left the house empty and drove to the mainland, traveling the familiar route to Willowcrest. Mimi's glass pendant was around my neck, and I kept absently reaching for it, just as she had on her last night with us. I'd found it in her nightstand drawer the day after she died, along with countless other things she'd been apparently collecting from around the house. Spoons. Slips of paper. An acorn. A button. I'd held it all in my hands, thinking if I stared at it long enough I would find meaning, a pattern, a reason these things had been gathered together. But there was nothing. Maybe this collection had held meaning for Mimi. Without her, it was just junk, and I felt a lump in my throat as I realized how true this was, and for how many things. Her house, her clothes, her furniture, her photographs. All pieces of a story that would never be told again, each of them full of meaning that winked out of existence when she did. The only significance these things held now was that they had belonged to Mimi—that in her last days on earth, these were the objects she wanted near her. These were the last things she touched.

I think that's why I kept them. Stashing them in my coat pockets, where they could gather meaning again. My grandmother's acorn. My grandmother's button. Mine now.

In the coming weeks, Mimi's whole life would be cataloged, sold, scattered. The pendant around my neck would be inherited by somebody, probably Diana, and the rest of my family was already on their way to Bangor for a meeting with the agent who would help us sell off the estate piece by piece. I had to assure my mother a half-dozen times that no, I didn't want to go with them, and yes, I'd be fine on my own for a night, but in the end she went and I was relieved. I was no good at comforting her; not just that, I was actively bad at it. All I could do was stammer and pat her on the shoulder, trying not to recoil at the damp heat of her skin beneath her shirt. She was making an effort not to cry too much in front of people, and it was like all the tears she was holding back were leaking out of her pores instead.

I picked up Adam in the same parking lot where we used to steal kisses behind my car. He had changed out of his uniform and was carrying a duffel bag, and everything felt almost normal, except that there was no grandmother waiting for me inside.

"Where should we go?" I asked. He peered out the window at the dark gray sky, the bare trees. There had been a foot of snow the day before the funeral, and the remnants of it were still lining the edges of the parking lot, filthy and crusted over with ice.

"I'm thinking California," he deadpanned, and I laughed.

"Have you ever been there?"

"Nope. You?"

"Once. To look at colleges."

He glanced at me curiously. "Not to visit your dad?"

"It was a quick trip, there wasn't really time." Or at least this was what my father said when he called me, days after I got home, to explain why he hadn't returned any of my messages. I didn't tell Adam that part, but he looked at me with so much sympathy that I think he must have guessed it. I put the car in gear. "Okay, let's go to California."

"Let's stop in Ellsworth first."

"What's in Ellsworth?"

"The past," he said, and took my hand, intertwining his fingers with mine. "And maybe something else."

An hour later, we walked down the little main street, huddled together against the cold. Most of the stores were closed for the night, but many of them still had holiday displays in the windows, ghostly and twinkling in the gloom. A mannequin wearing a Santa hat and trendy glasses stared blankly from the window of an optician; a white Christmas tree glittered in the lobby of a bank. Up ahead, the door of a pub with a blinking neon Budweiser sign opened, spilling out a group of laughing people and the tantalizing scent of fried food. Across the street, a gold and green deco theater marquee wished us a happy new year, the word *GRAND* looming over it in letters six feet high. Something stirred in my memory, a story I'd loved that wasn't mine.

"Mimi was here," I said. "This is where everyone came, after the fire."

Adam nodded. "But she came by boat, with Theo. So they were here together—"

"Unchaperoned," I finished, laughing a little. I pointed at the theater. "I wonder if that's the same one they went to." It had been one of the few perks for everyone from the island who arrived in Ellsworth with no home to go back to: free admission at the movie theater. My grandparents had used it as a meeting place, where they could hide together in a crowd, in the dark, safe from the prying eyes of Mimi's parents. When I'd asked my grandmother which movies she'd seen here, she said, "I haven't the faintest idea," and winked.

I used to laugh at the idea of my grandparents, young and in love and surreptitiously canoodling in the back row of a theater, gazing at each other and completely ignoring whatever was on-screen. An old-timey precursor to "Netflix and chill." But now I shivered, thinking of all the times I'd heard that story, and how I'd never hear it again. How the story itself would die, too, untold, gathering dust from disuse until you couldn't even see the shape of it anymore. Mimi had entrusted me with her memories, each of them better and more fascinating than anything I'd ever done or lived myself—but all the fascination in the world couldn't make them mine. How many details had I already forgotten? How many had I never known, because I didn't think to ask?

Adam nudged his shoulder against mine. "What are you thinking?"

"I was thinking . . ." I paused, debating how honest to be. And then deciding, suddenly and recklessly, not to hold back. "All those days I spent with her, it was like I was hoping some of whatever she had would rub off on me. Like she could teach me how to live. I was using her to make myself more interesting . . . and it didn't even work. Look at me right now: all I'm doing is retracing her steps, retelling her stories. Like I'm plagiarizing her life. She told my mom she was a parasite, but really—"

"Uh-uh," he said, cutting me off, and grabbed me by both hands. "Nope, I'm sorry, but you're not going to call yourself a parasite. Nobody talks about the girl I love that way."

My mouth hung open as I stared at him. "Did you just . . ." I said, and he replied, "Yes I did," and before I could speak again, he was kissing me. Right out in the open, as the cold and wind swirled around us, with one arm wrapped around my waist and his other hand resting against my cheek. Slowly and for a long time, as if he had all the time in the world. And then finally, finally, he pulled back and looked into my face. I smiled up at him. It took me a moment to realize that he wasn't smiling back. He held my gaze, his eyes dark and serious.

"So I love you," he said. "I wanted to say that first. Because I have some other things to say, too, and they're hard things. Just remember what I told you first. I love you. Okay?"

A chill ran through me as I looked at him. The wind was rising, the night was getting colder. I took a step back, crossing my arms protectively over my chest. I thought for a moment about taking another one, and another—about turning and bolting into the night, not even waiting to hear whatever it was that could make him look at me with so much misery in his face.

"What are you talking about?" I said quietly.

His shoulders slumped. "I've been lying to you."

"About what?"

"About everything."

17.

He told me everything then. The story I thought I knew, about how he'd been raised by his grandmother after his parents' death when he was seven, was a lie. He'd invented it: a past just sad enough to keep someone like me from asking too many questions, from ever probing deeper into the tragic, terrible truth that lay underneath.

Adam had been a mistake, he said. Born to an eighteen-year-old mother and a deadbeat father who had abandoned the family so quickly that his son had no memory of him at all. His mother, saddled with a kid she'd never wanted, had tumbled downhill into a life of needles and booze and bad men from the moment he was old enough to feed himself. Adam had tried to take care of her, doing the best he could—right up to the moment that the police, tipped off by a neighbor, kicked open the door and found the two of them watching cartoons at ten o'clock on a Tuesday. A woman in her underwear in a drugged-out daze, and her boy, seven years old, unwashed and malnourished, sitting on the floor with three fat cockroaches chasing up and down the length of his little legs.

He told me how his maternal grandmother swooped in then, how he was loved and sheltered for nearly five years before a heart attack took her, and the system took him. By the time he'd aged out of foster care, he had been in and out of a dozen different houses, halfway homes, and juvenile detention facilities.

Six weeks after his eighteenth birthday, he was crashed on a friend's couch when the police kicked down the door looking for drugs and guns. Everyone in the house was arrested. Adam's lawyer told him not to be stupid, to rat out his friends and keep himself out of prison. He did.

Then he fled—except that he had nowhere to go. No family, no friends, no plans, no prospects. His parents were dead by then, his mother of an overdose, his father in prison. The world had spent years chewing him up. Now it had spit him out.

"I'm not telling you this to try to make you feel sorry for me," he said. "I'm just asking you to understand how alone I was. I was so alone that I got certified as a health aide instead of becoming a janitor even though it's more work for the same money, because at least this way I could be around people. I started working in assisted living because that's most of the job, just being with people, talking to them. Listening to them. And I convinced myself for a long time that it was enough. But then I met you, and I wanted . . . more."

He stood there, hands stuffed in his pockets, misery painted over his face. The few feet of space that had opened up between us when I instinctively stepped back suddenly felt huge and cold and empty—and when I looked at Adam standing there on the other side of it, something twisted inside me. The expression on his face was so haunted, so hopeless. As if it was already over between us. As if he'd been left alone so many times that there was no other way it could end. I thought about the little boy he used to be, a kid trying desperately to take care of the woman who was supposed to take care of him. I had wondered so many times what would draw a guy like Adam to this kind of life, this kind of work, when he could have done anything. I didn't wonder anymore. This was his pattern. Taking care of people at their most vulnerable—he was making up for his old failure, doing for all these other people what he couldn't do for his mother.

"Why are you telling me this?" I said. "Why now?"

"Because you deserve the truth. And because . . ." He paused. "Because I deserve it, too. I've been so ashamed that I couldn't really live. All this time, ever since that day I ratted out my friends to stay out of prison—I was so busy running from my past that I never thought about the future. But then you came, and everything changed, Delphine. I didn't want to live like that anymore. I wanted to be a better man, the kind of man who is worthy of someone like you. But I could never be that person unless I told the truth about who I used to be."

"Because you love me."

"Yes. I love you."

Neither one of us spoke after that. I looked down the dark street, empty but for those pools of light spilling from the windows onto the sidewalk. I imagined Adam walking anonymously through a town like this, one of the many towns he'd lived in as he made his way north. A man with nothing—no friends, no family. A man too ashamed of his past to ever dream of a better life. I imagined the courage it must have taken to keep going. To bear that weight. To keep living each day, battling against the loneliness. And one day to find the strength to believe in someone else—and in a future where he wasn't alone anymore.

I only had one other question.

"Was it a ring? In the box you gave me?" I had found it on my nightstand hours after we'd found Mimi's body and stared at it, a relic of a yesterday so distant that I couldn't fathom it, couldn't touch it. The idea of opening a present in that moment, of celebrating anything at all, was obscene. I'd handed the box back to Adam before he left that night. He'd taken it with a wordless nod.

He nodded. "It was. I mean, it still is. I brought it with me, in case . . . well, in case this conversation didn't end with you punching me in the face and telling me you never want to see me again."

"Is that what you thought? You thought I would break up with you because you didn't have a perfect childhood?"

"The kind of stuff I got into is a lot worse than *not perfect*. Especially for someone like you."

"Someone like me," I said. "You mean someone with money."

"It's not just the money, Delphine. It's different worlds. You've never been alone like that. And you have a family who loves you. You think your mom would be okay with it if she knew we were together? You think she'd be okay with you ending up with someone like me?"

"My mother doesn't care about any of that. She would want me to be with someone who makes me happy."

"You say that now," he said. "The funny thing is, I've been telling myself the same thing. That if we both wanted it, it wouldn't matter how different we were or if anyone else approved. But now that I'm standing here, I can see so clearly that it's crazy. It's crazy to ask you to marry me, and if you said yes, that'd be crazy, too. I'm never going to be good enough. You deserve someone who can give you everything."

A chill ran down my spine, another echo of the past. "You know my grandfather said something like that to Mimi when he proposed."

He laughed at the look on my face. "Yeah, I know. I stole his line. But it's a good one, and it's true."

"But she said yes," I said. I thought suddenly of the first time my grandmother had told me that story, during an early visit when I was still reeling from how things had ended in New York, and Adam was just another member of the staff, albeit a little more attentive and a lot better looking than the others. I'd told her it seemed a little rash to me, that she'd marry a guy she'd been seeing for barely two months, one she knew her parents wouldn't approve of. She'd just smiled at me—and then glanced at Adam, as if she were trying to tell me something, as if she'd known before I did that something would happen between us. Then she'd leaned close and whispered, "When it's meant to be, you don't want to wait."

I'd thought then that she was crazy.

Now I understood that she'd simply known her own heart and trusted it, in a way I never had. Never thought I could.

I stepped forward, moving into the space between us, until it was gone and we were touching.

"Yes," I said.

Adam stared at me. "What?"

"Yes," I said more emphatically. "I'm saying yes. I'll marry you. Let's get married."

He leaned in, taking my face in his hands, his eyes deep and intense and so hungry that it was frightening.

"Don't say yes if you don't mean it. Because I mean it. I would do anything for you. Do you understand? Anything. So if you don't mean it or if you're not sure—"

I threw my hands up and practically yelled, "Yes! It's yes!" and in a single movement his hands slid around my waist, his mouth found mine. And for a long time after that, neither one of us said anything else.

Hours later, after we'd kissed on the street for what felt like forever and then drove to a hotel where we spent a second thrilling eternity having post-I-love-you sex, I felt him pull my hand out from beneath the duvet. I was curled up, nearly asleep, but my eyes flew open as I felt him slide the ring onto my finger.

"It's not a diamond," he said. "I looked for one, but they're really expensive." He looked so nervous that I laughed in spite of myself.

"Never liked diamonds much." I raised my hand, ready to fake enthusiasm no matter what was there, but I gasped with delight when I saw what he'd given me. It was a garnet, deep red and glistening, encircled by a lacy filigree setting, as if someone had spun a golden web to catch a drop of blood. "Oh, I love it. I love it. It's an estate piece, isn't it?"

"If that's how you rich kids say 'secondhand,' then yeah. That right there is the certified used car of engagement rings."

"Stop, I think it's romantic," I said. "I love thinking about who might have worn this before me."

"It was some fat lady."

"What?!" I screeched, and he started to laugh.

"I'm serious," he said. "That's what it says inside. It says *fat*."

I tugged the ring off my finger and peered at the inner band. The engraving on the inside was worn and hard to read, but sure enough, there it was: the ring was inscribed to F.A.T., from someone named Olly.

"Well, it's an honor to wear Fat's ring," I said. "I'll try to be worthy of it."

Adam was still grinning. "I don't know, girl, those are some big shoes to fill. For all we know, Fat was twice the woman you are."

I was laughing so hard I could barely speak. I took a deep breath and managed to gasp, "I see this as a growth opportunity," then collapsed into his arms. He had brought our bags in from the car and was dressed for bed in old joggers and a T-shirt.

"You'll stay with me tonight, won't you? I really want you to. And not just because I need you to drive me home."

I buried my face in his chest. "I'll stay."

"Is there anyone you want to call?"

"Call? What for?"

"To tell them you're engaged?" His voice was teasing. "No friends, no family? No crazy competitive girlfriend who'd straight-up shit herself if she knew you got engaged before she did?"

I cringed a little, imagining whom I might call; apart from the dutiful *so sorry for your loss* messages that flooded in after Mimi died, I hadn't talked to any of my old friends in months. "I can't think of anyone. Except my mom, and that's going to be . . . complicated."

"No hurry. We'll figure it out together," he said. I buried my face in his chest and breathed deeply. Thinking what a lovely phrase that was: *No hurry*. I wasn't in a hurry. I was exactly where I wanted to be. Wrapped in Adam's arms, warm and safe, smelling the soft clean scent of laundry detergent, the slightly zingy aroma of Old Spice, the heady notes of his sweat underneath. And then, just for a moment, just as I turned my head to rest my ear against his chest, one last thing: the light and slightly medicinal scent of lavender.

Lavender from a field in France. Lavender growing at the end of a dark path in the brackish mud.

Lavender on my grandmother's arthritic hands as I held them in mine.

My eyes flew open and I sat up so fast I saw stars. "Oh my god," I said.

Adam sat up, too, looking scared. "What? What is it?"

My breath caught in my throat. "Mimi. When they found her, I just remembered—"

"Oh, babe, you shouldn't," he started to say, but I cut him off with a furious shake of my head.

"No, you don't understand. She was wearing her boots."

He stared at me, his face blank. "Of course she was. It was freezing outside."

"Adam," I said. My heart began to race as gooseflesh rippled over my bare skin. "How did she get them on?"

18.

For two weeks, I kept the engagement a secret. More than a secret: it sat in my guts like a stone, weighed down by the horrifying possibility that Mimi hadn't wandered onto the ice by accident. I'd been so consumed by guilt, the sense that she'd still be alive if only I'd heard her get out of bed that night, it seemed like nothing could be worse. But there was something worse. More haunting, more horrible, and now I saw it every time I closed my eyes. A shadow shaped like a man, black and spectral, with long fingers and no face. I imagined him standing over my grandmother as she slept, whispering into her ear. I saw him bending low to tie the laces of her boots and stretching a skeletal hand to disengage the dead bolt above the back door. I saw him drifting alongside her as she walked the pine path, those long fingers wrapped around her arm. Sometimes he was broad-shouldered, wearing a peaked cap, like the silhouette I thought I imagined in the hallway. A shadow among the shadows.

He always comes at night, she'd said.

I thought she was being haunted by the ghostly fragments of her own memories. What if the ghost wasn't a ghost at all?

Even with so many of us in the house, even with Adam here, nobody could watch her every second. There had been so many times when Mimi was alone, and that one day, those many hours, when she'd disappeared completely. What if someone had been watching her, watching *us?* Creeping around corners, hiding in the shadows, filling the blank spaces in her mind with poisonous thoughts. Planting the seeds, biding his time. Waiting for the chance he knew would come, to lead her away into the dark. Someone who wanted to hurt her.

But I couldn't say that aloud. Just thinking about it made me feel hysterical, paranoid, insane. The more I imagined that shadow, the more indistinct it became, until it started to look like anyone—or everyone. It was Richard, getting the payback he felt he deserved for the weird grudge he'd been nursing since childhood. It was Diana, who wanted Mimi to hurry up and die so that she could claim her inheritance. It was my own mother, angry and exhausted by the endless grind of keeping the house and managing my grandmother's affairs, giving both herself and Mimi the gift of a quick release. They appeared in my mind one by one, lacing up Mimi's boots, taking her by the arm, disengaging the dead bolt, and leading her out into the dark.

I couldn't say that to anyone. Certainly not to my family or the police. And when I tried to say it to Adam, he stared at me like I'd grown a second head. "You can't really believe that," he said.

We were sitting in the parking lot at McDonald's, holding coffees that were too hot to drink as the wind blew furiously outside. He'd begun working extra hours at Willowcrest—so we could save up to get married, he said, which was so sweet that I couldn't bring myself to point out how unnecessary it was. But Willowcrest was the one place I had no reason or desire to go to anymore, and this was the first time I'd seen him in nearly a week, stealing an hour of time and a shitty coffee before I drove back to the island and he started his evening shift.

"I don't know what I believe," I said.

Adam shook his head. "Baby, I know you're grieving. You're looking for an explanation. Nobody planned—"

"Of course nobody planned!" My voice broke. "Who would plan for this? She drowned in the middle of the night, cold and alone, in her fucking nightgown."

"Yeah, but"—he grimaced, looking uncomfortable—"you and your mom, and your aunt and your uncle, you tried to . . . orchestrate. All families do. You wanted to control what was happening. So you make a schedule, you lock the doors, you do everything you can to make a bad thing less bad. But people die. They die no matter what you do and how much you try, and no matter how much you love them. All the planning in the world doesn't change how it ends."

I didn't answer. It was a pretty speech, one in which he'd said all the right things, but all I could hear was what he didn't say: that when Adam said *planning,* what he really meant was money. All the money in the world. And he was right: My family had tried to buy ourselves a sense of control. We tried to buy time, to buy a gentler, softer goodbye—not for my grandmother's sake, but for ours. And in return, we'd been taught a brutal lesson about what we could and couldn't control. Adam was trying to help me see that, to help me let go.

But I couldn't.

"She still had her boots on, Adam. Even if you're right about everything, how do you explain that?"

He sighed. "She must have put them on herself."

"But she couldn't. You know she couldn't. Someone had to have helped her."

"Who, though?"

I hesitated. "I don't know. Richard. Or—" I broke off, frustrated. "That's the thing. It could have been anyone. Everyone in the house had a reason to want her gone."

He raised an eyebrow. "Everyone?"

"Fine, not you. And not me. But everyone else? My uncle didn't even try to hide how he felt about her. My aunt . . . I told you what I heard. The will reading is tomorrow, and she's so impatient about it that she flew in today so we could do it first thing in the morning. I think she needs money, or her husband does."

"You said everyone. What about your mom?"

I shifted uncomfortably in my seat. "She left her entire life behind to move up here and take care of Mimi. Maybe she was angry. Maybe she just wanted it to be over."

"There's a difference between wanting something and doing something. Do you think she could have hurt your grandmother? Really?"

"If she was angry enough, or desperate enough, or . . ." I trailed off, thinking of the bruise on Mimi's neck. Wondering if it had still been there when they pulled her from beneath the ice a day later, dark against her frozen flesh. I shuddered. "It's not like I don't realize how nuts this sounds when I say it out loud. But we were so busy fighting with each other, we were all drunk half the time—and that house is so damn big. Maybe it wasn't someone in my family. Anyone could have been hiding there, even sleeping there, and we wouldn't have known. And she said there was someone. She said she saw a man—"

and so did I, I almost said, but didn't. I tried to sip my coffee instead, wincing as it seared my tongue.

"She said a lot of things. Hell, she *saw* a lot of things. You know that. Hallucinations, confusion, those are normal."

"And the shells outside her window? Did we hallucinate those? What if someone was watching her, messing with her head when she was alone?"

"Someone like who?"

"I don't know. Someone from the past, maybe. The people she knew back then, some of them must still be here. Maybe she had an enemy, or—"

"Now you're being ridiculous," Adam said, impatience creeping into his voice. "Anyone who was on the island back when your grandmother lived here would be as old as she was. You're talking about people in their eighties."

But that's not true, I thought, and felt gooseflesh rise on my skin.

"What?"

"Jack Dyer isn't in his eighties," I said. "And the last time I talked to him, I got the distinct impression that he wasn't exactly a fan of my grandmother."

"That's the guy whose mom worked for your family?"

"Yes. You saw them at the funeral."

"I remember. She had that iPad. I think she took my picture."

"Yeah, she took mine, too," I said. "Not at the funeral, though. At the bakery."

"Which bakery?"

"The one we went to, where I got that holiday cake? Jack was there when I went in." I shook my head, remembering. "God, he was such a dick. Thank god Mimi didn't want to come in. Who knows what he would have said to her? Anyway, Shelly was in his truck in the parking lot. She took my picture when I came out."

"You never told me that."

I shrugged. "I didn't want to upset Mimi. There was obviously some kind of falling-out between her and Shelly, something bad enough that her son is still angry about it."

"What could be bad enough for him to want to hurt your grand-mother?"

"Maybe someone should ask him." I paused. "Or her. Shelly. I wonder if she knows he's been coming around. Maybe I should talk to her."

"That'll be tricky. Shelly doesn't really do visitors. And she can't talk back."

"I'll figure something out."

"Yeah, of course. Tell me if I can help." Adam glanced at the dash-board clock. "I need to get back."

I put the car in gear. I felt him looking sidelong at me as I pulled out of the parking lot and headed back toward Willowcrest.

"Can I say something?" he said.

I felt a flare of irritation, and then felt bad for feeling it. It wasn't

Adam I was angry with. "You don't need to ask my permission to speak," I said.

He took my hand. "I don't want to tell you what to do. But the way you're obsessing over this, babe, it's not healthy. You know Miriam wouldn't want you tormenting yourself like this."

The turn to Willowcrest loomed ahead and I signaled, passing through the front gates and down the long drive that reminded me of the one that led to the Whispers, pulling into a space where nobody looking out could see Adam getting out of my car.

He leaned over to kiss me and smiled. "It'll be nice when I can kiss you in front of everyone at work," he said.

I smiled back. "It'll be nicer when you quit this job and we move to Palm Springs and open a cat café."

He winced. "I'm allergic."

"You are?" I blinked, surprised. "How could I not know that?"

"It never came up," he said, laughing. "Is this a deal-breaker?"

"I guess it could be a hairless cat café."

"Sounds disgusting. I'm in," he said, and kissed me again. "Get home safe."

But I didn't go home.

The idea of talking to Shelly had lodged itself in my mind, and I kept returning to it as I drove. It wasn't just that I wanted to ask her about Jack; it was that she knew things about Mimi, answers I had no other way of ever getting. She was the one person left who had known my grandmother when she was younger. She had stories, memories. Even her son had said so. And if she couldn't talk, there still had to be a way for me to ask questions and let her answer them.

The bridge that led back to Mount Desert Island loomed ahead, but I was already slowing, pulling a U-turn and driving back in the direction of Willowcrest.

Not long after, I was back in the parking lot where I'd kissed Adam goodbye just an hour before. I parked at the far end and considered my next move. Adam had said that Shelly didn't do visitors, which could mean one of two things: either that she didn't get many visitors, or that she was one of the residents with limits on who was allowed in to see her. I briefly considered texting him and then decided not to risk it; if I was breaking a rule by visiting Shelly, better that I didn't get him involved. I got out of the car, pulling my hood low over my head, and approached the entrance. I was in luck: Tasha, the receptionist, was standing at the opposite end of the sidewalk, hunched against the cold with her back turned to me. She was holding a vape pen in one hand, her phone in the other, and she was talking animatedly to someone on the other end. I caught a snatch of her end of the conversation ("and I was like, 'That is *way* too much puke for one person,'" she was saying), and then I was through the door, head down, hurrying around the corner and toward the residential wing where Mimi had lived.

It was just after five o'clock, dinnertime, and my heart sank as I realized that I had timed this poorly, and Shelly had probably already been wheeled down to the cafeteria. But when I turned the last corner toward what had been Mimi's room, I found I was in luck: her door was closed, and beside it, a small white light was glowing to show that she was still at home. Even if I had time to ask her only a couple of questions, it was a start.

I knocked and then tried the handle, which turned easily under my palm. "Hello," I called, slipping through the door. There was only one light on, a table lamp at the far end of the room, but I could see Shelly sitting in her wheelchair beside it. She was faced away from me, looking out through the glass sliding door that opened onto a small deck. In the summer the deck had a nice view, a small pond with a fountain where ducks swam. I'd sat there sometimes with Mimi, watching the birds while she reminisced. But the pond was invisible now, covered in snow, the fountain shut off for the winter.

"Hi," I said, hovering inside the door. "I'm Delphine. Miriam's granddaughter. We met—or, I mean, we saw each other. At the funeral. I hope you don't mind . . ."

I trailed off, waiting for an answer, then realized that of course I wouldn't get one. Shelly was half-paralyzed; she couldn't even twist around to look at me, let alone tell me if she minded whether I was here or not. I pulled the door closed behind me and moved quickly into the room, so she'd be able to see me.

"Anyway," I was saying, trying to sound cheerful, "I wanted to visit you. I was hoping I could ask—"

The rest of the sentence died in my throat as I neared Shelly's chair. She still hadn't turned to look at me, and now I understood why.

Shelly was dead, her head rocked back at an angle, her eyes open and bulging. Her face was a mottled purple, and her tongue dangled grotesquely from her mouth, where a thin foamy dribble of saliva tinged with something dark—blood, I thought—had escaped from one corner and run down toward her chin. I stared in horror, wondering if I should try CPR even as my rational brain pointed to that protruding tongue, that mottled skin, and told me it was much too late. For several long moments, I didn't move.

And then from the hallway came the sound of voices, a light knock on the door. "Miz Dyer," a woman's voice called. "Sorry, we're just a bit behind schedule. It'll be just another moment."

My guts twisted with panic. I told myself I could stay, let them find me here and try to explain—but my body was a step ahead, my hand already reaching for the handle on the sliding door. It opened easily and I slipped through without a sound, closing it quickly and hoping that the cold wouldn't linger in the room. A low railing ran around the deck and I climbed over it, brushing away the handprints I'd left in the snow, sinking shin-deep into a drift as my feet hit the ground. I gasped as snow filled the open tops of my boots, then clamped my hand over my mouth: in the room I'd just left, a light had come on. I slunk back against the side of the building, waiting. Wondering if they'd seen me.

But no shadow appeared at the glass door, no one opened it to peer out. Instead, there was a pause, and then another voice—male this time, and familiar—said, "Oh, Jesus. Is she—"

I hugged the wall, crept around the corner of the building, and ran. I knew how the rest would go. I didn't need to hear it.

19.

Adam called me the next day to tell me that Shelly had died. "I'm really sorry," he said before I could tell him I already knew. "I mean, I know you didn't really know her, but I feel bad that I didn't bring you in to see her yesterday when you said something about it. I just had no idea she was in such bad shape."

"Was it another stroke?" I asked, realizing as I did that I had decided not to tell him, or anyone else, that I'd been there last night.

"I think so. I was on movie night duty on the other side of the facility, so I only heard about it this morning." He paused. "Do you want me to find out?"

I thought of Shelly's mottled skin, the lolling tongue, and shuddered. Did I need to know anything else? All the questions I'd wanted to ask her were about her life. Her death, which I'd already seen too much of, was none of my business. "No. I don't need you to do that."

"Okay," he said. "I should go. Will I see you later?"

"Not today. Too much packing. And . . ." I hesitated.

"What?"

"It's just, my mom looks at me sideways every time I leave the house, and I'm running out of excuses."

"Maybe it's time to tell her the truth," he said, and before I could answer, he added, "Just think about it. I love you." There was a beep as the call ended, no time for me to say, *I love you too.*

I wove between the cardboard stacks as I found my way to the kitchen, where I poured coffee into a mug I'd decided I wanted to keep. The Whispers was in transition now, full of boxes and bags into which we had started putting the remnants of Mimi's life. We were supposed to organize it all into three categories—keep, toss, donate—but things kept finding their way out of the second two boxes and into the first. It was the most useless stuff that seemed suddenly priceless: a half-used lipstick, an old grocery list, a pair of ancient shoes whose brand-new soles meant they must have been her favorite.

My mother appeared, lugging a trash bag that looked ready to burst at the seams. "Someone has to take this to the church donation box," she said.

I looked around at the empty kitchen. "Someone?"

"Well, one of us. But since you always seem to be off somewhere, I figured you could take it on your way to wherever you keep going."

I shrugged, pretending I didn't notice that I was obliquely being asked a question. "Sure," I said, grabbed the bag, and left without another word.

In town, I stuffed the bag into the donation box behind the church thrift store and then walked back the way I came, pausing to gaze up at the church, its needlelike steeple rising high above the roofline so that it could be seen from anywhere in town. The gravestones in the churchyard cemetery were half-buried in the snow, jutting here and there like gray and jagged teeth. It was haunting, but meaningless: Mimi would never be buried here, not even when spring came and the ground was finally soft enough again to dig a grave. The plan was to scatter her ashes off the coast the following summer, as close as we could to the spot where my grandfather was supposed to have fallen overboard and drowned. The two of them reunited at last, the molecules of what used to be their bodies drifting together in the same endless sea.

"Hello," a voice said, very close behind me, and I jumped. I turned to see Reverend Frank smiling apologetically.

"I was sitting by the window and saw you pass by," he said, pointing back behind him to the small rectory beside the church. "The first time I thought you looked familiar, and the second time I realized why. And now here you are. Miriam's granddaughter, yes?"

"Yes."

"Are you here for the meeting? You're a bit early."

"Meeting?"

"Alcoholics Anonymous. Parish library, three times per week. First-timers sometimes do a few laps around the block before they can bring themselves to come inside."

I laughed nervously. "Oh no. I guess I'm just . . . loitering."

"Church is always a good place to loiter." He chuckled. "Perhaps you'd like to come in for a moment?"

"What for?"

He shrugged. "Whatever you might need. A cup of coffee. A rest. A conversation about whatever's bothering you enough that you're standing around on the street in this godforsaken weather."

I hesitated. "I don't want to bother you," I said finally.

He chuckled and looked at his watch. "I'm not bothered at all," he said. "And I need to be in the library in twenty minutes, so it would have to be brief. But if I can be of help . . ." The last part of his sentence was cut off by a sudden gust of frigid wind, so powerful it made me stagger backward. We both laughed.

"Okay, I'll come in."

Inside the rectory, the reverend poured me a cup of coffee and pointed to one of two wingback chairs that were set on either side of a farmhouse window. Beyond the patchwork glass I could see the cemetery and the sidewalk beyond, where we'd been standing a moment ago.

"So," he said after I'd settled in and taken a sip. "Is there something you want to talk about?"

My mind flashed on the memory of Shelly's open mouth and bulging eyes, and I shuddered. There was something I wanted to talk about, but the person I'd wanted to talk about it with was dead. All I had now was shapeless suspicion, grief, and questions that nobody could ever answer—but then, I thought, the priest was probably used to that.

"I guess I've been thinking a lot about my grandmother," I said. "There are things about her death, things I wish I understood."

He nodded. "But of course, you must know that how you feel is normal. Death is rarely tidy. There will always be loose ends, unanswered questions. Conversations you wish you had, things you wish you'd known."

"I know it's normal. It still feels . . ." *Like shit,* I almost said, and caught myself. "Feels bad."

He nodded. "We talked about this, you know. Miriam and I. Her past and her legacy. She had a very clear idea of how she wanted to leave this world, and about which of those loose ends she wanted to tie, so that she could move on without regret."

I frowned. Mimi had never talked to me about dying, and of course I never brought it up; it had never occurred to me that she might be making plans.

"When did you last see her?"

"Maybe a day or two before she left Willowcrest."

"I guess you can't tell me what you talked about," I said.

The reverend smiled. "Well, people have to be able to trust me to keep their confidences. I won't tell your mother, for instance, that we've spoken." I must have looked startled, because he chuckled again. "Not that she would ask. Purely hypothetical. But I can speak broadly. I can tell you that the seniors I visit with at Willowcrest almost always have the same concerns. At the end of a life, there are choices we've made, things we regret, things a member of the clergy can help a person come to terms with."

"They want to get right with God," I said.

"That's one way of putting it, sure. And I've heard every sort of story. Some of them are pretty banal, some small misdeed or misunderstanding that the person has become fixated on. Some are heartbreaking— the lost loves, the family estrangements. And sometimes . . . well, sometimes it's something far worse. It's rare that I hear something that shocks me, but even then I try to have compassion. Nobody suffers more than a person who's carried a terrible secret all their life." He looked somber. "So I try to offer solace. And your grandmother—I won't tell you which category she fell into. Some of what we discussed, she intended to take to the grave, and I have to honor her wishes. But I will tell you that when we last spoke, I believe she had found peace."

He paused, hesitated like he was going to say something else, and then didn't.

I found myself shaking my head. "Even if she found peace, she wouldn't have remembered."

"Ah, but God remembers. That's the beauty of it. We put our faith in God to know us, to be the guardian of our truth—and he forgives us, whether we remember asking for forgiveness or not." He paused. "Your grandmother had fallen away from the church, but she still had faith. And hope. I hope you can find some comfort in that."

I felt sheepish. "I don't know if it's comforting. I don't even know if I believe in God."

"What if I told you that was perfectly all right?"

"I'd think you were good at your job," I said, laughing a little. "But that's a lot of trust to put in something I'm not even sure is real."

"Do you struggle with that? Trust?"

"Maybe," I said, thinking of Adam. *You look for a way to control what's happening,* he'd said. *To make the bad thing less bad.* I twisted the garnet ring on my finger, then stopped as Reverend Frank looked at it, looked at me, and tilted his head as if he had suddenly understood something. The silence stretched between us.

"You know," he said finally, "there's a saying I often think of at moments like this. 'Let go or be dragged.'"

"That's in the Bible?"

He laughed. "Oh, I saw it on a bumper sticker. But I believe that good advice can come from anywhere. I'm afraid I have to start getting ready for the meeting, but if you'd like to talk more, my door is always open."

"Sure." We both stood.

I turned to go, and then turned back. "You were going to say something before," I said. "After you said that Mimi had found peace. There was something else. What was it?"

Sympathy mixed with sadness flickered over his face. "I was thinking of the last time I saw Miriam. She was looking forward to spending Christmas with you and your family at the Whispers, but she was a bit confused. She said her husband was going to be there." He paused. "And when she said goodbye, she told me we wouldn't be seeing each other again."

I spent the rest of the day thinking about what the priest had told me. About Mimi letting God do the forgiving while she did the forgetting. About the secrets, whatever they might have been, that she had taken to her grave. About the way she'd said goodbye to him, as if she'd known it was for the last time. My grandmother had found peace. She was ready, and now she was gone.

Let go or be dragged, he'd said. A bumper-sticker proverb—but one that rang embarrassingly true. How many times in my life had I done this, clinging desperately to a moment that was already over, refusing to say goodbye to someone who was already gone? I thought of the night my roommates told me to move out, the way I'd cried and begged to stay just a little longer, another month, another week, unable to stop myself even as I saw Clarissa exchange looks with Colin, her lip curling beneath her septum piercing as she mouthed the word *pathetic*. I thought of the boyfriend who'd broken up with me my junior year of college, and how I kept asking for one more conversation, one more shot at working it out, until he texted me back with a numbered list of all the reasons why he didn't want to date me anymore. (*Bad breath* was the first entry; the last one, number 15, was *Because you forced me to write this fucking list.*)

I thought about my father letting my calls go to voice mail.

Obsessing about the circumstances of Mimi's death wasn't about her. It was about me. Casting myself in the role of detective meant that I would never have to unclench my fingers and release what had already slipped away; I could dwell forever on what might have been, and tell myself I was doing something important, courageous, noble.

The worst thing, the thing that made me cringe, was realizing how close I'd come to buying into my own bullshit.

But I didn't have to. I could let go. I could move forward. I could live my life without the fear of falling—and I could start by being honest about the person I wanted to live that life with.

Until we tell them.

It was time. It had, I realized, been time for a while.

The reading of the will was the next day, and I woke up early, full of nervous energy. In the morning, we would drive to Bangor to meet with Mimi's lawyer. And in the afternoon, on the drive back home, I would tell my mother the truth about Adam.

The house was quiet as I slipped outside and found my way to the pine path, past the deadfall, all the way to the place where we'd found Mimi's body. Snow had fallen overnight, only an inch or so, but it was enough to blanket everything so that the whole world looked soft and clean. I stood there a long time at the mouth of the sea, gazing out into the bay that was half-frozen and half hidden by fog, and pretended I could see her there—not the way she'd been when we found her, dead and stiff, her eyes open beneath the ice, but alive. Her back turned, her head held high, walking alone into whatever lay beyond the horizon. In this version of her last moment, there was no break in the ice, no plunge into the frozen sea. She just kept walking into the mist until I couldn't see her anymore. She was gone, and I was alone.

But I wasn't, I thought. Not anymore.

We drove in silence to Bangor. My mother seemed lost in her own world, drumming her fingers on the steering wheel. I looked out the window at the passing landscape and thought about California. I'd only ever been there once, but the place, even just the word, was imbued with promise. I thought about clean slates, fresh starts. I thought that when I left this place, the only thing I would miss about it was the way it looked under a blanket of freshly fallen snow.

And later I would remember this, and think that I should have known better. That I should have seen that beautiful white landscape for what it was. The fresh snow was a lie, an illusion, the thinnest and most fragile layer of beauty laid over an ugly world. It wouldn't last, couldn't, wasn't made to. All it took was a single footstep to break the spell and reveal the dirt underneath.

The lawyer's office was a front seating area with a receptionist on one side and three closed doors on the other. The receptionist nodded as we came in, but she seemed distracted, and it was immediately clear why: behind one of those doors, the one with a gold plate that read *Bernard Stewart, Esq.,* a woman was shouting. My mother hesitated, looked at me, looked back over her shoulder to where we'd parked the car.

"Maybe we should . . ." she started to say, but she never finished. The shouting reached a shrill peak and stopped. The closed door flew open. Diana stood there, her face pale, her eyes blazing.

"What's going on?" I asked at the same time as my mother said, "Why didn't you wait?" but neither of us would get an answer. Diana crossed the room in five quick steps. She stopped in front of me. Her mouth was quivering.

"You conniving little bitch," she said, and slapped me across the face.

20.

1960

AUTUMN

She is thirty-two and awake again.

Theodora is crying. Again.

Miriam startles awake as she does nearly every night to the sound of her youngest daughter screaming. She doesn't reach out for her husband, because he isn't there.

Theo hasn't shared her bed for many months now, not since she banished him to a spare room during the last pregnancy, a terrible slog of restless nights, crippling nausea, an ache deep in her lower back that never went away, even after the baby was born. Sometimes, between the bouts of vomiting, she had lain down on the bathroom floor, her forehead pressed to the cool porcelain pedestal of the toilet, remembering with bleary disbelief how different the first two had been. How easy, how full of joy and wonder and only the most mild occasional discomfort, so rare that it was almost a novelty. She'd felt so beautifully and completely like a woman then, strong and capable, her body humming along in its purpose and everything working just as it should.

There was none of that this time. Not only did Miriam not feel like a woman, but she hardly felt human at all. She was a shell, an incubator, a chrysalis made of flesh, wrapped around something hungry and angry that felt like it was trying to tear its way out.

She'd been grateful, especially during those final exhausted weeks, to be sleeping alone. But somehow the temporary arrangement had become permanent. Theodora went from being a vampire inside the womb to a screamer out of it. And Miriam's husband had come back to their shared bedroom for just one night before telling his wife that he'd be good for nothing on the water the next day if he couldn't get some shut-eye.

It's been more than a year since then. A year of spending her nights alone, sleeping with one eye open, waiting for the moment that always comes. The silence split by a shriek, the long stumble down the dark hall to the nursery. She gathers her youngest daughter into her arms, already saying, *shh, shh,* rocking her gently and hoping that this might be one of the rare nights when she calms and closes her eyes again.

But it isn't. Theodora doesn't want to be rocked. She wants to scream, scream, scream.

Once a week, Miriam speaks by phone to her mother in Egg Harbor. She says it'll get better. She says some babies are just difficult and every marriage has its rocky moments, and that Miriam needn't worry. She also says it's not a bad thing for a woman to have her own bed, her own space, especially in a house with so much of it—that she should be glad for her privacy.

But Miriam wishes more with each passing day, and each lonely night, that they'd never come back to the Whispers. If only she'd insisted on a place of their own, one of those little houses in town, cozy and quaint. A couple living in a place like that couldn't help but stay close, not when they were always bumping into each other on the stairs or in the kitchen—and if they had a spat, then they'd have to see it through and kiss and make up before they went to bed together at night. There'd be no room for resentments to fester, for someone to carry a grudge into an empty bedroom and nurse it there for weeks or months or years, for a husband to vanish behind one of a dozen closed doors just when you thought you might finally sit him down and make him talk to you.

Miriam and Theo still talk, of course, but not like they used to. Not when one of those old grudges has a way of suddenly popping up from wherever it's been hiding, poisoning the air between them and turning everything sour. They don't fight all the time, but there's always something to fight about. The charter boat, and whether Theo should be allowed to sell it when her father gave it to him as a gift. Miriam's cooking, which she knows has never been much good, but couldn't he pretend to like it? They fight about Theodora's incessant crying and whether she ought to be seen by the doctor, and they fight about whether to take her to the doctor in town or the one on the mainland. Just last year, Papa told Miriam he'd like to pay for young Richard to attend a fine boarding school, and there was a fight about that—until Papa finally said, *Let me talk to him,* and Miriam handed the phone to Theo, who listened for a while, his jaw clenched, and then hung up without saying goodbye. He turned to Miriam and said, "Send him away, then, if that's what you want," and the look on his face was so sad and strange—a look he'd never given her once in ten years together—that Miriam wished she'd left it alone. Even as Theo walked away and disappeared into some empty room, she told herself she would call her father back tomorrow and say she'd changed her mind.

But she didn't. In the cold light of day, it all seemed so silly, so unnecessary. It was a very fine school, after all, maybe even the finest. And so she sent Richard off, and this year, she sent Diana, too. Even though it made the house feel quieter, emptier, even more haunted by unsaid things.

Thank god for Shelly. If not for her, Miriam thinks she might have gone insane.

Shelly is their nanny and housekeeper, a petite dark-haired woman of twenty-seven who lives in at the Whispers six days a week. Hiring her was the last thing Miriam did before the doctor told her she'd have to spend the remainder of her pregnancy in bed, and it was less a decision than a foregone conclusion: Shelly was the first to interview for the job, and Miriam had been just about to inquire after the woman's references when she suddenly lurched across the room and threw up into a garbage can. When it was over, Shelly handed Miriam a handkerchief and helped her back to the sofa.

"You have a lie-down right here, missus, and I'll just take care of this," she said, whisking the soiled garbage can out of the room and returning ten minutes later with a cup of tea.

Later, when Theo asked if Miriam had offered the young woman the job, Miriam would give a bewildered laugh and say, "I didn't have a chance to offer. She just took it."

What she didn't say was *Thank the Lord she did.* Shelly had been a godsend during those final weeks of her pregnancy with Theodora, keeping the house in near-perfect order without a peep of complaint, minding the older children and playing nurse to the bedbound Miriam. But in the time since the baby arrived, things have changed. Shelly is something more than a servant. Miriam never had a sister, but she thinks that this is what it might have been like if she did: a little sister, headstrong and stubborn, and impetuous in a way that reminds Miriam so very much of her younger self. Shelly has a wicked sense of humor and doesn't suffer fools gladly. And Miriam, initially grateful for the help, quickly came to appreciate her company. When she isn't socializing or entertaining, she finds herself seeking the younger woman out, following her from room to room as she carries out her duties, joining her out in the yard and holding the basket of clothespins while she strings up the washing on the line. Shelly knows all the best gossip on the island, stories that pass through the small underground network of women who work as maids or cooks in the homes of wealthier folks, and she has a way of punching them up with dramatic pauses and little embellishments so that Miriam will forget the book or newspaper she's reading and sit, rapt, gasping or giggling, while Shelly tells her which well-bred young lady fell down drunk and lost one shoe in a snowbank last New Year's Eve, or which prim and proper widow was rumored to have poisoned her husband's tea. Once she'd spent the better part of an hour listening to the story of how one of Shelly's friends, a housekeeper in Northeast Harbor, had forgotten her keys at her employer's home and returned late in the evening to get them, only to walk in on the master of the house sashaying up and down the stairs in nothing but socks, garters, and a very expensive pair of his wife's high-heeled silk shoes.

"No," Miriam had gasped. "You're pulling my leg. But what did she do?"

"Well, according to Doris, she looked him right in the eye and said, 'You'll want a pink silk hat to match, sir, if you're wearing those to dinner,'" Shelly said, and Miriam doubled over and laughed fit to burst, so long and loud that Theo eventually appeared from the other room to ask what on earth was the matter, which just sent the two women into paroxysms all over again, until Shelly finally caught her breath enough to say, "Nothing at all, Mr. Caravasios, we were only talking about the latest fashions," and Theo said, "Ah, well then," and left the room with a bemused smile.

That was the other thing about Shelly: she never gossiped in front of Theo or paid him much attention at all. It made Miriam feel oddly proud—not just that Shelly obviously understood when to be discreet, but that Miriam alone had the privilege of her friendship, of hearing those fantastic stories.

There was a time when Shelly would have been beside her now, here in the wee hours of the morning when the silence was shattered by Theodora's howling. She would appear in the door of the nursery with a warm bottle of milk for Theodora and another cup for Miriam, the latter spiked with a bit of brandy, and the two of them would take turns rocking the baby until she fell back asleep. But Shelly has been staying out more often lately, ever since late summer when she started carrying on with a young sailor from the maritime academy down the coast. The man keeps her out till all hours, so that Shelly spends her morning moving at half speed and yawning all the while, usually until Miriam takes pity and tells her to go lie down for half an hour, for Pete's sake. She won't scold the girl, it's not her place nor her nature, but she worries all the same. She can't help it. A fisherman, like her husband, that's one thing. But a sailor . . . well, she's never known one, but she's heard plenty of stories. And not the fun and funny kind, but bad ones. Sad ones. Stories about men who turned out to be good-for-nothing scoundrels, who fill a girl's ears with pretty talk and promises that turn out to be nothing but lies. A man like that would break your heart, ship out and leave you with nothing but wasted time and a tarnished reputation. But then it's not as if Shelly has so many options, twenty-seven years old and never married, her whole life spent on this little island. It's a shame, pretty as she is.

This is how Miriam's mind wanders as she rocks Theodora alone in the dark. Theo is far down the hall, as far as he can get from his youngest daughter's nightly disturbances. Richard and Diana are a hundred miles away at their very fine boarding schools. And Miriam, holding the fussing baby in her arms and staring into the deep night beyond her bedroom window, feels terribly alone. As if she and this baby might just be the only two people left in the world.

When Theodora finally quiets, Miriam tiptoes down the stairs and into the kitchen, pouring some milk into a saucepan and setting it to heat while she goes in search of the brandy. She's halfway down the dark hallway when the wind rises outside and starts muttering under the eaves, a sound so much like a human voice that it makes her hair stand on end. But as she hurries back, the sighing of the wind fades— and in its place she hears something else, the sound of a raised voice from beyond the kitchen, hissing.

Don't, it says. *Don't, damn you.*

A crack of light is shining from beneath the door to Shelly's room, and Miriam moves toward it. She sees a shadow moving there. Another step. Her hand extends toward the doorknob. She bites her lip, her brow furrowed with disapproval: for Shelly to carry on with her sailor out of the house is one thing, but to bring him back here! And then the floorboards creak beneath her feet and the sound abruptly stops, and the door swings open in front of her. Shelly is in her nightdress, her short hair tousled and her eyes at half mast, as if she's only just woken up.

"Missus?" she says, blinking. "Is everything all right?"

"I thought I heard—" Miriam starts to say, but stops as she peers over Shelly's shoulder. The door is open, wide open so that she can see every inch of the room. There's nobody there, no one at all.

"The wind," Shelly says with a smile. "It woke me too. Sounds like it's talking sometimes, doesn't it?"

"It does."

"I always wondered why they'd call a house the Whispers, but I sure understand it now." She pauses, waiting for Miriam to say something else, but Miriam just looks past her again and doesn't say anything. She hasn't been in this room since she can't remember when, and the sight of it makes her cringe. It's so small, so dark and drafty. Looking around now at the bare walls, the threadbare rug on the floor, she wonders how Shelly stands it, and feels guilty that she herself never thought to suggest she stay in one of the rooms up-stairs. Confining the young woman to the servant's quarters—what was she thinking?

The answer comes immediately: She wasn't. She was just doing what was done, what they'd always done, a bit of snobbery left over from when her father, always so obsessed with the trappings of class and status, was master of this house. He'd made Smith sleep here, too, even though the man was practically his only friend.

But that time is over, fading into the past if not entirely gone. She thinks again of those cozy houses in town, with their picket fences and pretty gray shingles, just made for a family. There'd be no space for live-in help, of course, but she wouldn't need that, and she wouldn't miss it, either. How nice it would be to snuggle in with Theo, hus-band and wife and three little children, how nice to have a home that might not be the finest damn house on the island but would certainly be a happier one than this.

"Missus?" Shelly is looking at her strangely. "Are you all right? Did you need something?"

Miriam opens her mouth to speak, not knowing what she in-tends to say. She does need something, she thinks. She needs time to think, to look hard at the life she's stumbled into, to ask herself before it's too late if it's really what she wants, after all. She needs to knock at the closed door of Theo's bedroom upstairs and tell him she thinks she might have been a fool.

And she needs to stand here for a moment, just one moment more, because there's something about this room. Something about its place beside the kitchen, something that made it different from the other small, dark places in the house. Something important and something terrible.

One day she'll remember. One day, in this very room, she'll whis-per the urgent warning she would have given to herself long ago. About this room and this house, and the things that hide inside it.

But not tonight. Tonight Shelly is waiting, and the silence has already stretched too long, and so what she says is "No, thank you. Good night."

As she climbs the stairs with the hot milk in her hand, she can hear Theodora: awake, again.

Screaming, again.

21.

The sound of the slap hung in the air. I lifted a hand to my cheek, more out of reflex than anything else, too shocked by the act itself to really feel the sting of it. I had never been hit in the face before; my own mother had never even spanked me.

Mom was the first to break the silence, rushing to my side and putting her cool hands on either side of my face. "How dare you," she said, glaring at Diana, who was in turn staring at her own hand as if she couldn't believe what it—she—had done. Her face was deathly pale.

"I—" she gasped. "I'm sorry. I was just—"

"I don't want to hear another word!" Mom was angrier than I'd ever seen her. "If you ever touch my kid again, I swear to God—" She broke off, looking at me. "Are you all right?"

I took a step back from both of them and took a deep breath. "I don't know. I don't know what's happening. What the hell is this?"

Diana turned to my mother. "Five thousand dollars. That's it. That's what I get. And I'm guessing it's what you get, too, baby sister, because this greedy little thing"—she pointed at me—"probably wouldn't think twice about stabbing her own mother in the back, if it meant she got what she wanted. Isn't that right, Delphine?"

I took another uneasy step back. I didn't like the way Diana was scowling at me, but I liked the incredulous, unhappy expression on my mother's face even less.

"I don't know what you're talking about," I said, but this was only half-true. No, I didn't know, but I also wasn't stupid: between her comments and our current location, I could make a pretty good guess. Behind Diana, someone cleared his throat. I looked up to see a man standing at the door of the office she'd just stormed out of. He was medium height and balding, and he was looking at the three of us like we were a trio of escaped zoo animals—not the kind you're afraid might eat you, more like the kind you want to steer clear of because when they're mad, they start throwing feces.

He also looked like a guy who was pretty good at dodging airborne shit.

"Miss Lockwood? Delphine Lockwood?" he said, and although I wasn't stupid, I pointed at my own chest in my best impression of an idiot.

"Me?"

"You," he said. "We'll need to talk."

And that was how I found out that the twenty-million-dollar elephant in the room now belonged to me.

An hour later, I stood in the parking lot and watched Diana lose her mind all over again. We'd been through it in the lawyer's office, where Mr. Bernard Stewart, Esquire, had patiently explained that Mimi's will—amended to leave me nearly everything, and witnessed by two of his own most trusted associates—would not be easily challenged, although Diana was certainly welcome to try. Then the lawyer had borne the brunt of Diana's rage. Now it was my mother she was angry at.

"Are you going to tell me you had nothing to do with this? You had power of attorney, she couldn't have—" She broke off with a strangled noise as Mom shook her head.

"I didn't."

Diana's eyes looked like they might pop out of her head. "How? How could you not?"

"It was on the list." She paused. "It was the next thing on the list. She kept saying we'd talk about it, but then she declined so fast, it seemed like there was no point. I was probably going to have to go to court."

"She was so demented that she couldn't grant power of attorney, but she could still get a lawyer to change her will?" Diana snapped. "I don't believe you."

My mother's face was stony. "You heard Mr. Stewart. He found her totally competent and reasonable, and frankly I'm not surprised. She hid it awfully well, Diana. Even after she'd moved to Willowcrest, she hid it." She paused, and then her next words came out in a flood. "Which is something you'd know if you'd bothered to visit or just called to ask how she was doing. I would have told you anything you wanted to know. You think I enjoyed this? Caring for her by myself? You think I wouldn't have liked to have some support? Do you think I'm not as hurt right now as you are?"

Diana shifted her weight and looked at the floor. "I've had my own life to worry about," she said, and her mouth started to tremble. "I'm broke, you know."

Mom stared. "What are you talking about? I know that Mother gave you—"

"It's gone. Long gone. All gone."

"How? How is that possible?"

"William made a . . . bad investment. Worse than bad. He owes money, a lot of money. I thought if we came for Christmas—"

"That's why you came?" I said. "To squeeze Mimi for cash?"

She glared. "Of course that's not the only reason. But—"

"But it's the main one. That's why you wanted to get her alone." I turned to my mother. "I heard her and William talking. They were trying to figure out how to get Mimi away from everyone so they could talk to her without any of us knowing."

"That's not—" Diana squawked, but Mom just sighed and said, "Yes, I figured," and fixed her sister with a long look. "You could have asked me. Or at least told me. I have money. I would have tried to help. That's the part I don't understand."

Diana let out a humorless laugh. "Of course you don't understand! Honestly, Dora. No matter how old you get, you're always the baby, aren't you? Always oblivious. You have no idea what it was like, growing up here, having to compete with Richard for a teaspoon's worth of attention because that was all she had to give. He was right, you know. All of us pretending that she was some great mother—such a repulsive fucking farce. He was the smart one, opting out. I wish I could have. But no, I had to show up and make nice and take a bunch of bullshit walks down memory lane, and hope that maybe I could somehow get Mother to be more generous with her money than she was with her love. And for what? Nothing. Twenty million, and she's left me nothing but a table scrap. Which I guess I should be used to by now, but I'm not." Another humorless bark of laughter, shriller this time. "And I needed that money. *I needed that money.*"

"How badly do you need it?" I said quietly.

Diana gave me a cautious look. "What?"

"Badly enough to lie, right? Badly enough that you were trying to get her alone so you could try and get it without anyone knowing? Is that all, or was there more? How far would you have gone?"

"Delphine," my mother said nervously.

I ignored her, ignored the warning note in her voice. I couldn't stop. I leaned in close. "Did you need it so badly you would've killed for it?" I said, and Diana blanched.

"I'm not listening to this. Not from you." She turned to my mother. "And I'm challenging this. I don't care what that man says. You'll be hearing from my lawyer."

• • •

We rode home in silence. My mother asked me to drive and then said nothing else for nearly thirty minutes, furiously typing on her phone so that the only sound was the haptic clicking of the keyboard. I gripped the steering wheel, thinking about the way Diana's face had turned pale when I asked if she'd needed the money badly enough to kill for it. Had she? Could she? I didn't know Diana well enough to answer that—but worse, I was starting to think I hadn't known my grandmother well enough, either. All this time, I'd taken for granted that her own children loved her as much as I did, if not more, because why wouldn't they? But they'd known her in a way I never did. They'd seen a side of her that she never showed to me. I thought of the day when she disappeared, the way her face contorted when she saw me with Adam, the way she called my mother a parasite. Even then I couldn't believe she really meant it. She's not herself: that was what I'd said, and I'd ignored Richard when he said that she was more like herself than ever. I thought he was just being hateful. What if I'd been wrong?

"Mom?" I said. She didn't look up, but the typing sound stopped. "Is it true, what Diana said? Was Mimi . . . a bad mother?"

She sighed. "I'm not sure I want to answer that."

"What? Why?"

"Because whatever she was to me, and to Diana, she was a good grandmother to you. She always wanted to take care of you. It's not even surprising that she'd include you in her will. I just don't know why she had to take it to such an extreme."

"I didn't know she was doing that."

"Are you sure?" She was looking at me now; my own eyes stayed on the road, but I could feel hers, fixed on me as if she was trying to decide if I was lying. "She never mentioned it? You never talked about it?"

"Mom, no. I told you. I was as surprised as anyone. I didn't know anything. And it's not like I need it," I said, talking faster. "I can just give it to you, or—"

"I don't need you to take care of me. That's not the point." Her voice was sharp. "It's a question of what's fair."

Neither of us spoke as the landscape flashed by outside: the bridge crossing to the island, the dark and curvy road lined on both sides with tall trees, the moon winking in and out of view behind the tree line and the clouds.

"I just wish I understood," she said darkly after a long silence. "What she was thinking. None of it makes sense."

I made the last turn before the Whispers, and the house loomed ahead of us. I meant to reply, but as my headlights swept across the piazza, I yelped and hit the brakes. I saw two copper eyes shining, then a streak of red fur as the fox ran off into the woods.

"Wow, did you see—" I started to say, but my mother hadn't seen. She was hurriedly gathering her things together and pulling her car keys out of her bag. I gaped.

"What are you doing?" I asked, but Mom only shrugged her coat on. "Mom?"

She put her hand on the door handle and I threw the car into park, watching incredulously as she got out without a single word of explanation. She turned and looked back at me through the open door, her gaze shifting from my face to my hand on the steering wheel.

"When did you start wearing that ring?" she said abruptly, and then shook her head before I could answer. "Well, no. Not now. But there's something . . . something we need to talk about."

"I'd say there's more than one thing," I said, and she blew out a frustrated sigh.

"Yes. But not now. I have to go."

"We just got back—"

She ignored me. "I'll be back late tomorrow or maybe early the day after. I'll let you know. I'm sorry. There's just something—"

"Mom, wait, please, I need to tell you—"

"—something I have to do. I'm sorry. I really am, I'm sorry, but this can't wait." She moved to close the door and then looked back over her shoulder, almost like an afterthought. "Shelly died, you know."

"I know," I said. I almost said, *I saw,* but I bit my tongue, and my mother didn't say anything else. The door closed, and she crossed the piazza in a few quick steps, not even glancing back as she unlocked her car, climbed in, started the engine. Her headlights flared and swept past.

I thought of putting the car in gear and driving after her, tailgating and honking the horn like a road rage freak until she pulled over. I thought of lying down in the driveway so that she'd have to run me over to get away. I thought about pulling her out of the car and shaking her until she started speaking, until everything she'd spent decades not saying to me was finally out there, out loud, out in the open.

But I didn't. Because I am my mother's daughter, after all, and if she had to talk, then so would I. Because I was suddenly afraid of what she might say, when all was said and done. And because in the time it took for me to think of everything I could do, her car had already passed the place where I sat, not doing anything. I hadn't even unbuckled my seat belt. Instead, I watched in silence as it rolled away, as the taillights disappeared around the final curve of the driveway. Behind me, the house loomed, huge and dark. I looked up at it, all those vacant windows with all those empty rooms beyond, and thought of the way I'd once called it "my house"—and the way Jack Dyer had laughed in my face when I said it. But it was mine now, I realized, whether I wanted it or not. A final gift from the grandmother I'd loved, but maybe never really knew. All those dusky hallways, mine; all the rooms with their dust-shrouded furniture and cracked walls; all the nooks and crannies where the wind whispered through like a human voice. A house with nothing and no one in it but memories, half packed into cardboard boxes. The emptiness belonged to me now.

I shuddered and went inside.

• • •

I had never spent a night in the house alone, and the idea of sleeping upstairs, in the bedroom where I'd once jolted awake in the dark to the sound of Mimi whispering "I see you," was too creepy to contemplate. I spent the night on the couch instead, wrapped up in a blanket, with lights on and the television playing at low volume. My mother sent a text message saying she'd be back late the next night and ignored me when I replied asking where she was and what she was doing. Adam called me on his dinner break, but our conversation was stilted. He was gloomy and distracted; I was preoccupied with staring at the dark doorways that opened onto the living room, imagining what I'd do if a ghost suddenly appeared in one of them. Mimi. Shelly. The grandfather, great-grandfather, great-uncles I'd never met. A stranger with pitted eyes and a stained smile.

He always comes at night, I thought, and shivered.

"Babe?" Adam said. "Are you there?"

"Sorry." I tore my eyes away from the doorway, the blackness beyond. "What'd you say?"

"I said I guess you didn't have a chance to tell them. About us."

"Not after everything that happened."

"Your aunt really hit you?"

"Yeah. Insane. It didn't hurt that much, it was just shocking. I've never seen her like that." I paused to touch my cheek, remembering the flash of her hand, the sting as she struck me. "Mimi didn't happen to say anything to you, did she? About leaving the house to me?"

He was quiet for a moment. "I don't know," he said. "If she did, I can't remember. But we didn't talk much about stuff like that. I was . . . oh, hang on a m—" There was a commotion in the background and then silence as the phone went mute. A moment later he came back. "I have to go. Love you. Talk to you tomorrow?"

229 / YOU MUST REMEMBER THIS

"Yeah, sure. Bye."

It wasn't until after I'd hung up that I realized I could have asked him to come stay with me, but I hadn't.

I also realized that I hadn't said, *I love you too.*

I woke the next morning to the sound of the ringing phone. Not mine, but the house phone, sitting in its cradle on the living room table just above my head. Sun was streaming through the windows. I fumbled for the phone, my back stiff from a night spent on the sofa, and got it on the fourth ring. "Hello?"

"Ms. Lockwood?" a chirpy and vaguely familiar female voice said.

"Yes," I said automatically. Then: "Wait, which one? This is Delphine."

The woman on the other end laughed. "Hey, Delphine. It's Tasha at Willowcrest."

Right, I thought. The receptionist. I almost asked her about the last thing I'd heard her say—*that is way too much puke for one person*—before I remembered that she hadn't seen me, that I wasn't supposed to have been there.

"There's a couple things here for you," she was saying. "Do you have time in the next couple days to pick them up?"

"What things? My grandmother's stuff has been cleared out for weeks."

"They're from that other lady, Shelly Dyer? She had a letter from your grandmother in with her papers. Her son said he didn't want none of that stuff and to just throw it out, but I thought you might want it. And there's some pictures, too."

I was on my feet. The house was eerily quiet, as if it was holding its breath. Shelly had died before I could speak with her—but somehow she was communicating.

"I'll come get them," I said.

"Great. When?"

"Right now."

•   •   •

An hour later, I was walking through the front entrance at Willow-crest. Tasha waved at me from the front desk.

"Hey, there you are. Here you go." She slid an envelope toward me. "What's your email?"

"What?"

"For the photos," she said, and laughed at my confused expression. "Sorry, my bad. They're digital. I think she took them with that tablet, you know, the one she always had?" Tasha clucked her tongue. "Her son didn't put a single app on there. Can you believe that? They make all kinds of tools for stroke patients, to help them communicate, even get their speech back. But you don't know what you don't know, I guess. Kind of amazing that she managed to send those pictures all by herself. I guess she could only figure out how to attach one at a time so it's, like"—she broke off, counting under her breath—"seven emails? She sent them all to the facility inbox. Lucky I even saw them, the system thought they were spam. Looks like photos from your grandma's fu-neral, maybe? Sorry, I had to open the one, just to check what it was."

I gave her my email address, and my phone buzzed immediately as the first one came in. The subject line read *4 Mrm Crvasos family,* and the attached photo was blurry—no surprise, I thought, remembering how Shelly's hands had trembled when she tried to lift the camera. I still recognized the shot, because I was in it: standing with Adam on the day of Mimi's funeral, me in my black dress, him in his Willow-crest polo shirt. He was leaning toward me, one hand resting on my shoulder, and my stomach fluttered nervously. I'd thought we were being careful, but even out of focus and on a tiny screen, you could see that there was something between us that wasn't strictly professional. There was a light *ahem* noise from the front desk, and I looked up to find Tasha grinning at me.

"I want to say I'm sorry for your loss, but I hear maybe congratula-tions are in order, too," she said, and winked. "Can I see it?"

"See what?"

"Girl. The ring!" She laughed and leaned in. "Don't be mad at Adam. It's not his fault I'm a nosy bitch."

I extended my hand with a smile. "Here."

"Ohhh, he did good," she said, nodding with approval. "What is that, a ruby?"

"No, it's—" I started to say, then broke off as my phone vibrated in my hand. I glanced at the screen and felt a flare of annoyance. It was a number with a 510 area code—Los Angeles—and the message said: DEL, IF THIS IS YOU, PLEASE CALL ME AT YOUR EARLIEST CONVENIENCE.

It could only be Richard.

"Everything okay?"

"Yes," I said, scooping up the envelope and putting it in my bag. "But I've got to go. It was nice to see you."

She smiled. "You too. I'll forward you the rest of those emails. And hey"—she leaned in, her voice dropped to a conspiratorial whisper—"congratulations. I'm so happy for you two."

The earliest convenient time for me to call Richard was right then and there, from the parking lot—so instead I left and drove around, going through the McDonald's drive-through for coffee and then parking at an overlook near the bridge back to the island. It was one of those cloudless, frigid winter days when the sun is all light and no heat, glaring so brightly off the hoods of passing cars and the pale sides of weathered houses that I could see green afterimages every time I closed my eyes. At the overlook, I sat with the engine running and the heat blasting, waiting for my coffee to cool and looking at the letter Tasha had given me. I recognized Mimi's handwriting, spidery and old-fashioned.

Dear Shelly,
The Reverend said he would help this letter find its way to you. I trust he will do it—he seems like a good man. I'm afraid my address book has gone missing, or perhaps I've mislaid it myself. I seem always

to be losing things these days. Sometimes I lose the days themselves. I wonder, are you the woman I remember from all those years ago? Are you there still in the same little house, with the broken picket fence on the outskirts of town?

I saw you there once. You didn't see me. It was after I sent you away, after Theo, before I left the island. I sat in the car with a kerchief on to hide my hair, sunglasses to hide my face, and watched you hang your washing on the line in the side yard while little Jack played with the clothespins. You were wearing one of my old sundresses, the one with a pattern of blue flowers, which I'd given you that first summer when you came to stay with us. I thought, wasn't that just a perfect metaphor for everything that had gone so wrong? Oh, it made me angry. I thought about getting out, walking across the street and into your yard, and ripping it right off your back, and that it would be only fair. Not that it would have made us even, of course. Not even close to that.

But I drove away from you that day, and afterward, I was glad that I did. I suppose I had learned at last not to be so rash, not to do the first thing that came into my head. If only I had learned it sooner, how different my life might have been.

I'm not sure what to say to you now. I'm not sure why I've told you all this, either. That little memory, of me in the car and you with your washing, that broken fence with no one coming to fix it, it only came to me as I began writing, and I wonder if it won't be gone again in a moment. Perhaps I am only remembering it now because I am thinking of you, and I don't like to think of you, Shelly. I despised you for a long time. Some days I still do. But today (I am looking at the calendar as I write this, it is December, in the year 2014) I mean to tell you not that I despise you, but that I forgive you. I couldn't bear to think of it back then, but the pain you must have felt—that is a pain I know well. A pain that burns a hole inside of you because to express it would also mean confession. It is a terrible burden. I have carried it all my life, mourning the husband I lost, the mistakes I made. I would never wish that pain on anyone. Not even you. Not then and not now.

This is what I wanted to say. I have said it.

Your son wrote to me some time ago, to tell me of your failing health. I didn't answer him then, but I hope you will not be too proud to accept my help now. The debt I truly owe is one that cannot be repaid with money, but money is what I have—the one thing I have always had, for all the good it's done me. I have placed a sum in trust for your care, with an additional stipend if you wish to be housed here at Willowcrest. Wouldn't it be funny, to be once again living under the same roof, here at the end of our lives? But we are both of us too old to hold on to anger.

I do not expect a reply as I understand you can no longer speak or hold a pen. Don't trouble yourself, as I may well forget having written to you. My clear days seem to be ever fewer, ever further between. I hope, before I lose myself entirely, that I may be forgiven.

Yours,
Miriam Caravasios

The letter was dated two weeks before Christmas.

I let my eyes drift down the page to the bottom, where a postscript was scrawled. The writing was looser, the strokes of the pen less certain.

Do you remember that pipe he smoked, with the flowers and vines? Sometimes I wake up at night to the smell of it, as if he's just been beside me—or am I dreaming?

I read the letter twice, feeling more and more frustrated at its vagueness. What debt did my grandmother owe to this woman—and what had Shelly done to be turned out of the house all those years ago? The bit about the money, I understood: this was how Shelly had managed to pay for her place at Willowcrest, not that she'd been able to make much of it before she died. I was about to read the letter again when my phone buzzed suddenly in my lap, and I jumped, spilling coffee on myself and splattering the paper. I looked at the incoming call and cursed, tried to decline it, and cursed again when my finger slipped over the wet screen and hit ANSWER instead.

"Hello?" came a voice from the phone.

I sighed. "Hi, Richard."

"Bad time?"

"It's not ideal. Didn't you ask me to call you?"

"I did," he said. "And then I realized that if I were you, I'd probably look at that message and decide *not* to call at my earliest convenience, or maybe not even for several days, just to show me who was in charge here."

"I would have called you."

"After how long?"

I paused. "Forty-eight hours," I said, and he guffawed.

"I should have guessed. Women have always been better at playing that particular game."

"What do you want?"

"You know, Delphine, you and I have never really gotten along," he said. "Do you know why?"

"Because you're an asshole?"

"Ha! Walked into that one, didn't I? But no, that's not why. It's because you and I are actually quite alike."

"I'm not an asshole," I said.

"No," he said, his tone surprisingly agreeable. "No such thing as a lady asshole. At your age, we call it sass. Another twenty years and someone might call you a bitch. Not me, of course. I'd never."

"Look, I'm not really in the mood—"

"All right, all right. All I mean to say is, you and I have certain traits in common. Including, I think, a slightly suspicious nature." He paused—for dramatic effect, I thought—and then said, "So I wonder if you've also wondered if Mother's death was really an accident."

Thank god I'd put my coffee aside; if I'd been drinking it, I would have done a spit take. I kept my tone neutral. "What do you mean?"

"I mean murder, Delphine. Money is one of the two biggest reasons in the world why people kill each other, and my mother, your grandmother, had a lot of it."

"What's the other reason?"

"What?"

"Why people kill each other."

"Love," he said, and chuckled. "But I don't see that being the case here. So, there, I've laid my cards on the table. Well, most of them. I haven't told you who I suspect."

"I assume it's me," I said.

"Why's that?" He sounded genuinely curious.

"Isn't that what this is really about? You know she left me almost everything."

"Yes," Richard said. "I did hear about that. But only because Diana called me, ranting and raving about it. I take it she was unpleasantly surprised."

I blinked. Something wasn't right. I'd assumed Richard hadn't come to the meeting yesterday because it was too far to fly, and that the lawyer would call him afterward. But—

"You already knew you weren't getting anything," I said.

"Bingo," he said.

"How?"

"Oh, Mother wrote me out ages ago. Told me she was doing it, too. She said she wouldn't leave me a dime, not when she knew I'd use it to fund a life of decadence and depravity."

"She disinherited you because you're an obnoxious drunk?" I said incredulously, and Richard said, "What?!" and then laughed for what seemed like forever and finally managed to choke out, "For god's sake, you idiot child, I'm *gay*," before erupting into a fresh round of hysterics.

For the next minute, I listened to Richard shrieking on the other end of the phone—at one point he was laughing so hard that he wasn't actually *laughing* anymore, just making this high-pitched *eee-eee-eee* sound like a squeaky dog toy—and wondered if I was the only one who hadn't guessed what seemed suddenly, painfully obvious. The thing was, Richard was so gifted at being an asshole that I'd never even bothered to wonder if there was something underneath, more ordinary and tragic, even pathetic. And the grudge he held against my grandmother wasn't petty at all. He'd only been lashing out at the mother who refused to accept him.

"Jesus," I said.

Richard had finally stopped laughing, at least enough to speak. "What?"

"But this means that Mimi was a, like—"

"A homophobe?" He sighed. "I forget sometimes how young you are. Mother was born in the 1920s. Of course she was a homophobe. But for whatever reason, she took it very, very personally when it turned out I preferred the company of men—although lord knows I tried to pretend otherwise."

"Your wives," I said. "Did they know?"

"Oh, I think Jillian has always suspected, but she'll never ask. Too polite. Natalie left me for a younger man before she could figure it out. Francesca, I told. She said she didn't care, but surprise, it turns out I did. It's exhausting. Pretending." His voice turned sly. "Of course, you'd know all about that."

The words were out before I knew I was going to say them. "We're getting married," I said. "Adam and me."

"Mazel tov. When?"

"I don't know. You're the first person I've told."

"Lucky me," Richard said, chuckling. "I've got to hand it to you, though. You played it awfully cool. Between you and your mother, you almost convinced me I was hallucinating all the sexual tension in the house."

"Wait, what? What about my mother?"

"Oh, come now. Don't play coy with me. And don't tell me you didn't notice. That ferret-looking fellow, the one always hanging around? You must have seen them at the funeral."

Blood roared in my ears, and I gripped the phone hard. Yes, I had noticed. Of course I'd noticed. But what I'd seen was Jack. There was no *them*.

"You're out of your mind," I said. "They're not dating."

"Oh, I think they're well beyond *dating*. My question, to return to the topic at hand, is were they *plotting*."

"What! Mom would never—"

"I know you're loyal to your mother, Delphine," Richard said. "But take a breath. She's been alone for a long time, and loneliness makes a person vulnerable. If that man wanted money and if he managed to ingratiate himself with Dora, how certain are you that she wouldn't go along with it? Especially if he convinced her that it was somehow for the best."

"You didn't see her that morning. You didn't *hear* her. When we found Mimi's body, she was—" I broke off. *Inconsolable,* I had been about to say, and she was. But was it because of what had happened? Or was it because of something she'd done?

"You don't know what you're talking about," I said forcefully, as if I could will it into being not true. "And why Mom? Why not Diana and William? They need the money more than she does."

"That's true," Richard said mildly. "Hell, maybe they all did it. Together. It would be very Agatha Christie of them."

"This isn't funny."

"Indeed. It's unsettling, isn't it? To think there might have been a killer among us. But if that was the extent of it, I doubt I would have said anything. As it is, you'll notice that I'm calling you rather than the police. And do you know why?"

"Because you don't care?" I snapped. "That's obvious. You're probably glad she's gone."

He paused for several seconds before answering. "*Glad* isn't the word," he said. "I have complicated feelings about my mother's death, and all things considered, I think I'm entitled. But dementia is a horrible way to go. It's awful and undignified and it takes goddamn forever, and I wouldn't wish it on anyone, not even someone I hated. And despite what you may think, I didn't hate her. I certainly didn't want to see her suffer a lingering death that turned her into a zombie with nothing left of my mom inside. But more importantly, I didn't want to see your mother putting her life on hold for god knows how long while she waited around for our mother to die. So if someone did help her into her grave a few months ahead of schedule . . . well, I'm not sure it wasn't a kindness. Maybe it's even what she would have wanted. I'm certainly not about to move heaven and earth to see that person brought to justice. But if that someone is a man who's also trying to seduce my littlest sister, who I wouldn't trust as far as I could throw him? That concerns me. And I have a feeling it concerns you too."

For several moments, neither one of us spoke. I wasn't about to tell Richard that of course it concerned me—or that I had no idea where my mother was now. There were so many questions I hadn't asked, things I desperately wanted to know now. Like who she'd been texting last night and all those other nights. Like where she'd been all day on Christmas Eve.

I thought again of the way she'd fallen to her knees in the cove, slamming her fist against the ice until blood ran, the horrible keening sound she'd made. But behind it was another thought, rising up unbidden from a darker place: that she was the one who found Mimi's body because she was the one who knew where it would be.

I would not say any of this to Richard.

"I have to go," I said, and he sighed.

"Of course you do. Look, just think about what I said. We both know Dora isn't going to listen to me. I could send her an entire dossier—hell, I could probably send video evidence of her boyfriend playing soccer with a severed human head—and she'd just tell me to fuck off and mind my own business. But she might listen to you."

"Fine, but you're wrong."

"Wouldn't that be nice," he said. "I'd prefer to be wrong. But I don't think I am. As you well know, I have a bit of a sixth sense for this sort of thing. Not that I really needed it when it came to you and the nurse."

"What are you talking about?" I said. "We were super careful—"

He cut me off with a snort. "Oh, you were. But a word of advice, honey. At night, in an old house like that? Sound carries."

I should have asked what he meant then. If I'd been listening more carefully, I would have. But it was at this moment that my gaze drifted back to the letter, now stained with coffee, and the postscript, that tentative handwriting. I could picture Mimi so vividly in that moment— waking up and reaching for her pen, trying to capture a thought that was already half-gone, so faded it seemed like it might be nothing at all. And then I pictured her again, that night at the house, the night she'd woken up and run from her room.

I see you, she'd hissed, but when I'd gone to investigate, there was no one. No one and nothing, just a cold room and her unmade bed— only that wasn't quite right. There had been something else, too. That strange odor, unplaceable—dusky and slightly sweet.

Or am I dreaming?

Something cold and dreadful uncoiled in my stomach.

Because she hadn't been dreaming. I was sure of that because I had smelled it, too. That night at the Whispers, and at other times. Unplaceable then, unmistakable now. Drifting down the dark hallways, lingering in the air.

Wafting off Jack Dyer's coat when he came close to me at the Northeast Harbor bakery—and curling above his head as he stood smoking beside his truck.

The scent of pipe tobacco.

"I have to go," I said, but Richard had already hung up.

I sat immobile for minutes, my mind racing. *He was there,* I kept thinking over and over. Not just that first day, when he'd frightened Mimi and there'd been all that commotion, but other times. Times we hadn't seen him, times we hadn't even known someone was there. I thought of the strangeness in the house in those days before Christmas. The attic, where photographs and mementos had gone missing. *Everything's tossed around,* Adam had said—and I remembered him opening up the stairs, the way the dust had drifted down to join the dust that was already there, beneath his feet. Why? Because someone had been up there before him. Someone who wasn't one of us. And that morning, when Jack had come to the house and there had been so much commotion . . .

Mom said she'd called him, I thought, and my hands gripped into my knees. Yes, she had said that. But not before. Not ahead of time. Not like you would, if a strange man was coming to your house early in the morning to look at the furnace and you didn't want your family to be freaked out. She'd said it only after we'd all seen him—and only when I asked.

I picked up the phone and opened my email. I had six more messages from Tasha, the rest of Shelly Dyer's photographs, but I just wanted to look at the first one again. The picture of me and Adam, except that as I looked again, I realized that the picture wasn't just of us. We were standing to the side of the frame; Shelly had aimed her camera at a spot over my shoulder, where one of the long windows on either side of the front door offered a view onto the porch. Two people were framed there, talking with their heads close together. One was her son.

The other was my mom.

I looked again at that subject line—*4 Mrm Crvasos family*—and then shifted my gaze to Mimi's letter, to the part where she told Shelly about the trust, and the line that read: *We are both of us too old to hold on to anger.* Shelly couldn't get a message to my grandmother, but she had found a way to communicate all the same. To show us that she, too, had let go.

And maybe also to warn us that her son had not.

A horrible thought was taking shape in my mind.

Tasha answered the phone on the first ring.

"Willowcrest Senior Living," she said. "How may I help?"

"Tasha, it's Delphine."

"Heeey!" she chirped. "You got the rest of those emails?"

"Yes, thanks," I said quickly. "I was wondering, I know it's a morbid question, but how did Shelly die?"

"Oh, I'm not really supposed to—" She hesitated and broke off, lowering her voice. "Okay, between us. She suffocated. You know how she couldn't talk? She also couldn't swallow that good. You'd think her son would be more careful—"

My breath caught in my throat. I thought of the voice I'd heard as I stood huddled against the wall outside the room where Shelly was dead. I thought it had sounded familiar, and now I knew why. "Her son. He was there?"

"Uh-huh," Tasha said, her voice dropping even lower. "He came to visit with a box of chocolates, but I guess he stepped out to take a call or something? He only left her alone for fifteen minutes, but I guess she couldn't wait. He came back and found her slumped over with her face all purple. He hit the alarm fast as he could, but there was nothing we could do."

And now all the money my grandmother had set aside for Shelly's care would go to Jack instead. I didn't think he had hit the alarm as fast as he could have at all.

"Thanks, Tasha," I said, and hung up before she could continue. I was already putting the car in gear. Already tearing out of the overlook parking lot.

And I was already too late.

His truck was parked on the piazza outside the Whispers, right up next to my mother's car and at a strange angle, as though he'd pulled up in a hurry—or was trying to box her in. I got out cautiously, gathering my things, fighting the urge to run inside. I needed to be smarter than that. I needed to think this through.

He doesn't know I know, I reminded myself, but rather than being comforting, the thought made me shudder: I was pretty sure that if he didn't know, he wouldn't hurt me or my mother. But what if he figured it out? What if the knowledge was written all over my face? I couldn't let him see it. It would be better, I thought, if he didn't see me at all.

I opened the front door and called out, "Mom?" hoping she would appear immediately, praying she'd be alone. I could make her come outside, maybe even ask her to get in the car. I could drive a few miles away, show her the letter, tell her what I'd found, before Jack even knew what was happening. The brightness of the day made the inside of the house seem murkier than ever. I stood still, straining to hear footsteps, an answer, anything. The usual creaking and muttering of the Whispers had paused; it was like listening at the door of a tomb.

And then in the silence, I heard it: a single, strangled sob.

I bolted through the door and toward the sound, all notions of caution forgotten, then froze as I rounded the corner into the parlor. They were together there, the two of them, sitting on the green sofa where Mimi used to spend her days, sitting close enough to touch—only worse, they *were* touching. My mother had her hands over her face, and he was leaning toward her, one hand resting on her knee, the other on her shoulder. My stomach turned over.

"Don't you fucking touch her!" I screamed, and they sprang apart, my mother's hands flying out in front of her as if she were trying to stop traffic. But it was Jack Dyer I was looking at, and he was looking at me. He was on his feet in an instant, moving toward me quickly, his face contorted with anger. I backed up. He kept coming. My back collided with the doorframe, and he kept coming—and I looked down at the objects in my hands and did the only thing I could think of.

My shitty McDonald's coffee, black and bitter and barely luke-warm, hit him square in the chest and exploded in every direction, splattering his face and his shirt.

"What in the goddamn hell!" he yelled, but he stopped walking toward me, and I turned to my mother, the words pouring out of my mouth in a shrill cascade.

"Are you with him?! Because whatever he's told you, it's a lie!" I yelled. "He's been in the house, he was here, he was hiding here, and he was trying—he's still trying—I think he killed her, Mom, he killed her and"—I whirled to face him, my hands balled into fists—"I swear to god, you bastard, if you lay a hand on my mother, I'll—"

"Delphine, stop!" my mother screamed, and I did. Not because of the words, but the noise: a metallic shriek, so loud I felt my eardrums buzz, so loud I stopped in midsentence and stared with my mouth open. I'd never heard her make a sound like that. I didn't know she even could.

Jack Dyer had his mouth open, too. He put his hands up and backed away from me like you'd do from a rabid animal, not stopping until we had fifteen feet and several pieces of furniture between us. "I think I should go," he said.

"Yes," I said.

"No," my mother said simultaneously, and crossed the room to put both her hands on my shoulders. She peered into my eyes and gave me a funny half smile.

"Jesus Christ, honey," she said. "Jack isn't my boyfriend. He's my brother."

22.

AUTUMN

She is thirty-five on the day it all falls apart.

It will be many years before she understands the truth: that it was all falling apart long before this moment. The life she built had been rotting for years, from the roots on up, from the inside out. But that revelation isn't for Miriam now. It's for the old woman she'll someday become, peering back through the fog of her memories, her mind clouded but her eyes clear. She will see herself for what she was, a foolish young thing who took too much for granted, who couldn't understand the harm she was causing until it was too far gone to be undone.

Someday. Not today.

Today, there's only the gut-wrenching sense of the earth suddenly vanishing beneath her feet. There's nothing to do but fall.

She's watching the children when it happens. Theodora and little Jack, whose presence in the house feels entirely unremarkable, the tears and shouting and ultimatums over Shelly's unfortunate situation long since forgotten. Miriam doesn't even regret anymore that she kept silent about that sailor, though he had indeed turned out to be every bit the scoundrel she'd feared, and more. It was the winter of 1961 when he left for parts unknown, and left Shelly heartbroken and carrying his child; the arguments between Miriam and Theo over whether to send the girl away went on for three months after that. But this was one fight Miriam refused to lose, no matter how her husband blustered and complained, and no matter how people whispered behind their hands when they saw her in town. If Shelly could bear the scorn of being an unwed mother, Miriam said, then surely her employers could weather the comparatively minor scandal of having her remain in their home.

In the face of her stubbornness, Theo had no choice but to relent. Perhaps he remembered that it was only for his wife's stubbornness that he'd been able to marry her at all—or perhaps he was simply used to losing arguments by then.

Regardless, Miriam could never have sent Shelly away. And even Theo had to admit, eventually, that it was nice to have another little family in the house, and for their youngest daughter to have a playmate closer to her own age. The Whispers felt so much fuller, so much less lonely, with the sounds of children's laughter and footsteps echoing off its walls.

On this day, Miriam is sitting on the veranda to enjoy the autumn sunset while Shelly fetches an ashtray for their evening smoke. The two women are alone, as they have been for most of the week. Richard and Diana are back at their schools, and Theo is hardly home; two men have chartered his fishing outfit for a span of several days, but they're more interested in carousing with their captain at the local pub than in actually catching anything. Here at the Whispers, there's not much to do but smoke and gossip, keeping half an eye on Jack and Theodora as they play. They're tumbling around in the grass tonight, the light golden all around them. Shrieking and laughing, happy and safe.

But Miriam doesn't see the beauty of the scene, the lovely glow of her daughter's cheeks as the sun kisses them good night. She doesn't see her daughter at all. She is looking at little Jack. She's been watching him often lately, watching him without knowing why. Of course he's a handsome boy. Growing up fast, too: at three and a half, he has lost the generic pudginess that makes babies all look the same, his own unique features beginning to emerge and take shape. Shades of the man he'll someday become. She can see already that he'll have his mother's glossy dark hair, her pouty, downturned mouth—an unfortunate thing for a boy to inherit, she thinks. It's a feature far more flattering on a woman. But his eyes, his brow line . . . those are not Shelly's eyes. Not Shelly's brows. And the way his face scrunches in frustration as he chases after Theodora, the scowl as she outruns him—there's something about this, especially, that makes her unable to look away. For the first time in a long time she thinks of Shelly's beau, the damnable sailor who knocked her up and promptly disappeared. What had his name been? Donald or Daniel, one of those two, but she remembers his face better than his name: round and friendly, with a high forehead and a broad smile. No, there's not even a hint of that man in this dark, intense little boy, and a terrible thought is beginning to tickle at the back of Miriam's mind. Something she's avoided knowing for too long, something that has grown tired of being ignored. She leans forward. Gazing at Jack, who is scowling at Theodora, who is twirling circles against the setting sun. A single line creases the little boy's forehead, just above his brows but slightly off-center. It's comical, a furrow that deep on the face of someone so young, and Miriam knows it will etch itself into his face early and forever. This one line, before any other. How does she know?

The answer comes immediately—too fast for her to swat it away, too fast for her to do anything but stare at the boy and struggle to breathe, her heart pounding, her mind reeling.

She knows because she has seen it. She's seen that line all her life, every day since she was eighteen, on Theodore Caravasios's handsome face. An identical crease above an identical brow line, arching above deep brown eyes that are the same size and shape.

Like father, like son.

The cigarette she's holding snaps in two.

An eternity seems to pass before Shelly comes back with the ashtray. Miriam tosses away the broken cigarette. Reaches for another. She takes her time lighting it and takes a drag. Her hand shakes. Her voice doesn't. She has that odd sense, just as she did at the pond years before, of floating above the scene like a curious observer. Watching the betrayal unfold, wondering what's going to happen. "It's funny, isn't it," she says.

"What's that?" Shelly says, her voice light. She doesn't yet see the look on Miriam's face, the ice in her eyes.

"I was just thinking about that man you used to run around with. That sailor. What was his name?"

"You mean Dennis?" Shelly lights a cigarette, takes a drag. "Gosh, what are you thinking about him for?"

"I was thinking that Jack doesn't look much like him." Miriam pauses. "Nothing like him, really. Not a whit. It's quite strange."

Shelly has gone very still, her body tense, the smoke from her cigarette gathering in a cloud above her head. Like a tiny mouse, frozen in the grass as a hawk swoops overhead; if she doesn't move, if she doesn't breathe, perhaps the circling predator will forget she's there and simply disappear. But the silence stretches between them, and Miriam is looking at her, waiting for an answer, and she lets out a nervous little laugh. "Well, I don't know about that," she says.

Miriam stands. Unfolding to her full height, so that she looms over Shelly, who seems to shrink and squirm in her chair. Trapped beneath the shadow of a predator who sees her, who was always going to see her sooner or later. It was only a matter of time.

"Oh, but I do," Miriam says. "I do know." She sucks in air through her teeth—and she wishes, for a brief and furious moment, that she could exhale fire instead of air. She wants her next words to hurt, to blister, to burn right through the soft pink flesh of the other woman's face and leave nothing behind but a black and smoking ruin. She leans in close.

She hisses, "I know what you've done, you bitch."

She waits in the library for Theo to come home, with a book in her lap that she isn't reading and a whiskey in her hand that she isn't drinking, only swirling around and around in the glass, watching how the amber liquid catches the light. Her uneaten dinner, the one she was supposed to have with Shelly, is still in its pot on the stove, untouched and slowly congealing. Theodora is in bed, sound asleep. And their now-former housekeeper is gone, long gone, taken away in a taxi with her few paltry belongings packed into an old suitcase and her wailing, confused child clinging to her hip.

Jack's were the only tears. As much as Miriam would have liked to make a scene, to scream and sob and drag the woman out by her hair, she thought Shelly would have probably liked that, too. To see her not just humiliated but unwound, out of control. And so she said as little as possible until Shelly's things were collected and her taxicab called, and then watched them go from the library window, standing back to stay hidden behind the drapes. She noticed only at the very last moment that the woman was making her exit still wearing one of Miriam's own dresses—one of those little gestures that had made Miriam feel magnanimous at the time, offering some of her prettier old clothes to someone who had so few nice things of her own. *Doesn't that just serve me right?* she thought, watching Shelly gather her skirt to keep it from catching, exposing one slender ankle just before the cabby closed the door behind her. Theo had always liked that dress. Perhaps Shelly had even been wearing it when—

"No," she hissed through gritted teeth, and slapped herself hard across the face.

There was already so much that was beyond her control. She was betrayed, humiliated; people were surely laughing at her behind her back. All those times that people had tilted their heads together as she passed, whispering to each other; all those looks of pity she'd never quite understood. She understood now. The most salacious story on the island, and she was the last to know. Her best friend had fucked her husband. Her husband had fathered Shelly's bastard child. And Miriam, oblivious idiot, a prize fool, had let it all happen right under her nose.

These were things she could not change.

But she would be damned if she allowed herself to imagine the two of them together, their naked bodies intertwined. If that picture tried to worm its way into her brain, she would knock it back out with her fists, and she would do it as many times as it took to make it stay away.

It is after ten when he finally comes back. She sees his headlights sweep across the driveway, hears the front door open and close. His gait is unsteady as he crosses the foyer, his shoes scuffing on the tile. *He must be drunk,* she thinks, and the realization makes her feel slightly giddy despite her misery. Drunk means uninhibited, more easily provoked—and oh, she wants to provoke him. She wants him to get angry, to shout, to fight her, because a fight would mean there was still something left. Of the man he used to be, of the love they had together. It means there's still hope for them yet. For the first time in years, she thinks again of a little house in town, the one she's fantasized for too long about buying and moving the family into. Of all the impulses she's chased over the years, why didn't she ever chase that one? Why doesn't she?

"You're still awake," he says, and she turns to look at him. He's leaning against the doorway, his cheeks flushed, his hair mussed. She'd wondered if he might look different to her, uglier somehow now that she knows what he's done, but he's the same as ever—and as handsome as ever, she thinks, and shudders. It's not just that she can still want him after he betrayed her; it's that she wants him more, and more desperately, her desire tainted by revulsion and heartbreak that somehow makes it all the more intoxicating.

"I wanted to talk to you," she says.

He stands up straighter. "What about?"

"I've let Shelly go."

The silence stretches between them, punctuated by the ticking of the clock. She stares at him, unblinking. Daring him to ask why, daring him to say anything at all.

He looks over his shoulder, down the hallway. "Is she—"

"Already gone."

Another long pause. "I see," he says, finally, and frustration gets the better of her.

"Aren't you going to ask why?"

He takes a deep breath, holding her gaze, and lets it out with a sigh. "No. And not just because I know why. It's all over your face, Miriam. I don't know if she told you or if you guessed it, or . . . but it doesn't matter."

"That's rich, coming from you. After what you've done." She pauses. "Or what you're still doing. How long, Theo? How long have you been making a fool of me?"

"That's all over. It's been over."

"Don't lie to me." She makes a strangled sound, the breath caught in her throat. "My god. You were going to her at night, weren't you? I thought I was crazy, hearing things, but I wasn't. I heard you in there with her."

His face twists. "Ayuh, you did. That night—it was the last time. Because I wanted her to leave. I begged her to leave, Miriam, and do you know what she did? She laughed in my face and said, 'I don't take orders from you.' She said, 'This here is your wife's house. You and I, we just live in it.'"

"That's not fair," she says, and he lets out a little bark of laughter.

"Fair got nothing to do with it. She was right. So when you tell me you let her go, what's the point in asking why? You do what you want, don't you? You get what you want. You take what you want. You always have. The only reason she was ever here in this house in the first place is because you insisted."

"Don't you dare," she hisses, her voice rising. "Don't you dare try to turn this around on me. This isn't my fault."

He shakes his head. "No, it surely isn't. I don't deny what I did. I did it and I have to live with it—but boy, have I been living with it. Living with it right here in this house, sitting down to dinner with it, staring it right in the face every single day. I was tested and I failed. But who put me to that test?" He pauses. "You did, Miriam, and I wonder if you didn't do it on purpose. I think maybe you even wanted it to happen."

"Why?" Her voice is small, barely a whisper. "Why on earth would I want this to happen?"

He shrugs. "It just proves what everyone already knew, doesn't it? I'm no good. Never good enough. Never was. Not for the likes of you."

Miriam stares at him, searching for words and finding none. The expression on his face is the most terrifying thing she's ever seen because it's no expression at all: not angry, not sad, but defeated, and resigned to the defeat. She will not be getting the fight she wanted, because there's no fight left in Theo, and that's her fault. She drained it out of him herself, indignity by indignity, over the course of sixteen years. The space between them seems suddenly huge and dangerous, as treacherous as the water that once stretched between them all those years ago when she'd been a girl on the pier, watching at sunset for his boat to pass by. If she reached for him now, would he still take her hand and pull her to him? Or would he only watch as she sank, arms outstretched, into the drowning emptiness?

There was a time when this question would have been no question at all, when the very notion would have made her laugh out loud. *You're wrong,* she thinks desperately, and tears fill her eyes. She had never tested their bond in hopes that he might break it; she had never tested him at all. And that's been her mistake. She puts her face in her hands.

When she looks up again, he's gone.

Miriam cries for a long time then, sobbing between sips of the whiskey until both the glass and her eyes are dry. Then she pours herself another and sits quietly. Thinking—but she doesn't think for long, and this is her next mistake. If she'd taken another moment, even had another drink, maybe she would have thought better or just fallen asleep before she could do her worst.

But then Miriam has never been one to think better. *Always jumping into things, aren't you?* The man on the truck had said that, the day of the fire, and he was right: jumping into things is what she does, it's who she is. A little impulsive, a little wild, a woman who follows her heart. Why not? Her heart has always been trustworthy, always steered her true.

It will only occur to her much later, when it's much too late, that today was different than those other days.

Today her heart is broken.

She picks up the phone. The dial spins beneath her finger and she listens as it clicks and connects. It is very late, but that won't matter. Not to him. Not tonight. And not when she made a promise.

If the worst comes to pass, you come to me.

Five hundred miles away, in a grand home in Egg Harbor, Roland Day looks up from his reading at the sound of the ringing phone. His body is stooped, his hair bright white and nearly gone, but these are merely the trappings of age. The qualities that made him the man he is, fierce and feared and fearsome, are qualities not dulled by the passage of time: He is still the same man who made his fortune against the law and under cover of darkness, who was known in low places and high society alike as someone you'd be wise not to cross. He is still the man who built and then rebuilt the finest damn house in Bar Harbor, raising it up like a phoenix from the ashes while softer, richer men slunk off with their tails between their legs.

He is still the man who put a bullet between the eyes of the double-crossing son of a bitch who was fixing to squeal on them to the Prohibition men back in 1928, who stuffed the body in a bag weighted with stones and pitched it overboard thirty miles off the coast.

And he is still the father of a daughter he loves with everything he has. A daughter he held in his arms on the wild night when she first came into the world, when he looked into her face and knew that he would kill any person who ever harmed her. Her pain is his pain; her heartbreak is his rage.

Miriam knows this. She fights back a sob.

"Tell me what's happened, my girl," her father says, and then for a long time, he says nothing else.

23.

When I was in first grade, I learned a rhyme about secrets. We'd sit at our little desks and chant it in unison, clapping on the first and third beat like cheerleaders.

Secrets, secrets, are no fun!

Secrets, secrets, hurt someone!

I always thought it was funny, because the secrets of your average six-year-old are nothing special. Usually they're not even secrets. When your best friend cups a hand to your ear and whispers that Marybeth Bell's new haircut looks like a porcupine butt, it's not like she's telling you something you don't know. It's not secrecy but intimacy that makes it magic—the way your friend's breath tickles your ear, the way you laugh together afterward until someone asks what's so funny, and you both say, "Nothing," and then start laughing even harder. The sharing of whispered confidences that sets you apart from the rest of the world. Being inside that circle of trust was glorious, and being outside was a cold and lonely hell, and that was the lesson we were supposed to learn: not to tell secrets, or at least not in front of other people, because it hurt to be excluded.

But as I looked from my mother to Jack Dyer and back, as the words *He's my brother* hung in the air, I felt that stupid rhyme echoing in my head. Only I knew now that what really tore people apart wasn't telling secrets.

It was keeping them.

Jack went home then, declining the offer of both a fresh shirt and any part in the conversation to come. I felt him watching me warily as he left, as if I might throw something else at him. I thought that I ought to apologize, but thinking was as far as I got. The embarrassment and confusion were paralyzing. I couldn't have spoken if I wanted to. And what would I say? *Sorry for hitting you in the face with a coffee, but I thought you were a thief and a murderer—for which I am also, incidentally, sorry, except that I'm still pretty sure you're guilty of something, even if it's just being a general creep.* Instead, I stared at my shoes, studiously not looking at Jack and my mother as they said goodbye. Now that I knew the truth, the vibe between them couldn't have been more obviously nonsexual. I couldn't believe I'd let Richard convince me that she might be dating him, let alone plotting with him.

My mother couldn't believe it, either. As Jack's truck pulled away outside, she settled next to me on the couch, sighed, and gave me a bewildered look. "Dear lord, Delphine," she said. "Did you really think I was seeing him? Romantically? How in the world?"

I kept my eyes on my feet, my cheeks burning. "I don't know. It's not like you'd tell me if you were, right?"

She looked thoughtful. "All right," she said slowly. "Maybe I've been a little closemouthed about that part of my life. I decided early on that I wouldn't introduce you to anyone unless it got serious enough that I was thinking about marriage again, which none of them ever did. So . . ." She trailed off and winced. "Look, Jack's not a bad man. But for god's sake, I've never been that desperate."

I laughed a little, and so did she, and the tension in the room lifted by half a degree.

"And that would be true even if we weren't related," she added.

"Are you going to tell me about that?"

"Yes, I'm going to tell you everything."

It was Mimi who had triggered my mother's suspicions, on the day she'd come back to the Whispers. *That's Shelly's room*, she'd said, but it wasn't all she said; when Mom helped Mimi into the bed that day, in the moment before she fell asleep, she'd suddenly gone wide-eyed and grabbed her by the arm.

"He was hiding inside the wall," she'd said, her voice low and urgent. "I should have known. I should have known, because the baby was screaming."

If it had been me, I would have dismissed this as spooky but meaningless, just like the old songs Mimi sometimes sang under her breath. Like her trip to the moon or the man with the brown teeth: just a scrap of flotsam briefly surfacing from the depths of her memory, maybe a snippet of some scary old story she'd once read about a haunted house. But my mother knew better because she'd been there. She was the screaming baby, waking to the sound of her father's footsteps as he sneaked past her nursery and down the stairs.

"I'd always suspected that things weren't wonderful between them when my father died," my mother said. "She'd had such a difficult pregnancy, and I wasn't an easy baby—it puts a lot of stress on a marriage. But once I realized that my father had an affair with Shelly, I realized there was also a good chance he was the father of her child. It's why I hid those photos."

"And let Richard take the fall for it," I said, and Mom looked chagrined.

"I suppose I owe him an apology. But I couldn't say anything, not then. The last thing we needed was for your grandmother to go paging through those albums, having her memory jogged. It wouldn't have been good for her. And I also didn't want to have that conversation with my brother and sister just yet."

"What about Jack? Did he know?"

"He might have suspected," Mom said. "I found several letters from him mixed in with Mother's correspondence when I started looking through everything. He had written to her several times, asking for money for his mother's care. He clearly felt that a debt was owed."

"It sounds kind of like blackmail," I said.

She shook her head. "He was just desperate. Shelly eventually married another man, but apparently he died a while back and they never had any children, so when she had her stroke, there was nobody to help except Jack. He had to put his life on hold to move back here and care for her."

"I guess you knew how that felt."

"Of course I empathized," she said. "But I also wanted to be smart. Your grandmother didn't have long, and if Jack was connected to the family by blood, it could have made things complicated. Once we'd confirmed his paternity, assuming he was my half brother, I thought we might be able to come to some sort of arrangement. But—"

"But Mimi had already taken care of it."

"That's right," she said, and looked at me curiously. "How did you know that?"

I dug into my bag, finding the letter and handing it over. "She sent this to Shelly, right before Christmas."

I waited while she read it, watching emotions flicker over her face until she reached the postscript, and her eyebrows went up.

"Huh," she said.

"Yeah," I said. "Mom, how many times has Jack Dyer been at the house? Apart from that first morning, when he scared Mimi."

She looked cautiously at me. "Why?"

"He smokes a pipe. I've seen it. And that thing she mentions at the end, about the scent of tobacco? I've smelled it, too, here in the house. I smelled it that day when she went missing. If he was coming around here when we didn't know about it, messing with Mimi's head—"

"Oh, god, I'd almost forgotten about that," she said, cutting me off. "He needed a wheelchair for Shelly and I told him he could stop by and take ours, since your grandmother was so intent on not using it. Apparently he was getting it out of the closet, but then you all came back from your walk, and he thought seeing him might upset her, so he just took off rather than try to explain. He's been by a few times, actually."

"To see you?"

"And to see about the furnace," she said with a laugh. "He's actually a very good handyman. He'd park on the road and walk up through the woods so he didn't disturb anyone."

"Those pistachio shells Diana found—"

"He leaves those everywhere." She grimaced. "I guess he eats them while he works. He's kind of a slob, all told."

I thought back to the one conversation I'd ever had with Jack, the strange way he'd looked at me when I said that Mimi never talked about his mother. As if I was lying or crazy—*my ma sure remembers her*, he'd said—but now I finally understood. He thought I knew, and what I'd mistaken for anger was just confusion.

And I'd been wrong, not just about Jack, but about everything. My grandmother's great love—that gorgeous, tragic romance like something out of Hollywood, so incredible that all I wanted was for a little bit of its magic to rub off on me—was just another ordinary drama, full of disappointments, complications, betrayal. The man who'd saved Mimi's life, captured her heart, kissed her in the anonymous darkness of the Ellsworth movie theater, vowed in front of their families and God to love her, honor her, comfort her in sickness and in health: he was a liar and a cheater who had broken every promise he ever made. The beautiful stories Mimi used to tell me were nothing but a highlights reel with all the dark parts clipped out, as fake and filtered as a lifestyle influencer's Instagram feed.

It made me furious. Not at Mimi, but at myself, for being duped by it. For *wanting* to be duped.

"Is it for sure?" I asked. "That Jack is your brother, I mean."

My mom squeezed my knee. "Yes. That's where I've been since yesterday. We did a paternity test. My father was his father."

"So there's no way . . ." I shook my head, still unable to believe how wrong I'd been. "I thought maybe he hurt her."

"Your grandmother?" She looked aghast. "Good lord. Is that what you were shouting about when you came in? Where on earth would you get that idea?"

"It's just, they said her death was an accident, but—"

Her face fell. "But you didn't think it was," she said, and hesitated. "The thing is, I don't think so, either."

"You think someone hurt her?"

"Not exactly." She took a deep breath. "I think she hurt herself. It wouldn't have been the first time she tried to. She talked about it, you know. Suicide. When she first got her diagnosis—it was terrifying to her, the idea of losing herself that way. That was one of the reasons I wanted her to live at Willowcrest, so that there would be someone to monitor her. But the truth is, nothing was going to stop my mother from dying if that's what she wanted to do. I've made my peace with that."

I hesitated, and my mother squeezed my knee again. "What is it?"

"It's just . . . when she died. She had her boots on. Her winter boots. And I thought . . ." I trailed off, painfully aware of the quaver in my voice. I sounded pathetic, childish, the amateur true crime podcast listener who thought she was a detective. My mother looked confused—and then anguished.

"Oh no. So you thought—fuck, this really is my fault," she said savagely, and looked up at me, smiling but with tears in her eyes.

"Don't you understand? She could have tied them herself. She always could. I just made a big deal about doing it for her because I knew it embarrassed her. Having to need someone else, depend on someone else, she hated that. And after everything she'd put me through, I liked having that little bit of power."

We both cried then, but only for a little while. Then we opened a bottle of wine, lit the fire, and my mother talked for a long time as the sun went down and the wind picked up. She told me things I'd never known about her childhood, her life, her marriage, and what came after. She told me what it was like to be my mother, and to be my grandmother's daughter. She told me she wasn't sure what to do with herself now that she had nobody to take care of. She laughed when I said that she could always get a dog.

The muttering of the house was a constant as our voices rose and fell, until I threw another log on the fire and said, "I just can't get over it. The way Mimi talked about your father, he sounded like, I don't know, something out of a movie. The perfect guy. And he cheated on her. How could she make it all sound so romantic when that was how it ended?"

My mother took a long sip. "It ended because my father died. Who knows what would have happened if he hadn't? Maybe they would've reconciled, or maybe not." She paused. "But your grandmother lived without a husband much longer than she lived with one. She had a whole life after he was gone, and I think it was a very good life. It's a shame she didn't remember more of it, latch onto one of those pieces instead—but I guess that's the thing. You don't get to decide what stays with you at the end."

"You could have told me," I said.

"What? That her marriage wasn't the fairy tale she made it out to be? Why would I ever do such a thing? You loved her stories, and she loved sharing them with you. If she made things up or left things out—well, so what? That doesn't make it worth any less. It was your time with her that mattered."

"I miss her," I said and drained my glass. My mother reached out and refilled it.

"So do I."

We sat in silence for a while. I allowed my eyelids to droop. I was drunk but comfortable. Cozy. It was nice to listen while someone else talked. To let my mother take over the storytelling, to untangle the knotted history of so many intersecting lives. I was nearly asleep when the quiet was interrupted by the sound of my mother's phone buzzing. I opened my eyes to see her pulling it from her pocket; she looked at the screen, frowned, and looked up at me.

"What?" I said.

"Do you know what this is about?" she asked, holding out the phone. My stomach sank as I looked at it. It was from Richard. *Can't stand the suspense,* it said. *Have you talked to Del?*

"I—" I started to say when the phone buzzed again. She pulled it back, reading aloud.

"'Do tell the young fellow I said welcome to the family,'" she said, knitting her brows together. "What on earth? I haven't said a word about Jack to anyone, how could he possibly—"

She stopped talking as a strangled noise rose from the back of my throat. I opened my mouth. Closed it. Opened it again. My mother stared at me, confusion flickering over her face—and then slowly her gaze shifted to the ring on my hand. Back to me. Back to the ring.

"Delphine," she said, and because I thought I might scream if I opened my mouth, I just stared back at her and nodded imperceptibly. In a few moments, my mother would be peppering me with questions, and it would be my turn to talk. But in this moment, she just said, "But *who?*" and I said, "Well, first of all, Adam's not gay," and watched as understanding dawned on her face, as her eyes opened wide, as she started to laugh. I thought again of that rhyme, the one about secrets. Mimi had tried to keep hers, wrapping it up in a fantasy of how things could have been, hiding the shame and heartbreak just like she'd hidden her valuables away. Out of sight, out of mind, until she no longer remembered where she'd left them, until it was like they'd never been hers at all.

She thought the truth would die with her. She'd wanted it to. But that was the thing, I thought.

Secrets, secrets, are no fun. Somebody always tells.

24.

FEBRUARY

"Well, if you do decide to get married here on the island, I would be delighted to help," said Reverend Frank, smiling at me over the top of his coffee mug.

It was my third visit in as many weeks, but this one would be my last. My car was already packed for the cross-country drive: I would head south tomorrow, stopping to say hello to friends in New York and spending a night with my mother in New Jersey, then turning west and heading toward Los Angeles. I had no itinerary and no firm plans. The next mark on my calendar was weeks out, at the end of the month, when I would meet with a friend of Richard's whose production company had an opening for a script reader. It was the least he could do, Richard had told me, given that he felt at least partially responsible for inspiring me to what he would not stop referring to as "an act of caffeinated violence." He also seemed to think we were going to be friends once I arrived, inviting me to move into his pool house for as long as I liked until I found an apartment. Weirder still, I was seriously considering this offer. It sounded . . . fun.

I had long since finished my own coffee and was nervously twisting the garnet ring on my finger, something I seemed to do every time I talked or thought about the engagement. There was space in my car for Adam's bags, and room for him in both the passenger seat and Richard's pool house, but everything else about our future together was an open question. It wasn't that I didn't want it; it was more like I couldn't imagine it. A cross-country road trip had always been on that list of things we'd do someday—we'd fantasized about eating greasy drive-in food, taking cheesy pictures, stopping to see offbeat attractions like the World's Largest Taxidermied Bat—but now that it was actually happening, it didn't feel real.

Reverend Frank was wondering if I was falling into old patterns, those same old trust issues. I was telling him that on the contrary, taking a leap like this—new state, new fiancé, new life, and no plan— was entirely a new thing for me.

"You know you make a face every time you say that word," he said.

"What?"

He laughed. "Fiancé."

"It's weird. It sounds weird when you say it, too."

"In old French, *fiance* meant a promise." He paused. "From the Latin *fidere*. To trust."

"Well, I didn't know that," I said. "But that's not why it sounds weird."

"Does it feel weird? That's what's important."

I shrugged. "Everything feels weird at the Whispers. It always did. But that's nothing to do with Adam. It's the house, the memories. It's like it's not really my life I'm living there."

Which was why I had to leave. If I didn't know exactly where I was going from here, I was certain that I couldn't stay. I had barely even seen Adam, who was finishing out his last two weeks at Willowcrest while I readied the house for the estate sale. It was exhausting, my phone going off constantly, five new tasks piling up for every one I managed to check off the list. The reverend set his mug down.

"Have you talked to Adam about this?"

"Not really. Not yet. He really wants to set a date. You know, for the wedding. Actually, he wants to get married on the way to California."

"Vegas?" He laughed. "Well, I would have liked to do the honors myself, but if you decide to give Elvis the job, I'll understand."

I smiled. "You'd understand. I don't think my mother would."

"I'm sure your mother just wants you to be happy. If you wanted to elope—"

"I *want* to want to." I began to gather my things. Outside the window, the first arrivals to the Alcoholics Anonymous meeting were coming through the front gate and walking toward the church. I pulled my gloves on. "I mean, I'd like to be that kind of person. I'd like to have that kind of crazy love where you know it's right and you just go for it. Like Mimi did . . . except minus the part where my husband cheats on me with the maid," I added quickly, with a weak laugh. "But I'm not like her. She would just jump into things, consequences be damned. I wish I could be brave like that. But I guess I'm not."

When I looked up, Reverend Frank was looking at me intently, his hands pressed together like he was praying. I saw his Adam's apple bob as he swallowed, and cleared his throat, but he didn't speak.

"What?" I said.

"I was thinking that what you call brave, some might call impulsive," he said. "Or reckless. A decision made in the heat of the moment or the heat of emotion . . . recklessness gets people hurt. Or worse."

I stared at him. "Are you still talking about me and Adam?"

"I'm talking about . . ." He trailed off, shook his head. "I'm talking about the difference between being bold and being foolish. Whatever your grandmother's great romance might have seemed like to you, you must realize there are parts of her story you still don't know. Things that would make you think twice about imagining her life was something to aspire to. Nobody ever knows what really goes on in someone else's marriage, and nobody can ever truly know the truth of another person's life or"—he hesitated again—"or death," he finished quietly.

I thought of Mimi out there on the ice. An accident or a suicide: there was no way to know. The truth would stay buried. And either way, she was gone.

"I think I understand," I said. I extended a hand, and he clasped it in both of his.

"I hope you'll visit me when you're back in town," he said.

"I will," I said, and he squeezed my hand.

"Best of luck, Delphine," he said.

The reverend was a good man.

I would never see him again.

"I still can't believe you're going to let your family sell this place," Adam said as we pulled up to the Whispers for the last time. Last summer, I'd driven through the front gate and been awestruck by the sheer size of the place, the way it loomed above the bay, a relic from a different time. The time I'd spent living here had done nothing to diminish this feeling. If anything, it seemed bigger now, replete with even more memories and mysteries, and I would be relieved to lock the doors and leave it behind. I'd told my mother she could handle the sale and divide the profits between herself and her siblings—and that hopefully this would resolve any lingering resentments about how Mimi had changed her will. I did not tell her that I hoped Diana would use her share of the money to divorce her idiot husband rather than paying off his debts. It was, in the end, none of my business, and I thought of what the Reverend Frank had said during our first conversation—*Let go or be dragged.* Whatever it had once meant to my grandmother, I had to let go of the Whispers. The house was too huge, too heavy; trying to keep hold of it it would only pull me backward, pinning me with the weight of its history when I needed to break away.

"It's for the best," I said.

Adam peered at me from the passenger seat. "Are you sure? Your family has so much history here."

"The history is why I want to let it go. Someone should make good memories here."

"Don't you have good memories?" He smiled and took my hand. "I know I do. Being here with you and your family, walking the pine path—"

I grimaced. "When I think of the pine path, I just think about the day we found Mimi. I remember my mom down there in the cove, screaming, trying to break through the ice. It was so clear, you could see—"

Adam squeezed my hand and said quietly, "Delphine, don't," but I couldn't stop.

"—her eyes," I finished, and shuddered. "Her eyes were frozen open. That's what I remember." I opened the car door and looked at him. "I just need to do a final walk-through, make sure everything is closed up. Do you want to come? Take a last look at the place?"

Adam waited in the foyer as I made my way through the north wing, opening doors, looking through every room without really seeing anything. The drapes were all drawn, the furniture covered with dust cloths, and I thought of the last time I'd done this, peering into the shadows in search of my missing grandmother, feeling all the time as if I was being tracked by unseen eyes. I thought of Mimi's wheelchair, tipped on its side where Jack Dyer had hurriedly left it, one wheel still spinning in space. I thought of the fox I'd seen on the terrace, the way it sat unmoving and stared at me. The house had never felt more haunted than it did that day—and it had been, I thought. Not by ghosts, but by secrets.

I left the north wing and passed back through the foyer, checking the library and the parlors before moving toward the back of the house. Adam wasn't standing there anymore, and I thought about calling out to him, then thought better of it. Maybe he was saying his goodbyes to the Whispers, too, and if he wanted to do it alone, I understood. Jack Dyer had done the same thing when I asked him if there was anything in the house he wanted, something to help him remember his mother and the time they had spent living here. He'd said no, nothing. "Except I wouldn't mind taking a walk through the old place," he said. "Just by myself, just to really see it. I always wanted to go exploring in there, but Ma never let me out of her sight."

He'd come the next day while I was working in the library, sorting through the documents I was leaving behind for whoever became the new owner. Ledgers, photographs, blueprints, a photocopied list of the heirlooms that Mimi had stashed somewhere and that we'd never found. At first I thought he might leave without ever mentioning what had happened the last time we saw each other, but in the end, he poked his head through the door and deadpanned, "I'll be off, then . . . unless you wanted to offer me a cup of coffee."

I hiked my bag higher on my shoulder and felt it vibrate: another email from the lawyer. One more bit of unfinished business. I sighed, scrolling back through the dozens of messages until a familiar subject line jumped out at me and I felt a chill run down my spine.

4 Mrm Crvasos family.

Speaking of unfinished business, I thought. Shelly Dyer had been dead for a month, but she was still haunting my inbox.

I scrolled absent-mindedly through the rest of Shelly's unread emails, dutifully glancing at the attached photos before deleting them, feeling vaguely guilty as I did. Maybe this had been her way of saying thank-you to Mimi, to us, but the photos were all too blurry and off-kilter to be legible, let alone worth hanging onto. All they reminded me of was Shelly herself, the way her hands shook as she held the tablet, the way her eyes blazed in her half-frozen face—and then bugged out of it after she was gone. A choking accident, after all. It seemed like a horrible way to go.

I wandered through the kitchen and then took a final turn into the small bedroom that had been a servant's quarters before it was Mimi's. I deleted another photo from the funeral, this one taken on the way into the house: I could see the roofline at one end and a chunk of Shelly's forehead at the other. But in the next message, the setting changed, and I found myself staring at my own face. Looking back at the camera across the hood of Jack Dyer's truck, holding a bag that contained a cranberry holiday cake. Only two months had passed since then, but I hardly recognized myself. I looked startled and a little bit spooked. The woman in the picture had no idea what was coming and wouldn't have believed me if I told her.

I turned back toward the open door, already thinking a step ahead—I'd take a quick run through the upstairs and then get going—but the thought died in my mind as I opened the last message, the last photo. I glanced at it but then looked at it, really looked, and the blurry shapes resolved into an image. A captured moment.

My feet had stopped moving. The last breath I'd taken was caught in my throat.

The world spun and swam around me, fading away, so that nothing was left but the picture. Out of focus, badly framed, but unmistakable. I closed my eyes, but it was too late. *Once you understood what you were looking at . . .*

I opened my eyes. The picture was still there.

. . . you couldn't stop seeing it.

I clutched the phone and sank onto the bed in Shelly's room, staring into space as the minutes ticked silently by. Outside, the light was beginning to fade and the room felt cold, just as it had that night when I brought Mimi back to bed after something—someone—had frightened her. A figure I knew couldn't be real because it was like something out of a nightmare, a man with brown teeth, and I'd been so focused on that horrifying image that it never occurred to me to tease it apart. I never stopped to think that even Mimi's most outlandish stories, like the one about going to the moon, were always based on something real. Something she'd seen or heard that lodged like a stone in the darkness of her broken mind and gathered moss until it turned into a false memory. Something like a man who came at night, who hid inside the walls, who brought her presents and promises of forgiveness.

My sweetheart gave it to me.

Dread sat like a stone in my guts as I worked Adam's ring off my finger. I looked again at the inscription, remembering how I'd laughed when he said it belonged to "some fat lady"—laughed so hard that I'd forgotten to wonder ever again about who its previous owner might actually have been. But as I stared at those faded letters etched in gold, I realized that I didn't have to wonder. I knew. I could have known anytime: it had been staring me in the face for weeks, three-quarters of the way down a page I'd shuffled past countless times as I organized the paperwork for the house sale. *Lady's inscribed vintage yellow gold ring with one 2ct round almandine garnet,* just one more item on the list of things that Mimi had hidden away. One more story lost, forgotten, for lack of telling. This one was about a woman I'd never met, but whose blood ran in my veins. A chorus girl who'd married a bootlegger, a man who wooed her with pretty words, lofty promises, extravagant gifts—including a ring she'd worn so often that pieces of the inscription inside had all but disappeared by the time she passed it along to her only daughter. The story already beginning to fade away. But if I looked, if I looked closely, I could still see where a horizontal line once extended from the bottom of the F in F.A.T.

Not an F, but an E.

I put the ring back on.

The servant's quarters were sparse, but the wall was paneled with the same intricate millwork as the rest of the house—inlaid wood with a motif of decorative rosettes every few feet—and I saw the seam in the wall before I even knew I was looking for it, half hidden behind a coatrack in the corner of the room. I grasped the nearest rosette, felt it turn under my hand. There was a faint click, then a rush of cool air as the door swung out, and on its heels, something else.

The scent of pipe tobacco.

To my right was a narrow staircase that rose six steps and then turned, spiraling toward the second floor, the kind that the staff would have used to deliver breakfast trays to the upstairs bedrooms while sparing any guests the horrors of having to meet a servant on the main stairs. To my left was a small cubby with a shelf and two hooks. Hanging from one of these, an old canvas coat and a cap, the kind that fishermen used to wear. The coat was missing a button, and I reached automatically into my coat pocket, feeling the jumble of objects there, the things I'd taken from Mimi's nightstand drawer after she was gone. A slip of paper, an acorn. A tiny spoon.

A brass button.

I knew even before I pulled it out that it would match. I could picture it: the button coming loose, its ancient moorings starting to fray. Maybe it had snagged on the doorframe as he passed through, tumbling unnoticed to the floor where Mimi had found it and picked it up. Or maybe she'd plucked it off herself surreptitiously, a keepsake from the nighttime visitor whom nobody would ever believe was real.

I turned, gazing around the room. Thinking of the times I'd been in here with my grandmother, and then further back, to my first weeks at the Whispers, when the house had seemed like a giant box full of props, little bits of the lives of everyone who'd lived here scattered in every room. A collection of mismatched dining chairs nobody had sat on in decades; stacks of old magazines someone had once intended to read; fussy little hats all trimmed out with velvet and flowers and feathers, hats that used to advertise you as a lady with good taste and money to burn, suddenly rendered useless when people stopped wearing hats altogether.

I thought of how easy it would be, in a place like this, to drape yourself in the leftover pieces of one of those lives and pretend to be someone else.

Behind me, the hidden staircase beckoned.

I began to climb.

The stairs turned twice and ended one floor up, where I fumbled for the latch and a second door swung open to reveal the upstairs hallway. To my right was the window that looked out on the bay.

To my left, down the hall, standing exactly where I'd been on the night when I saw the man-shaped shadow that I'd convinced myself was only a dream, was Adam. He stared at me, his eyes wide. Startled, I thought—but not surprised.

After all, we had both been here before.

"Hi," I said.

"Wow, hi." He flashed me a weird lopsided smile, as if half his face couldn't quite pull it together to make the right shape. "Where'd you come from?"

"There's a staircase."

"Oh," he said. "How about a secret toilet?"

He laughed. I didn't.

"It goes to that back room downstairs where Mimi stayed. It's probably how my grandfather used to get into Shelly's room at night without anyone seeing," I said. "That room, my room, it used to be the nursery. So he would walk down this hall, past the room where his baby daughter was asleep in her crib, and go downstairs to fuck the maid."

"Yeah. Wow," he said, again.

I stared at him. "Adam, where did you get my ring?"

The smile stayed plastered on his face. "What?"

"My ring. You said you got it secondhand. Where?"

"Oh." He hesitated. "Some antique store."

"Antique store. Which one?"

"I don't know." He shifted his weight. "I don't remember. Why?"

"Because it was my great-grandmother's."

There was a long silence. "I thought her name was Evelyn," he said finally.

"It was. Evelyn Alice Teasdale. E.A.T. The E had gotten worn down. My great-grandfather gave it to her when they were dating. Olly, it's a pet name. Short for Roland. But you wouldn't have known that."

He didn't answer. I didn't need him to.

"My grandmother, when she started getting sick, she hid a bunch of valuables. Mostly old jewelry. We were never able to figure out where, and obviously she didn't remember. I had a list of everything that was lost so that I could submit it to the insurance. All those heirlooms, we had records of them, you know?"

"No," he said finally, and a note of bitterness crept into his voice. "I wouldn't know about heirlooms. That's not really my area, is it?" His shoulders slumped. "All right, I guess there's no point in lying. It was in the attic. When you guys sent me up there to look for the photos, I found a bunch of stuff stashed in one of those trunks, and I thought . . . well, it doesn't matter what I thought. I shouldn't have taken it. I know that. I just, I couldn't afford a ring. And I kinda convinced myself that it wasn't really stealing if I gave it to you."

"I understand." I paused. "It's just funny, because another one of those missing pieces, we found before she died. You know that day when she disappeared? She came back with a necklace. My mom and I figured she'd stumbled on her hiding place while she was wandering around the house and pocketed it. But when I asked, she said her sweetheart gave it to her."

"You know that's normal," he said. "People with dementia—"

"Oh, I know." I cut him off. "They make up a story. But I don't think she made this one up, Adam. I think she was telling the truth. The problem was that I wouldn't believe it."

I beckoned him to come stand beside me, rummaging among the objects in my bag until I found the phone. "I want you to look at some photos. Starting with this one. And then just scroll back through."

"Why?" he said, but I just held the phone out, and finally he shrugged, taking it and swiping his thumb over the first picture: the funeral.

"I can hardly see this," he said. His voice was guarded. "Is that . . . us?"

"Yes. Keep scrolling."

He did, reluctantly. Through the next funeral photo and the next. Past the shot outside the house. The next picture: me outside the bakery. Staring at the camera with a bag in my hand. He lifted his thumb away. "Okay, cool," he said a little too loudly, then tried to hand the phone back to me.

I almost laughed. As if he could keep what was going to happen from happening if he refused to look. It was a desperate, childish impulse, like clapping your hands over your eyes when the killer in the horror movie raises his knife overhead. As if it would just hang there in the air forever; as if the killing stroke would never come.

As if we both didn't know what the next picture would show.

"You're not done," I said.

"Delphine—"

"Come on, Adam."

The tension went out of his body then. His shoulders slumped forward in defeat. Silently, he scrolled to the next and last photo. I thought he might refuse to look at it, but he didn't. He looked and didn't say anything. And he didn't ask what was in it, of course he didn't, because he knew. He knew because he was there, and because this wasn't the kind of moment a person could ever forget. Not ever. Not even if he wanted to.

I was in the picture, too, just barely, a slice of my hat and coat visible at the edge of the frame as I walked into the bakery while Mimi and Adam waited in the car. But it was the car that was the focus. There was the Subaru, with its center console, the one Mimi thought was there to keep young people from canoodling. And here were its two passengers, their heads filling the space between the two front seats. The back window was dirty, but you could see Adam's gray beanie and Mimi's white hair. You could see the curve of his arm where his elbow rested on the console, and one of his hands, nearest the camera, resting against her cheek.

But most of all, you could see that he was kissing her. Not briefly, not a peck, but deeply and on the lips, holding his hand against her face in the same way that he had so often held it against mine.

Outside, the light was almost gone.

Adam turned to me, the glow from the phone lighting the stubbled curve of his jaw. There were deep hollows beneath his eyes. "He told me what she was like, you know," he said. "He said she was the kind of jealous that destroys everything it touches. He said any man who crossed her path should run the other way. But I didn't believe it could still be true. Not after all this time. And by the time I realized, it was too late." His voice turned pleading. "I had no choice."

"Who?" I said. My voice sounded strangled. "Who told you that?"

He smiled a little bit then. Wearily, like he'd been telling a long, unfunny joke, and here at last was the punch line.

"The man who killed your grandfather."

25.

1964

AUTUMN

Miriam wakes the next morning on the sofa in the library, still in her clothes, her mouth dry and sour. Something is tugging at her arm, and she opens her eyes to see Theodora. The child's eyes are huge and serious. Miriam bolts to a sitting position, running her hands through her hair and groaning. Her head has begun to pound. The details of last night are hazy, like a bad dream—but the pain, the dreadful pit deep in her stomach, the look on Theo's face, those are vivid enough. She can tell from the brightness of the room that it's long past dawn, which means that Theo left for the marina without waking her or saying goodbye.

Theodora is staring at her. "Where Shelly?"

"She's on vacation," Miriam says, and stands with a groan. Breakfast was one of Shelly's responsibilities; the child must be starving. But Theodora isn't crying, not today. Only gazing at her with a disappointed expression that's far too grown-up for her little face.

She fixes breakfast for both of them but barely touches hers, staring out the window while her eggs get cold. She thinks about the night she sat at this table, the taste of Smith's blood still on her lips, and prepared herself to fight for what she wanted. For the man she'd chosen. She had been so sure—of him, of them, of her own heart. Would she have made the same choice if she'd known how it would end?

Morning turns to midday, and midday to afternoon. Theodora seems to sense that something is wrong and sets up at a table in the library with a sketch pad and a box of crayons, humming to herself while Miriam sits nearby and stares into space, lost in thought. When the child goes down for her nap, she puts on her coat and sets out down the pine path.

At first she can only trip over more memories. Walking this path alone in the dark, to meet him at the mouth of the cove. Strolling hand in hand with her husband, the two of them laughing and leaning into each other, while Richard and Diana scampered ahead. Alone again, arms crossed against the bitter wind, on the day she realized there would be a third baby.

But then she reaches the end of the path, where the sea lavender grows, and exhales. The trees across the cove are a symphony of red and gold, blazing against the sky, defiant in the face of the coming winter. The air is clean and sweet and salt, tickling her nose. And her mind, after so many clouded and chaotic hours, is finally quiet. Finally clear.

It won't last. She knows that—just as the brilliant display across the water will soon be scattered, dead and brown, by the winter wind. To every thing, a season. A time for every purpose.

And in this moment, it is time to choose.

She thinks of leaving. She could take Theodora and go to her parents. She could weather that: the disapproval, the disappointment, the way her mother's lips purse together when she's about to say, "I told you so." She could abandon this life and this pain and this man; she could start over in a place where the people smiled more freely, where the winters were gentler. She could find happiness somewhere else, maybe even with someone else someday. It would take time, of course. It would be hard.

Staying, though . . . that would be harder.

She drifts back along the path. The leaves crunch beneath her feet, the wind rustles her hair. At the edge of the forest, the trees fall away and she looks up, past the garden, where the house looms like a giant. Her breath catches in her throat.

Just ahead, from atop the garden wall, a pair of amber eyes are tracking her every move.

She stops to watch the fox. Fascinated at first—she's never seen one so close—and then increasingly uneasy, because the fox seems to be watching her, too. Waiting to see what she'll do. But she doesn't know herself what she intends to do, even now, and a desperate little laugh escapes her throat. There are no good choices, but not just that: there's no excitement, no possibility, no great leap into the unknown. Miriam's days of jumping into things are over. Whichever path she chooses, she can see quite clearly where it will lead, the miserable work that awaits. And still the fox watches her.

"Shoo," she says, but it doesn't move. She stoops, fishing a pebble out of the grass, and throws it as hard as she can. Her aim is good; the stone pings against the wall just inches from the creature's feet. But it still doesn't move, doesn't even flinch. It only stares, and she stares back, and then she laughs, because this is her lesson: that sometimes the only choice is not to choose, but to wait. To wait and see. She loves her husband still, in spite of everything—and in spite of everything, he has not left her. Maybe that will be enough or maybe it won't, but she has been making all the decisions for both of them for far too long. Let him tell her if he thinks it's too late. Let him decide what sort of life he wants. Maybe they can set the sky aflame again.

After all, she thinks, they still have so much time.

She's wrong, of course. There's no time, no time at all. Theo has been dead since morning, when he stepped aboard his boat to begin preparations for the day's fishing. The *Red Sky* ran aground in Brooklin just before noon, where two local boys climbed aboard and found some tangled nets, some spilled liquor, and no sign of the captain—save for a smear of blood on the starboard coaming. The police will conclude that Theodore Caravasios was likely drinking, tripped on a net, and went overboard, hitting his head on the way. An awful accident and a damn shame; you'd think a man with a wife and three children would take more care. At least the woman would be well taken care of, being who she was.

Theo's body will never be found.

And for all but a few, this is where the story will end. Nobody will ever stop to wonder at the boat ending up in Brooklin, an odd location considering the tides and the fishermen's usual routes. Nobody will notice that the spilled bottle of liquor is a Kentucky bourbon, when Theo was rarely known to drink anything stronger than beer. And nobody will ever remember the strange car that was parked at the pier at dawn, the tall stranger who slipped out of the shadows and onto the *Red Sky* in the last moments before sunrise. He had driven all night to be here before sunrise, a man with sunken cheeks and stained teeth, and a funny-looking scar on his hand that you'd recognize for what it was only if you happened to know that he'd once tried to interfere in a young woman's life and been bitten for his trouble.

One day, many years from now, this man will lie dying in his bed in a state-owned nursing home, telling a story with his last labored breaths to the stranger who sits beside him—a young man whose dark hair and dark eyes make him look just enough like Theodore Caravasios to make a person look twice. He'll talk about the thrill of running bootleg whiskey through the harbor under cover of darkness. He'll talk about the great stone house above the bay and the man who lived there, the closest thing he ever had to a father, whom he served loyally until the bitter end. He'll talk about the foolish young man he killed, a man who found out the hard way how the Day family deals with traitors. He'll talk about the girl, Miriam, who knew what she wanted out of life and would take it with her teeth if she had to.

He'll say that if the young man sitting beside him ever leaves this place and makes his way north, he should go and see it with his own eyes: the wild sea, the fetid mud, the boats rocking gently in the wind. The finest damn house in Bar Harbor, standing like a sentry high above the bay.

Miriam will see Smith only once more, years from now, at her father's funeral. She will force herself to meet his eyes and see the truth that lives there: that whoever held the knife, whoever did the deed, it was her choices, her recklessness, that cost her husband his life. This is her burden to carry, and she will. She will spend a lifetime carrying it. Waking up next to it in the morning, curling around it in bed at night. Someday, as her memories begin to fade and falter, its horrible siren song will bring her back to the place where it happened—the end, the beginning, and everything in between.

But here, now, she still has hope. As she makes her way back through the garden, she hears the sound of a car coming up the drive and hurries her pace. *Theo,* she thinks, her heart soaring, but already she knows that it can't be. It's too early, the sound of the engine not quite familiar, and as she rounds the corner of the house she feels dread crawling over her skin. The car is a police car. And the man getting out to stand beside it is holding his hat in his hand.

"Mrs. Caravasios?" he says, and oh, those two words are enough. They are more than enough, she doesn't want to hear any more. She wants to run to him, clap both her hands over his mouth, and force the rest back down his throat.

But she doesn't. Instead, her knees buckle, and she sinks to the ground. The police officer begins to walk toward her, reaching out to help her even as he opens his mouth and says, "I'm afraid there's been an accident."

Miriam lets him talk. There's no stopping the words now, and no changing what's done. The vow she made a moment ago was nothing but a fantasy. She gazes back toward the place she came from, but the garden wall is empty, the fox gone. Theodora will wake from her nap soon, and Miriam will have to see to that. Indeed, there's no one else to see to it. Only the two of them in this great house, with all its many rooms, its memories, all those dark windows like watchful eyes. She looks up at it and remembers: the games of hide-and-seek she played in its secret spaces. Those lovely young ladies in their silk and pearls, strolling the veranda on her brothers' arms. Papa in his library; Mother in her parlor. A house that held her family. A house that tore it apart. *But no more,* she thinks.

She will leave this place. She will never come back.

She wishes she could burn it to the ground.

26.

FEBRUARY

He told me then: about the old man with tar-stained teeth who lay gasping for breath in his final days, telling the story of who he'd been and what he'd done. A story that connected him forever to my family; a secret he and Mimi had kept separately for years, holding it close. But at the end, neither one could leave it completely unspoken. My grandmother had unburdened herself to the Reverend Frank, who had kept her confidence even as he tried to warn me away from the same reckless love that cost her everything.

Charles Smith, on the other hand, had made a different sort of confession. On his deathbed, in between fits of coughing that racked his brittle body, to a young man who listened raptly and remembered every word.

"I've heard so many stories, but god, that one," Adam said. "It was like he'd planted a seed in my brain. So after my contract there ended, I just went north. I could have gone anywhere, but . . . I don't know. It was like something was pulling me to this place. And when I ended up at Willowcrest, and I realized that the old woman in the room down the hall was the girl from that story? I knew it was meant to be. I believe that, Delphine. Fate sent that man to me, so he could send me to you. That's how I know we're supposed to be together."

We stood at the window for what felt like hours, watching as the sky deepened from violet to slate, as shadows crept across the fresh-fallen snow. Adam was breathing in sharp little bursts beside me, and I wondered if he was angry, and then realized I wouldn't know what it looked like if he was. I had never seen him angry. I had never seen him at all, not really. I had decided to spend my life with him not because of who he was, but because of how he made me feel: wanted.

I didn't feel wanted anymore. I didn't feel anything at all. Not the fluttering of my heart in my chest, not the cool air on my skin. I felt like the snow-covered landscape outside, twilit and silent and still. I felt like the ice that wouldn't shatter under my mother's fists. I felt that I could have stood there forever, like a spectator, waiting to see what would happen—and I thought that whatever happened, I would always remember this moment. The way the last of the fading light kissed the curves of Adam's face. The wavy glass of the window, feathered at the corners with curls of frost. The absolute quiet that lay heavy over everything, because in that moment the whispering wind that gave the house its name had finally fallen silent.

The certainty, in the coldest and darkest part of my heart, that whatever came next would be something I'd carry for the rest of my life.

"I'm glad," Adam said finally. He kept his gaze straight ahead. His hands, one of them still holding my phone, hung limply at his sides. "I'm glad you know. I hated lying to you."

I almost laughed. "For something you hate, you do a lot of it." I paused. "So you planned this. How much? All of it? You and me . . . was any of it real?"

Now he did look at me, and on his face was genuine hurt. "I can't believe you'd ask me that. Do you think I would have done this if it wasn't real? Everything I did, I did for you. So we could be together. I wanted to give you everything." His voice turned fierce. "And I did. You have the money now to do anything you want, and that's because of me."

My breath caught in my throat. "I don't understand."

"Yes you do. You were the only one who came to see her. The only one who ever spent any time with her. The rest of your family, they're fucking vultures. All they wanted was for her to die so they could get her money. Even your mom—you saw it, I know you did. She couldn't wait for it to be over so she could go back to her life."

"But how, how did you—"

He shrugged. "I told Miriam she should leave it all to you. She was already meeting with her lawyer, to set up the thing for Shelly. That whole week, I told her she should think about who really deserved to inherit the rest. Who was there for her every day? I don't have to tell you that she put a lot of stock in loyalty, do I? Look what happened to your grandfather. It wasn't hard to convince her. Sometimes I think she might have done it anyway, even without me working on her."

I shook my head. "You lied to her. You tricked her."

"No I didn't. Delphine, I didn't need to. I just needed to help her remember. And show her the visitor logs and your name in there every single day. Even the lawyer didn't ask questions after he saw that."

"I don't believe that. The lawyer? He must have wondered—"

"Why would he? There was nothing suspicious about it. She wasn't leaving her money to *me*. I was just a random employee, totally uninvolved, saying oh yes, Miss Miriam had spent all week talking about changing her will, that she wanted to leave her entire fortune to her devoted granddaughter."

I swallowed hard. "But I wasn't devoted. Half the time I went to Willowcrest, it was because I wanted to see *you*. Or because I just didn't want to be here."

"Do you think that mattered to her? She didn't care why you were

there, just that you were. You played the part she needed you to play."
He paused. "And so did I."

"That's not the same thing. We're not the same."

"Sure we are. There's a reason she never told you the truth, you
know. About what he did and what she did. About how he really
died. She wanted to forget. She wanted a different story. I just helped
her tell it. I made it real. I was the only one who could."

I thought of my mother, the desperation in her voice as she begged
Richard to just tell Mimi that her husband was out and would be
home soon. *When she doesn't remember and you tell her that he's dead, it
breaks her heart just like she was losing him for the first time.*

"When did you start pretending to be him?" I asked quietly.

"It wasn't like that," he said. "Not the whole time. At first it was
part of the job. The residents get confused, they think you're someone else, sometimes it's easier to just play along. But when I saw how
much it calmed her down, yeah, I encouraged her. It wasn't hard. She
still had really powerful sense memories, like if I played old songs or
touched her hair a certain way. And smells, too—"

"My grandfather smoked a pipe."

"Exactly. So I got a little bag of tobacco and kept it in my pocket,
or sometimes I'd put it under her pillow. It worked great. It's just,
when I came back here for the holiday, it was like a switch flipped.
She started getting clingy. Jealous. I think she could tell I was distracted, you know, because of you. And being back here in the house
where all those things happened, it wasn't good for her. I had to do so
much just to keep her from flipping out."

My stomach clenched. "So much. Like what you're doing in that
picture."

He winced, and I did, too, remembering that dreamy look on
Mimi's face that day at the bakery. At the time, I'd thought that
whatever happened to make her look like that, it must have been
good, magical. Now that I knew, I thought I might be sick. All those

nights when Mimi had paced the room, talking to someone I thought wasn't there. All those long days when he sat with her, walked with her, holding her by the arm. I thought of the necklace and the thumbprint bruise on her neck. Not a mark made in anger, but something else. Something worse.

I thought of the smugness in Richard's voice: *At night, in an old house like that? Sound carries.*

"You were in her room at night," I said. "That was you in the hallway, coming out of the staircase. Jesus Christ. *You were in her room.* Did you . . . did you—"

He looked disgusted. "No! It wasn't like that. I mean, it wasn't like *that.* We just, you know, kissed and stuff, and sometimes I'd hold her until she went to sleep. You don't understand, I had to. Or she would've gone all over looking for me. Like that day when she got lost."

I thought of the look on Mimi's face when she'd seen us together on the sofa, and then again, moments later, when I found them together in the foyer. The smile on her face as she turned to me: *Have you met my husband?* I had been so panicked about being caught with Adam that her meaning had slipped right past me. She wasn't asking if I knew her husband; she was asking if I'd been *introduced* to him, the man standing next to her.

He's explained everything, she said.

My breath caught in my throat. "And then you killed her," I said.

"I *helped* her," he said fiercely. "She was dying, Delphine. When she went back to Willowcrest after Christmas, she was going into memory care. Do you know what that means?"

"It means she had more time."

He shook his head. "More time, sure. More time to ruin everything. Memory care is the last stop before they die, and the people they were are long gone. It's just bodies walking around. They lash out, they shit themselves, they say horrible things to everyone who tries to help them, and they don't remember any of it, but you do. That's how it works at the end. When they're done forgetting everything, they ruin *your* memories, too. Don't tell me that's what you wanted. I know it's not. Jesus, your whole family practically begged me to do what I did."

I stayed silent, and Adam started talking again. Faster now, his eyes glittering. "Do you know, on her clear days, she said she wished she could die just so she could see him again? Just so she could say she was sorry? All she wanted was to be with him at the end. I gave that to her. I gave him back to her."

"But it wasn't real," I said.

"It was real to her."

I thought of the way he'd laid his hand against her face in that photograph. Tender. Gentle. Something made of ice moved horribly in the pit of my stomach.

"Shelly, she knew what you were doing. She was trying to warn us. Tasha said her death was an accident. She said she choked." I hesitated. "Was it an accident, Adam?"

"You should think about what you're asking me," he said quietly. "You're the one who told me she was there that day, Delphine. That's how I knew she knew. And you're the one who wanted to talk to her about Miriam. So think about it. If it wasn't an accident, think about whose fault that was. Do you really want to know? Because I'll tell you. I won't lie."

The house had begun to whisper again, the wind moving under the eaves and around the corners. Adam's question hung in the air. Could I bear to hear him say what I already knew must be true? Could I bear to leave this thing between us, unspoken?

"Tell me," I said.

"I was just going to make her delete the pictures. That was all I wanted. But she'd already sent them." His face darkened. "It was cruel, what she did. And she was so damn pleased with herself, too. Laughing at me with her mouth all lopsided and hanging open. She was going to ruin my life, *our* life, and she was *laughing*. It just made me so angry, I . . . I grabbed one of those chocolates and stuffed it in her big ugly open mouth, as far back as I could get it. And I watched her choke on it." He stopped, looking into the distance. Lost in the memory. "I didn't think it took so long for someone to choke."

I thought about running. Hiding. Snatching my phone from his hand and calling for help. I thought about how alone I was here, in this huge and empty house surrounded by acres of wood on three sides and miles of ocean on the fourth. If I called the police, it might take thirty minutes before they got here.

I thought about the look on Adam's face when he said, *I didn't think it took so long for someone to choke.*

"What are you thinking about?" he said. He reached for my hand again, and I let him take it. As if it made a difference now, whether or not I let him touch me. But when I looked at his fingers intertwined in mine, I felt like I wanted to vomit.

"You killed my grandmother. You killed Shelly. What now? Are you going to kill me too?"

He actually looked hurt. "How can you ask me that? I killed *for* you. How many other men can say that? Everything I did, it was for you."

I looked at the ring on my finger. "Was it? You knew I was going to inherit this money. And god, you've been in a hurry since then. Wanting to get married in Vegas. What was going to happen if we did? Would we have even made it to California before something bad happened to me?"

"It was never like that," he said, desperation creeping into his voice. "I'd die before I ever hurt you. I just wanted to start my life with you, that's all. Nothing has to change, Delphine. We can still be together, we can still go to California. All I want is to go to California with you. I'll take care of you just like I promised I would. It'll be just like you wanted."

"None of this is what I wanted," I said.

"Then what do you want? Just tell me. I'll do anything."

"Would you? What if I asked you to turn yourself in? What if I want you to pay for what you've done?"

He stared at me for a long time. "I don't believe that," he said finally. "If that's what you wanted, I don't think we'd be talking right now." He looked down at his hand, my phone still in it. "And I don't think I would be holding your phone. Can't call the police without this, can you?"

"You could give it back to me."

"I could," he said. For a moment, I thought he might actually do it. But then he frowned, shook his head, and shoved the phone into his pocket. "No. I know you. You don't need this," he said. "You don't *want* this. There must be another way."

I still think about this moment. The look on his face, the sound of his voice, the certainty that I wouldn't turn him in. The muttering of the house behind us that became more urgent as the wind rose.

Maybe it was because he did know me, and I knew him in the ways that mattered most. Or maybe I was starting to believe in spite of myself: in things that were meant to be, in stories that come full circle.

What I know is that I never felt closer to my grandmother than in that moment. I never felt braver, colder, or more reckless.

I took a deep breath. "You're right," I said. "There is another way. Let's take a walk. One last time. Down the pine path."

"And then what?"

"And then we'll see how this story ends."

We walked without speaking: down the stairs, out the door, around the back of the house and through the garden, leaving silent footprints in the snow. The night was thick with fog and either one of us could have bolted, but we stayed close, as if we were still tethered to each other, bound together by a story that wasn't finished yet. I thought about him walking here with Mimi, on that last night. Her last walk. How had he done it? A kiss to wake her, maybe. A familiar silhouette in the dark. An old woman wrapped up in a young woman's memories, rising at the touch of her sweetheart's hand. The house quiet around her. Her family, sleeping blissfully through it all so that

she never even remembered they were there. If only I'd woken up . . .
but I didn't.

He spoke as though he'd read my mind. "It wasn't your fault, you
know. I put something in your wine so you'd sleep."

I remembered stumbling up the stairs that night, how I'd felt suddenly, terribly drunk. "You drugged me."

"I'm sorry."

The moon was rising, cold and distant against the sky. We had
reached the entrance to the pine path. His breath hovered cloudy in
the air.

"Tell me what you did," I said. "Tell me how it was, at the end."

He hesitated. "I could tell . . . she knew the way," he said. "She kept
getting ahead of me and then teasing me, saying I needed to catch
up. She could still move so fast. And in the moonlight, she looked . . .
young. But not like a kid, not like a girl. Ageless. It was like you could
see who she was and who she'd been, all at the same time. All these
different versions of her, looking out through one set of eyes. She really
was beautiful."

The wind moved high in the trees, the forest tossing and creaking
around us, a carpet of frost and dead leaves crunching beneath our feet.
The fallen tree loomed ahead. I thought he might hesitate there, but
he climbed over easily and so did I, the bark slimy beneath my palms.
My armpits were soaked with sweat.

"When did she think it was? What year?"

"She asked if the children were sleeping. I guess that means the
fifties, at least. I don't know. But she wasn't afraid."

Ahead of us, the trees parted to reveal the dark cove, a tiny patch
of sky, a few glittering stars that vanished as I looked at them, the
fog rolling in and growing thicker by degrees. At my feet the open
mouth of the sea.

"That was her mistake," I said.

He turned to me. "What?"

"She should have been afraid of you. She would have been if she'd known the truth about who you were. What you were doing. What you would do."

"Everything I did was—"

"For me? For us?" I shook my head. "When you watched Shelly choke to death, who were you thinking of then?"

He didn't answer, and I looked at him for a long time, my eyes streaming with the cold. Willing myself to stay strong, to see this moment through. Realizing as I did that it was already over.

My grandmother hadn't been afraid of Adam—but I was.

I didn't want to be afraid anymore.

"Then what happens now?" he said finally. "How does this end?"

"I'm going to give you a chance," I said. I raised my other hand, pointing: into the cove, into the dark, where that distant island stood hidden in the mist. "I'm going to give *us* a chance. You know this story, right? Crossing the ice to that island, that was hers. Her love, her memory. But you took it from her. You used it against her. You made it yours—and mine."

He took a nervous step backward. I moved toward him.

"So now we're going to finish the story. We'll cross the reach. We'll start over together, if that's what you want. You wanted another way. This is it."

"Delphine—"

I shook my head, baring my teeth against the wind. "Maybe we'll both get a new beginning. But this—everything you've done, all the lies, all the death—it ends here."

I stepped onto the ice.

27.

He stared at me, his face twisted. I took another step.

"It won't hold us," he said.

"It might. It's been cold," I said, and marveled at the grit in my own voice. I sounded so brave, so sure. And I wasn't lying: It had been cold. Cold enough that I had stood by the shoreline just that morning and observed that the ice stretched much farther into the reach than it had a few months before. Cold enough that a person could walk very far out indeed—if she was careful and if she didn't weigh too much.

But he hesitated again, and in that moment I wondered if he would change his mind after all. If he would run, run away from the promises he'd made and the terrible things he'd done. I still wonder what would have happened then. Maybe I would have let him go. Let him live with it. A lifetime of looking over his shoulder, wondering when fate might come to collect the debt he owed. But as I watched him watching me, something flickered over his face. Love, maybe—or just something that disguises itself as love, a spark of that madness that makes even prudent men foolish, reckless, dangerous.

The madness that makes a bland, devoted husband gamble away

every penny in his joint bank account on a series of bad investments. Or a loving father willing to kill for love, for money, for the sake of protecting what he holds most dear. Or a young man willing to risk the frozen reach for a chance to hold his love in his arms—or bold enough to imagine he'll find a way out, as the walls close in.

The madness that disguises itself as courage, that you don't recognize for what it is until it kills someone you love.

The ice was firm beneath my feet as I began to walk. Carefully but quickly, opening the distance between us.

"Wait," I heard him call. I turned.

"Come on," I called back. He was on the ice now, twenty feet behind me. His face was obscured by shadow and fog, but I could see the shape of him, the cadence of his movements. Tentative, but getting bolder.

He was starting to believe.

He took another step and another, and I watched for a moment more before I turned away. Kept walking. The fog was thicker than ever, and while I wasn't the one who believed in signs, in fate, I did believe in this one: as if the sea itself knew what was about to happen and wanted to shield it from view.

When I heard him call out again—"Delphine? Where are you?"—I turned back and saw nothing but gray.

Beneath me, the ice had turned dangerously dark.

I dropped to my knees and then my belly, spreading my weight as I began to crawl laterally back toward the shore. I took shallow breaths, the damp cold of the frozen surface seeping against my body. I willed my teeth not to chatter.

The fog was disorienting; he had lost track of me, and when he did pass by, it was at a distance, just a shadow stumbling in the direction of the distant island, arms outstretched. He didn't see me and I didn't speak, and then the fog closed around him and he was gone.

I waited, listening. A beat passed, and another—and then, below the light whistle of the wind, somewhere in the dark, came another sound, low and sinister.

The ice, not nearly thick enough after all, was beginning to groan and crack.

But I didn't call after him, and if he called out, I didn't hear it. It was too late for that now, or perhaps it always had been. We had always been destined to come to this precipice and to take this leap. There was nothing to do now but fall.

I slithered backward until the ice was white again beneath me, climbed to my feet, and walked back to the shore.

I sensed them before I saw them, tracking my movements as I neared the tree line. Two coppery eyes stared at me, unblinking, and then the fox trotted out of the woods, its paws soundless on the snow. It stopped only a few feet from me, looking back to the place it had come from. My breath caught in my throat as a movement flickered in the shadows, and a second fox appeared. Running to stand beside its mate, shoulder to shoulder. They paused there, together, staring straight ahead—and then slowly, one at a time, each head with its black-tipped ears swiveled toward me. I stared at them and they stared back, and nothing moved but the wind. We looked at each other even as the groaning of the ice grew louder, even as there was a second sound that might have been a low cry, a splash, a story ending somewhere out there on the frozen reach.

But in this moment, I stood alone on the shore and knew nothing. Felt nothing. Clung to nothing. I watched the foxes standing with their heads high, ears forward.

I imagined standing in this place, this moment, until the sun rose sparkling over the empty cove.

I watched as they turned away and ran together into the dark.

EPILOGUE

2015

MARCH

Richard plopped two ice cubes and a thick slice of orange peel into a tumbler and poured out the cocktail shaker, drowning the cubes in red. "Negroni," he said, handing me the glass. "That's Italian for 'I told you so.'"

"You didn't tell me so," I said. "If I remember correctly, what you said was mazel tov."

"Did I?"

"You know you did." I took a sip. "It's bitter."

"It's a metaphor. The next sip will be sweeter." Richard winked at me, but then leaned in, putting a hand awkwardly on my forearm. "But let me be serious for a second."

"Please don't," I said, and he laughed.

"I'm impressed, you know. You've put on a hell of a brave face about this. What I want you to know is, you don't need to. If you want to have a nervous breakdown or do a bunch of peyote or spend three weeks in Sedona writing angry man-hating poetry, you've earned it."

"Why do I have to go to Sedona for the poetry writing but not the peyote?"

"Because even I have limits to the depravity I'll allow in my pool house," he deadpanned. His hand was still on my arm, warm and heavy. I was starting to sweat. "Look, just tell me honestly. Should I not have shown this to you? Would you rather not have known?"

I looked at the table in front of us, where a manila file folder lay open, the papers inside stacked neatly. The page on top held the name of a private investigator. The rest held the life story of the man I'd been planning to marry.

I shook my head. "No. I'm glad you showed me. It makes this easier."

He grimaced. "I hope so. I'll tell you, I'm furious. That son of a bitch pulled the wool over everyone's eyes, including mine. If he knows what's good for him, he'll stay gone."

I nodded. I hoped he would stay gone, too.

I tried not to think about the cove or the coming spring.

I wondered where the tide had taken him—back to the shore or out to sea.

I had arrived in L.A. three weeks before, unannounced and ahead of schedule. The drive was a blur. I had stopped only to eat and sleep, and then only when I had to. In over three thousand miles, the only landmark I remembered was the strip mall where I'd stopped to buy a new phone. I'd made it to Pennsylvania before I remembered that I didn't have mine anymore.

It was also when I realized that his duffel bag was still in the trunk of my car.

Richard had come back from a meeting to find me parked in his driveway, still in the driver's seat, staring into space. I had prepared myself for this moment—I would tell anyone who asked that Adam had dumped me with no explanation, leaving me to make the trip to California alone—but in the end, I didn't need to. Richard had looked at me and at the empty passenger seat and said, "You look like you could use a drink." His nose wrinkled. "And, more urgently, a shower."

That night, I slept for eighteen hours. If I had dreams, I don't remember them.

Richard called the investigator that night, but hadn't told me until this moment, after the report arrived. When he did hand me the envelope, he apologized. Not just for being nosy—of course he'd already read it—but because he thought I would be disappointed. For all the information it contained about who Adam had been before I met him, the places he'd been and the things he'd done, the detective had come up short on one crucial front: he couldn't tell us with any certainty where Adam was now. The trail went cold in Bar Harbor, as if he'd fallen off the face of the earth.

This wasn't the first time that Adam had disappeared without a trace, or the first time he had left a trail of lies and betrayal behind him. In the years before we met, he had made his way up the coast under a series of aliases, working at the type of posh assisted living facilities where wealthy middle-aged women tended to install their parents. He had a sixth sense for the damaged ones, so desperate to feel loved, wanted. So susceptible to his charms. He had fleeced two of them for a sum in the high five figures, and had blackmailed another with photographs that he threatened to send to her children. The investigator's report noted that these were just the women who would talk to him, that there were almost certainly more. All of them were racked with shame, blaming themselves for being taken in. Nobody had gone to the police.

I was the only one he'd ever asked to marry him.

I wondered if that meant anything—or if I even wanted it to.

And I wondered if Adam was right: that he was drawn to Bar Harbor for a reason. That it was meant to be. Maybe the man who killed my grandfather was an instrument of something bigger, the hand of fate reaching out to balance the scales and make Mimi pay for the terrible wrong she set in motion all those years ago. Or maybe it was something less poetic, more banal: a criminal at the end of his life who recognized a little piece of himself, a kindred spirit, in the eyes of the young man at his bedside.

Maybe it didn't matter. Either way, the ending would have been the same.

Richard's voice broke the silence. "The most important thing," he said, "is that you dodged a bullet. I know it probably doesn't feel that way now, but man, you really did. One of these days, you'll stop feeling shitty and start feeling lucky. And then one day, further down the road, you'll realize it's been ages since you thought of him at all."

I nodded, and he smiled.

"Wait," he said. "I know, how about I float some Prosecco in your drink? That'll cut the bitterness."

"Okay."

"Just take a few sips, make some room for it. I'll be right back."

I watched him as he strode back to the house. I thought that he was half-right: I did feel lucky. Lucky to be here, facing west, with the sun on my face and family beside me. Lucky to have a life ahead of me, full of possibility. Lucky that I never had to return again to the Whispers, the frozen reach, that cold, dark water.

There had been a clothing donation box next to the strip mall where I bought a new phone. Nobody had looked my way as I stuffed the duffel bag inside. Letting go of the last thing that might have tied me back to him.

That was lucky, too.

But letting go was not forgetting.

The door slammed: Richard was back, holding a sweating bottle in one hand. A breeze, warm and arid, blew across the yard, ruffling the surface of the swimming pool and lifting my hair away from my face. I raised my drink in his direction, the cubes clinking, and took a long sip before setting the glass down, half-full. But the flavors of juniper, cherry, and bitter orange lingered on my tongue, and I shuddered as I swallowed.

Not because of the bitterness.

Because of the ice.

ACKNOWLEDGMENTS

So much gratitude to everyone who offered support (moral or other-wise) while I worked on this book: Leigh Stein and Julia Strayer for their invaluable feedback, chapter by chapter. My mom, Helen Kelly, for reading every draft including the bad ones. My brother, Noah Rosenfield, for the conversation that sparked an idea that became a story. My mother-in-law, Peggy Anderson, for letting me steal her grandma name and give it to a morally ambiguous senior citizen who is nowhere near as sweet as she is.

Yfat Reiss Gendell and Rachel Kahan, thank you for pushing me toward certain edges and reeling me back from others; we've got a good thing going on here.

Attorney Paul Black answered all my stupidest questions about elder law, the execution of wills, and other miscellany. (He did, for the record, explain that a "will reading" only happens in the movies, but he also agreed that it's more dramatic to pretend they're really a thing.) Thank you to Andrew Fleischman for introducing us.

A note on the history: There were indeed a rash of forest fires across the state of Maine in October of 1947, which destroyed nearly a quarter million acres statewide. The devastated areas included much of Mount Desert Island and its Millionaire's Row, marking the end of Bar Harbor's reign as a summer playground for the rich and famous. These things happened, and insofar as they are accurately represented in this book, it is thanks to the online archives of the Bar Harbor Historical Society, the Northeast Harbor Library, and the New England Historical Society. I am also especially indebted to filmmaker Peter Logue, whose documentary *Fire of '47* was an invaluable resource.

Insofar as the history is inaccurate, it's because I made a lot of stuff up.

Finally, thank you to Brad Anderson for all things, with love.

ABOUT THE AUTHOR

Kat Rosenfield is the author of the acclaimed *No One Will Miss Her*, which was nominated for the Edgar Award for Best Novel. She partnered with the late, great Stan Lee to coauthor the *New York Times* bestselling *A Trick of Light*. She also wrote two acclaimed YA titles— the Edgar-nominated *Amelia Anne Is Dead and Gone* and *Inland*. Her work as a pop culture writer has appeared in *Wired, Vulture, Entertainment Weekly, Playboy, US Weekly,* and *TV Guide*. She is a former reporter for MTV News.